LAST WRITES INK
A NEW BREED IN HORROR
lastwritesink.com

PRESENTS

THE DAVIS BROTHERS

WHEN IT REIGNS
BY TODD ANDREW DAVIS
&
SHADOW Of THE DEVIL,
THE DESECRATION OF PETER
CAMERON
BY DEAN JULIAN DAVIS

Brothers Todd & Dean Davis developed their style of storytelling over many years and now they're proud to announce the release of their debut novels - When It Reigns & Shadow Of The Devil, "We greatly appreciate our family, friends and fans for their support. Join us as we delve into the darkest corners of the human psyche."

In the sleepy community of Ravenswood Illinois, Detective Logan Crenshaw becomes entangled in the brutal slayings of two sisters. When the body count rises, secrets buried deep within his subconscious begin to surface. His only salvation is a childhood friend turned priest.

When It Reigns is a psychological horror linking a killer, detective and priest; with sexual taboos, demonic possession, religious strife and paranormal activity.

The names and locations have been changed to protect the identity of those involved, for these horrific events have not yet taken place: Todd Andrew Davis.

Senior Editor: Jade Eunice Davis
Editor: Dean Julian Davis
Artwork: Michelle Pawula
Like us on Facebook @ lastwritesink
Website: www.lastwritesink.com

TODD ANDREW DAVIS
WHEN IT REIGNS

THIS BOOK IS DEDICATED
TO
MY MOTHER EUINCE KIRTON DAVIS (RIP)
MY FATHER HARVEY V. DAVIS Ph.D.,
IN ORDER OF BIRTH
SISTER CAROL
SISTER SHEILA
BROTHER DEAN
NEICE SASHA
FRIEND BRYAN MILLER WHO RECEIVED FIRST
READ
SPECIAL THANKS TO
FRIEND CHRISTINA NELSON WHO TOLD ME TO
PUSH THE ENVELOPE
AND RICK DENZ THE ONE WHO INSPIRED ME TO
MERGE TWO GENRES
MY DAUGHTER JADE EUINCE WHO I LIVE AND
BREATHE FOR
AND MY TWISTED ANGEL THE LOVE OF MY LIFE
MICHELLE PAWULA WHO NEVER ALLOWED ME
TO GIVE-UP THE DREAM; ALWAYS SUPPORTIVE
ALWAYS BY MY SIDE
WHOM WITHOUT THIS WOULD BE A BOOK FULL
OF EMPTY WORDS
SHE HELPED TREMENDOUSLY WITH EDITING
AND DESIGNING THE COVER
SHE DEDICATED THE FOLLOWING POEM

DEATH BECOMES HER BEGINNING

PALE WHITE SKIN ILLUMINATES UNDER DIM
LIGHTS
REACHING OUT, I SLOWLY CARRESS THE
COLD HARD FLESH UNDER MY FINGERTIPS
SO FRAGILE YET SO PRESERVED
SUNKEN EYES STARING FORWARD IN HORROR
BUT SOMEHOW AT PEACE
DRIED BLOOD LITTERS THE SKIN
ACCMULATING MOSTLY ON HER TORSO
AND WRISTS, WHICH WERE BOUND
THE STINK OF ROTTING FLESH BEGINS TO FILL
THE AIR
HER CLOTHES SHREDDED AND OPENED
SHOWING HER PHYSIQUE;
PETITE, SLENDER WITH SMALL CURVES
GASHES ON HER TORSO SHOWS THE PAIN AND
ANGUISH SHE MUST'VE FELT UPON HER FINAL
MOMENTS ON EARTH
LOOKING ONCE MORE AT HER FACE
A FEELING OF DEJA-VU WAS OVERWHELMING
STUDYING THE CONTOURS OF HER FACE
I REALIZE A FAMILIARITY ABOUT HER
ALL TOO FAMILIAR
SHE LOOKS EXACTLY LIKE.....
SHIT! THAT'S ME!

TODD ANDREW DAVIS
WHEN IT REIGNS
PROLOGUE

Golden brown leaves mixed with lava red and pumpkin orange splashed across the canvas of the landscape; the main portrait, a mangled masterpiece of white flesh. Her face so disfigured and swollen by her attacker, it was an impossible task to picture her once being part of the human race. Her legs sprawled out; broken pieces of ivory bone highlighted purple bruises. Her nude body was a hellish mess from head to toe. Her clothes tossed carelessly in a heap next to this empty shell. It was torture trying to envision the last moments of her life. What had been done to her was unconscionable; way beyond my mind's comprehension. Frozen on her face was a contorted expression of pure horror; it screamed out, 'What did this to me is not human, not of this world.' Little white polyps littered her skin; steam emanated from her blistered flesh as clear liquid seeped from the open wounds then dissipated into thin air. A mixture of fog and light rain lingered over the crime scene. The onlookers were kept back by police tape and resembled extras in a Hollywood horror flick while her nude pale corpse exposed to the elements began to deteriorate. Two plain clothed officers fought feverishly to protect her vanity by shielding her with flimsy black rain slickers.

I could feel a razor-sharp spasm shoot into my hip from all the squatting I had done. Normally, I would block out such a thing but for some reason my mind couldn't focus on the task at hand. It was hard to disguise the fact that I didn't want to be here; I prayed my face masked the truth. If you believe in God, the heavens above and all the good people who inhabit the earth, then you have no alternative but to believe the opposite is true. There is no other explanation when death is thrown in your face. No sane person could justify the carnage I stood over. The essence of evil; its soul lives, breathes and walks among us. What immediately came to mind was that she had been boiled alive, her body methodically arranged and dumped in the woods. He must have used an acid based chemical thinking it would destroy any and all trace evidence. He may have just outsmarted himself; a paper trail linked to the buyer of the chemical or linked to its origin may possibly unveil our killer. My job was to find her voice. In these situations you force yourself to become numb and yet, I found myself wiping away tears. This senseless murder made me a true believer that the devil is walking the earth in human form and has just begun to quench his insatiable appetite. I felt as if I was caught in a time warp and the world was spinning off its axis. My movements were in slow motion and everything relative blazed past at an accelerated speed.

"Detective! Detective!" Tamara Webb screamed. She had just recently been promoted to Lead Detective on my task force and this mess was her first official case, "Logan!"

She waved a thin gloved hand in my direction; concern was etched deep within the contours of her face.

Could I possibly be so transparent? My gaze focused in her direction, I made sure my voice held steady and measured.

"Tamara," her name was all I could muster.

"Logan, follow me," she said in an unsettling tone that sent shivers down my spine. Confident she had my full attention, she turned and walked deeper into the woods.

The ashen moon rinsed in the backwash of the fleeting hours of darkness blazed a trail alongside the dirt path. Webb's ghostly figure floated in and out of my line of vision. The sound of rushing water temporarily fazed out the bloody crime scene from my subconscious. It was a welcome relief, but I knew even before we hit the water's edge that it would be short lived. Branches and thicket impeded our progress; forewarning us of the secrets held within. Three plainclothes officers and two CSI techs stood in astonishment near the crime scene. An ordinary thorn bush in every account, but upon closer examination showed it had been bathed in blood. The amount of blood the human body holds astonishes me and I could only imagine that if all this blood actually came from one source then every drop must have been spilled. The CSI techs donned in moon suits stained with scarlet covered evidence worked ominously side by side. The tall one turned toward me with an apathetic look. Webb paused, giving me time to soak in the horror before she resumed her descent into the nightmare that would forever haunt her. We pushed forward; an opening in the woods unveiled a pair of divers in wetsuits. A cop held his head in his hands while a River Patrol's yellow beam light knifed into the water searching for additional lost treasure.

"Are you squeamish?" asked an officer.

I ignored the words of the young pimple faced kid as I passed him by. A white sheet concealing a female torso rippled and danced in the slight breeze mocking my curiosity. I knelt down beside the body.

"Logan she's been decapitated," Webb's voice said passionately.

"Did you find the weapon?" My words fell upon deaf ears. I left the sheet momentarily in place. I looked up from my position and the pimple faced kid's six-foot frame towered above me.

"If I were to offer a guess," he said, "I'd bet her head had been yanked off."

TODD ANDREW DAVIS
UPON A BED OF LEAVES
CHAPTER I

I was listening to the sound of my hemi roar as the engine pumped out four hundred horses of unadulterated power. I raced down the highway; no radio, just the sound of wind whistling through the cracked bug infested windshield like a freight train howling in the distance. My eyes half glazed from a hard night of drinking, a fresh bottle of bourbon at my side with nowhere in particular to go. A faint but audible rhythm captured my full attention; I backed off the accelerator. Boom-boom-boom. My eyes transfixed on a soft amber glow off in the horizon. I left the comfort of the four lane highway and crossed onto a narrow gravel road. A multicolored beacon of light hovered above the treetops, drawing me in like a moth to a flame. The next several sensations were impossible to illustrate and neither words nor meaning could do them justice.

I couldn't remember leaving the safety of my car or opening the rustic barn door that revealed a mob of people so overwhelming that I almost turned away. The blaring music added to my already burgeoning migraine. I sat in the corner listening to Emo music, belted out by teenage wannabe rockers. The stage could barely accommodate a novice stripper yet alone five gangly fucks and their rent-to-rock equipment. The club was inhabited with painted faces donned in black leather and white lace. Mock feedings took place in darkened corners where groupies would moisten their lips by sipping gently from one or more hosts. Like always, I felt awkward and out of place but then I saw her; long golden hair resting gently upon her shoulders, piercing green eyes and a face to die for. My eyes darted away instinctively when she glanced in my direction. *Should I risk another gaze?* My fleeting courage was rewarded with an angel's smile. She was now the only person in the room; she was my obsession. The music faded and the hoard of people transformed into gravestones that plagued the path in front of me. There is a magical moment that sometimes happens when two people first encounter one another; not all of us are blessed with this phenomenon but for those who have experienced it, cherish it. Summoning the bravery I fought my way closer without hesitation.

A stuck-up black haired chick with a distasteful smirk gave me the once over, before excusing herself from the table.

"Never mind her," the angel spoke to me, her emerald eyes were soft and inviting. "You're new to this scene," she motioned for me to sit next to her. Her sweet perfume reminded me of fresh cherry blossoms. "Jessica," she extended her hand.

"Jack." *A name I'm fairly positive I never used before.* I took her delicate hand in mine. I hate when females greet you with handshakes, it portrays them as being less feminine. I could feel the warmth of her blood flowing from her palms to the end of her manicured fingertips. She didn't jerk her hand away or react repulsed the way some do. No, she was quite different from all the others in every aspect; absolutely breathtaking.

"You're a man of few words. Shy I suppose, huh?"

"I'm anything but shy," I realized I was holding her hand perhaps a little too long and a little too tight. I quickly released my grip. The devil's grin I'm famous for must've reared its ugly head, yet her demeanor had shown no evidence of the fact. She smiled, ignoring my devious intentions. *Could she possibly be so innocent or just naïve?* "I'm the guy your mother warned you about," not my words, not my thoughts; I spoke in a low seductive tone. I felt the change begin to creep inside of me and tried desperately to fight it off for her sake. *Why now? Not this one.* I was powerless; every sensation, every feeling, every thought turned to black.

"I need a smoke," she said as she took my hand and led me outside.

Every man makes a choice of who they want or hope to be. I was tormented, teased and spat upon. I was nothing; until one night everything changed. Whether I made a conscious decision or was merely seduced by the devil himself, I will truly never know. I had watched myself sleep; my mind consumed with murder. I took my own life that night and was born anew. I awoke intolerant of weakness, intolerant of what made me what I'd become. I had to rip away the core and accept who I was now; at times being in control made me feel powerless. His thoughts, his actions, his movements, his revenge became just as much mine. For he is me and I am him, we are one, but not the same. Immersed in moonlight, we breathed the freshness of the invigorating September air. I inhaled deeply, filling my lungs and electrifying my senses. The radiance of the moon swept down upon us; beckoning and pleading us to heed its summons; to show mercy. *I control even you tonight.*

"Can you hear the river?" I placed my arm around her waist and pulled her close.

"What river?" she replied with an inquisitive look and lit up a cancer stick.

"Those can be detrimental to your health. I can too by the way."

She tossed it to the ground and snuffed it out with a designer heel, "Is that so? I suddenly lost the urge," she mused.

The barn door flew open unexpectedly; I recognized the stupid bitch. She stumbled down the steps obnoxiously drunk with her disheveled dark mane flowing. She recaptured her balance but lost her dignity and blurted out something so incoherent I thought she was speaking in tongues. Jessica nodded her head and the creature promptly returned to its lair. I affectionately took her hand and led her deeper into the woods; I was completely amazed how little coaxing it took. Not often am I intrigued by someone's willingness to embrace the inevitable. The footing was treacherous; however I managed to navigate the trail without peril. I found a secluded clearing just off the pathway where we wouldn't be disturbed.

My hands moved toward her breast and she halfheartedly fought them off. I grabbed her by the scruff of her neck, pressing those sensuous lips close to mine. I felt her heartbeat trying feverishly to escape her bosom. I slipped my hands between her thighs…

"No!" her eyes blazed at me. "Stop it!" her words laced with fury.

"Sweet little Jessica why do you fight me so? You're going to die; this night is preordained. Why disavow yourself the ultimate pleasure of an honest tribute. Tonight you'll sing with the angels, tonight I'll set you free."

"Let go of me you sick fuck!" Stunned, perhaps a sudden change of heart, she screamed into my ear.

I slammed my fist into her skull so hard she began to hemorrhage. A trickle of blood materialized in the corner of her mouth; it tasted like copper wine as I placed another tender kiss upon her lips. She bit me, sending me into an orgasmic combination of pain and pure ecstasy. I felt the white hot pain in my knuckles; instantly my hands were engulfed in warm sticky crimson. I saw the other one before she could comprehend what had taken place, before that orifice under her fat nose could form a word. The shock on her pasty white face was comical. The sobering realization of events took hold, catapulting the big black haired beast into flight.

"Sleep darling Jessica," my boot collided with her cranium and with an unabashed force I crushed it beneath me.

I ran after the raven haired cunt. The thorns cut deep into my flesh purging my soul as I pursued my prey through a wicked labyrinth of branches and wild brush. The sound of rushing water over riverbed stones caught my attention. *How did I know about the river?* To my advantage in her haste she headed in the wrong direction. It was a critical mistake that would cost the bitch her life. She stopped and turned around at the end of the trail. She stared at me in dismay; her hands rested on her hips out of breath and totally exasperated. She tried to acquire her equilibrium when the realization and the full weight of her error finally seeped in. Step by step I approached and cut off her only means of retreat. Her eyes were nonstop waterworks. She made a mad dash for the water in a futile attempt to escape. I overtook her on the river's edge, quickly seized her by the throat and lifted her several inches off the soft sandy ground. She kicked wildly which only infuriated me more. I squeezed with all my might and within mere seconds held my souvenir up to the heavens.

"This world has shown no mercy on me, nor shall I upon it!"

I was drenched in the blood of the dead; my memory of the night began to fade. The golden leafed bed, the baby blue skirt, the lifeless Jessica along with the headless bitch… all vanished. The only sounds and sights were of the hemi as it roared to life, gravel to pavement, howling wind and the moon. My soul was jarred back to life by an ambulance's blaring siren as it passed in the opposite direction doing well over eighty miles an hour.

𝒯amara climbed into the passenger seat of the sport utility. Before she was settled, I tossed a file onto her lap.

"Billy Dugan."

"Vic's boyfriend; you want to interview him?" she said inquisitively raising her eyebrows, "I thought Santiago gave him a pretty good once over."

"It's been forty-eight hours. Why hasn't he paid Jessica a visit or called her parents?"

"You think he knows she's dead?" Tamara peered up from the file.

"You haven't been sleeping much have you?"

She made a small attempt to straighten herself up. "It's not easy being alone at night. The girl…" she glanced over at me, "the one who was beheaded, I see my face in hers. I know eventually the images will fade, I'm just…."

"I can do this solo if you prefer?"

Her demeanor changed in an instant, "And what, go back to

the house, no thank you! I don't care to be alone with my thoughts either."

The murders had the whole department shaken, but she was honestly petrified. I have always been too overprotective of her. For an instant I rethought her promotion, but we all have demons to face. I figured as long as we were teamed up no one else would be in jeopardy. Besides, it would be much easier to monitor her. Human teeth marks were found underneath the left breast of Jessica Foster. The flesh had been partially eaten yet no saliva had been detected. Disturbingly, no signs of a chemical agent had shown in the test as I had originally hoped. Her pale color and massive blood loss had been attributed to this one particular wound. In any ordinary case the nature of this salacious crime would have had the station animated with cryptic tale s of the undead. However, these killings surpassed the brutality that any of us had ever witnessed and the tension in the department was palpable leaving far more questions than answers.

We pulled into the Dugan's driveway. A marked squad car was parked across the street. We approached the two-story brick house with no intentions of disguising our purpose. A sleepy, barefoot, middle-aged, obese woman with kankles blocked the entrance to the Dugan's home.

"They've already talked to my boy," she said rebelliously.

"They have, I haven't." I didn't try to subdue her fears, instead I used them. "I'll take Billy with me if you don't step aside."

She stood defiantly, perhaps she was eager to call my bluff; she then moved aside. Once inside, the home was what I had imagined. A typical European household; lived in but very clean nonetheless. There was an aroma that assaulted my senses upon crossing the threshold and it made me think of a real life gingerbread house. Spices and a variety of baked goods ran the gambit of the spacious kitchen counter. Wood floors interlocked with stone and marble. Miniature statuettes and grand chandeliers that swashbucklers could only dream of flying flamboyantly through the air accentuated the grandiose entry. A beautiful angel waterfall with mystical cherubs welcomed visitors as they watched over your every move. Prominently displayed in the foyer were religious artifacts, golden framed portraits of our Lord and Savior, several depictions of Mary and baby Jesus with an over abundance of silver and gold crosses. It gave the house such an intrinsic feeling; so authentic that it felt as if you had literally stumbled into a Cathedral. The home oozed with old world charm and spiritual grace, almost making it a separate entity from its inhabitants. Two beautiful little girls with blonde locks flowing past their ears bobbed their heads out from behind a wooden door; one of them reminded me of my Elizabeth.

"Billy!" The woman bellowed, "Billy we have company, get your ass out here now!" Her Polish accent more pronounced the further she became irritated.

"What mom?" his voice was clearly agitated.

We walked down the narrow hallway filled with family photos and porcelain figurines to what I presumed was his bedroom. Without hesitation his mother flung the door wide open. Ravenswood High Aztec Warrior's star quarterback was in the midst of pulling his pants up. He noticed Detective Webb right away.

"What the fuck ma!" Billy was fully aware of the

impending slap from his mother for his disrespectful response.

I felt the sting reverberate within my body. I had lived with an overbearing mother as well. Her eighty-four pounds soaking wet frame packed quite a wallop back in the day. But he didn't even flinch when his mother laid into him. I got the sense the fear was long gone, but respect for her was still clearly evident. I gave him a sympathetic grin full of understanding and compassion as our eyes briefly met. Billy, with his dirty brown hair and uncaring stare was a man-child of six foot three, one hundred and seventy five pounds of raging testosterone. His room was an eclectic blend of posters ranging from Michael Jordan, Sammy Sosa, Marilyn Manson, Static X and a few other icons I didn't have the time or pleasure to pursue.

"Billy, I'm Detective Logan Crenshaw and this is Detective Webb."

"Don't get up," Tamara said amusing herself.

If looks could kill; he ignored her and finished zipping up his blue jeans.

I quickly intervened, "Ma'am, we have some personal questions to ask Billy, we'd like to talk to him in private."

"Nothing is too personal for me to leave my boy alone." His mother's pose mimicked the one she gave at the front doorway, arms folded and face emboldened.

"Ma, I'm almost eighteen…" his voice wisely trailed off, not wanting to re-cross their invisible boundary.

"First things first," Tamara started the questioning. "What's with the cast on your left foot?"

"Doc says partial tear of my Achilles. Don't you cops read the paper? I'm kind of a big deal."

"When Bill?" I asked. His smugness gradually diminished my sympathy for him.

"I dunno, three weeks ago, give or take."

"Jessica's a college girl, how'd you two become acquainted?" Tamara moved closer to Billy, her tone infused with skepticism.

"Varsity football my sophomore year," he said as a matter of fact, "she was a senior cheerleader. We traveled in the same circle I guess."

"So you two were just infatuated with each other," I stepped in, "played it hot and heavy from the start huh?"

"No, we had an open relationship; we'd see other people on occasion."

"When was the last time you saw her?" I asked.

"She came over the night before last."

"What did you do? Where'd you go?" Tamara pressed.

"I've answered all these questions already. What, you don't even read your own reports?"

"What and where Billy?" I reiterated her question.

"Nowhere, we stayed here."

"Did you ever hit her?" Tamara chimed.

He sheepishly looked over at his mother.

"Answer the question?" she prompted her son.

"You think I did this? I've been laid up in bed staring at the ceiling. Just because I won't cry in front of you pigs... I told her not to go," his voice had a hint of compassion intertwined with anger. "I got scholarships, I got dreams. I wouldn't trash them for anyone, not even her.... Okay so I hit her once; the night she left.... We argued and... she didn't deserve what happened to her. She's a sweet kid."

"Have you ever been to the bar where the incident took place?"

He took a moment and thought about my question before phrasing his answer, "A group of us went there a few times. We all had fake ID's. Almost half the crowd is underage."

A deep sigh escaped his mother; however, I didn't believe she was as ignorant as she led on.

"That scene's a little dark. You partake in that underground shit do you?" Webb focused in on his black painted nails. Before he could answer she fired off another question, "Those go over well in the locker room?"

"I can handle myself. I know what you're thinking; what a combination, me being a jock and a freak right? Well Ravenswood is a small town. We all need to just cut loose now and then."

"Did you know she was going to the club Saturday night?" asked Webb.

"Yeah, that's what we fought about… Kyle."

"Last name," I prompted.

"Anderson."

"I don't see anyone named Anderson," Webb scanned the report.

"Nobody asked about him before."

"Phone and address?" Webb asked exasperated.

"Seven twenty-eight, forty-six, ninety-five; he lives off Collins and Wilshire; three-hundred something? Three-twenty six Wilshire Avenue. That's it," he said confidently.

"He lives in this area code?" Webb continued writing.

"Yeah, that's his cell number. They never answer their home phone."

"I don't either," she said sarcastically. "So your failure to mention Kyle to the other officer's was because if he were responsible for what happened to Jessica you planned on exacting some type of revenge?"

"Kyle wouldn't hurt her."

"And you know this how?" I couldn't help but to smile.

"He's a jerk, but he's also been my best friend since grade school. Besides, he's scared of me."

"If he's such a boy scout, what was the argument about?" My patience was wearing thin.

"Drugs. Kyle got hooked on coke and wanted my help," he paused, "I don't mess with any of that shit."

"You want us to believe you're a counselor, Billy?" I tried to aggravate him; throw him off his story. I listen intently to his voice, observing his demeanor, searching for tattle signs of deception.

"He dated Jess's sister. Everyone knows she's one messed up chick. I warned him several times about her, but he never listened. He got caught up in the life, you know what I mean? Man, he even asked me for my piss during a surprise drop; I told him I barely had enough for myself," he chuckled. "His test came back positive and that was the beginning of the end. He was suspended from the team. She screwed his life up big time."

"Why would he throw it all away?" Tamara's voice said mockingly in disbelief.

"Simple; seventeen years old, got himself a twenty-two year old. Truth be told, she wasn't much to look at, but I guess when you're strung out on dope you lower your standards."

"Did you have sex with Jessica Saturday night?" Webb inquired.

"Jesus," the question blindsided Billy but he answered it nevertheless. "Yeah, we had sex."

"Did you use protection?" Webb pursued her line of

questioning.

"No. We never used protection," his head hung low, ashamed of being anymore forthright in his mother's presence.

"Was it consensual?" again Webb asserted herself.

"You fucking dyke! She was my girlfriend! I didn't rape her or nothin'," he fought back tears and reflected on his words. "She was raped?" His mother comforted him as he wept.

Without another word, we vacated the Dugan's home. I walked down the driveway side by side with Tamara; I could still hear Billy sobbing.

The sky was a bright sunshine filled crystal blue, I took several deep breaths; crisp fall air invaded my lungs. Billy Dugan semi convinced me of his innocence; however I'd have Tamara follow up with his physician to confirm the diagnosis of his injured Achilles. I also wanted to alleviate a nagging suspicion of possible steroid abuse.

"He's got a nice size cock," Webb crudely blurted out. She slid into the passenger seat beaming with self-indulgence. "How'd you think he got all those college girls? Hell, I don't even like the kid and I'd do him."

"Feeling better I see." We headed west on Cousins Avenue toward Belmont.

TODD ANDREW DAVIS
JAGGED EDGE PUZZLE
CHAPTER III

My fingers were encased in blood; I fought feverishly to shut off the ignition. I felt exhausted; I desperately needed to recharge. I sat motionlessly; my aching body cradled by black leather bucket seats. My hands and clothes were saturated with thick cranberry syrup. God, I'd never seen so much fucking blood. My shirt was plastered to my chest and stunk of sweat and filth. The pungent aroma of vomit and whisky rose from the stained carpet floor lining. Without warning, I became racked with convulsions. My eyelids fluttered, pupils dipped and rolled then spiraled back. My body imitated a roller coaster ride at Six Flags; kaleidoscopic images of the previous night's events flooded in. I only achieve true clarity during these episodes. A fucking bloodbath, no doubt both those bitches lay dead and to think I played an integral part. I had been a wild animal whose primal instincts had surfaced. I had zero control and zero remorse. Why should I; it hadn't really been me.

A window framed the inhabitants of the redneck dive like a picture. I was in the early stages of my awakening; parked outside a Mom and Pop truck stop when I notice the waitress milling about. She was a middle aged woman, stocky build, hairnet and bleached white apron with ribbon tied neatly in a bow. She poured a steaming hot cup of Jo. My head throbbed as the beat of distant drums banged away throughout my skull. Second occupant; an overweight man, blue overalls, long greasy brown hair, two day old beard and a tattoo on his upper left forearm that was indistinct from this distance. The third and final patron was a real fat assed male with a short cropped military styled haircut. I spotted his gun tuck neatly under his fleece button shirt. *Fuck how did I not see the cop?* My heart felt as if it were about to seize; a vein pulsated sadistically in my throat. I searched the lot for his car, sure enough an unmarked stood out like a sore thumb on the other side of the hillbillies rig. *Did he notice my suspicious behavior or that I was plastered in human waste? If I drove off would he follow? I'm fucked.* I opened the door slowly and eased out of the driver's seat. Kill the cop first, redneck second and then have fun gutting the bitch. That was the plan. I made my way to the rear of the car, popped the trunk and disengaged the spare. Through the six inch arc, I could see past the rear window and beyond the windshield into the truck stop. I removed my shirt, wiped my face, arms and chest. I found the car jack and as luck would have it there was enough grease ingrained among the threads to smear onto my skin. I pretended to change a flat; never shifting my gaze off the pig. Fifteen minutes passed as I tightened the last lug nut. I turned my shirt inside out, soaked it in a puddle of oily water, wrung it out and slipped it over my head. I summoned up the courage, shut the trunk and proceeded toward the diner.

The tiny copper bell rang as I opened the glass door; *an angel must have gotten their wings.* I spotted a sign that read restrooms and without breaking stride I headed toward the men's. I felt their eyes on me like flies on shit; the cop's stare lingered. I flung the door wide open and checked each stall. Satisfied I was all alone, I began devising the plan; it had been a fools bet to even ponder. I guess the act of slaying two individuals tends to heighten one's paranoia. *If I ambush the cop first, snap his neck in one motion I'd have the gun before I had to deal with Hoss.* I acquired quite the treasure trove of goodies during my travels; one I particularly admired was a pearl handled hunting knife. I was mesmerized by its weightlessness and balance; it molded seamlessly to the contours of my hand almost becoming another appendage. This simple blade of steel had the power of transforming me into a violent and highly efficient killing machine. I realized it had been quite some time since it last saw the glory of battle. I opened the door and found the three piglets entrenched in deep conversation. They were oblivious to the stranger who crept inside their little sanctuary. I quickly rushed the cop. My blade slid across his jugular; ketchup like tentacles streaked down his double chin and drenched his scrambled eggs. His hands instinctively darted upward toward his throat ignoring his gun belt. I yanked the pistol out of his holster. Hoss backed off his stool so fast that the tub of lard fell flat on his fucking ass. I tossed the pig to the ground and he squealed like the swine he was. I watched the cop shiver and shake as his life blood decorated the white linoleum.

"You're next Hoss," I remarked. What a fucking speechless piece of shit he was. I had planned on saving the little cunt for last, but she stupidly made a beeline for the phone. I squeezed the trigger on the Glock 9 and the shell somersaulted in midair as the bullet tore through her frontal lobe. "Hoss, I grew up on a farm and every morning I had to slaughter pigs. The decent thing was to be humane, but that just ain't gonna fly for me today. See the thing is, those pigs put up much more of a fight than the three of you. I guess their natural instinct for survival kicked in. But your dead cop friend here," I kicked him as I passed; he twitched, "sorry dying cop friend, your stupid redneck fat ass and that little bitch haven't made this much of a challenge. So we're gonna play a little game called… who wants to see tomorrow?"

"Kid," the bathroom door unexpectedly opened and Hoss walked through. "Are you okay kid?" he asked. "I saw you working on your hot rod. You were already finishing up, otherwise I would have given you a hand," he stared at me for a second or two. "That nose of yours is a real geyser; you should go see Marge she'll pack it with ice."

Kid? I gripped the edges of the porcelain sink; the color drained from my knuckles, making them appear bone white. It was difficult to process and just as maddening to tolerate; I couldn't even kill if I wanted to. He controlled me, he set things in motion and he made the final determination of who, when and where to strike. All I had was pure fantasy but I hungered for far more. I deserve my share of the conquest. I could barely associate the blood suit I was wearing with the bloodletting I've been made to perform. I smeared my bloody nostrils on the back of my hand, pushed past the blob and wandered back into the dining room. The cop's bar stool was vacant and his car long gone.

"Are you okay son?" the waitress asked in a mothering tone. "Do you want some grub?"

I pictured her dead corpse lying against the far wall; the phone still pressed to her meaty ear. I visualized a blackened bullet wound oozing forth a mixture of ruby and yellow pus. The bacon still sizzling and her white stocking legs sprawled out in front of her identical to a broken doll. The flashback was so vivid, so intense that I felt truly saddened to see her standing, hand on hip with her hairnet enclosing a gross salt and pepper mane.

"Nope," I said bluntly, "I've suddenly lost my appetite." The stupid bell above the door clanked as I strolled toward my ride. I hopped into the driver's seat, adjusted the rearview and watched the truck stop fade into oblivion.

TODD ANDREW DAVIS
CHASE THE RAT
CHAPTER IV

*A*fter phoning Kyle Anderson, we were informed that he was out visiting friends in Chicago and would be gone till evening. I decided to follow a hunch. Detective Santiago had scribbled down the name of one Chase Stevens. For a short time he worked as a bouncer at the Double Door in Ravenswood. His current job was as a personal trainer at Apollo's Gym in Newhaven and he also had a connection to Jessica. Santiago felt he had been given the runaround; since the interview more information had surfaced.

"Logan. Why didn't you tell the kid she was dead?" Tamara asked curiously.

"He didn't ask."

The drive to Newhaven took less than a half hour and like any cop who's worked the beat, there were several questionable events that caught our attention.

"There's a drug deal going down!" Webb screeched. "Where are you taking me? I don't feel safe on this side of town."

"Cute." It was a relief to see her smile. Shit, it would've been a relief to see anyone smile. The past forty-eight hours were the most intense I've ever experienced, including the birth of my five-year old daughter Lizzy.

I wanted to surprise Mr. Stevens at home. The neighborhood was upper middle class, filled with children taking advantage of the unseasonably nice weather. The address, 4729 Prairie Lane was at the end of a reddish cobblestone driveway. A blue and white Colonel stood amidst a well manicured spacious lot surrounded by towering oaks. A grape colored Porsche was parked near the garage and sparkled in the brilliant sunlight. Tamara, with her yellow note pad in hand followed me to the front entrance. After several rings of the doorbell, a pair of dark beady little orbs peeked out through narrow slots.

"Hello. Who's there?" asked a female voice.

"Police ma'am," I answered back. We held our badges up. The door promptly opened revealing a tiny Asian woman.

"We're looking for Mr. Stevens," Tamara stated politely.

"I'm his wife, Helen," she replied in semi-curious broken English. Her expression was that of pure puzzlement. Apparently the loving husband, neglected to tell his adoring wife that the police paid him a visit. She motioned for us to come inside.

"Take off your shoes please," she scooted in the direction of the kitchen. A gray tabby cat curled atop a Grand piano and peered out the bay window to soak up the last vestiges of the sun. "Sit, please. Can you tell me what this about?"

"I'm Detective Webb and this is Detective Crenshaw, we're with the Ravenswood Police Department," she looked unimpressed as Tamara dispensed with the formalities, "Is Mr. Stevens in?"

"No. He works until seven at the gym," her eyes jetted from me to Webb. "Fuck! Fuck! I told him not to sell to kids! I knew he'd get caught. Shit," her English miraculously improved. "I just opened Pandora's Box, didn't I? Please leave."

It was so sudden that I couldn't tell if she was being candid or honestly flustered and blabbered before thinking. "I believe you'd rather talk to us in your home than at the station," I retorted.

"You're not here because he's dealing are you?"

"No, we're not," I replied.

"I need my lawyer."

"You just confessed to two detectives that you're aware of your husband dealing to minors. I promise you, lawyer up now and I'll do everything in my power to charge you as an accessory, because as far as I'm concerned, you're complicit and that makes you just as guilty." I had an opening so I exploited it. Our eyes locked.

"You don't frighten me!" she spouted.

"It would be a shame to come back with a warrant and tear up your lovely little home." I tossed in for good measure, "What will the neighbors think when they see police cars sitting in your driveway and along the street. There will be so many cops pouring in and out of your home, seizing all of your personal property that it'll make your head spin. Paints a pretty picture, doesn't it?"

There was a brief silence when somewhere in a back room a baby cried. She looked bewildered. I've found that the threat of DCFS worked better than water boarding. She stood silently for a second, weighing her options before admitting defeat.

"Okay, what do you want to know?" she let out a sigh.

I wish all interviews were this easy. I knew she was petrified that he would eventually be caught, but she was undoubtedly desperate to protect herself as well. Of course she could always reason with him, leave him or turn him in. The romanticism of having a family and children often clouds people's judgment. All I know is we had her and she wasn't about to wiggle off the hook that easily.

"What product is he pushing and who is he selling it to?" Tamara sensed her trepidation and pounced on what could be her only opportunity to get her talking.

"Shit! You don't even know what he's selling? Goddamn it, I'm so stupid! I can't believe my fucking big mouth!" She paused briefly; exasperated she divulged, "Steroids, HGH and coke."

"Who's his supplier?" Tamara asked.

"I don't know. Truthfully I don't. He's so going to fucking kill me!"

"He never told you that Detective Santiago had interviewed him Sunday afternoon?" Tamara shook her head in dismay.

"No! Now can you please tell me what's going on?"

"We're investigating a homicide and need to verify your husband's whereabouts," I informed her.

"Murder? You think Chase is involved in a murder? That's impossible! Who? Are you talking about the girls on TV? That's what this is all about?" she said answering her own question. Her fears seemed to quell as she pondered her statement, "Chase may not be a model citizen, but he's no killer either. He has a heart of gold. The other shit he got involved in was because he figured the only way he could make extra money fast was for him to deal until we got back on our feet. The baby, the doctor bills, that damn car, we're way over our heads in debt. My…"

"So far this information rests in my hands," I wasn't in the mood for a sob story. "Solving this crime is my first priority. I'm gonna find your husband, so you would be well advised not to tip him off. Don't work against me on this; right now everything else is irrelevant. If I discover that the drugs and murder are tied together, both of you will need a higher deity to save your asses! I've got no tolerance for drug dealers. The Jessica Ann and Jennifer Leigh Foster case takes precedence, so don't fuck with me!" I glanced out the window in the general direction of the squad car, "I'll leave an officer with you until we get a hold of your husband. Make no mistake; any attempt to signal him will have extremely dire consequences. Now tell me somethin' I want to hear."

Twenty minutes later we pulled into the parking lot of Apollo's Gym. A one-story brick building fitted with handicap gunmetal gray guardrails and a concrete ramp led to the entrance. Stenciled in red, black and gold letters was the name of the establishment, owner and hours: ***J.P. Taster, founder and owner of Apollo's Gym since 1972.*** **Open 6am to 10pm Monday-Saturday and 6am to 6pm Sunday.** The lot was filled with exotic cars, pickup trucks and ten speed bicycles; a virtual cross section of clientele. I held the door open for Tamara; a plush red carpet led us like celebrities to the receptionist's desk. Sitting behind the counter was a smiling half-woman/half-man; for the love of god I couldn't tell by looking which half was which and even its voice kept the secret hidden well.

"Can I help you?"

We flashed our badges simultaneously.

"I didn't think you were here to sign up for our introductory rates," she smiled again.

"Chase Stevens?" The second I spoke his name, her expression altered to a somber but calm sadness that resonated in her eyes.

In partial disbelief, she repeated his name, "Chase?"

I didn't get the impression she was aware of his illegal activity, more like a notion that a man with Chase's integrity might be involved in anything untoward took her completely by surprise.

"I'll buzz him. Did Chase do something...?"

"Is he on the floor?" I interrupted.

"Yes with a client."

"Point him out."

She stepped from behind the counter and collectively we walked in the direction of a large floor to ceiling tinted glass wall. Dozens of people were lifting, straining, walking, running and sweating profusely to new age music.

"That's him, the black guy standing near the elliptical machine wearing the blue and white striped shirt."

I gestured for her to return to her station; Webb followed me inside. He never indicated he was aware of our impending approach. I stood directly behind him.

"Chase Stevens?"

He glanced at me over his left shoulder at the sound of his name being spoken, "I'm busy, come back later." His focused turned back to an attractive young Latino woman he was training.

"Chase!" I said with more authority.

"What, are you two selling something?" he said contemptuously.

"Are you?" Webb shot back.

Her quick retort registered with him immediately and his body noticeably tensed up. The only question now was will he or won't he run. His brain ticked away as he contemplated his next move.

"Excuse me Deidra," he stepped away from the machine and turned to face us. His expression; a deer caught in the headlights.

The searing acknowledgment of being ensnared in an erroneous web he wove abetted his escalating fear. True, he had been previously interviewed and probably thought he'd given enough satisfactory answers that would shield him beyond reproach. You have to be a combination psychologist and chess player thinking three moves ahead to untangle the reality from the falsehoods your adversaries set before you. The criminal mind is fascinating from the standpoint of validating their wrongdoing. Intellect is not a barometer that separates criminals from law abiding citizens; it just segregates the degree in crimes from those who commit them. White collar criminals are no different from your run of the mill petty thief. Killers however, are an exceptionally dissimilar and perverse breed. What makes them tick and still operate completely unnoticed is astonishing. Those who have a conscious often are led to their own demise, but then there're others with counterfeit emotions who harbor so much contempt for mankind that it's hard to believe they can remain undetected. Only by being inside their realm can you identify some idiosyncrasy that may hint to an aberration or defect in their personality. Every one of us is capable of killing. The majority of us can easily suppress our murderous impulses; it's instinctual and centuries of breeding and societal rules only keep this instinct dormant.

Chase guided us into a tiny office with a small hand crank window. He sat on the edge of an antique mahogany table and spoke of Jessica before we posed a single question.

"I knew Jessica," he stated dryly, "we met one night while I was working at the Double Door." Just like his wife, when feeling snared in a trap they eagerly spilled their beans; a little too easy for my taste. "We hit it off right away. Typically, I wouldn't go for that type. Gothic, Vampire or whatever the hell they call themselves." I didn't want Chase to feel empowered by dominating the conversation and ultimately misleading us, but I had to give him enough rope. "Jessica was different," he continued.

"Different? Meaning young?" Webb interrupted bluntly.

"Look, my job was simple. I flirt with the girls. I let the hot ones slide on in with no cover and kick the homely ones to the curb; i.e. the prettier the babes in the club naturally the more guys. It all equates to more revenue in the end. Jess was a free spirit with an old soul. She was waiting for a ride one night after club hours so I introduced myself. We talked a little and I ended-up driving her home. Nothing happened. It was just innocent, you know."

"Why'd you get fired?" Webb inquired.

"The Night Manager Colleen is nothing but a racist bitch! She didn't like all the attention I was getting; she had it in for me the day I started."

"According to her statement, she walked in on you while you were receiving a blow job in the stockroom," her eyebrow raised in antipathy. "Were you donating blood to your vampire fiend or were you all out?"

"My wife and I were having problems. We separated for a time. Jessica made me feel alive when I was dying inside. Even though we weren't technically together, I still felt guilt ridden." Chase sat down in a hardback wooden chair, "Look, I only had oral sex with Jess, never sex. I know how absurd that may sound but in my mind, I was staying faithful to my wife Helen. I always knew we would reconcile."

"How often were you with Jessica?" Tamara continued.

"Only a handful of times."

"How bout Saturday night?"

He paused, "No."

"Let me rephrase Detective Webb's question. Did you see her Saturday or any time during the week? I know you were no longer working at the Double Door, but did she ever visit the gym?"

"Yeah, I saw her Saturday afternoon," he was uncomfortable.

"Why?" I prodded. He knew we knew about the drugs.

"Money problems; I just got fired and have a baby and…"

"Excuses aren't going to save you but the facts may go a long way in determining which way this investigation turns."

"She didn't have a drug problem. Her sister was the coke addict and her boyfriend, a huge HGH and coke freak. Both of them couldn't get enough. I think they were reselling most of it to their friends." He confessed, sensing that it was his only way out from underneath his man made hell.

"You've met Billy Dugan in person?" asked Webb.

"Billy?"

"Jessica's boyfriend, you know tall, long shaggy hair, good looking."

"Her boyfriend was Ken…Karl or something like that."

"How does the name Kyle grab you?" said Webb.

"I didn't really deal with him, only her; so basically he was a non topic. The hormones didn't do his ass any good anyway. But one thing's for sure, he was hooked on dope. He didn't have long hair or was that good looking for your information either," he remarked sarcastically. "Jess was only indirectly part of the drug culture; she's smarter than that. It's... what do ya call it? Oh yeah, peer pressure, that's it! Her sister and that dude pressured her into it. I had connections and helped her out now and then. My wife doesn't know anything about our little fling and I'd appreciate as much discretion as possible. I'm a decent enough guy, honestly. I just got caught in a fucked-up situation. I'm done with all that shit now." He gazed downward, "How's Jessica doing?"

"She's still in a coma," I said. I knew lying was contagious, but giving the illusion that one of the girls had survived might flush the killer out into the open. "Where were you Saturday night?"

"I was with my wife," he said unequivocally.

"You were with her the whole night?" I asked skeptically.

"Sunset to sunrise; Sunday morning."

"You ever sample your own product?" asked Webb.

"Not exactly mine; I am more or less the middle man. But no, I'm just tryin' to make a buck. Besides, I think that would be pretty counterproductive."

"It takes all kinds," Webb punctuated.

"Listen. I'm not proud, but I did what I had to. Now I'm

trapped and have to deal with the consequences. I got no loyalty to the guy I purchase the shit from…"

"Save it Romeo, I'll send someone up and you can give them a full confession. You're lucky I don't have the time to focus on you at the moment. But, if I find anything, no matter how minute that leads me back in your general direction, you'll find out just how much I detest someone like you." I stared indignantly.

He came off unbelievably smug and phony. Exerting pressure on him would have only divulged mindless gobs of information. I was growing increasingly impatient. I've dealt with killers and I have dealt with assholes and he was the latter. Nothing really in what he said or did; it was just his persona that irritated me. From the very second I set eyes on him, I battled the urge to drive my fist into his smug face. I felt mentally and physically exhausted. I wanted to go home and hibernate for the winter but I promised these girls on earth soaked knees that I would bring their killer to justice. Chase was a small time drug dealer only capable of stroking his own ego and the only other suspect was a high school punk who lived under the thumb of his imperious mother. Were they both capable of committing a double homicide; probably. However, I had the explicit feeling these murders were from the mind of someone far more maniacal. I wasn't utilizing the task force or my own capabilities adequately. I didn't want to diminish our collective endeavors. I had no explicit knowledge; I just felt that we were going about the case too much by the book. We needed to take the blinders off. I realized from the start that we needed to match our report with Detective Santiago's and only then could we decipher the truth. I thought about Stevens again, but I knew he was a joke. An ex high school jock whose memories of yesteryear were no more than just a collection of failed dreams. He, like most people who floundered in the purgatory of a small town community lived vicariously through the eyes of his youth. This town was no different from the plethora that lay scattered throughout the country. Chase was no more a killer than I was.

The highway sign read '**RAVENSWOOD ILLINOIS 7.5 MILES**' in green and white lettering. I watched a bleak and drastic change occur right before my eyes. I drove further west and the night's humanity devolved into an infestation of mud people that scoured the streets. Throwaways and do over's as my brothers and I so compassionately referred to them. Blood pulsated in their veins just the same, but the beat they lived to was in the seedy underbelly of society's wasteland. They were displaced, far enough away as not to tarnish the connecting neighborhoods. There should be warning signs; *'Leave the highway at your own peril'*. These people had no real purpose, no goals; they sickened me, but I needed the cover of anonymity and for that reason alone these droids served a useful function.

I found a shady motel on the outskirts of town. Even the camouflage of darkness couldn't disguise the sleaziness of this fine establishment. I needed time to wind down; to think on things a bit. I took my key from an unwashed hand, drowned out the attendant's irritating voice and made my way up the staircase to room 309. Simple: made bed, brown covers, yellow sheets, wall mounted air conditioner and a tiny bathroom with a combo tub-shower. I locked the door behind me and spread out on an unforgiving bed. I sat a black duffle bag on the floor; just another souvenir I'd acquired. I tried to conjure up the events of the past several days but for the life of me I couldn't recall the girl's name. I had never even learned the name of the raven haired bitch. This time the memory came via old black and white still photos. Time always brought a terrible disconnect. Even those few memories I was afforded were steadily eroding and drifting away like a child's breath upon a dandelion. *Why can't I be rewarded for my deeds?* I peeled out of my clothes and headed toward the bathroom. I leaned over the tub and turned the knob on the shower head. I stared deep into a wall mounted mirror, within minutes the steam quickly distorted my image; as long as I could remember I never saw myself clearly. After a ten minute shower, I placed my blood stained clothing in the tub to soak. I turned up the heat and pressure then submerged them. I walked back into the bedroom; it was time to thoroughly inspect the contents of the bag. With the towel draped around my naked torso, I shuffled aside several fresh pairs of underwear, a white tee, black pants and a navy blue short sleeved button down shirt. I unzipped a cleverly hidden interior pouch and found a Velcro wallet; the driver's license read; *Dr. Gregory H. Lowry.* I had no recollection of such a person. I tossed the license and credit cards atop the dingy brown comforter and found myself staring dumbfounded at five crisp one hundred dollar bills. I remembered a saying my dad used over and over, *'Never look a gift horse in the mouth or stand too close while he's taking a shit.'* I now had new clothes, money and no reason to stick around this joint any longer. I hurriedly dressed, turned the water off and returned to the beckoning call of the night.

The parking lot was alive with unscrupulous characters. I fired up my cherry red Chevelle and eased out of the parking space; five minutes later I turned eastbound down

Central Avenue. Scuttle bums, crack whores, vice; the night was alive with weirdoes. Within two miles I spotted a pretty little white hooker and drove around once to check her out. When I was confident she was legit; I cautiously approached.

"Are you working tonight?" I said smiling.

"I'm looking for a party," the bitch replied unequivocally.

"What's your name?" I was already growing impatient.

"Candy," her eyes searched the interior of my car. "Hey, are you a pig?"

"My girlfriend thinks so."

"What do you want?" she gave me an unamused smirk.

We were in the open and she was making me nervous. I produced the wad of paper money I had acquired and waved it in front of her like a magic wand. *Abracadabra!* She jumped into the passenger seat so fast you would've thought she just won a trip to the Bahamas. She had no clue she was about to become a part of my illusion and I was going to make her disappear into thin air.

"Do you have a spot? I can get us a room if you want? It will cost us a little more but you can afford it. Or we can go to the alley across the street?"

Her constant yammering made me realize that she was a lot younger than I had previously thought. Her hand quickly moved between my legs, I returned the favor.

"How old are you?"

"How old do you want me to be?" she said in a giddy little voice.

I slapped her so hard that spit splattered across the passenger window. Bloody saliva snaked its way downward leaving white, red and brown dirty streaks in its wake.

"Fifteen, I'm fifteen!" she shouted back without hesitation as her lip quivered.

I could see the formation of a budding welt through the dimly moonlit interior. Crazy thoughts flooded my head. *Would she jump from a moving vehicle?* I sped up. *Should I take her back to the motel or find a dark place on the side of the road and take care of business?* I placed my hand on the back of her neck and squeezed hard, really hard. "Sorry," I uttered a sympathetic apology to an underage whore.

Her entire body relaxed as my grip loosened. She immediately proceeded to unzip my trousers and earn her living; apparently we were both under a lot of stress and tension. Almost five minutes later, we arrived back in the parking lot of The Paradise Inn; which I infamously dubbed *The Parasite Inn.* I knew that I wasn't the first Einstein to come up with that nickname.

"Do you wanna go in first and I follow?"

"We go together," I replied. I walked around to the passenger side and took her hand in mine, like I had done with what's her face and escorted her to my room.

"Do you have any coke?" her puppy dog eyes stared up at me as she balanced ever so precariously on the edge of the bed.

"Get undressed. I gotta take a leak," I shut the door and locked it. I left the bathroom door slightly ajar just in case she bolted. An underage prostitute fleeing a motel room doesn't look good in any circumstance not even in a fleabag place like this.

"Hey, you're not such a big stiff after all!" she proclaimed, "You've got coke? Party!"

"Where'd you find it?" I asked as I shook myself dry. I flushed then entered the bedroom.

"Don't look so serious," her eyes were glued to the wallet, "we don't have to do any lines."

"You shouldn't go through a man's personal belongings. You're not going to be a problem?"

"I'm a naughty little girl aren't I?" she thrust her supple bottom heavenward. "Are you going to spank me now daddy?"

I truly saw her for the very first time. A petite brunette, face marred by years of drugs, alcohol abuse and the hard life. Although her voice was young and immature she was definitely a pro. I could see that now as plain as day.

"Do you want me? Bought and paid for," she flashed the money I had used to entice her.

I crawled onto the bed and positioned myself next to her. I clutched a fistful of tangled curls and tilted her head back as far as humanly possible. My teeth tantalizingly close to her jugular, my mouth wet with anticipation. I covered her face with the palm of my hand and effortlessly lifted her up onto me. My hands moved to her waist, her eyes engaged mine the whole time. My fingertips glided over her nude firm breast. I did my best impression of an anaconda, slide my fingers around her windpipe and squeezed. She bucked upward trying to dismount, but I held a tight grip. I was deep inside her wet pussy, hammering away, clutching her throat and cutting off her oxygen. She violently gasped for air, mimicking a fish out of water. *I was intrigued and wondered; would her life finish before I did?* I almost laughed aloud at the prospect. I astonished myself and actually turned the little vixen free. She kissed me and bought herself more time.

I lay on my back, my brain consumed with hellish images and every bit recorded in hi-def. *Is this truly the onset of insanity?* I heard a distinctive pinging noise that sounded like raindrops on a copper tin roof. My palms itched fiercely and the taste of hot black licorice lingered on the tip of my tongue. I experienced the onset of vertigo and tried with every fiber of my being to keep the room from spinning. I had little control over my actions no matter how repetitive they were. Kill, feed, sleep, kill, feed, sleep and fuck. *What had become of the inner me? Do I no longer exist? Was I fading into nothingness? Having control over madness is still control. Right? Or am I becoming obsolete in this body?* I was always surrounded by blood and violence. Heaven will surely shut its gates in my face as my bloody fists pound frantically on those pearly whites. *What will become of me? Will I be forever lost in purgatory searching for a forgiving God?* Not even he can absolve the sins I have executed upon his children. I was damned; condemned by my own self righteousness and must bare my own cross. I shall never gaze upon his likeness. Not when the hunger grows more intense with each passing day; nothing else matters. *I will deny the Devil his trophy for as long as I can.* When your body cries out for nourishment and nothing but human flesh can satisfy you, you're only left with two options: feed the hunger or commit suicide and suicide wasn't very appealing. A trail of stark misery and severe panic washed over Ravenswood and its neighboring suburbs and I was the root cause. This power that is unattainable by most was lavished upon me with such great brilliance. The transformation would be pointless for mere mortals. I was a God in the making; a king who amused his servants by keeping them bathed in a shroud of mystery. At first I was reluctant to create my prophecy. I became him; the one they whispered about in coffee shops, grocery stores, schools, work and the like. I won't hide in obscurity waiting to strike. They languish in the shadow I cast over them. *No. I'm not insane. I am their God and I shall cast out all who dare commit blasphemy against me.*

The days and nights bled together making each indistinguishable from the next. Her naked body was still warm to the touch. I was pleasantly pleased to find signs of life. She had been immunized to the goings-on in the criminal underworld; half the things I did to obtain extra cash didn't raise an eyebrow. For the most part, I continued to let her trick and trusted her to return by daylight. She turned me on to my first taste of heroin; it was crazy to allow her to inject anything into my bloodstream. However, the high was like no other and it actually curbed my hunger tenfold. In all honesty, I figured she'd be long dead by now. *Why did we continue to grant her life? Had we become a sadistic spider teasing its prey?* Truth be told it had been nice having someone else to converse with, but I knew that I needed to remain emotionally detached. I shoved her off the bed; her body made a loud thump as she collided with the floor.

"Shit!" she hollered in a semi-giggle-snort sort of way.

"Shut the fuck-up," I stepped over her on the way to the toilet. *Little bitch little bitch, how shall I kill thee?*

Her nude body squeezed passed mine, "I'm taking a fricken shower."

Stay distant, we both know she'll eventually have to be terminated. There's seldom an occasion when I could actually differentiate my thoughts from his and at times trying to isolate who thought what or who spoke what became a task within itself. *Did he hijack my subconscious too?* Some day's I'd grasp at anything tangible just to prove to myself that I was still alive. *I've questioned little because he might decide to eliminate me altogether?* There were times I'd found myself inexplicably in different rooms or places. I had no sense of time passed or how I ended up somewhere strange. In most cases I had complete reign over the mundane. It's surprising that I'd been granted the privilege of enjoying my little Lolita. *Was he only able to take control of me in small increments? Was he lying in wait or did he just need me to face the world?* My main objective was to remain viable even to the point of cloaking my thoughts in a thinly veiled disguise of ambiguity. As reprehensible as it sounds, the time spent delving into my inner thoughts kept me from the task at hand.

I removed a ceiling panel and hoisted Candy's tiny limp body through a small gap. I anchored her to a cross beam using my belt and the bed sheet. Once I was confident she was secure; I replaced the panel. It was a relief that he spared me the gruesome details. I was actually somewhat fond of her even if I had killed her with as little afterthought as it would take to tie one's shoe. I tried to convince myself that eventually she would've been nothing but trouble. I sat on the floor Indian style with my back firmly against the cold plaster wall of the motel. I puked and the entire contents of my stomach heaved up a river of maroon bile. It was more blood than my stomach could possibly consume. *What have I become?* I quickly scrambled to my feet and retrieved the comforter. I tried to soak up the mess, but smeared the blood and guts across the floor. A slimy stream of thick drool frothed from my mouth. I spat a reddish rainbow hue of phlegm into the bathroom sink then meandered back into the bedroom. My muscle spasms continued to surge producing painful fits of dry heaving. I stumbled toward the unmade bed, draped my aching body in the over starched sheets of The Parasite Inn and wept. My soul had been kidnapped and I had no way of paying off the ransom. I brought this upon myself; my deeds unleashed the beast that now harbored inside this empty chassis. These scars were all self-inflicted; I was infected and rotting away from the inside out. I had been relegated to a petulant child. The monster inside deliberately kept my mind occupied while he devoured her and left me to tidy up; as usual. I took the bedspread with me into the bathroom, rang out as much of the slimy fluids as I could then dampened it before I returned to cleaning the rest of the floor.

Hunched over, I could still taste the thick syrupy sludge that coated my abdomen. *Not only am I murder, but blood consumption?* My hands shook uncontrollably and my lungs burned. *Had I ever drank their blood before? Conceivably I had and the whore's was tainted and that's what had induced the vomiting.* I was left to try and rationalize everything. I guess he spared me the killings because I was so pathetically weak. My esophagus felt as if a branding iron had seared it and my legs could barely support my weight. I did my best to clean the horror show with the toiletries stowed beneath the tiny bathroom sink. I knew that I would need to buy bleach, gloves and a mop to complete the job. I checked my appearance and made sure that I wasn't a walking exhibit of blood and guts. I scooped up the duffle bag, hung the 'Do Not Disturb' sign on the door, and was instantly submerged in the glorious radiance of the morning sun. I intended to cover my tracks by washing the entire room top to bottom, but I was subservient to his wishes and his will. I walked to the rear of my car, popped the trunk and retrieved a one gallon red container half filled with gasoline. I didn't smoke, but was positive the whore had left matches on the nightstand. I returned to the room and spotted the matchbook on top of her purse. I felt conflicted; oddly unhinged upon returning to the room. I splashed the gas all about the furniture and carpeting, blocking out thoughts of the previous night's carnage. I struck the match and stood there only for a moment, feeling a slight pang of remorse. Suddenly, there was nothing but emptiness and the soothing radiance of a towering inferno raging all around me.

TODD ANDREW DAVIS
CHANCELLOR'S MANOR
CHAPTER VI

Kyle Anderson, our final interview of the day wasn't scheduled back in town for a few hours. The sky had turned from a spectacular blue to an ominous gray. As darkness set in, we rounded the corner of Park Street and headed south on Seventh. A vagrant had been spotted loitering near Chancellor's Manor, an enormous old Victorian that blocked out the sky to the west. As a former native, I had no previous recollection of the house ever being inhabited. This was the house where legends were born, death, misery, ghost stories, and hauntings; rumors abound. I had always believed it should've been condemned and torn down decades ago. Over the centuries the foundation had rotted through, but it remained as a historical testimony to the timeless ingenuity of our forefathers. The description of the individual on the premises didn't cross match any homeless person known to the department. I understood my reservations about this place were predominantly colored by childhood fantasies and urban myth, but I could not shake the unassailable angst that always would materialize whenever I saw this place. The ghostly mansion was enclosed by an eight-foot brick wall and cast iron fence. I slowly drove up the cobblestone driveway.

"And why are we here?" asked Webb.

"I want to check this place out."

"Why now Logan? We could always come back in the morning."

Why now? Because this house haunted my youth and every child who walked past it on the way to school. As boys, we often dared each other to enter and relentlessly ridiculed those who refused. Why now, because those awful memories need to be dispelled. Even now, I felt anxious as I parked outside the gate. It was the crime scene and seeing this place after all these years that gave me the same eerie disposition it did many moons ago.

"Stay here."

"Logan," she saw the seriousness of my face, "remain in radio contact."

"Give me a half hour to check her out."

"I'll contact you every five minutes. So you better respond!"

"It's just a house Tamara," I gave her a smile; "the bogeyman doesn't reside here. Trust me; I'll be fine."

"Very funny Logan, the house is dilapidated. Just be careful."

"No worries baby face."

I walked around the rear of the vehicle and retrieved a flashlight from a hidden compartment in the lift gate; closed the door, winked at Tamara and headed toward the house. A rusted padlock and chain interloped the bars of the gate; the wall was my best bet. Webb, realized my dilemma, slid into the driver's seat and inched the SUV closer. I waved her forward until she was less than half a foot away from the brick wall. I maneuvered into position atop the hood and prayed that it wouldn't collapse beneath my weight. I hoisted myself up onto the edge of the wall then glanced over to visually inspect the hood for damage.

"What the hell are you doing?" Webb stuck her head out the window.

"Stalling... I guess," I swung my body in the opposite direction.

The towering oak trees shielded my view of the house. I saw nothing that could endanger my well being, so I closed my eyes and took a leap of faith. I crashed to the ground in pain; my knees buckled the second I hit the ground. It triggered an incident from when I was a young boy. My best friend Tim, whose family adopted me, devised a brilliant scheme one winter's night, to turn the roof of our house into a ski jump. When our dad arrived home after a long day's work, he couldn't figure out what in the hell had created the tracks. We used to joke saying it was Santa and his reindeer. One day our nosy neighbor showed him a video of us doing tricks off the roof, it was the day I fell and thought I had broken my ankle; among other things. The pain in my left foot combined with the beating I received later that night, rivaled the pain I now felt reverberating throughout my body. I pressed my back against the cold brick wall. One thing I knew for sure was that I had to find an easier way out. The drop was more treacherous than I anticipated and in hindsight I should've tried to lower myself down.

It truly sucks when you get older and realize you used to be able to achieve physical feats that would not even rise to a mere afterthought. I braced myself against the wall and hoisted up my forty-year-old aching body. I tested the ankle, winced; it felt tender but not broken. The last remnants of light morphed into a colorful rainbow that melted into the horizon from the west end to the north end of the mansion. The house stood majestically hovering above the town; acres upon acres of field lay hidden from the outside world. The majority of land was unkempt, covered with overgrown weeds, wild grass and trees as far as the eye could see and in the distance I could see the rooftop of a small cabin in the woods. When you reflect upon the past, things tend to always feel bigger and more intimidating. The things bordering on supernatural seem … natural. It's not until maturity plays a sobering part of your life that you realize how ridiculous your fears once were. Unfortunately, my fears weren't going away. I was a teenager the last time I remembered setting foot on Chancellor's Manor and the same trepidation that paralyzed me then had imprisoned me now. My heart hammered frantically as I wrestled with my inner child. I walked with a slight limp and ascended the narrow driveway that zigzagged in the direction of the mansion. I was startled by the chime of my cell phone and its ring caused a dozen bats to flee from their steadfast perches.

"Logan," it was Tamara. "Are you okay?"

"I'm fine, headed up to the house now."

She turned the headlights on and the beams cut rudely into the rapidly approaching night. I signaled to her with my hand in appreciation. Unfortunately, I had to make my limp vanish before she could see the pain I had endured.

The walk was excruciating. Thankfully, whatever wild animals were roaming the woods remained cautiously at bay by the light's silvery beam. I still felt as if something or someone was watching me and felt it with every fiber of my being. The halogen beam grew weaker as the distance widened. I fought the urge to make a mad dash for the front door; I could have outraced the hounds of hell. All sorts of hoots and howls welcomed me into the sanctuary the darkness provided. Heroically, I braved my way to the doorstep. The wooden porch protested noisily beneath my weight. Congratulations, fear triumphs over pain. I grasped the knob; one hard turn and the door moaned open. I frantically searched my jacket for a flashlight before I found it in my rear pants pocket. My heartbeat steadied. Cool air surged forward as though it embodied an unwelcoming spirit. The flashlight sliced through the darkness as if it were a saber seeking its intended mark. The light bounced from one crook of the room to another. To the right a chasm led to an unknown abyss and to the left; yellow pealing wallpaper which encompassed a small passageway that had once been the entrance to the kitchen staff's quarters. A moldy and musky smell lingered in the air. My eyes stung, eyelids became heavy and my head began to swim. I entered a large room where a fifteen foot skylight cast shadows over an empty Olympic sized pool decorated with tiny marble tiles. A dank oily smell assaulted my senses; I choked on the putrid air and fought the urge to vomit. I delicately tried to establish to my satisfaction, the hyperbole in which the manifestation of ghosts dwelled within an imaginative teenage psyche and was miserably failing. My knees knocked, goose bumps rose and sweat emanated from every pore.

I used a trick I learned from back in the day when I worked construction; when estimating a project always start at the highest point then work your way down. It was easier to finish in the basement and walk up one flight of stairs when the job was completed than go up flight by flight, only to come back down in the end. Imagine an awkward teenage girl making her first attempt to walk in high heels then you could envision the lack of support my legs gave me. I walked into the giant living room and was met by the stone faces of two lions that hung over the colossal fireplace. *Fuck this.* I unholstered my gun; it never felt this good in my hands before. I brimmed with a newfound confidence and made my way up a rickety spiral staircase to the third floor. The stench of rotted flesh that hung in the atmosphere was reminiscent of decaying meat in a third world market. My eyes still burned and began to water as I approached the first of the three rooms. The nausea I felt in the pit of my stomach pitched back and forth. I wiped away the perspiration from my forehead with the sleeve of my jacket and covered my nose. I twisted the doorknob, crossed the threshold and entered a tiny ten by ten incubator. Newspapers and musty boxes had been haphazardly tossed about the room. The headlines depicted stories that defined the decade from gas shortages, President Jimmy Carter, Roslyn, Amy and Billy Beer. I briefly scanned the room: a rusted bedspring, a child's dresser with faded pink and baby blue bunnies painted on the drawers and a few moth eaten dresses ambiguously summed it up.

Exactly twelve steps from the doorway lay a second room. I peered inside a boy's room that was not age specific but didn't belong to a young child either. There was an old oil stained mitt that rested atop a baseball bat in one corner and a ten speed bicycle turned upside down displayed a single flat wheel on a bent rim. I had this notion that the family who once lived here had left in a hurry; tattered clothes still hung in the closet. Maybe they never left at all. I heard something; movement caught my peripheral line of vision and I concentrated in the direction of the sound. My gun was at the ready with every intention of doing harm. A mud brown rat slinked over a half eaten shoebox and carried something in its mouth as it went about its business. I promptly secured the door before proceeding down the hallway to the last room. It was cleaner than the others and had the disturbing feeling of being lived in. A pair of brown khakis, a white shirt neatly folded and a pair of socks rolled in a ball were sprawled out on an unmade bed. A bottle of cologne on an end table, steel toed boots, sneakers and cowboy boots were neatly organized in a row. A novel written by a less than famous author and an array of men's toiletries were situated atop an antique cherry wood armoire. I slid open the top drawer; men's boxers and clean white tees lined the inside.

An apparition had manifested into human form and I immediately became more alert. My phone rang; it was Tamara. I quickly silence it realizing that I may no longer be alone. I listened attentively wondering if the sound had given me away, but it was quiet. An unsettling hush persisted for the next several moments until I reminded myself to breathe. I slowly backed out of the room, carefully making sure everything was exactly the way I had found it. I crept down the steps allowing my gun to lead the way. I saw her for only a fraction of a second; a blur was the most uncomplicated way to describe her. She was a young child out of place, dressed for bed and probably searching for her father or mother to tuck her in. When she saw me, she bolted. I'd guessed she was following the strict instructions of her parents to avoid all contact with outsiders.

I have visited houses of squallier on many occasions and had been confronted with absolute cruel poverty that intrudes itself into people's daily lives. I would kill for my daughter; sell my organs if I had to if found in a situation of dire hopelessness like this. Anything would be better than to allow my child to suffer the indignity and humiliation. This diseased infested shithole was unbearable to me and bled me of all compassion for those who subjected their children to this lifestyle. The second floor was as desolate as the first. I listened but heard nothing; she couldn't have eluded me that quickly. I wanted to call out, but thought wiser of it. There must have been a million places to hide. I rationalized that if a little girl could run around in this mausoleum with no fear then I could brave it as well. A smoldering orange glow glimmered beneath a toothless gap in the floorboard.

After trying to steady myself, I visualized images of fire and brimstone. I had the odd suspicion that I was being observed from below. I found a wooden door that led to the basement hidden in a corner behind the spiral staircase. Jagged splinters capable of impaling Dracula jutted out from door and frame; I carefully opened it and slowly made my descent into Hades. The risers and railings were forged from steel and made my approach known. It grew noticeably warmer the further I plunged. The staircase wound then unwrapped revealing a space heater, kerosene lamp and a vacant cot. I turned just in time to be confronted by a huge white male with a shaved head. He towered over me; shirtless, barefoot and wearing only faded jeans. However, it was the sawed off shotgun that held my interest.

"Put her down," said the stranger.

My fingers tightened ever so slightly on the trigger, "And if I don't?"

"Nothing is predetermined," he motioned for me to toss my

gun on the bed, "only you can save you."

"I'm detective Logan Crenshaw of the Ravenswood Police Department."

"You're a trespasser is what you are," his eyes flamed, "I 'm not gonna tell you twice."

"You're making a mistake; shoot a cop and you're permanently fucked for life."

"My fence was padlocked, the door was shut and I didn't hear you knock. I'll take my chances, even if you're who you say you are."

"I'll show you my badge," I eased my hand....

"I wouldn't if I were you."

"Listen, I got complaints that a man was wandering around this place at night. All I was doing was checking things out."

"First and foremost, I bought this place and being a cop, you'd have checked that out before barging in."

"I'm investigating a double homicide, not casing homes," I said. Although, I wanted to say, '*You have nothing worth fucking stealing anyway*' but thought better of it after all, his gun was bigger than mine. "We can stand here playing with our dicks or we can resolve this," I reached for my badge... shit; I left it on the dash of the truck so I wouldn't lose it when I jumped the fence. *Why did that thought materialize in my mind?* Fuck! I hate getting old; by the looks of him my worries would soon be over. His trigger finger twitched uncontrollably. This fucker had hands the size of a professional athlete and was built like a brick shithouse and if humanly plausible he could probably tear the head clear off a person. If he were a killer it was no time for me to be right, "Looks like we have ourselves a Mexican standoff huh? Someone always loses."

"And somebody always wins."

"Be reasonable and put the shotgun down. You have every right to defend yourself, but why jeopardize your freedom by making the biggest mistake of your life?"

"And what if I think the biggest mistake is putting the gun down?" the giant remarked.

Footsteps overhead suspended the negotiations. The basement door opened. His partner would discover us in a matter of seconds and if he had a weapon, I was done for. I tightened my grip on the gun and steadied myself for the impending onslaught.

"Logan?"

I never felt so relieved to hear Tamara's sweet voice,

"Shoot him!" I yelled.

"Uh, shoot who?"

The giant stood there with an insipid smirk on his face.

"Logan, please look at me!" She appeared at my side; her gun rested on her left thigh, "nobody's down here but us."

I don't know if it was the words she spoke or the nonchalant way she stood there, but the room spun. I lost my balance and fell to my knees. I tried to stand as I looked up I saw him there. I knew he would kill her and I was completely powerless. He produced a silver serrated knife with a pearl handle. The kerosene lamp flickered, orange flames danced sardonically upon his blade. I could watch her die or close my eyes and hope to block out her screams until it was my turn. She remained completely oblivious to him. I tried to fight the weight of my eyelids, but in the end, I gave way to the darkness.

TODD ANDREW DAVIS
LAURA JEAN MILES
CHAPTER VII

After twenty minutes of driving, I almost did something unthinkable.

"Red light dumbass!" shouted a kid standing on the sidewalk.

I slammed on the brakes and nearly hit a girl walking through the crosswalk. Inches from her, she turned and bitterly scowled; her facial expression filled with ridicule. She made a terrible mistake; she should've kept walking because I sure as hell noticed her now. I knew right then and there she would be my next conquest. I watched her strut across the street and enter Marcel's Coffee Shoppe. I parked kiddy-corner from Marcel's and vacated my car as a bone chilling arctic blast rushed past me. I fetched a black leather jacket from the back seat along with a red on black ball cap and pulled the cap low to hide my eyes. I navigated my way to the sidewalk in front of the Coffee Shoppe, peered in and saw my prize possession mingling with a few patrons. She kissed a tall redheaded individual who gave me the impression that he knew her intimately. He gently placed a hand on her ass then wrapped his arms around her and lifted her slightly off her feet. His body language spoke loud and clear, warning all bystanders that she was his sole property. Surprisingly, I entered the small establishment. I found a corner booth and initiated my infiltration into the life of my new subject. I focused exclusively on her conversation blocking out all other interferences. She sensed my presence, but refused to acknowledge me. She'll regret that mistake as well.

"Allen," she spoke coquettishly. "What time are you swinging by tonight?"

"Shit!" he replied. "That thing-a-ma-jig is tonight? I thought…"

"Oh hell no Allen!" her voice cracked like a whip as it jumped an octave. "You promised me!" her demeanor took a radical detour. "You're a real asshole!"

"Shush, keep your voice down," he none too gently grabbed her by her elbow. "Are you trying to get me canned?"

She yanked her arm away in disgust, "Don't you shush me!" she said with a quiet intensity. "I'm not always going to be around Allen," the way she punctuated his name relayed the seriousness. Disgusted she spun around on her heels and marched toward the exit.

"Laura!" the expression on his face displayed a sheer sympathetic request for forgiveness. "Laura!" he overtook her; their voices now a whisper. Her glossy lips forced a barely detectable smile. He gently kissed her anticipating lips with all the passion of a dead trout.

Through dirty blinds, I watched her crisscross the street. The cold put an extra boost into her step. *Should I risk following her or would that be too obvious?* Within seconds, she was beyond sight. Allen was apparently unaffected by what had transpired and openly flirted with one of the females at the counter. *Don't worry Laura. Soon all your troubles will be put to rest.* A young freckled face girl with a pencil tucked behind her left ear leaned over and asked me for my order.

"I'll have a coffee, black," I said.

"Do you want anything else?" she muttered; her pencil paused on the scratch pad awaiting another command.

"No thank you, just the coffee," I replied.

I waited five minutes for the worst tasting mug of java I've ever had. I remained hopeful of making sweet Laura's acquaintance. That thought and that thought alone brought comfort. I had to devise a game plan; something that wouldn't just bring excitement but would ignite a long lasting memory. I wanted to lie down at night and fantasize about my excursions. Now I think I've found a way. I needed to learn every intimate detail about her life and become a full fledge hunter, not just a predator or an executioner. I'd learn the things that made her tick, her relationships and her deepest darkest fears. I beamed with eagerness excited to start my new foray; my new mission. In the meantime, I'd find someone insignificant to satisfy my hunger, perhaps another whore, a pretty runaway or one of the walking dead. I left a couple of bills including the tip, stretched my legs and exited the booth. I was inadvertently tracked by security cameras but didn't allow it to capture a full glimpse of my identity. Sometimes, just out of pure instinct, he protects me. However, I still try to be cautious but to be fully honest, he picked the booth, the cap and the girl. I made my way toward the door.

The first snowflake of the season floated downward from the heavens and I stuck out my tongue to taste it. I headed toward my car and Laura magically reappeared. She had hastily left Colleen's Book Emporium located next to the Ravenswood's Downtown College Campus. The sign above read, **'Turning Young Minds into Tomorrow's Future Leaders.'** *And for some, tomorrow will never come.* She headed for the parking garage elevator. Seven minutes later, a red compact convertible darted out onto Bellaire Parkway. I eased the Chevelle into first gear and eagerly embarked on my pursuit. I watched her attentively and kept my distance; not that a college girl would realize she's being followed. She was like most stereotypical female drivers; the fact that she hadn't sideswiped, rear-ended or totaled her vehicle with every turn or bend of the road was just dumb luck. The sky opened and the snow fell down upon us. The roads were becoming more treacherous with each and every passing moment. The stoplight morphed from green to yellow, I tapped the brakes and slowed to a stop. She made it through and I kicked myself for not running the light. My eyes strained to focus on the world beyond the street light. A black and white stationed on the opposite side of the intersection slightly protruded from the adjacent alleyway. He tapped the radar gun mounted on the dash while his eyes vigilantly sought violators; I was thankful I stopped when I did. It took an eternity and a day before the signal rotated back to green. I couldn't contain my eagerness to reengage the hunt. The car promptly fishtailed as I pressed the pedal. My gaze shifted from the streets to the sidewalks; rows of four foot tall two-hour meters stood at attention. The townspeople dashed in and out of the little town square; women folk bundled in faux fur coats and knockoff Gucci handbags with children, husbands or boyfriends tightly in tow. Christmas décor was hung, nativity scenes erected and colored bulbs were strewn by the Public Works employees as the town ushered in the holiday season. Their hustle and bustle kept the quaint little community of Ravenswood's economy flowing. They were all unaware that I was about to liven up their humdrum existence forever.

Caught by a red-light three blocks down, Laura was an omen wrapped in the perfect package of human flesh. She'd been delivered to me and I need to be mindful and appreciative of the gifts given. I had hastily accepted my status as executioner but never thought about the repercussions. I've considered at great length; God, morality and the Devil. But what if I were arrested? The misery of being caged by gray steel cobalt prison bars would turn me into a wild beast longing for freedom. I had to take more precautions. Two towns and six and a half miles later, we arrived in Tella Hute. These sleepy towns were all connected by a labyrinth of ensnarled streets and eclectic cafés. Laura pulled recklessly into a parking lot outside a string of condominiums. Scattered vehicles accented the snowbound lot. She parked her little red coupe out front in the compact only section. The condos were individually numbered making things relatively easy to find. I found a spot further back and assimilated to the new surroundings. She lingered in the car for several moments before leaving her vehicle with her arms tightly wrapped around books and packages clenched close to her bosom. She dashed across the blacktop while her red coat flapped in the wind. Immersed in a halo of snow, she placed a key in the lock of condo 728. *Things to learn: Does she live alone? Is this boyfriend Allen's little love nest?* I climbed out of the car and scanned the front of the building. The cold weather was irrelevant; I'd been fueled by a powerful combination of self-righteousness and obligation. I passed the condos to the left hand side and walked eastward toward the back lot. Gazing down, I tried to reassure myself that I wasn't leaving any identifiable footprints. *Don't be overly cautious; the snow will obliterate them anyway. Besides, I haven't done anything yet. This isn't why he tolerates your existence. Stay vital and for God's sake, cease giving him ammunition or he will eradicate you if warranted.* The ground steepened; I found myself climbing a hill as the terrain became overgrown with vegetation and trees. I seized an outstretched branch and negotiated my way to the top. My new vantage point not only gave me an unobstructed view, but incredibly from this position I could glimpse into the homes of the unsuspecting. And then there was Laura. Her back window was draped in a sheer white curtain designed purely for decoration or vanity but definitely not privacy. Through a high powered night scope, I'll enter her home at will. The smile on my face must have beamed from ear to ear. I chanced a voyage deeper into the woods; no longer would I park in her lot. I needed an escape route. I paid close attention to my footing until I came to a point where I spotted a school; Tella Hute Junior High Fighting Rebels. A perfect dwelling that would be unoccupied after nightfall. I could park close, slink around the building and disappear up the other side of the hill. I was truly inspired and more engaged. I carefully retraced my steps down the hill and towards the parking lot. Laura was a vibrant, intoxicating, youthful, beautiful little angel and now she's become a self indulgent orgasmic quest of prophesized bliss. I shed my ball cap and allowed my curly flowing locks to dance wildly in the crisp breeze. I gazed heavenward; my adversary the moon had not yet shone his brilliant face, but I suspect he knows my objectives by now. I reveled in glory before I re-entered my car.

Laura: "Mom, mom, please I beg you, will you let me talk now?" the phone was welded to my ear and it actually made my eardrum throb. I was in the process of cooking, listing and burning my dinner. "Mom, we're being safe."

"I want grandkids sweetie, before I die."

"Oh my God, you lecture me for fifteen minutes on birth control and not being a whore like Sharon…."

"Laura, I never said your sister was a whore. I just meant she should be more discrete."

"Okay mom, I give-up; I've gotta go."

"You're upset with me now aren't you Lamb chop?"

Ugh, I hated that nickname, "I'm not upset with you. Allen canceled our date tonight. I just want to eat, take a bubble bath and curl up with a good book. I don't plan on discussing my sex life with you. I appreciate you and daddy paying for the condo but….." *I thought I spotted a kid outside my window horsing around; someone that I've never seen before.* He was young with long curly dark hair and fixated on something beyond my sight. "Hold on ma," I couldn't get a good look at his face because he quickly tucked his head inside a ball cap. I could tell he was tall though; maybe six feet or taller. He ventured into a blind spot when he moved toward the parking lot.

"Laura!"

"Sorry mom," I hurried into the living room, peered out the window and stared into the parking lot. I lost him. "Shit! I burned my Ramen noodles."

"You never put enough water in the pot dear."

I repeated her words silently to myself mocking her

verbatim.

"Dad just pulled into the driveway. You want to talk with him honey?"

Laura: "I'll call back later, promise," my breathing was unbelievably erratic; I grabbed an inhaler from my purse. It always took a few moments to return to normal after conversing with family. I searched the lot for signs of life; it was an odd feeling seeing someone in the backyard. *There's literally nothing out there.* Well, unless of course he's working for the cable or Phone Company or the dreaded cocksuckers who work for gas or the electric company. *He must've been a utility worker. Why's my heart still racing? Jesus, my mom has me on edge, even two thousand miles away.* The noodles were unsalvageable; I turned the sink on and soaked the burnt waste under cold water. I was still hungry, but I didn't feel like venturing back out into the arctic cold. *I guess he could have been wearing a vest of some type underneath his leather jacket?* Even though I couldn't make out the features of his face he still seemed somewhat familiar.

I found a store that had everything I needed for my late night excursion. It was juvenile to have exposed myself as I did. I rattled off in my mind the factual, concise methods I needed to adhere to in order to maintain my viability. I unnecessarily jeopardized myself in an attempt to feel a modicum of dignity and significance. It's no consolation that he didn't castigate me for it. Perhaps I was being molded in his image, or perhaps he gave me a license to shape the outcome but remained capable of interjecting at any time. I want that power. *So why am I so damn determined to sabotage myself?*

Laura: "I am taking a bath, Allen."

"Can I join you?"

Why did I reach for the phone? "I thought you were working late?"

"I am baby, I just miss you."

You mean you miss mistreating me no doubt. "I'm tired; I'll probably turn in early tonight."

"I'll come over and tuck you in."

Laura: *Had he always been this desperate and I just overlooked it?* "No thanks, goodbye Allen," *click.* Funny, I really didn't want to be alone this evening but I didn't want to be with him either. I closed my eyes but felt uneasy soaking in the tub. I listened to every ping; every reverberation of the pipes rattling as the thermostat automatically turned the heat on and off. I remember the first night I spent alone here; I got no sleep. The howling wind only contributed to my anxiety. I imagined that my humdrum life was being invaded by some dark mysterious being, who I might add, would die of boredom if they wandered into my mind numbing life. *Gee, I made myself smile. That's more than Allen's done recently. Why am I thinking of him? Okay, whatever made that noise just freaked me out.* The door is locked, so were the windows. I listened more intently. My mom would have a heart attack if I died in the nude but why ruin a half decent bubble bath for a clumsy ax murderer, right? *Chill Laura; fuck, you're not sixteen anymore. Breathe in breathe out. I'll loufa the fucker to death.*

I watched the outline of her naked body as she paused then entered the bathroom. *What would it be like to experience Laura?* She'd been carefully sculpted into a flawless statuette of feminine exquisiteness. *Was I being sanctimonious in believing that only I was worthy of this heavenly creature?* I highly doubted anybody else saw her true essence. In return, she'll reciprocate her undying love and embrace me with an understanding of who I truly am. Together with unbridled passion, we will undergo a remarkable sacrifice. She'll fight, but eventually she will succumb and be submissive and obedient. I'll convince her of her purpose; it's a harsh lesson when you find that your dreams were just that. We all search for our station in life however, not all of us are meant to stay the full term on earth. Sacrifices have been a part of mankind's creation since time and memorial.

TODD ANDREW DAVIS
THE DEVILS PLAYTHINGS
CHAPTER VIII

Tamara was at the mercy of her rapist and I was unable or unwilling to intervene. She was only feet away, if I only had the courage to save her. I loathed myself for my pathetic disposition. I blocked out her shrill shrieks and unbearable cries and painstakingly surrendered to unconsciousness but before the last remnants of darkness eclipsed my dying soul; I etched his hideous image into my brain.

"Get up," the monster snarled.

Dazed and confused a dark coarse voice cut through my stupor. *How long had I been out; minutes, hours, days?* I'd been physically pulled to my bare feet by giant paws that used my ears as handgrips. Tears flowed from my eyes and a river of blood flooded my inner lobes. Sweat streaked aimlessly down my face as intense heat scorched my skin evaporating the salty discharge. With my head swimming, ears deadened and vision blurred, I tried to regain focus. Remarkably, my body yearned for the cold damp concrete from which I had laid. An ill fitted iron collar choked off oxygen as I wheezed to fill scorched lungs.

Fashioned around my wrist were heavy rusted iron cuffs that dug deep into my flesh. The monster jerked the collar and laughed as I gasped for air and raised my hands to my throat.

"You…" my vocal cords seized; temporarily repressing my thoughts.

He threw a rock hard fist that blackened my left eye. His toothless grin, his breath, his oil stained face and body, all stunk of low grade diesel fuel.

"Come!" the sadist barked as he tugged on the metal leash once again. He was draped in a cloth tunic fastened at the waist and wore Jesus shoes, though he was anything but a prophet.

"It's time for you," he yanked down hard on the chains and his garbled voice hissed. "Struggling prolongs your fate; acceptance is honor."

The words clamored in my head and I struggled to make sense of them, "Am I to die?" I sounded incoherent with words spoken by an alien tongue.

"So others can live," he vomited forth. "Your life has meaning, despite its tragic end," he struggled to open a heavy steel door that was set on wheels. Exalting tremendous power the system engaged and the twenty-foot high barrier crept open inch by laborious inch. "Stay close to the wall," he chided.

I wrenched backwards so not to plummet to my doom.

The narrow winding staircase led into a dark chasmic abyss of tortured souls. Embedded razor sharp spikes alongside the wall tore vehemently at my naked flesh and I moaned in anguish. His back was turned toward me as I visualized his bucktooth smile. I wanted to bash the heathen's fucking head in.

I peered over my left shoulder briefly. My mind converted the spikes into ivory teeth attached to animated skulls surrounded in loose fleshy tissue. Dark orbs shunned away whimsical spirits who dared attempt to Christianize their ill fated souls. My bruised and aching body was a validation of everything I was experiencing. I began to sway side to side from exhaustion and heat. Open bloody wounds added to my weariness and I had to tightrope one foot precariously in front of another as the stairwell increasingly narrowed. The semi-human wall shrieked in a maddening chorus of insufferable heartaches that resounded throughout my body. The damage done to my eardrums had been astronomical and probably irreversible. I was exasperated and took my destiny into my own hands and leapt into the great beyond. The metal chain links strained in protest. I thought my neck would surely snap and I felt him thrashing about in an effort to maintain his balance. I caught him off guard and smiled at the prospect of the monster clawing at thin air. He tried desperately to save his miserable existence; within seconds, he lost the fight and we were both in freefall. I yelled at the top of my lungs; the most guttural vitriol scream I could summon.

A greenish glow fought back the edges of darkness. The beeping of the EKG machine was proof that I was still among the living. My arms and feet were strapped down to a gurney; a clear tube was rooted deep inside my nasal passage and an I.V. drip made the vein on my left hand itch so wildly, it nearly drove me mad. Beyond the safety of the light, a ghostly figure stoically watched. *Jesus Christ?* I slowly came to the realization that it was nothing more than a white sheet draped over the back of a chair. My over active imagination caused my heart to fluctuate and almost got the best of me again. That was until she moved. I was awake and aware despite the concoction of drugs being pumped into my veins. *She's Lizzy all grown-up, or perhaps Kathy waiting patiently by my side. Maybe Tamara's raped and beaten corpse was haunting me for not saving her.* No. None of them; Jessica Ann Foster cradle the severed head of her sibling Jennifer. Her swollen disfigured face and the pale, maggot infested skull of her sister were just beyond my vision. I was positive it was her just the same. She drifted closer as I shut my eyes. The room smelled of putrid death and damp earth. It grew drastically colder with every broken step she took. With her face centimeters from mine; her rancid breath washed over me. Heavily sedated I had to convince myself that ghosts didn't exist. My eyes remained tightly closed. *Make it until morning light Logan.* The bed sheet was encapsulated with sweat, but I remained resolved in my convictions. *Eyes stay shut until someone saves me. Was it early morning or late night?* I yearned to know. *Had there been a clock in the room?* I still felt her rotted face lingering above mine. Her shimmering green eyes turned into dull black orbs and her flesh bubbled with pockmarks. Her breath was stained with death and the all too familiar scent of formaldehyde. Maybe I died and had been too afraid to accept it. Yet I'm still cognizant and still have a sense of being connected to the living world. *Open your eyes Logan.* Perhaps I feared I had succumbed to death? *Had Jessica been an Angel of Mercy or an Angel of Death? She might have been watching over me to make sure I returned to the living to avenge her. She was a living corpse, an oxymoron; impossible. So what the hell was she?*

"Logan…. Logan."

I felt a disturbing weightlessness. *Was I still falling into the pits of hell?* I awaited the brutal thud my body would make; eventually it would strike something solid and shatter my bones into a million pieces. I was terrified by Jessica's late night visit and still dreaded the thought of opening my eyes. When I did, I muttered to my dutiful wife Kathy the name Tamara. Instantly my wife released my hand; diluted by the haze and unfocused clarity that was my world I still recognized how deeply I had hurt her. I reached out for her as she fled my bedside. Tamara's perfume preceded her; it was a scent I had grown well accustomed to. She wanted that speck of femininity in a world predominately dominated by male officers, male criminals and the like.

"I thought you were dead?" I blurted out.

"When you didn't answer your phone, I went inside the mansion," she sat beside the bed. "You were on the floor screaming that someone... something attacked you. I searched the house, but I found no one," she said compassionately. "You don't remember anything else?"

I heard my wife's voice in the background ether, "I'll leave you two alone."

I hadn't realized she was still in the vicinity. I felt too ashamed to acknowledge her words when I had failed to acknowledge her presence.

"Logan, what happen back at the house?" Tamara spewed forth in a dark sardonic tone.

The house tainted my memory. A warm feeling swelled from my frozen soul hearing Tamara's voice. I wasn't quite up to reliving past events. I had to separate reality from fantasy and deal with it internally. My simple self-diagnoses; acute pneumonia accompanied by dehydration and a raging fever. Theoretically, that would explain away the delusions, however I knew better, much better. "How long have I been laid up?" my voice was gruff. "What's wrong Tamara?" her body language betrayed the façade.

"It's been nearly seventy-two hours, Logan... I promised Kathy I wouldn't tell you. She moved to the edge of the gurney. Her face flustered, she took several deep breaths then exhaled and said somberly, "Logan, there were two other murders. A young female prostitute was found stuffed in a motel ceiling after a fire was set. The firemen retrieved her before her remains were scorched behind recognition; right now the pathologist is giving her the once over. Originally, I thought it was unrelated, but now it looks like her murder parallels the Foster sisters with massive blood loss."

"Postmortem?"

"No Logan, she was very much alive."

"Alright then, tell me about the second killing?"

"Um, I'm headed there now."

I painfully disengaged the I.V. and hose. Tamara helped me dress without too much protest and five minutes later, we were out the door. We were like drunken teenagers encountering their parents and Kathy's wide eyed expression sobered us up instantaneously I placed my left arm around her waist and whispered, "There have been two more homicides. If I feel too weak, Tamara will bring me back. I have to do this." I placed a kiss on her lips and gently patted her belly, "I love you sweetheart; I'll be okay."

Kathy's gaze pierced Tamara's soul and cut her profoundly deep with resentment. Tamara tensed up, braced herself for the onslaught of expletives sure to come, but Kathy remained silent as we headed toward the elevator. During times of crisis it's amazing what your body can accomplish. I was flying high with the adrenaline surging through my body but by the time we set foot in the hospital's parking garage I began to rethink the wisdom. Tamara was certainly competent enough to run the investigation. We finally reached the car and I was somewhat embarrassed to ask for assistance. The car roared to life and we sped off towards downtown Ravenswood. The fever worked my body over like a boxer striking a speed bag. I was burning up inside while being tormented with bitter chills.

"When did it snow?" I remarked.

"The zombie stirs."

"Tam."

"Sorry, it flurried a couple nights ago, then off and on throughout the night."

Glancing at the dash, I realized it was only one-thirty in the morning not the middle of the afternoon as I assumed.

"Kathy hates me," Tamara bluntly stated.

"Were you under the impression she liked you all these years?"

"You're a jerk!" she flashed a glib smile after noticing mine.

"Never mind Kathy, the right thing was getting me outta there. Maybe the fresh powder will provide us with a breakthrough?"

TODD ANDREW DAVIS
THE LIBERATION OF LAURA JANE
CHAPTER IX

Liberating might be an accurate description. Being in Laura's home unknowingly to her caused a sense of power to wash over me. She left her condo just thirteen minutes ago and today, I decided to make my third entry into her home. I wanted to dissect every aspect of her life no matter how miniscule. There are aromas that permeate throughout one's dwelling that initiate a different thought process. I immediately identified soaps, laundry detergents and a plethora of scents that I associated with her everyday routine. I could tell Laura had bathed in lavender honey oatmeal body wash today; made eggs, wheat toast, pork bacon and had washed it down with a cup or two of finely ground fresh gourmet coffee. There was this sense of realization as though I was beginning to know Laura quite well. It is of great importance for a hunter to know what their prey digested before devouring them. I was mindful of her habits and made mental notes of where things were in her apartment and never tried to intentionally disturb her environment. However, there were times I needed to quench my thirst, make a sandwich or even indulged myself in a hot shower. I was always aware of the ripple effect my presence could inflict upon her little paradise. No one misses a slice of bread, a strip or two of bacon and egg or a cup of coffee. Sometimes it was for nourishment and other times I just needed to treat myself.

I'd create my own dialog as I watched television with the sound muted. I'm sure she was bewildered when I clicked the close caption and had forgotten to reset her TV. I even used the vacuum to clean up the dirt left behind by my shoes. The use of noisy appliances is never a wise decision, especially when paper thin walls are shared by multiple tenants. But sometimes you have no other practical alternative. However, I never once contemplated sleeping in her bed and would never intentionally do something that would alter her sense of security. Honestly, how many times have you arrived home and found your bath towel still damp or your toothbrush wet and thought absolutely nothing of it? Have you ever sworn you had more toilet paper or paper towels only to discover you miscalculated and then had to make a mad dash to the corner store to restock? Humans have natural flaws and chalk a minor inconvenience up to forgetfulness. What you don't want is clumsiness; breaking a family heirloom or a glass that was part of a collection. You need to familiarize yourself with the surroundings and the placement of things and always be cognizant of abnormal sounds and movements. It's all an integral part of the wider spectrum.

Today was abnormally warm. I walked into the bedroom and entered the diminutive adjoining bathroom. I pulled my jeans and shirt off, reached for the faucet and ran the water. Staring back at me from an antique mirror was a man that at first I didn't recognize. His eyes were a vibrant hell red, his hair full of long loose curls and his youthful face was somewhat pleasing to the eye. Being trapped inside this flesh and bone cell was not such a horrifying dilemma after all. I realized I'd have to make the best of my situation. *Maybe my survival instincts kept me from allowing him to fully take over? Would it be easier just to give in? Would I fade away or continue to be a witness to his crimes?*

At the moment I hungered for participation instead of total inhalation. I looked away before he noticed. *Why was this mirror different from any other? Why did it capture his image?* I climbed into the shower and was instantly soothed by a rainfall mix of heat and pulsating energy. *I'm going to install the same exact shower head in my bathroom.* I used just a dab of shampoo and a dollop of conditioner. Sometimes it's easy to find yourself addicted to the smallest of amenities however; I never ran the risk of shaving for fear of leaving behind traces of blood evidence. When I finished I toweled off. I stuck to my routine and wiped down the shower walls and tub basin. I could smell the coffee even before the timer went off. After dressing, I poured a cup of the steaming hot brew. Her bed had been made as usual and the curtains were drawn letting the sun infiltrate her room. She was a fairly neat young lady with no posters plastered on the walls or CDs strewn about. Her dresser drawers were tidy as could be and all her clothes painstakingly folded. After I downed the last remnants of coffee, I rinsed the mug and returned it to the rack. The clanking of metal keys echoed in the chamber of the front door. *What possessed her to show up now?* With the sound of the keys still jingling, I sprinted to the door and retrieved my shoes from where I had kicked them off. I scooped them up in one motion and hustled to the hall closet. I peered through quarter inch slats and watched the front door spring open. She entered and locked the door behind her. She kicked her shoes off and they bounded one over the other almost landing in the exact spot I had left mine. She froze for a second or two as if sensing danger.

Laura: I could still smell the bacon and coffee from the morning's breakfast. As I crossed the threshold for whatever reason, I felt like suddenly fleeing from the apartment. My skin was plagued with goose bumps. I wanted to check under the bed and all my closets for an unfounded unsubstantiated fear. *Knock it off Laura. You should be happy. You did well on the exam and now you have the whole afternoon to yourself. The world is your oyster; whatever the hell that means.*

Kill her, I thought as I watched her through the closet. My plan was unraveling right before my eyes. I almost regretted the shower but I was feeling rundown and desperately needed to replenish. She removed her jacket and headed directly toward me. I reached into the back of my jeans and clutched the pearl handled knife. She slammed her hand so hard against the door that it shook in place for several moments.

"I've got you!" she proclaimed as she stared at the palm of her hand.

It was a mosquito, fly or some sort of vile insect she crushed beneath her cuticles. It almost caused a certain fatal response. Instead I waited, for what I'm not exactly sure? I couldn't comprehend why I didn't just strike. *Pounce on her and drag her lifeless body into the bedroom.* She tossed her coat onto a pink leather couch and proceeded down the narrow hallway. Seconds turned into minutes and minutes lingered painstakingly and agonizingly by. The aroma of coffee hovered in the air and I was sure the pot was still warm to the touch. She should be dead already. I was cramped, hot and extremely uncomfortable. I had the power to put my misery to an end. However, without him I wasn't exactly a highly efficient killing machine. Without the keys to turn the ignition, I remained sadly in idle. *Was he making a statement?* She waltzed past me once again, swept up her coat, slipped her feet into rose colored shoes, opened the door and disappeared.

Today I waited for Laura; late as usual. It had been two days since our little episodic encounter in her apartment. I had become a horrible malfunctioning robot with crossed wires; I never should've allowed her to draw another breath.

"Can I borrow some ketchup?" a little boy of five or six with puppy dog eyes appeared tableside.

"Bobby!" his mother yelled from the corner booth.

"Oh yeah," his gap toothed smile was in full view. "Please," he stared up at me.

I smiled and without another word handed the bottle to the little shit. I wanted to tell him that his mother was a cunt and would set precedence for all the bitches that would scar his life throughout the coming decades. Instead, I patted him gently on the head and sent him skipping back to his miserable life. The door opened and Laura casually walked through, stunning as always. She strolled over to the counter and ignored me in her customary way. It was actually an unspoken joke we shared.

"Sorry Allen."

"I'm the one who should apologize," his arms outstretched in a compassionate pose. "I hate when we fight."

"You know what tonight is don't you?"

A loaded question if there ever was one. Once again the charming little Laura had him completely baffled. The expression on his face was absolutely priceless; a blank and clueless stare, completely oblivious to the anger that was sure to follow.

"Seriously Allen?"

"Baby…"

"Fuck you!" she shouted back.

It was so unexpected coming from sweet little Laura, that I accidentally chuckled. It stunned Allen as well. I chose that particular moment to look over in their general direction; stupid me. I broke the cardinal rule. I was a man that did everything possible not to attract any attention; a man who tried to be as inconspicuous as a fly on a wall. Now, I was visible. I was a piece of twine that unraveled just enough to be clipped. I had foolishly exposed myself and would bear his wrath.

"What the fuck are you looking at?" Allen's face grew beet red as he glared at me.

I lowered the rim of my baseball cap, hid my eyes and sheepishly departed the table.

"That's right you little jag-off, keep walking. Mind your own business you god damn pussy!"

"Allen, knock it off you jerk!"

She defended me and a smile crests my lips. *Allen, we shall meet again.* The Coffee Shoppe was now off limits; I would have to spend the majority of my time staking out her apartment. It was foolish of me to interject myself into her life. I had been content with hiding behind library books and watching her do a load of laundry six machines away. I even sat through a god awful chick flick in a late night cinema and had spied on her while she flirted with a clerk at the local grocery store. I spent almost a week in and out of her apartment trying to break up the monotony. And now, *Could I be identified? Did my clumsiness give me away?* I drove three miles in absolute astonishment and agonized over my compulsion to gain access to every crevice of her being. All the while, I blatantly ignored the warning signs. *How could I have allowed this to transpire?*

12:01am

I sat blankly staring out the windshield of my car in a dark alley. The moon echoed my sadness or maybe just mocked my error. We had sought out one another often during these past few months. Enemies, rivals or maybe allies, that was yet to be determined. Had he been this much of a presence in my life before? I didn't pretend to know that answer, but all the same he envied my power; that I knew beyond a doubt. My window was slightly cracked open and exposed my skin to the cold. I felt nothing, just numbness, calmness.

12:13am

A metallic gray door violently flung open and put an abrupt cease to the boredom. The sound drew my full attention. And then he materialized; the swirling snow gave him an aura of a majestic God orchestrating the winds. I could feel the change come over me; a tingling sensation that awoke my senses. The smell of burnt cinnamon filled my nostrils, my eyes itched and my head swam as my migraine had me teetering on the verge of another blackout. I wanted to participate; I tried to prolong my stay. We silently approached our prey with a tire iron in hand. Still conscious of every movement, in unison our arms rose and in one downward swoop we brought the iron bar crashing down upon his right temple. The cold made my hand vibrate with excruciating pain. I delighted in the shock and terror that flooded his face. His hand instinctively rose and for the moment protected him from another attack. It was an utterly useless defense; the heavy metal bar came crashing down once again and staggered him. He wore a pathetic frown on his clown face, which begged the question why? He wouldn't bleed to death from those blows alone and a couple of strikes weren't nearly enough to blunt my rage. Our hands snaked around his throat and his survival instincts kicked in. His body pivoted; a semi-defense mechanism initiated by fear and training. Allen actually thought he had a fighting chance and thought he might live after all. Adrenaline fueled his punches but their stings were weak with little to no effect. His voice was stifled making it impossible for him to let out a single yelp. He squirmed but couldn't kick free of our grip. I wanted him to feel the pain that I felt having to deviate so drastically from our goal. Warm blood continued to shower our face as we stared into his eyes and watched his life slowly slip away until there was nothing left. I took a healthy drink of his blood then finished beating him to death.

1:55am

We drove slowly and crept through the back alley of Marcel's Coffee Shoppe. Three squad cars with their cherries flashing gave birth to a virtual human puppet show. Red and blue lights danced in a macabre ballet of shadows along the brick wall. Both ends of the alley had been sealed off and mostly badges prowled the premises. Snow fairies tangoed whimsically about as the temperature continued to rapidly plummet. Three inches of fresh winter snow blanketed the concrete and made the footing extremely treacherous. Raspberry droplets publicized a nightmarish slaying. I watched the first responders quiver from beneath fleece blankets as they stood outside the crime scene tape. I knew their discomfort was due to more than the harsh weather. The setting was a sequel in the making. Allen's body had been broken and was a jigsaw puzzle like mess composed of twisted arms and legs. The blood kept your mind from imagining that you were staring at a mannequin. *How on earth did no one hear his cries?* In a circle of authority and composure, mass anarchy brewed just beneath the surface. It yearned for an accelerant to ignite it and set the whole scene ablaze. Blood had coated the metallic green dumpster and turned portions of the snow into strawberry Italian ice. Bloody handprints and frozen blood with shards of ice matted Allen's red hair and intertwined with the exposed gray matter that poured out of his skull. His limbs, wrenched from their sockets were twisted and disjointed with broken fingers that protruded from his mangled right hand. Here lies Allen Benjamin Gross, bloodied and bludgeoned to death. He was twenty-two years young, a college senior who stood nearly six foot five. Among other things, Allen had wrestled for Ravenswood's varsity team and played second string linebacker for the Ravenswood's Titans. Allen was no slouch, in fact he was quite the physical specimen and he was someone who could take care of himself. So you'd think; so he thought.

"You look like shit Logan; comparatively speaking of course."

Ross Hayward was in his mid-seventies and strictly professional. Mistakenly, he was also thought to have been retired. He was a tall lankly black man with a dark sense of humor who stood ridged, strong and proud. He knew his shit and if he didn't, he'd learn it. He was held in great esteem by every agency across the country and I had the unenviable task of relieving him and his department of their duties.

"Ross...."

"A sanitation worker found the body," he interrupted. "Isolating one distinguishable shoe print would be nothing short of dumb luck. This poor soul's been eviscerated. His flesh seared, bones broken, fractured and pulverized. See this crude gash near his right temple?" He pointed to a hole still caked with blood, "I believe it was probably made by an ordinary tire iron. We suspect the onslaught he endured until finally succumbing was created by a human or not so human fist. His neck's broken in several places. His collarbone was dislocated and both eye sockets were shattered. Three fingers on his left hand were severed and two on his right seem to have been mauled and I'm guessing… eaten. We haven't found all of his remains and if not for the brutal cold and snow; we'd all be wearing hip waders. We found the partial impression of human bite marks on the right side of his throat and neckline. I've just started working on him Logan, so if you're going to tell me your crew is pulling rank; partner he's all yours. You don't have to ask this old fool twice." He peeled off a latex glove and extended his long bony mahogany fingers in an understanding yet remorseful handshake. I didn't have to say another word. "Logan, keep me informed," he appeared grateful and almost sympathetic to my plight.

Several fresh tracks surrounded Allen's torso. He had fought vigilantly to no avail. *How could one individual catch him so off guard?* I watched as Detective Hayward climbed into his jet black Chevy Suburban. My first impression of Allen's corpse was that it had resembled a deflated rubber doll; an observation I made from about fifteen feet away. Hovering over him, my impression didn't change much. His perpetrator stored so much vitriol and animosity that his rage was irrepressible; just like Jessica and Jennifer I feared we wouldn't find any chemical or trace evidence. For the first time I felt the frigid air the storm had brought. My eyes caught sight of the moon just before a cloud obscured it from view. Allen's large intestine had been wrapped around his neck like a noose. He may have died from the loss of blood caused by the six-inch gash behind his right eye. He may have died from the tremendous beating he took at the hands of a lunatic. Maybe he died from shock as his fingers were broken and partially devoured. Perhaps beyond humanly feasible, he staved off death long enough to be choked with his own intestine. Whatever the case, long after Allen inhaled his last breath his attacker continued the onslaught. His big toe on his left foot had been crushed and both ankles damaged. I searched the interior of his mouth; his teeth resembled a picket fence. His throat had been cut by a serrated edge knife. He was meant to feel this pain well into the afterlife. His knuckles bruised and bloodied, defensive wounds scarred the palm of his hands and several of his fingernails had been torn away. God, the pain he must've endured. *Who the fuck did this to you Allen? Just give me a clue.*

TODD ANDREW DAVIS
THE DARKSIDE OF ANGER
CHAPTER XI

My anger got the best of me. How cliché that sounds, but in retrospect it summed up Thursday night to a T. I woke up in a tremendous amount of pain, partly due to my hunger and partially because of Allen. To my astonishment, my survival was more blood dependent than I had realized. Allen, to his credit was able to inflict some minor wounds; in the heat of battle warriors sometimes underestimate the strength of their opponents. Allen was an imposing figure in his own right and would've been a pass in most circumstances, but in my defense he had made himself a necessary target. I wanted Laura; deserved her and Allen's death was of very little consequence. He was an insignificant piece of shit who had attempted to lead me away from my ultimate goal. I could have resurrected and slaughtered him a hundred times over and still would have yearned for Laura. I behaved as though she was the one lying in a pool of her own fluids. I can never allow my anger to blind me again. After I finished taping my ribcage a new idea was born; I could take full credit for this one.

Connie Jefferson was seductive, lanky, ebony female with a nice butt and a great pair of tits. As part of the overall illusion, I would venture outside my circle in an attempt to hinder the Police Profiler and not allow myself to be easily categorized. At the very minimum it would force them to take an eraser to their chalkboard. Today a black chick, tomorrow who knows? Maybe I'll feel like Chinese or a kid or two. Connie's normally not the type that would typically trigger my killer instinct but unfortunately, she was a pawn who got caught up in a virtual game of cat and mouse. I tracked her in much the same way I did Laura; knowing with all certainty that my next kill would be spontaneous and random. I even dabbled with the idea of leaving clues. I'd buy shoes one or two sizes bigger then leave conspicuous footprints. That's when an even brighter idea emerged; an idea that brought me back to last week.

Ryan was a good looking fast talking kid who was a bit rough around the edges. He had a muscular build and short curly black hair. Unbeknownst to him, he had just won a starring role in act V of my jeu macabre. He'd been shooting pool and tossing back brews with his buddies for nearly three hours. If he wasn't drunk now he was doing everything possible to get there. The plan I had conjured up was a relatively simple one but grew in complexity with each and every passing moment. I spied on Ryan from my bar stool; he was loud, arrogant and an over aggressive parasite with an offensive personality. He would never be missed and killing him would be doing a valuable service to humanity.

"Last call ladies and gentleman, last call."

They were words that I'll forever cherish. Our friend Ryan was the type to close a bar down long after his group of five departed. Each of them were subjected to his heckling chorus of pussies, losers and wimps. I started to become ever so reluctant to elevate this miserable prick's status. *He's not worthy of portraying me, not even for a second*; yet still I sat in wait for hours. I even sent his crew two pitchers of amber ale to contribute to their intoxication.

Ryan drank more than his counterparts without complaint. Yeah, he won't be missed; he's just another blotch on society. He made his way around the bar giving hi- fives and fist bumps to all the guys and hugs and kisses to all the ladies. He chatted with the bartenders, barmaids and bouncers and with pinky and thumb extended, he whispered *'call me'* to a little brunette waitress. From my car, I watched as Ryan and a couple of stragglers lit-up cigarettes while they hung out underneath the veranda and were mesmerized by the icy rainfall. He whipped out his cell and made calls. Twenty-three minutes after Hanna's bar closed, he was finally on the move. *No taxi or late night drop offs? I guess none of the pussies, losers and wimps were going his way.* He took a shortcut through the woods; thank god, this night finally began to show promise. I parked the Chevelle at a nearby church, got out into the swirling rain and reveled in pure delight. I entered the woods and sought out other forms of life; I found none and had my fun.

"Ryan," I called out to him. "Ryan," my voice was barely an octave above a whisper.

"Who's there?"

His head jerked around as I stepped off the trail and out of sight.

"Ryan!" I yelled louder, "You're going to die!" He fought to keep his balance and staggered forward; running might've caused him to stumble and break his neck. "It's Allen," I said, "Allen Gross; back from the dead."

"What?" he stared right at me, walked backwards and tried to gage the distance between us.

"Ryan, I can make you immortal."

"Fuck you scumbag!"

For a fleeting second I thought he'd shown some balls and fight, but in predictable Ryno fashion, he ran. His pace quickened and his steps remained uncertain. My eardrums were being pierced by a wailing crescendo of sound that threatened my sanity. The treetops swayed back and fro and my balance eluded me. I began to overheat and sweat dripped profusely. I felt the neurons pulsate in the back of my eye sockets. Lightheaded and weak, I fought back a violent wave of nausea.

"Watch your step Ryan, I don't want you to hurt yourself," I said. "Don't make me chase you. I promise I'll kill you quick."

He bobbed, weaved and staggered forward seeking refuge, "I'll kill you fucker!" he shouted gallantly back as he continued to wobble down the path. He had reached the lip of the woods and was mere yards from safety. He dashed left towards a house illuminated by a single porch light. "Help me! Somebody, please help me!"

A kitchen light sparked to life, the oak door opened to reveal an elderly Caucasian woman in fluffy white slippers and a raggedy yellow cotton robe. Her face bewildered and sleep deprived. My cap concealed my true identity; I made the obligatory universal hand gesture and slowly dragged my forefinger across my throat. Ryan physically sagged when she slammed the door shut. He tried in vain to reach the next home. Stretching out through the darkness, I caught him in a Half-Nelson and dangled my trusty pearl handled knife inches from his throat. He stopped struggling immediately.

"What do you want?" he pleaded.

How could I allow this ingrate to become me? He could never hold the title of legendary killer. I plunged the knife deep into his chest; digging out his soul with the tip of my blade. Warm blood saturated my hands as his body violently spasmed. His lungs expelled his last gasps of air and traded each breath of oxygen for warm liquid. I held my grip tightly, until I was positive the last remnant of Ryan's fire had been extinguished.

"Why me? What did I do?" his voice shuttered in protest.

He startled me. I'd lost once again. I wanted to kill Ryan for his weakness; I didn't want this pathetic individual to garnish any undue glory. He wasn't entitled and the very thought made me ill. I produced a vile of clear scentless liquid from my jacket, applied it to a rag and covered his nose and mouth. It was an arduous task transporting Ryan's dead weight from the woods and into the trunk of my car. Hopefully it wouldn't be as problematic stashing him away.

3:45am

"Who's there?" Kathy was lying naked next to me with Lizzy on the opposite side of her. I had slept through the storm and the little one crawling into bed sometime during the night. What woke me was the smell. Once again, she boorishly intruded into my sanctuary and her abhorrent presence still lingered in the room. I had become part of a morbid anecdotal tale and was beguiled by her raw refusal to be vanquished. I surrendered to the notion that she would ever leave by her own volition; I knew I had to dispel her spirit once and for all. Hidden under a cloud of darkness, she motioned me to follow. I gently extricated myself from beneath Kathy's arm and left both my angels fast asleep. She paused briefly in the hallway unsure if I would follow. The front door stood wide open and rain ferociously pounded the brick pavers. I entered into the unyielding rain and chased her battered and tormented soul. We ran barefoot through the wet grass; two lost souls pursuing the night. She danced and rejoiced in the moonlight like a spinning dreidel. She possessed the youth and carefree spirit of a child. We headed for the woods; her golden mane fought the wind as it threatened to wrestle free from her rotted skull. The neighbor's motion detector activated and flooded the backyard with artificial light. I should've gained some solace as the pathway was bathed in light; instead it gave me a clearer view of my ghostly guide. Her body was wrapped in a yellow stained nightgown. She was a young female; her skin as pale as wedding rice and her movements robotic. She reveled in the violent weather as though it personified a fleeting sensation of once being alive. Her dead eyes caught mine and sent me a jealous glare as if to utter that I had taken my life for granted.

An alien with slight human characteristics is the best way to describe her. I felt a twinge of empathy; her spirit was imprisoned in a world she could no longer be part of. *How can anyone cope with their own demise?* I continued to tag along as we melted further into the woods. We came to a fork in the path; she hesitated for a moment then darted left. I madly pushed away branches and twigs; beneath me were the sounds of a black lagoon rippling in the midnight air. Like Jesus before her, she walked on the water's surface. I slid down the muddy embankment wearing only boxers and a tee shirt. I knew I'd be risking hypothermia as I launched into the frigid black water. The surge of pain was an excruciating sensation like soaking in a tub of ice. I was on the verge of blacking out and my head slipped back under the dark water. My eyes fluttered open as I stared through the muck. She swam towards me, took my hand and towed me across. I lay at the water's edge for several moments; a feverish red moon hovered high above. I willed myself to my feet and she celebrated my courage; my will to survive. I absorbed her strength and soldiered onward. It felt as though we had covered miles, half-running; half-staggering. My lungs fought for oxygen as the rain continued to pummel our flesh; ahead of us an ancient barn came into view. Rows of headstones were concealed behind it and she weaved in between them before coming to rest at one particular grave. Slowly I made my way in her direction. The gravestone was worn; the lettering almost completely washed out read, '*Sara Jane Carter*'.

I pointed to her, "Are you Sara Jane?"

Her face lit up in recognition of a name that hadn't been spoken by a human tongue in decades. I'll never know what possessed me to move closer, I reached to clean off the stone with my hand. She let loose in a low animalistic growl and I slowly retreated. She gnashed and snarled with razor sharp teeth before lunging at me. She found her target spot and chomped down hard on tendon and bone; my wrist was caught in a deathtrap.

"Fuck!" I yelled as we thrashed about on the frozen tundra.

I tried to scramble to my feet. My blood sprayed her face as she fed. I kicked hard, my right heel caught her square in the jaw but it didn't discourage her. I wanted to stop fighting and give into the pain. I thought of my wife and Lizzy left unprotected and alone. I picked up a fallen branch, reared back and with all my might stabbed her in the eye. Greenish purple pus gushed from her wound as her head fell back.

I launched into her with a front kick that caught her under the jaw line and wrenched my bloody hand free. I found a rock and unleashed a second assault with all the unrestrained force of Allen's killer. I bashed, slammed, elbowed, kneed and punched her in an attempt to send her dead fucking corpse back to hell.

Wake-up Logan. I staggered away from her and came to rest my full body weight on a headstone. I ripped the sleeve of my tee shirt and crudely bandage my wrist.

I wanted to turn her over and get a better look but thought better of it. The rain was unrelenting and the only option was to seek shelter. *Wake-up Logan.* I was freezing; I watched as each breath I took floated into the night and couldn't help but wonder if it would be my last. I searched the edge of the woods seeking shelter. A light flickered from a mansion in the distance and it was a welcome alternative to the ancient barn. In my condition; beaten, bruised and half naked, I had little hope anyone would dare take me into their home. I decided to make my way back to the barn. I had to find something to wrap around my body. White hot pain raced up my leg and stopped me in my tracks. A piece of wood jetted out from my thigh. I didn't have the stomach to look at it for long; instead I hobbled the rest of the way in excruciating pain. A single wooden beam secured the barn doors. I removed it and flung the double doors wide open. I half-heartedly expected to be trampled by livestock. The barn was at least forty feet deep yet I could barely see two feet through the darkness. *God, did I really want to search blindly and risk impaling myself on a nineteenth century pitchfork?* Half-naked man it is. The wind howled as it bounced around the graveyard and by the light of the moon I watched her vanish. I panicked, but was inspired by a tiny shimmering beckon coming from the oasis on top of the hill. Movement in the distance caught my attention and a strange sound came from an unidentified direction. I headed southward; the sound grew more intense and I braced myself for another attack. Whatever's stalking me, waited, watched and was itching for me to make a lethal mistake. Unfortunately, I chose a path with no discernible markers. A branch full of razor sharp thorns sliced my flesh just below my eyebrow; the blood stung my eyes. I could hear her as she pursued me. Ahead of me danced a flickering reddish orange flame and in the distance I could see the familiar contours of Chancellor's Manor.

'*Run!*' my thoughts screamed but the constant throbbing in my leg made that prospect impossible. Slow and steady, nice and easy. My last resort would be to test the leg in a dead run. *How far off was that fucking light anyway?* The treetops swayed and drenched me with frozen rainwater. I leaned against a giant red oak and that's when I saw the eyes. They were hellfire red and floating six feet above the ground. *This ain't Sara.* I grazed my thigh with my hand and a low whimper escaped me. The eyes suddenly shifted in my direction and I heard sniffing. Whatever lay beyond the tree line was attempting to pick-up my scent. I listened intently, but the crackling thunder and rain drowned out the creature's movements. *This has to be a dream.* The leaves on the right began to rustle and move in a suspicious pattern and I was off and running. I ignored the pain and fought the blitz of obstacles ahead: trees, branches, bushes and brush. A small log cabin situated within the nucleus of the woods came into insight. It sat in an open green patch of field a hundred yards away. I'd be exposing myself to anyone or anything that wanted to do me harm. Without breaking stride, I kept running. I heard the hooves pounding away in hot pursuit and rapidly close the distance between us. My lungs burned and eyes watered. I wanted to glance back and see the beast that had been gunning for me but didn't dare. I leapt onto the porch and slammed my body violently into the door. I twisted the knob as I regained my balance; opened and shut it all in one motion. I slid down the door and came to rest on the wood splintered floor. I took full stock of my injuries and surveyed the room then took several deep breathes allowing my lungs to refill.

A pungent odor that came from something boiling atop the cast iron stove alerted me to some other presence. White smoke curled near the ceiling and a single candle sat in the center of an antique table set for two. Moth eaten curtains framed the windows. It was obvious someone had been here recently; I wanted to call out to them but remained silent. I had lost a considerable amount of blood from my leg; the sight of my wounds sent chills throughout my body. Suddenly, my attacker rammed the door and I was forced back into battle mode. A door in the far corner of the tiny cabin sprung open. I sat with my back up against the front entrance; I was completely defenseless. Sara staggered into the room; her twisted smile displayed the hunger gnawing away at her empty stomach. Her head severely damaged and her left eye dangled from its socket. This bitch could definitely take a beating. She sensed the gravity of my wounds and I sat crippled as she crept closer. Her ghastly leg dragged miserably behind her; pungent saliva trickled down her chin in anticipation of a fresh meal. She placed her hand on my face, straddled my legs then inched her face closer; her breath was vile. Her tattered and stained dress brushed against my cheek; an opaque lifeless eyeball stared back at me. I would've thought after our last go around, she'd be more skittish, but my poor condition must have emboldened her. Her muffled raspy growl grew louder with each passing second. She reared her head back and I pulled the piece of splintered wood from my leg, let out a war cry and plunged it deep into the soft underbelly of her throat. I pushed away her dead weight and with my back against the door, rose to my feet. I opened the door and tossed her screaming corpse outside and listened to the perpetual sounds of bones breaking; jaw snapping and bloodcurdling cries. A horrid moaning and low petrified whimpering begged me to let her back inside. Whatever was out there ripped and tore at her rotted flesh. I was safe for now.

BREAKFAST

SUNDAY 8:00am

The bed was drenched and the sheets and spread were soaked with perspiration. I could hear the soft drone of Kathy and Lizzy's voices over the television in Elizabeth's room. I scooped up the linens and tossed them in the washing machine then snuck downstairs and made Lizzy's favorite: French toast, eggs sunny side up, turkey bacon and freshly squeezed orange juice. I smiled; there was a time I could get away with cinnamon toast and a juice box on the weekends. Now all I had to do was learn the secret of why I was being haunted. My wrist was swollen twice the normal size and scratch marks ran from my forearm to my elbow. My leg throbbed and was painted with a small purplish welt; of course there had to be a logical explanation. I had to allow my mind to heal. I had spent the previous night and subsequent morning with Allen Gross. Last night's storm washed away the snow and the morning's sunshine ushered in fifty-eight degree weather. In the early morning light, I still felt the presence of Sara Jane Carter and my new mission was to find that graveyard.

TODD ANDREW DAVIS
CAUGHT IN THE WEB
CHAPTER XIII

Along came a spider and sat down beside her.
Connie was none the wiser as I cut her insides away.
I spread open her legs. I aborted her eggs and laughed as I
played.
'Why me?' she screamed.
Her brown eyes dripping bloody tears, as I rudely wipe
them away.
You are among the chosen. That makes you all so very
golden my dear.
So remain ever frozen and I will become beholden to you
throughout the years.
So forget your fears my sweet little Connie
As I eat your liver, heart and gizzards on this beautiful fall
day.

I thought I was going to burst out in laughter as I sat next to her on the bus stop bench. Connie was a Sixth Grade English Teacher and if my little ditty wasn't about her she may have actually enjoyed it. I know, I told myself not to get to close until it was time. Taking alternative transportation made it easier for me to ride with her rather than follow, although I had to find seating where I could. I could at least maintain a close proximity to her without creating suspicion. She had a gorgeous face and it would surely be a shame to have to disfigure it. There were five people waiting for the bus to Glenmoore Heights that day.

Most of the riders were of African descent, one Mexican and one wannabe gangsta. The weather changed as much as my mind did lately. I was deep in thought and understandably concerned that Ryan had managed to free himself. *Could he point the police in my direction? Would they think the prodigal son returned home with murder on his mind? Would they think a deranged maniac was on a rampage?* I didn't kill him like the others. *So why would they link his kidnapping with any of the killings? How would they? Because I said I was Allen?* Ryan was so heavily drugged he'd never be able to ID me. The bus slowed to a stop and I transferred to another keeping pace with Connie. I kept my distance and tried to remain inconspicuous. She was tucked away in her own world. Her head was buried in text books as she graded papers with a red highlighter; I had never been fond of school. I watched her as she meticulously plodded through the stack of exams and even that act became too laborious for me. *I had always wanted to kill my teachers. Maybe this was the next best thing?* I placed a hand over my mouth to disguise a smile.

Just when you envision an Indian summer, a snowstorm comes barreling out of nowhere; it was Illinois after all. Today a feverish sun shined down and last night's rainstorm substantially melted most of the snow that had accumulated. The seasons were fighting an eternal battle as well. I kept a pocket map with me to track the bus driver's route and glanced at it every so often. I did my best to familiarize myself with the surrounding neighborhoods. Connie tugged on the blue strap above and the bus slowly eased to a halt. She had neatly stowed away the children's work and made her way up the aisle. Connie and a handful of other indistinguishable minorities mindlessly congregated at the front of the bus.

I waited my turn and kept a watchful eye on my prize. She fled the bus, happy to be rid of the degenerates she was forced to commute with on a daily basis. She meandered through a complex maze of clothing racks, street merchants and penniless window shoppers which cluttered the sidewalks of West Munster Avenue. The task of keeping her from blending into the herd became increasingly complicated. She stopped outside Olivia's Urban Clothing Boutique and an older woman with remarkably similar features rushed to give her a hug. They stood arm and arm conversing for several moments until Connie gently placed a loving kiss upon her cheek. The two departed and I continued to shadow her along Pence Boulevard where she made a stop at Chong's Vietnamese Food Market. We shopped for nearly twenty minutes before exiting. At times, I felt she knew that I had been following her, although her body language never gave it away.

She was a fascinating woman with diverse interests and seemed so out of place. She was better than them, it was a recurring theme. I guess in many ways she was a lot like me. I got my share of stares and glares but I just ignored them and continued my quest. *I mean, I couldn't kill them all.* A thought and a ridiculous one at that, but one that crossed my mind countless times wading through the cesspool of humanity. We headed north; three blocks later Mexicans and Indians added to the color collage. At one point it was almost more than I could tolerate; the rodents and peasants could not appreciate the presence of the greatness they were among. Connie continued across the hallowed grounds of the Saint Vincent's Church. I wasn't willing to tempt the wrath of the Holy Ghost, so I waited outside one of God's churches for her return. Maybe, it was worth the risk but the thought of spontaneous human combustion didn't appeal to me. *Perhaps I should venture inside. I'd turn wine into blood or do other preposterous tricks.* The devotion to her faith or high standing in the community wouldn't deter me; in fact it bolstered my conviction that Connie was the perfect speck of righteousness in an unjust world. *I am an unholy disciple. A fallen angel cast in the devil's image to rage war and become the enemy to all who have abandoned him. With each soul I rip away from its host's body, my strength grows. My obedience and loyalty will earn me great rewards in the afterlife. I will sit at the feet of my savior, dine on the flesh of the forsaken and bask in the glow of hellfire with great satisfaction. I will not be part of the lost flock of sheep and you won't find me begging for God's unmerciful hand. I embrace my destiny.*

Connie was just part of the path that I must travel. Speak of the devil; she emerged from a shrine of inept graciousness, of false love and false hope. The eighteenth century façade stood worn but unyielding and the steeple flirted with the heavens above. I gazed too long at the golden cross perched high above and it made me dizzy. These were the symbols of society's losing battle. I grew weary of Connie's insistence to being a pillar of the community buried among thieves. *What was she trying to accomplish in this wasteland anyway? Save a ho; save a soul. They're all degenerates and festering sores on the asshole of life.* Perhaps she was searching for the golden key; one good deed that in turn would unlock the gates of heaven. *Your Lord and Savior won't save you from me. No matter how much you pray. No matter how much you beg for his mercy. Oh my sweet little Connie, I'm going to love hearing you beg and plead.* Blood entwined with tears, panic, sweat and utter disbelief. *Oh yes Connie, we will see just how strong your resolve and how deep your faith and unwavering duty to the Lord really is.*

The bitch crossed within five feet of me and gave me an

uneasy smile that sent ripples throughout my being. *Does she know? Preposterous! Wasn't it? Why hadn't she fled if she was aware that I had her in my sights?* Connie's soul was pure, untouched like a young virgin. She was unaffected by the mass of vulgarity and cynicism in which this earthly world had trapped our bodies. *I wanted to be the one to reveal her destiny. I'll lay her nude body upon a bed of bloody thorns and if she denies me, her suffering will be unparalleled. This I swear.* The chase, the pursuit of Connie invigorated my soul and gave life to the inner me; the original host of this flesh. She walked the campus of Darrin Hall and took the elevator to the fourth floor. She knocked on door 438 and unlocked it with a silver key. She sat the brown paper package from Chong's just inside the doorway. I took the stairs down to the lobby and waited mere seconds before resuming the hunt.

As the day grew long and the blue sky darkened, the birds sang through the winter's sting. The morning glow gave way to an afternoon chill and the sky shifted gray. Connie was cloaked in an oversized navy blue pullover that concealed her body. *I'll unwrap all your fears my love. By the time I'm finished you'll realize that you've mistakenly chosen the wrong God in this fight.* The Emerald Park Residency apartment 22-B, in the heart of Glenmore Heights was our final resting place for the evening. It was renowned for its magnificent turnaround from worst- to-first in reducing crime. Too bad I was going to place a blemish upon the quaint community and once again tarnish its immaculate reputation. Its status carved from shit and blood had eventually bloomed roses; roses render thorns. This setup was going to be exceptionally challenging; all I needed was the reassurance that she lived alone.

TODD ANDREW DAVIS
THE RETURN OF LAURA JEAN
CHAPTER XIV

*T*amara tracked down Allen's girlfriend Laura on the east end of town. She had seen Allen earlier that evening and was pretty much nonresponsive since learning of his death. She exuded a sense of purity and remarkable innocence and was figuring out fast what the world had in store.

"Take a breath sweetheart." Her beauty was stunning; a Hollywood starlet without the airbrushing. Perhaps another time or under different circumstances, she'd be well worth the risk. I asked the obligatory standard question, "Did Allen have any enemies?"

Laura: "I guess he must have," my voice was shaky, nervous and immensely sad.

"You stated you dated for nearly six months?"

Laura: I've been asked the same questions over and over but what really made me depressed was the fact that I should have felt more pain for Allen. Sure, on the outside I was a torrential water show but inside I felt like an imposter masquerading as Allen's lover. I was ashamed his murder hadn't affected me more. What the fuck was wrong with me? Jesus. Detective Crenshaw was handsome, about six-four, athletic build and with his short curly hair bore a resemblance to Justin Timberlake; all grown-up of course.

Again Laura, what the fuck! He repeated his question after realizing my brain went on a short holiday.

"You dated for six months?"

Laura: "Six months last Tuesday," I politely responded.

Six months she's said as a matter of fact. *I had difficulty remembering Kathy's and Lizzy's birthdays let alone an anniversary. She had an angelic aura about her, and here I was questioning her about the brutal murder of her former lover. I was becoming lost in her,* "Ms. Miles, I understand how difficult this must be for you. We all want to catch this son-of-a-bitch."

Laura: "I'm just…" *I just don't care. What an awful thought; those couldn't have been mine because I do care. I loved Allen.*

I placed my hand on top of hers; she was warm to the touch and her blue eyes were laden with tears.

Laura: "Detective Crenshaw…"

"Logan." *Shit Logan, don't get personally involved. She's just another case victim.*

Laura: "Was Allen killed because of me?"

The beating Allen took was personal. My initial theory was there had to have been a love triangle between Allen, Jessica and the killer, but I quickly realized something more than mere passion and jealousy sent this subhuman monster on a rampage. The mangled bodies, the extraction of blood, suggested a cult satanic in nature. There were plenty of kids in Ravenswood and surrounding area that pushed back against the outer limits of society and inhabited the underground subculture lurking amongst the shadows. Even clean cut Billy Dugan could attest to that fact. She moved her hand from beneath mine.

"I seriously doubt this has much to do with you. Why do you ask?" I tried to atone for my embarrassment with another question. She told me of things forgotten; things unsaid to the other investigators.

Laura: "Allen was stubborn, his confidence was often confused for being conceded but he was well liked nevertheless. I'm sure he made enemies. Anyone who's lived long enough probably has one or two," I gazed toward the window. "There was a guy with a baseball cap," I paused, pressed my hands to my lips as if in prayer, "at the coffee shop, Allen and I were arguing and Allen none too politely, told him to mind his own business." *Why am I just remembering all this?*

"This guy defended you?" I was moving on from my adolescent crush.

Laura: "No he didn't speak; maybe it's nothing. I was just..." *I was making a fool out of myself; just talking to hear myself talk.*

"No please continue." *A hunch, a woman's intuition; perhaps it was nothing, but the case was fraught with a lack of evidence.*

Laura: "Allen being Allen laid into the guy. He laughed; I think at something one of us said and Allen's ego got bent out of shape," *shut up Laura while he still thinks you're sane.* "Lately, I've had this strange sensation of being watched; just a feeling, I never saw anyone." *Oh for*

God's sake I should just flash my tits; maybe he'll forget everything I said. Sorry Allen, that was disrespectful. My thoughts clamored madly. "Well that's not entirely true, I saw a man outside my window a few days ago, but I don't think….?"

"You saw someone outside?" Webb stood near a four foot window thinly veiled in a white laced curtain that overlooked the backyard of the complex.

Laura: "Yeah, but he must've been a utility worker." *Cause he wasn't in a uniform or caring a toolbox or any visible tools. Dumb, dumb, dumb, Laura!*

"Approximately where was he standing?" I gestured to Laura with my hand.

Laura: God he sounded so condescending. I'm not some stupid little bimbo who can't fend for herself, "He stood there only for a brief second; staring up at the sky or something off in the distance," I was irritated or was it that I noticed the band on his ring finger for the first time? *Figures, men are such pigs.*

"Can you give me a description?" *Her tone had changed; maybe she was becoming more comfortable.*

Laura: "White or maybe Mexican; big you know, kinda built." *Cute, hopefully single, maybe if I leave my window open he might come back and molest me. Shit, sorry again Allen.* "He had long curly hair, brownish I think." *Wherever Allen's spirit was, I'm sure he had better things to do than listen to my brain implode.*

"What time of day?" Laura walked over to her house phone and scanned the caller ID.

Laura: "One fifteen Wednesday afternoon, I was having a conversation with my mother."

"Great Laura; we can backtrack with the utility companies and see if any of them had a man in the area. Okay Laura concentrate, the guy at the coffee shop, any similarities?"

Laura: "Right now I can't even picture Allen's face! Shit I'm so sorry, I didn't mean anything by..."

"It's alright Laura."

Laura: *God, he says my name like he's known me forever. What gives him the right? I wanted to crawl back in bed and sleep the rest of my life away. Do you cheat on your wife? Do you have any children? I bet it's a yes on both counts.* "I really didn't get a decent look at either person."

A defeated sigh escaped her. She hugged herself; her body language was becoming increasingly irritable. *Maybe I misread Laura? I really haven't been in sync with anyone lately. Between the killings, Kathy's pregnancy accompanied with her titanic mood swings, Lizzy and my nightmares; I was a psychological mess. Now I'm practically undressing this girl with my eyes. She's only four years removed from shaking her high school pom-poms.* As I tried to refocus, she said something that shook me out of my stupor.

Laura: "I've had this odd suspicion that someone's been inside the apartment. It's probably nothing," *you've rambled on so much Laura; you might as well seal the deal,* "I can't prove it; nothings gone missing." *Sure that sounds plausible enough, an intruder who window shops. Verbalizing things made me wish I left them unsaid.*

There it was again, intuition versus fact but I truly believed every word she spoke. She'd been severely shaken. I stood up, looked around the apartment then made a beeline toward the hall closet. I turned the knob; a rank stench of scented body odor ravished my nostrils. I knelt down, brushed my hand over the carpet; it was dry. "Laura, come here please," she appeared by my side within seconds. "Is this brand of cologne familiar to you?" Revolted, she cupped her mouth and nose with her left hand and shook her head no.

Laura: I became nauseated by the sweet stench. *I was right; someone has been inside after all.*

I sent an officer out to canvas the backyard and wooded area. *If this was our killer, why had he been stalking Laura? Why is she still breathing?* I placed my arm around her waist and led her back into the living room area. Her body trembled as she curled up in a magenta colored loveseat. I was at a loss for words; fortunately for me she restarted the conversation.

Laura: "Someone hid in my closet and watched me?" I felt as if I were about to vomit. "Why me? Why Allen? It doesn't make sense."

"Let's not jump to conclusions Laura. There's a lot we have yet to establish." She was petrified and I had no way of consoling her; I hadn't even satisfied my own suspicions. *Why couldn't this just be your average degenerate intruder?* That's the way I should've approached this but my gut told me differently. She believed differently. "Have you noticed anything unusual? Um, things moved or perhaps misplaced in the past several days?"

Laura: "The egg carton, I think..."

"Excuse me?" I was astonished.

Laura: "A couple of days ago I smelled fried eggs and thought... I don't know what I thought, but I hadn't cooked breakfast; I ate a bowl of cereal and a slice of apple butter toast." *Paranoia; dementia.*

"Have you had any interruptions regarding your cable or your phone service; computer, etc.? Any visitors..."

Laura: "I'm monogamous..." I said, my eyes flashed a stern warning.

"I'll check with the property manager and make sure they haven't called anyone out." The conversation had turned in an entirely different direction but I was relieved she said it without me having to probe deeper into her private life. "Often times when tenants aren't home and there's a problem such as electrical or plumbing, they'll let someone inside to deal with the situation and inform you later."

Laura: "They can do that? Is that legal? Isn't that an invasion of privacy? I haven't even had the chance to grieve." *Shit what if I was... Okay, why would that hideous smell be so concentrated in the closet? He was either grasping at straws or trying to ease my fears. It was infuriating being treated as if I was a child. I'm tired of having this man trample through my thoughts. He's trying in a roundabout way to gain more intimate details of my life, maybe it's for the investigation but it felt more like personal use. The way he stared at me and groped me wherever and whenever he could. It's all disgustingly inappropriate and I'm not a damsel in distress. I should call him on it; fuck him. Allen played that kinda game with me all the time. Allen... shit; I need to call mom and dad. They'll flip and demand that I take the first flight back to Nevada.* There were still officers milling about when I wanted them all gone.

"Okay Laura, you've been tremendously helpful. I am awfully sorry about your loss," I thought if I continued to push, she might clam up entirely. I'd find the link between Laura and the murders; if there was one. Her arms remained tightly folded. I didn't extend my hand to her or unintentionally make things anymore uncomfortable for her by placing a hand on her shoulder. I just smiled and excused myself and my team.

Laura: Poof; just like that they were gone. I returned to my bedroom, crawled into bed and suddenly leapt to my feet. I pulled the sheets and comforter off and retrieved fresh bedding from the linen closet. *I'll wash everything tomorrow.*

TODD ANDREW DAVIS
MONKEY BRAIN
CHAPTER XV

Ryan had been gagged and his ankle chained to a steel post in the basement. His hands were expertly tied behind him. I had scored a set of syringes that would now serve a dual purpose. I'd plant his DNA at various crime scenes to provide the police with their first vital and tangible pieces of evidence to date. His subsequent disappearance and the bodies that were found would make him a prime suspect.

The Market collapse and unscrupulous loans had people buried neck deep in the mortgage crisis with no immediate end in sight. That in turn made vacant million dollar homes sit on the market for months without buyers in sight. I went to an open house listed in the papers, found the universal garage remote and disengaged the security system all on a Sunday afternoon. I had a modicum of safety in a risky line of work. Sure there would be other openings in a week or two but that's all the lead time I needed anyway. I walked down into the basement and could smell the stink of sweat and urine.

"You defecate on yourself to Ryan?" I inquired. I walked over to where he was bound and slowly pulled the tape from his mouth. His lips bled tiny cherry bubbles. He was too apprehensive to talk at first.

"Are you letting me go?"

"If I had any intention of letting you walk out of here, I would've blindfolded you, covered your head or worn a mask."

His eyes averted mine, "I won't tell anyone." Hearing no response he said, "I'll do anything; even oral…"

"You can't even die with dignity you faggot! I should kill you right now!" It was amazing; he didn't even attempt to scream. He must've thought the walls were soundproof or that we were in the middle of nowhere.

"Why are you doing this to me?"

"You're my alibi; well your DNA anyway. It'll be left behind for others to ponder. A suicide note confessing everything will be pinned to your body." I waved a ballpoint pen and white notebook pad in front of his puzzled face.

"I am not writing shit!" he spouted boldly.

"Oh, I think I'll be able to convince you."

"You can torture me all you want; I'll never write a fucking word."

"I'm going to torture you regardless. Besides Ryan, you still have time to rethink your answer. See this jar? Fill it with semen before I return. I untied his right hand and promptly secured his left with handcuffs."

"You're fucking insane! I'm not doing a goddamn thing!"

"Are you fond of your cock Ryan? Because if you disobey me," my face was inches from his, "I'll cut it off and feed it to you." I let that little gem float around inside his monkey brain. Ten minutes or say goodbye to the first of your two best friends."

"I can't," he said dejected.

"Then in ten minutes you'll be giving yourself head; happy thoughts Ryno," I handed him the bottle, walked upstairs and laughed the whole way.

I unscrewed every light bulb in the place. I unplugged the power bar that fed life to the television, VCR/DVR and cable box then disconnected the microwave, bedside lamp and clock radio. I unplugged the computer in the hallway and snuffed out the last bastion of electrical life and waited in the darkness.

I listened to tenants rehearsing their phony day to day dramas on life's stage. I waited patiently like a dog awaiting its master next command. Suddenly the door sprung open reveling a small black child with food stuffed in his mouth. He couldn't have been more than four years old. I hit him with a right cross and his eyes went dead. She screamed, I'm almost certain of it. I grabbed her by her weave and dragged her inside as I kicked the door closed behind me. She stared at me in shock while I hauled her into the bedroom. I threw a white gown at her and motioned for her to slip it on. At first she didn't quite comprehend my actions, but then embarrassingly complied and stripped to reveal an exquisite body. She haphazardly dressed in the present I laid before her. She pushed her entire body firmly against the metal headboard and realized the horrors were just beginning.

"Obey and the boy lives," I said; *if he wasn't dead already.*

I placed two vials of Ryan's DNA on top the dresser. Even without the heavy brush of make-up she was remarkably beautiful. I grabbed her by the throat and with my free hand taped her mouth shut. She struggled as I knew she would. A hard strike to the temple squashed her enthusiasm. I tied her hands and feet without too much effort. It's working; I'm still in the moment. I lit several candles she had decorated the room with. I reached for my black duffle and produced a needle and thread. *I wasn't the only one who needed to witness this.* It was like catching a fish with your bare hands as I tried to grasp her eyelids; she blinked and bucked. I slipped the needle through the fleshy layer of skin and placed the point of the needle precariously close to her left eye.

"I'm not trying to blind you, I want to make you see. You're making things more difficult than they need be Connie." Her face went ashen when I spoke her name. I pressed hard on her throat with my forearm and thought her neck would bust wide-open. I had to make her relax and accept things, but she was a fighter. I'd learned a great deal from our little friend. I was more than just a mere casual participant. "Stop it Connie," I whispered as I stroked her hair. Her eye was twitching. The needle's double looped thread, danced across her cheek. I wanted to have fun with her while she was still alive. My knife felt weightless and my fingers clutched her throat. I began to gut our God loving, God fearing, God blessing and now I'm positively sure, God damning Connie. "You stupid insipid fucking whore!" my body was soaked with her piss.

My teeth tore into her fleshy tissue; blood filled my mouth as I bit into her nipple. I pinned her down and slowly began draining her of her lifeblood. When I reached my threshold I climbed off the slimy bitch and viewed my handiwork. The white nightgown clung tightly to her blood soaked figure. I had envisioned things working out differently, not that I'm complaining. I just wanted her to appear pristine when she was found. I used Ryan's gift and planted his semen inside her, his blood on her and finally strategically in the bed and bathroom. Boom! I heard somebody enter the apartment. I pressed my body close to the far wall, just beyond the light of the flickering candles.

"Connie. Connie you home?" a man's voice bellowed. "Con-n-i-eee," his voice trailed off. He must have stumbled over the little nigglet lying on the floor. "Connie!" he sounded more incredulous as he entered the room.

His mind tried to comprehend the possible scenarios that had taken place. I was surprised that he hadn't gone screaming into the night. Instead he took too much time distrusting his lying eyes. The child's unconscious body lay on the floor near the entrance way and Connie's bloodied body hog tied to the bed. And that's when I made my move. In one motion I sprung from the dark shadows and sliced his jugular while grabbing his right arm. I slung him toward the window; a stunt man couldn't have done it more gracefully. The window exploded upon impact and his body flipped head over heels. He slammed thunderously down on the metal fire escape then bounced off and plunged two stories to the hard cold ground below. Without hesitation, I followed him out into the night.

I stared back up to my dark angel's windowsill. A crowd began to form and I disappeared as the shadows embraced me. I hurried alongside a wooden fence, only to be trapped in a dead end. I turned slowly with toxic fire filling my lungs; hundreds of the faceless mob blocked my escape.

In this desolate part of the world called Emerald Park the apes ruled the planet, but I refused to show fear to these monkeys. I slowly approached them and with each step I took, they took a step backward. A woman clutched a bald headed baby to her bosom. I wanted to grab the child from her flabby naked arms, throw the infant to the ground and stomp its life out. I would rape their daughters and butcher their sons. Like Moses, it became a biblical reenactment of the Red Sea as they parted an allowed me passage. Their guns, knives, baseball bats held in hand and at the ready posed no threat to me. *These people; these humble, pathetic, forgotten souls were more enlightened than I'd imagined. They recognized me and understood the full extent of my power. I was their God and they my dutiful servants, a maestro conducting an orchestra of slaves.* The simple act of taking Connie's life paled in comparison to the recognition of this new found glory. I fired-up the beast and road my stallion hard like a white knight fading off into the horizon.

TODD ANDREW DAVIS
BLIND FAITH
CHAPTER XVI

In my line of work you meet a whole host of unsavory characters; some you needed to lean on and some you formed a bond with. My informants ranged from the low end prostitutes, small time drug dealers and a vast array of petty criminals. Gaining their trust or trusting in them was an extremely precarious task. However, a guy like this was in a category all to himself. I extended my hand and he gave me a warm bear hug embrace.

"Tim."

"You still can't bring yourself to call me Father," his enchanting smile lit the small interior of the Mom and Pop pancake house.

"It's hard to call anyone Father when you're older than them."

"Logan you only beat me by six months."

He was always very loud and verbose and exhibited a magnificent sense of self awareness.

"Table for two, gentleman?" the greeter, a young overweight girl met us at the door.

"Preferably a booth if you have one open," he replied then turned to me. "It's good to see you again Logan. How are Kathleen and the baby?"

"Kathy's pregnant and the baby's almost six."

"Here you go gentlemen; window seat okay?" she handed us the menus.

"It will do just fine thank you," I said.

She didn't seem to notice his collar; it was something that took me years to get used to. The priesthood was not something you would associate with kid Daugherty, it was hard to understand and I never fully figured out.

"Lizzy's six? Wow, it's been forever since we've seen each other?"

There is always an anchor to an event that measures time passed. It wasn't just Lizzy; it was much more than that. Timmy was the same kid I spent every summer's day with from kindergarten to high school graduation. Nobody could have asked for a better friend than him. Even without his white starch collar and his black button down, Timmy was Timmy buried in biblical text. He stunk of righteousness and his devotion to the Lord was absolute. Timmy was now Father Tim, but still took delight in taking me down a peg or two whenever he saw the chance.

"I will have the six stack apple topping, turkey sausage, sunny side eggs and coffee, black," Timmy addressed the waitress all smiles.

"And you sir?"

"Number three, coffee two sugars."

"How would like your eggs sir?"

"Over easy."

She collected the menus than scrambled off in the direction of the kitchen.

"My Achilles' heel has always been a free breakfast," Timmy's laugh was boisterous and somewhat bogus. It had been rehearsed many times over the years than adopted as part of his new persona. "Obviously I don't get too many chances to indulge myself," he chuckled.

It was the same laugh with subtle inflections only noticeable to the trained ear. I guess in my own mind I was calling him out; a counterfeit cloaked in the robe of God. We all have our own crosses to bear and he felt the need to make atonement. Maybe I was too hypocritical or too cynical. He wore the cross, I wore the badge and nobody from the old neighborhood could have seen any of this coming. We had made a pack that together we'd join the academy and for many years I thought Kathy was the reason we parted ways. They dated for two months senior year before we fell in love. I guess it's possible this holy man still held resentment towards me. He had shut me out, turned his back and betrayed my faith in him. He was the closes thing I ever had to a brother, a friend. Six years ago in a moment of weakness I cheated on Kathy with Tamara and confided in only one person, Father Timothy Daugherty. Outside of the affair itself, telling him was the single fucking biggest mistake I made in my life. I knew the man beneath the robe, before he found God he was the arrogant kid I grew up with. His soul hadn't changed and God, the church; none of it truly changed him, not at the core anyway. Even though he emitted a holier than thou façade, he was still a good man in every sense of the word, or at least better than any that I'd ever known. That's the rub; I knew him. Six years later I reluctantly needed another favor from him.

"You seem lost Logan."

"Just deep in thought that's all."

"You should come to the church."

"I prefer to do my praying on a more one on one basis."

The food arrived during idle chit chat; we were either trying to figure each other out, or truly had nothing more in common but old war stories.

"I saw Barry the other day."

"What a fucking jag-off he was."

"Please Logan."

"He was?" I said with as much disdain as I could muster. Barry was a tag along, a moocher; never a true friend. From time to time he tried to insert himself into my life to no avail.

"What do you want from me Logan?"

"I need to know what you saw."

"Okay, um could you help me out a little? I'm not following you."

"Remember the time we found a gun back in Westchester Park," I said. His face was stoic but his eyes proved to me that he knew very well what I was talking about, "We robbed Connors liquor store." He was increasingly uncomfortable; his eyes shifted downward fearing the walls had suddenly sprouted ears.

"Am I under arrest?" Timmy's smile was smug as if he had just one upped me, "We're talking well over two decades ago. Aren't the statutes of limitation up?" a quiet snicker escaped his lips.

"We were something back then. How we made it this far is beyond me."

He noticeably relaxed and I wanted to make sure I could read him before delving any further. I had never had much of a home life, so most summers I spent at the Daugherty's. When my parents were killed I became a permanent fixture in the Daugherty household.

"I've been having nightmares."

"Logan have you seen any one; a professional or just sought out counsel?" he relaxed after realizing the conversation wasn't about him.

"And lose my badge, not a chance. I've been working through it on my own."

"Sorry, but I don't see where I can be of any help."

"I've seen things; ghosts. I've been afraid to even close my eyes at night and the odd thing is it's so real that I swear I'm awake."

"Logan…"

"When we were teenagers a group of us dared each other to go inside Chancellor's Manor," I cut him off, "you were the only one who had the balls to go inside. You disappeared for hours. What happened to you Tim?"

He looked as if were about to puke. His face was flushed and his eyes blinked wildly. I thought he was having a heart attack.

"Logan, nothing happened," Timmy eased out of the booth. "Thanks for the late night breakfast," he excused himself and left me to wallow in my own misery.

"I had always assumed you flaked out on the academy because of Kathy."

"You knew how I felt about her," he stopped in his tracks; his eyes were fueled with anger and hatred. His reaction betrayed the stature of a priest; it was of pure an utter jealousy from a self pitying little man.

"You dated for only a couple months."

He sat back down, lowering his voice, "Maybe your conscious won't allow you to get over what you did, but I forgave you a long time ago."

"It was a fair trade: I have a beautiful wife and daughter; a son on the way and you found God."

"You're a fuck Logan!" he wanted to say it under his breath but it was a couple of octaves too high.

"Father!" an elderly lady scolded him from the opposite

booth.

"Sorry," he whispered apologetically.

I was somewhat amused. A person acquires an innate ability to push the buttons of anyone they've known for a substantial period of time. I was needling him; trying to get him out of his comfort zone. I didn't want a long conversation with Father Daugherty; I wanted to talk with Little Timmy D.

"You saw something didn't you? Something that made you abandon everyone from your childhood. It made you choose the church and if you are going to tell me that the church was your calling, I'll rip that fucking collar right off your neck and make you choke on it!"

"Keep your voice down Logan," a murmur resonated throughout the little pancake house.

"I want you to go to the house with me. I'll bring the gun and the flashlights; you bring the cross and the Holy water."

"I wouldn't go to dinner at your house."

"I wasn't inviting you. You're the one person who can help me…"

"I didn't see a thing Logan."

"You're lying, not very becoming of you Father Tim."

"You need to grow up Logan and if you're having nightmares maybe you need your mommy to tuck you in," he regretted his words the moment he spoke them.

"I need your help."

"You need help, that's an understatement."

"Tim I know you're in there," I grabbed him by the arm, "after this we can part ways forever if that's what you want, but don't give me the God shit! You were never this much of a pussy! Now I know you shit yourself after you left Chancellor's Manor. You wouldn't talk for days, so something happened. I didn't understand or care back then but now I have to know; and don't tell me you can't remember. Everything that's happening to me stems from that place, so I want you to... "

"I want you to let go of my fucking arm; that's what I want," he mumbled with controlled anger. "God can help you Logan, I found him to be a good listener."

I turned him loose; he paused to retrieve his overcoat and crept out of the Pancake Palace with his tail between his legs. It occurred to me that I probably could have handled it a little better, but I probably wasn't going to get anything useful from him anyway. I guess I might be the one who had some pent up anger. It didn't solve my problem, however I felt much better now. Unfortunately in this business, Tim still ranked as the finest man I ever knew. Worst comes to worst I'd pay him a visit at the rectory, handcuff him and drag his fat ass screaming and kicking to the mansion on the hill. I dropped some cash including a healthy tip down on the table and made my way to the front door under weighty stares. The one thing I liked about this place is that they stayed open until midnight and served breakfast from sunrise till close. As I stepped through the doorway, my body was enveloped briefly by the light of a full moon; my gaze turned upward seeking wisdom. A dense fog had been born from the inclement weather. I was not a religious man, but even the theater back there was out of character for me. The amount of contempt I had for Tim and the church even surprised me; well quite frankly it stunned me. My thoughts, my words seemed influenced by deep seeded feelings that I didn't know I possessed. I guess somewhere inside the crevices of my subconscious my true emotions had emerged. Everything I said to Timmy was so convoluted and laced with rage. There was a point where I fought with every fiber of my soul not to strike him. I hadn't slept in days from the nightmares, the killings; fuck me. I dodged light traffic and made my way over to a creamed colored sport utility. The moon had me under its spell and I was questioning my mental stability, my sanity.

After driving for a half hour, I sat for several minutes in the leather bucket seat. I counted the snowflakes that landed on my windshield then melted away and mused over the radically fluctuating weather. The car's heater was on full blast but had no effect. I reached for the door and focused on the digits seven, two and eight. Winter's grip tightened around me like an ill-fitting sweater. I walked around the condominium to the back lot. *Had it been the moon that set this monster off? Was there any correlation between it and the murders?* I climbed the small wooded hill to the east; all the fallen leaves enhanced or broadened my vision. I glanced at my watch; 1:00 am. Most of the lights were off; the inhabitants long ago snuggled away underneath their comforters and electric blankets. The light from her apartment guided me through the storm. She was understandably paranoid, or suffered from insomnia, or maybe she was just too terrified to sleep with the lights off. Her slight frame passed by the window. I wanted to rundown and knock on her door but I had no excuse as to why I was here. I hadn't thought much of any of this through. I lit a Cuban and watched her from afar. I thought about my relationship with Tamara and what it was that drove me towards Laura. *Did my infidelity revolve around Kathy's pregnancy? Did I find her less attractive? I loved her, Lizzy and the baby. So why did I lust after another? It's this town.* I had been a New York City Cop for so long that I missed the action. Kat had made me put in a transfer seven weeks after we discovered Lizzy was on the way, but Ravenswood was a place where dreams came to die. We both had grown up here and knew the pitfalls. We knew the community and still had 'friends' here. I had been ambitious and quickly rose through the ranks.

The murderous evil that was inflicted upon the town of Ravenswood was never supposed to happen here. Honestly or should I say disgustingly, it was exactly what I needed to electrify the boredom of my soul. It awoke my spirit and gave me purpose again. The spilling of blood satisfied the killer's hunger and was essential for both of us. I was more concerned about my life returning to its humdrum conformity. I was gonna put this son-of-a-bitch down even if I'd never killed anyone before. There would be no remorse; no second guessing. *I'd spill his blood and become a legend, a fabled hero; the slayer of a mythical beast. Would the adulation be enough to fulfill me? If these murders continued, every law enforcer, every politician who took the oath to serve and protect would be ripped to shreds for their lack of competence.* I was cold and buried deep in the heart of the woods. How did I end up here? *What was I searching for? Was I here to catch him or had I come for her?* A sick synergy had formed between us. She was something that I never should have considered. The depravities of man; lust and murder were sins that blemished our race and elevated God and demons alike. I walked down the hill with purpose; three minutes later I arrived at her front door and without hesitation rang the doorbell.

Laura: The doorbell rang three times before I even moved. I'd been lost in thought, but they quickly faded away as I stared through sleepy eyes at my clock radio; 1:45am. *Who the fuck could it be this late?* My nerves were on edge. I feared it could be Allen's killer, my intruder; one in the same back to finish me off. I grabbed a butcher knife and slinked towards the door. Peering through the peephole, I instantly recognized the unshaven face on the other end; the cop. *Was there something else? Did someone else get murdered?* In a panic I opened the door to where the chain lock held it in place. 'Officer Logan,' he said back to me in an assuring tone. I put the knife down and I unhitched the lock and allowed him in.

In the soft glow of shimmering light she was even more angelic, more desirable than I remembered. She wore a navy blue men's pinstriped button shirt; Allen's I surmised. She unhooked the chain; I opened the door then shut it behind me, turned the deadlock and hooked the golden latch. I took two steps toward her, grabbed her by the scruff of her neck and kissed her hard. I leaned her back sweeping her off her feet and headed in the direction of the bedroom. It was something I wanted to do from the moment I saw her, but something I dare not act upon. But here I was walking down the halls of her apartment intent on ripping every button off Allen's tailored made shirt. I could feel my heart working overtime. *Did I really want the guilt?* She remained speechless as I gently laid her down. I gazed deep into her eyes and realized I needed her as much as she needed me.

Laura: It had become a movie, a fairy tale. I'd been speechless yet wet with anticipation. I hungered for him; I wanted a real man not a conceded frat boy who was afraid of taking control. Allen had always been so easy to manipulate, boring, unimaginative in and out of bed.

I became a tongue tied mute and he became my escape. School, Allen, family, life in general; nothing felt real. We were lost in one another.

Tears rolled down her face, I gently wiped them away. Her body warm to the touch. My head buried deep in the nape of her neck. Her perfume was intoxicating; never before had I'd been this bold. I felt free. It felt right. There wasn't much afterthought, but I was mindful of how badly all this could have turned out.

Laura: *Why was I crying? Were they tears for Allen? I can't fucking believe I'm doing this.* I felt like a little girl trapped in a woman's body with adult desires I didn't quite understand. His fingers lovingly crested my face as he wiped away my tears. He smelled like a man should. '*God save my soul.*'

Sex is a curious thing. It has intrinsic value; an essence of you always remains with the other person and the meaning can be diluted. You can convince yourself that it is as animalistic as hunting for survival and you can detach yourself like a killer to their victim. The mind is capable of many things. Her guilt will be far greater than mine. Her dead lover lay in a fresh grave, while mine is months away from giving birth to my first born son. *Does this make me evil? Or just put me in a category of unfaithful men who use the excuse that they've been driven to cheat. Will I seek out another vapid man of the cloth? Hell no! I am going to enjoy fucking her.* My brain flushed out all abstract distractions as I thrust deep inside her. She was the embodiment of youth and sexuality and I embodied a soldier returning from a tour in an ill-fought war. I regained control of me, no longer was I having an out-of-body experience. I tasted the sweet sweat that formed in the crevasse of her neck. I inhaled her warm breath and ran my fingers over her erect nipples. She started biting my neck, my ear and my lips. I slid downward licking her flat stomach than her inner thigh. She began thrashing in ecstasy even before my lips touched hers. No not guilt; a conquest perhaps but never guilt. I could feel her blood coursing through my veins. Some things in life are just predestined; she was one of them. Enthralled in passion and consumed in pure lust our bodies mirrored each other's rhythmic motion. Our shadows danced upon her bedroom wall. Our breathing, our heartbeats all magically synchronized, in a crescendo, we rose and fell as one. And in the end maturity forbade me from remaking the great escape. Lying in her arms I thought about that poor bastard Allen. He would never have the pleasure of experiencing this beautiful creature again. My cell rang saving me from an awkward disengagement. Her pouting face reluctantly handed me the phone. It was Webb. Her words were fast and furious.

"Tamara, slow down." I needed time to rejoin the outside world.

TODD ANDREW DAVIS
STAGE OF BETRAYAL
CHAPTER XVII

The sound of my footsteps bounding down the staircase awakened my prey. I heard the rodent scurry about. He knew he had been living on borrowed time; the last particles of sand had sifted through the hourglass and time was no longer his refuge. I wanted to skin Ryan alive and let him choke on a cocktail of severed body parts and vomit. I had real hardcore plans for Mr. Beliford; a portion of his soul would be forever mine. I walked toward him, stuck out my hand, clutched the pathetic bitch by his throat and lifted him out of the chair. My eyes dared him to turn away as he let out a whimper. I let go of him, his head snapped back and I undid the duct tape muzzle.

"I can help you," he struggled to speak.

"What could you possibly do for me?" I laughed.

"I'll serve you. I know a lot of chicks who'd never be missed."

It was a desperate attempt to appeal to the demon that stood before him, "I'm listening," I replied as a cat to a mouse. He thought he had detected a flaw. *Adorable; this pea brain came up with a fascinating game of deception. He'd turn his friends and love ones over to the Devil. I was honored but not fooled.* I handed Ryan a bottle of water from the duffel bag. After taking a few wild gulps of water he was more confident and I wanted to hear him beg.

"Thank you," he said graciously, "You killed the girl in the woods and that Allen character right?" he smartly avoided eye contact and I smiled. "Um… I um just figured that you need to be insulated; protected from prying eyes. Shit like I said I know a bunch of airhead chicks; one call and it's as easy as pizza delivery."

He was pretty fucking high of himself. Instantly it all turned to mud and my rage was ignited. His words were so explosive and damning that I lost control. My hand locked onto his jugular, his eyes bulged and the blood vessels threatened to explode. I reached into his back pocket with my left hand and his face registered that all hope of survival was gone. No explanation needed, no apologetic bullshit, just the acceptance of his fate. I didn't take all the necessary precautions; I fucked-up the impetuous fool that I am. I held up the cell phone I took from his pocket. I flipped it open; twenty-four miss calls and nine new messages. I cycled through the menu and scanned the outgoing calls: #11, 011, 811, 822, 922 and 911, after several attempts at dialing blindly he was able to call 911. How much longer would I let him live? The battery was low and his phone set to the all sounds off position. I checked the length of his incoming calls. Carrie 4:30 am Mon. Oct 12. 01:26 min; Beth, 10:45 am Mon. Oct 12 03:13min. Raydogg, missed call 12:00 pm Mon. Oct 12, Shannon, missed call 1:30 pm Mon. Oct 12. 911 incoming call 2:15 pm Mon Oct 12 length 01:03 min. There were many more calls. I threw his phone across the room and it struck violently against the faux wood paneling that covered every square inch of the basement walls. This was just the kind of negligence I couldn't afford. I released my grip, the chair roared up on its hind legs, toppled over and made a dull thud as it hit the ground. Ryan's face slammed into the cement floor, but no sound escaped his lips. I guess he intended to die with some dignity after all; blah, blah, blah. My plan was straightforward; incriminate Ryan. I'd make him write a suicide note in his own blood. I intended to take him to the attic and had bought a rope just for the occasion. I'd toss it over one of the rafters, make a hangman's noose and watch him struggle to maintain balance on a three legged chair. I walked over to where he lay and gave him a sharp kick in the ribs. Ryan's face contorted but he remained silent. Unfortunately for him, I loved a challenge. I knelt over him, placed a knee firmly against his cheek then produced my trusty pearl handle jagged edge blade of justice. I cut away at his right ear. He squirmed and muttered under his breath.

"Ryan, I am gonna enjoy dismembering you." His body thrashed; the pain excruciating. I dug the tip of my blade deep into his left earlobe. I was amazed at his fortitude and determination to survive. I had mistaken Ryan for someone who lacked courage and conviction. Still, I'd get my satisfaction. I was incredulous as I watched the earless subhuman try mightily to block out the pain. "If you're going to remain quiet, I'll remove your tongue?" I wanted him to visualize it well before I started in, "That's right Ryan embrace the pain. I'll hold your beating heart in my hands and feed it to you while I dine on your flesh. It doesn't matter if you fight it or not. You might think this is some sort of macho way to go out but I'm going to send you screaming through the gates of hell! So pray to your God; mine awaits your eternal soul and I'll deliver you to him! Where is your fucking Messiah? Your false prophet who sold you a book of lies? You seek him in your darkest hour. Where is he? His son's suffering will pale in comparison to yours. You're proof all mankind is deceitful and should be rendered extinct."

I cut away his shirt and carved some prime rib. He screamed as I made my second incision. I turned him over and devoured the fresh meat before his eyes. With another agonizing yelp, I broke his index finger and pulled flesh from the bone ala jerk chicken. He screamed and I forced his left eye open then plucked the little olive from its fucking jar. He vomited and in a desperate attempt tried to choke himself on his own bile but I saved him.

"Ryan you're a fucking bloody mess!" I fought the hunger building in the depths of my soul. My mouth salivated. I needed him to suffer. And suffer he did. I rolled up his pant legs and cut deep enough to expose his femur. Blood flooded his pants and his screams pierced my ears. I pulled off his shoes and socks then sliced off three toes on his left foot and two on his right. I cut off a pinky toe and tossed it in the ever-growing pile of meat and bones; he screamed. "Ryan, pretty soon you're gonna wish you had more toes to cut off." I laid him flat on his back with hands and bloody feet bound. He was unchained from the chair and his constant struggling made it difficult to work. *Hmm, this was gonging out with dignity?*

The fluorescent lights flickered for a millisecond; little white floaters clouded my vision. A howling and whistling noise rattled my body and the pain lit my brain up like a match. My stomach churned and I convulsed as blood gushed from my nose. The air was choked with smoldering ash, my tongue swelled and I couldn't breathe. A vision appeared before my eyes and a golden ray of light so radiant and soothing; it hovered at the far end of the basement. A young teenage girl appeared in the center of the halo with her feet suspended in midair. Her pale face belied the gruesome sight on display. Her blue eyes were unwavering and I felt the burning white hot heat on my skin. She had the aura and a strange familiarity of my advisory the moon but was much more than that. Her presence tested my patience. *Did Ryan see her? Was she a figment of my imagination; an angel?* I wanted to take the knife and plunge it deep into her heart. She drew my attention away from the task at hand. Suddenly, all the oxygen was sucked out of the room and I was drunk with dizziness.

"What are you?" my dark voice bellowed. She didn't respond or give any inclination that she would provide an answer. Her ghostly and transparent form contradicted her existence. *Had my mind been so warped that it conjured up a fucking demon witch?* I continued dismembering the traitor Ryan despite the little jackal's prying eyes. *So what was she accomplishing? All she's did was provide me with an audience.* "Fix your virgin eyes on me bitch! This is just the fucking beginning!"

I left Ryan and the little demon to purchase a plastic roll of six-inch poly and a hacksaw. I changed my clothes before I entered the tiny hardware store. Blood under the fingernails, a scarlet drop on a shirt sleeve or raspberry jam footprints on wooden floors would spell my doom. No I was too smart to be that careless. I bought heavy duty cleaning supplies, a plastic pale and rubber gloves. It had been nearly twenty four hours since Ryan dialed 911 or quasi communicated with friends. I hadn't seen any signs that the house was under surveillance when I left and I wondered how much time would elapse before the pigs found his body. *I should never go back; I've had my fun.* It was the last thought I had as I pulled into the driveway. I needed to cleanse my soul of Ryan but little did I know his betrayal was only the first in a series of lies.

I watched her nude breast rise and fall in rhythmic swells of uninhibited passion. Beads of sweat pooled on her flesh, her skin radiant from perspiration and her body taut with anticipation. Her eyelids embodied butterfly wings, fluttering open and shut. She was immersed in pure ecstasy. Her fingernails plunged deep into the folds of the mattress and seized the only thing that kept her from thrashing wildly about. Internally I burned as their naked bodies intertwined with one another. My mind on the verge of shutting down made it difficult to process it all. *How could she do this to me? I should've been more assertive.* I would have done anything for her. I watched as the two remained oblivious to their audience of one. They performed for nearly a half hour and I physically ached. No doubt, she hurt me plain and simple. Watching them together had caused an overwhelming state of disbelief to wash over me. The human mind is capable of many things. How much pain, stress and sorrow could it entertain before your natural defense mechanism engaged and forced it to snap? There're legal alibis for those who kill in the heat of passion; frailties of the human condition are well known. *Why did I feel this way? I thought I had successfully detached myself from all emotions.* I'd been forced to watch, I wanted to march down there to murder the both of them. I had to remind myself; *simply adhere to the Master Plan.*

I watched him eat her pussy. I watched him kiss her bare feet and melt in the warmth and softness of her inner thighs. His tongue forged its way across her stomach. Her legs wrapped around his lower torso as they re-engaged and once again began to fuck. With every stage of betrayal, I watched as a hapless voyeur not able to turn away. The pain and anger had been sown and grew into a strictly vengeful state of mind. I watched the two lovers playfully interact. He pulled her hair and she clawed passionately at his bare chest. They continued their love making and I knew beyond a shadow of a doubt what had to be done.

Without warning, the mystery man promptly sat on the edge of the bed answered a phone call and pulled on his boxers. She reached out for him, but he ignored her. I made my way down the ravine and pass the home of the Fighting Rebels. I hopped in my car, drove a block and a half and waited at the edge of the parking lot. I thought about running him down, beating him to death but they were short lived fantasies. He emerged from her condo; Laura followed draped in a white satin sheet and this time was rewarded with a soft kiss placed ever so sweetly upon her inviting lips.

TODD ANDREW DAVIS
APARTMENT 2206-B
CHAPTER XVIII

"The Messiah has risen!" cried out an old leather faced African man.

"He died for our sins!" a charred skinned teenage girl bellowed before melting into the background.

These people were a pack of zombies, incoherent and lost. They crawled out of the woodwork by the hundreds and drifted into the streets from the surrounding apartment complexes. As daylight slowly approached, rays of light glistened upon the crowd showing the repulsive variety of characters scattered along the block. A pale fog added to the eeriness. We entered the building and hoards of black faces with blank stares shouted down from the balconies above.

"He's our savior!"

"He was sacrificed for the good of all of us!" a woman cried.

"Leave us alone!" I held the gaze of an old gray haired woman with deeply etched crow's feet and wrinkles, "you're not welcome here!" she cursed.

My team ascended the staircase. Mounds of flesh were

pushed up against the wall so tightly you'd think their bodies were nailed in place. I could feel the warmth of their breath as I passed by. The scene was reminiscent of a particular reoccurring dream I had; the descent to hell lined with festering skulls displaying their dagger like teeth, or perhaps it was an ominous premonition of what was yet to come.

"He's coming for you, Logan!" a child's voice rang out.

I spun around and searched the crowd for him but he had vanished. I witnessed the surreal and completely irrational; I could no longer differentiate between the world of dreams and reality. I knew if I acted out of character that I wouldn't be the only one questioning my mental stability. I had to break through and distinguish fiction from fact.

"You'll all die here!" belched another anonymous voice.

I lead Detective Webb, a uniform and two plain clothed cops pass the wave of ghouls. We silently entered apartment 2206 fully prepared to confront any and all hostiles. The smell convinced me this was a real life nightmare; I posted a uniform by the front door.

"No one enters or leaves got it?" I said and he nodded his head affirmatively. Under normal circumstances I would've preferred Tamara at my side but this time I needed to see the crime scene before subjecting her to any further brutality. "Carson, follow me, Webb and Donnelly process the living room."

I entered the bed room; an icy breeze chilled me to the bone and caused the candles to flicker. I crossed the room intending to close the window and found it shattered.

Glass sparkled from the top plank of the fire escape. I scanned the grounds but found nothing else amiss. Connie was sprawled out on the bed in a blood soaked nightgown; on each side of the bed were the bodies of two nude young girls displayed in a position that mimicked one another. Their arms were folded over their chests and their ankles crisscrossed. Both girls had been asphyxiated and the clear plastic bags remained tied around their heads. The deaths were horrific but at least they had been spared the cruelty Connie was subjected to. I examined her body first, straddled her mutilated corpse and tried not think about the dead children lying at my feet. All the candles were relit and the lights were turned off; I wanted to see Connie the way he did. Her bronze body was cloaked in a white nightgown soaked in scarlet. A crude gash ran from her esophagus to her pubic bone and was clearly visible through the caked blood. She had been torn open and left to rot. The massive amount of bite marks suggested that it was the same animal we had been searching for. The Department deemed the graphic details surrounding the victims' deaths were similar enough to alert my task force. Was it possible that he wanted to communicate with us by sending bizarre messages? Or was he getting off by mocking us? The brutality was equal but the symbolism and uniqueness showed an astronomical evolution from the embryonic stages. This neighborhood was outside his comfort zone and the whole methodology placed the killings in an entirely separate category. *Why kill the girls? And why were they suffocated and not butchered as well.* I leaned closer to Connie's face; her hazel eyes were cloudy and her eyelids had been painstakingly sown open. I physically recoiled at the discovery and lost my balance as my right shoe was entangled with one of the girl's feet. No doubt the sadist stuffed a message deep inside Connie's open torso or down the throat of one of the girls. He's making it a game; taunting 'Catch me if you can.'

"Logan."

I glanced over my shoulder; Tamara held her arm around a young boy who had a massive bruise on his face. An elderly man, possibly his grandfather, stood next to them. I shot her a vile look that didn't faze her. *Something's wrong.* I walked over to them and shut the bedroom door behind me.

"Logan, the little boy saw him," stated Tamara.

"Did the man you saw do this to you?" I asked the boy in a fatherly tone. My heart fluttered and I prayed that we had a solid ID.

The boy's left eye was severely blackened; full of fear he hugged Tamara's waist and refused to answer.

"He's Connie's son. He saw a tall white man with curly dark hair," she looked at me with sad eyes. "There's more Logan, the girls… his sister and her best friend."

"They died for our sins," the old man chimed in.

"He's confessed to killing his granddaughter and her friend and placing their bodies in the room with Connie."

The old man's septum shattered as I drove my fist into his face. I pulled my arm back to throw another punch but before I could, I was wrestled to the ground. A cop's knee was placed firmly in the back of my skull and my left arm pinned behind me as my right hand searched for my gun.

"Logan!" Donnelly's Irish voice shrieked, "Easy there,

Logan. I'm going to release my grip slowly. Okay?" His 5'10", 260 plus lbs frame was squarely on top of me; I relaxed and didn't give him any further excuse to rub my nose in the rug.

"The old man isn't going anywhere; we've got the situation under control. Okay?"

No one put me in such a vulnerable position since the academy. Impressed but pissed, I subdued my rage, "Let me up Pete," and with those four unambiguous words he helped me to my feet.

"Things out there really escalated with the tenets, Logan," Tamara spoke, "it's an angry mob scene and they're armed."

I was livid she defied my orders and had ventured outside the apartment. I surveyed the room but the old man had disappeared.

"Barricade the doors and radio the station for backup," I barked out the orders somewhat confidant that my mental stability had returned. "Oh and Tam, tell tactical they need full riot gear; anybody comes through those doors not wearing a badge you shoot to kill."

Donnelly unholstered his gun and headed for the bedroom. Carson and the other officer placed barriers in front of the door while Tamara talked to command. The little boy clung valiantly to her side and the old man lay incapacitated on the floor. There was no way to know the severity of the threat we faced; the hypnotic stares we encountered posed more concern than relief. The doorknob turned a couple of times as they kicked and pounded on the door. They screamed and yelled threats and promises of death. Other than that, the next half hour was uneventful. I knew command center would take time to mobilize and time was a luxury we didn't have. I put the passing minutes to good use and resumed the examination of Connie's corpse.

The girls were disregarded; they were victims of the old fuck. I found specks of dried blood under the index finger on her left hand. *Why did he get sloppy? Maybe he had been interrupted by the boy?* I knew we had to get her back to the lab as soon as possible. I collected the sample, performed a vaginal swab and tagged the evidence. I photographed everything in the room: the bed, walls, rug, furniture, Connie and the dead girls. I took pictures of the lit candles, broken window, a nightstand with a half-filled glass of sour milk, photographs, slippers and everything in sight. I moved to the bathroom and found more droplets of blood in the sink basin. Maybe she fought him, drew blood and he hadn't realized or he didn't have time to clean up. I made notes for the forensic team to cut the pipe under the sink below the elbow. I removed portions of the carpeting down to the sub-floor. I wanted the whole sha-bang, bed and bath area resurrected down at the lab. A rock was hurled spraying the remaining glass and causing it to rain down inside the apartment. Tiny shards struck Donnelly directly in the face and bloody tears crawled down his cheekbones. I grabbed my gun, headed for the fire escape and blindly fired a shot into the courtyard below. Tamara raced into the room and comforted Donnelly. My eyes darted wildly as I searched the yard. A dog barked then two, then three. The stress was too much and the tumult induced Officer Carson to yell at the top of his lungs.

"Don't leave your post!" I hollered back while I cleared the remnants of broken glass from the window pane with the butt of my gun. There were marks on the window frame that indicated it had been previously splintered from the inside. I stepped outside into the early morning dew; knelt down and found what appeared to be smeared blood on the grates. I should have focused on the killer but instead I wanted to catch some rogue individual who had tossed a rock through an already broken window. It was my responsibility to protect my team at all costs even if it meant jeopardizing my own safety. "Webb, you're in charge!" I shouted to Tamara as I departed the safety of the rat hole.

My brown leather loafers clanged down each step of the fire escape; I periodically peeked down, estimated the distance to the ground and let go with an audible grunt. I searched the streets but saw no one. The garages, homes and trees gave cover to whoever started the mêlée. I was disheartened an angry; I wanted this fight and wanted blood spilled. It's funny how an emotion such as rage can impair your judgment. If I had a clear head I would've thought about Kathy and Elizabeth and would never have charged out of the apartment. I would've chided any officer who recklessly behaved as I had. I felt a chill form inside my bones. Dawn hadn't fully lit up Emerald Park and all I had was my gun and no backup in sight. I holstered my weapon and jogged toward a six foot wood fence that rose from the earth. I leapt as high as my aging body would allow, secured my grip on the top of the weathered fence and hoisted myself up as the planks screeched under my weight. I peered over the top and stared in astonishment at the sea of black humanity. Mothers, daughters, sisters, fathers, brothers, sons, worshipers, sinners and killers alike littered the earth with their lifeless gaze. *They're not real Logan.* The fear that crept into the corners of my subconscious would not allow my mind to rationalize and sent my heart racing. I wanted to shoot madly into the crowd, drench the earth with their blood but I didn't have enough bullets to fight them all. The image of David Koresh and his followers clouded my mind. *How could one man cause mass hysteria? How could someone be so influential yet so detrimental to so many ordinary lives? How could one man convince hundreds that he was the son of God? Perhaps these people were convinced otherwise that the son of Satan had visited them.*

The rustling of leaves alerted me to an attacker just before he was able to strike. He realized he'd been made and the young black male was off and running. I chased after him and my eyes fixed on the crude knife that dangled from his chocolate colored fingers. I was not much of a track star and knew that I should've just shot the punk. I was bound to lose him; he shamed my old body as he accelerated in speeds that mocked my heritage. I cautiously tracked him through the woods; he had plenty of time to double back and set a trap. I drew my gun; *tonight wasn't my night to die*. I slowed my breathing, quietly crept forward and listened for the slightest peculiar sound. I could sense him nearby. He dashed from behind an old oak tree and ran with purpose deep into the forest. I trailed in hot pursuit and weighed my options carefully but my thoughts couldn't keep up with my body. The cabin in the woods materialized like a Mayan Temple. A flickering candle, unkempt graveyard and weather beaten barn beckoned me back into its hellish confines. At the top of the hill was Chancellor's Manor creeping out of the depths of childhood nightmares and into real world fear. I wasn't positive if the boy had sought shelter inside and truthfully didn't give a rat's ass. I stood mesmerized then the child within took action and in a lung burning breathless sprint I fled, northward and terrified. My nostrils flared; the damp air threatened to… "Logan!" Startled it took me a moment to register Tamara's voice.

"Logan!" she yelled again from the top of the fire escape. In that moment it became abundantly clear, I was submerged in a drowning pool of insanity. I'd been standing just yards from the building and seemingly hadn't moved since jumping from the fire escape. My eyes trained on her face. *Steady Logan, it'll be okay.* The last rung of the ladder was suspended eight to ten feet above my head. Webb motioned for me to stay put and vanished from the window like a puff a smoke caught in the breeze. I felt feverish, my eyes irritated and face flustered. *Were the hallucinations sparked by the medication, fever and a lack of sleep?* Tamara reappeared and waved one arm as she held the back door open with her hip.

"It's too dangerous…" I muttered.

"It's secure Logan; they took Connie away twenty minutes ago," she realized I was straining to comprehend. "Swat arrived and was gone without incident… they think they found another crime scene.

TODD ANDREW DAVIS
LIFE'S BLOOD
CHAPTER XIX

The secret to tailing someone successfully is to not follow too closely or linger too far behind. Normally people have little reason to be overly cautious; they feel safe in their two ton vehicles and are immersed in their own worlds. Their minds are consumed with talk radio, top ten countdowns, cell phones, makeup or other various distractions and being hunted is the last thing they'd ever expect. The streetlights hovered like a spacecraft in the misty paleness of the daylight hours; low lying fog hid the ever changing scenery and left the sun unable to place its imprint on the day. Beyond the edges reside the people whose lives and lifestyles had been drastically eroded by economic unfairness. The familiarity of this place congealed within the confines of my subconscious. *How could this be? Unless our mystery man...* my mind refused to complete the thought. I found a somewhat safe and inconspicuous place to park miles into our adventure and blocks away from our destination. I snatched my black leather jacket from the rear seat and entered into the morning haze.

God was crying tiny droplets and it felt wonderful on my face. I proceeded with the rest of the odyssey on foot. The area would make any average pale skinned individual feel an unsettling degree of angst strolling around in the hood, but I had a purpose and an overall 'don't fuck with me' attitude. The neighborhood was something to behold. It was actually quite charming, in a niggerish way. You had to look beyond the bald landscape, the ironclad bars on storefront windows, the diseased night crawlers who solicit their souls for fifty bucks and the blue and whites who were paid to look the other way. A decent person wouldn't stand half a chance in this cesspool, but then there was Connie; she floated high above this unflushed toilet called Emerald Park. This was progress? This was the city's shining light of hope? Shit, I say flick the lever and flush them all. But they showed me something that night Connie and I became one and for that, I will not reign down upon them; even rats have their purpose. The brisk air quickened my pace. The horizon flirted with the sun and produced an early morning tango of orange and dull gray.

I didn't kill Allen so this whore could fuck another blasphemous soul; Laura was my reward. *Was I envious?* In less than a week after her dead lover was butchered another man had entered into her life so effortlessly. *Was he hidden in plain sight?* I wanted to gain insight into this hedonistic intruder and make them both suffer, but the Plan needed time to take root. Ryan and Connie were initially pawns to buy time; time for Laura and me to finish become more acquainted. Now this stupid vile bitch-in-heat sickened me! I could not act solely in rage; it would only spell my doom. Through the murky green haze of my scope, I watched the both of them unwittingly seal their fate. I imagined myself lying next to her, caressing each curve of her nude flesh. Laura liked her hair pulled, liked to slap and bite; I made a mental note. Thunder without lightening or rain, clapped loudly in the horizon; it was shaping up to be an interesting day. Blue and red strobe lights assaulted the early morning that resembled a seventies disco tech, minus the coke and abhorrent clothing. My intuition had been proven right and I learned another noteworthy fact; our new friend was in fact law enforcement. That however didn't make him any less of a target. I was aware of the danger I was inflicting upon myself; cops routinely photograph bystanders who gather around crime scenes in bewilderment. They sought out individuals who seemed out of sorts and in this neighborhood they'd find a baker's dozen linked to other transgressions. The skin I'm in was a burden indeed, but I needed to accumulate a great deal more information about our mystery man. What role did he play? Was he a low level subordinate or a great deal more? He was however, a pig ballsy enough to fuck someone intimately associated with the case. Maybe he was a rogue warrior marching to a different rhythmic beat and thought himself invincible. I prayed this cop was a worthy opponent; boredom could be ever so frustrating. The moon with its infinite wisdom sits in judgment; knowledgeable but forever silent. However, a human adversary with all its flaws could conceivably provide me with an admirable foe.

I scaled a six foot weather beaten wood fence, landing in the common grounds of Connie's apartment complex. A dark cloud of humanity greeted the police and Connie's makeover into a modern day masterpiece was the venue. The artist should be praised not vilified. The candles were hers; I only used them to add to the ambiance.

Planting Ryan's DNA and posing Connie's body was ingenious. Unfortunately, my anger with Ryan had gotten the best of me and he suffered the consequences. True she'd been gutted like a catfish and there would always be that fragment of doubt; one killer or two, copy cat, infinite possibilities. There would be many more questions once they found Ryno; the cop just added a new layer of intrigue. Someone relit the candles in Connie's bedroom and I hid behind a red Oak. I kept my eyes trained on the broken window. A man's shadow moved about then held steady; his chiseled physique unmistakably identified him as Laura's lover. He was poking and prodding, examining Connie's half naked torso for clues. *Seek and you shall find my friend.* I fought the urge to scale the fire escape and peer inside the window. It was like watching a movie and knowing the ending. *Check the bitch's pussy for seminal fluid, it'll be there. You'll find blood under those nails, on the floor, in the sink basin. What will this do to your hypothesis? Was I getting sloppy? Was it the work of the Suburban Slasher?* It was the name the Ravenswood Times had admirably dubbed me. Out of the corner of my eye materialized a caramel-colored skin boy wandering the back lot; he quickly drew my ire. He paced around irritating me as a mosquito would. I needed action; after several minutes, I found a nice sized rock and hurled it through Connie's window. Within seconds our hero appeared and with gun drawn fired a warning shot into the air. He paused to shout something to the other officers inside then dashed down the fire escape and peered in my direction. The boy sought refuge and dashed behind my tree. A crude metal shank dangled from his monkey paw; his body pressed firmly against mine.

"Run nigger!" I growled in his ear.

His body tensed with fright; he didn't dare turn and face me. He ran off in absolute terror with a speed that embodied his slave forefathers and was quite the sight. Our hero alerted, made a mad dash and chased the jungle bunny deep into the woods. I couldn't contain myself and burst out into laughter. *That boy smelled freedom; he aint's gonna come back easy Massa.* I entered the woods with all the agility of a jaguar and could smell the stink of human sweat. The boy still clutched the shank; wanting to do bodily harm to our man of the hour. I couldn't have that.

I spotted his unkempt shaggy afro; he'd cut his pace and found himself the ideal killing position. He had the element of surprise, but thankfully the pig had me as an ally. I crept ever so closely to our menace; my hand covered his mouth just before the bug eyed little bastard expelled a death shriek. I easily overpowered him and flashed my pearl handled blade in front of his wide nose. Predictably he squirmed. Expectedly I cut. Within this tiny yarn lies my dilemma. My craving for blood, made my hunger intolerable and I was a junkie in desperate need of a fix. I could drink from the fountain of blood his throat gushed or maintain visual contact with the pig. He was preoccupied and appeared to be in a trance. Whatever had him hypnotized gave me the luxury to snack before dinner. I didn't take the proper time to truly indulge myself, tossed the little nigglet aside and moved in closer to our hero. There seemed to be a moment of recognition as our eyes locked. His gaze slowly turned from mine as he was mesmerized by something unseen. I could have slit his throat with the greatest of ease; somehow, somewhere we'd cross paths again. His constant erratic behavior was a real nuisance. The fear that griped him had a deeper hold than any terror I could inflict.

I turned my attention back to the boy's open wound. A sexy little black bitch called out to our cop friend. Bacon never looked so good. Our hero entered the building then dashed across the main lobby. I took off northbound headed for the main street and I approached the roadway in time to observe a rather large congregation of coffee drinking, donut eating swine. My two little piglets broke free from the rest of the lemmings and hopped in the infamous cream colored SUV. My heart pounded as the fresh blood I'd consumed coursed throughout my veins. I charged down West Highland Avenue like a wild beast and it triggered memories of the time I ran with the bulls in

Spain. A repressed memory I think. *Maybe I'm not that far removed from my host body.* The pig brigade took the main boulevard; exited this crown jewel and headed west towards civilization. I resumed the chase but was mindful; tits was driving and might have been more alert to a tail. I checked the rearview myself, nobody behind me; I focused my attention on my prey. The most vigilant and skilled assassin can still be had by the element of surprise, but anonymity gave me a distinct advantage.

TODD ANDREW DAVIS
WISHING WELL
CHAPTER XX

"What's going on?" I stammered. If I wasn't on edge before, I was now on the verge of madness. I almost tripped head over heels as we dashed thru the building towards the SUV. "Fill me in." I reached the passenger door, popped it open and waited for her to climb in. I could feel beads of molten sweat cascading down my face.

"Logan you don't look so good."

"I'll get a second opinion from someone in the medical community; talk and drive."

"Two young girls, thirteen and twelve saw a man tied to a chair in the basement of a for sale house. Mrs. Heidi Page, mother of the thirteen year old is a Real Estate Broker."

"Let me guess. The little Hiltons cased one of mommy's properties and were seeking a rad place to throw a party."

"Bingo. Shit you're going to love being the father of a teenage daughter."

"I plan on being dead long before then," I joked.

"Of course the little darlings waited two days before alerting the authorities. We also have cell phone usage calling 911 coming from inside the house. Dispatcher chalked it up to pranksters. Quote: Nobody was ever on the other line."

"Okay when do things get interesting?   And for the record

I'm dying not dead; keep your eyes on the road."

"Prick," responded Tamara, "Dorothy Hastings, a friend of Ryan Beliford called him on several occasions and hadn't heard back.   She went to file a police report and was informed that since he was over twenty-one she'd have to wait the customary twenty four hours.   She stated that she had to work the next day and opted to forgo the paperwork. He texted her several puzzling messages; she thought he was playing and didn't follow up on the missing persons. Thankfully, she left her name and number with one of the officers."   She glanced over, "You sure you're feeling alright?"

"Well enough continue."

"A couple of uniforms checked out the house with the mother of the kid.   There was the unmistakable stench of death mixed with bleach and industrial cleaner. They also found traces of blood and a cryptic message in the basement.   The call came in fifteen minutes ago and the patrol officers were as careful leaving as they were entering; real pros. Santiago is there now holding down the fort until we arrive."

"So you think Mr. Beliford is our number one suspect?"

"One and only real lead Logan, he's better than nothing."

"He could be a victim. How about the two little cat

burglars?"

"In their own words they were freaked out. Their statements two days later bore little similarities to one another. They were more concerned with giving believable alibis of their own. Kids gotta love um."

Through the entire ride we were in a dueling battle of hot and cold; I'd roll down the window as she blasted the heater. I was burning up and as she so politely put it, 'freezing her goddamn ass off.' Twenty minutes later we pulled up to the palatial gated community of Kings Crossing.

"If this is our guy, how the fuck did he manage to get inside undetected?" I said in amazement.

A pretentious guard lay in wait, coiled and ready to strike. The five by ten enclosures housed one Winston Howard V. He was the gatekeeper to the affluent and ostentatious. I imagined the little prick would bellow, *'Who goes there?'*

"And you would be?" asked Winston in a classic drag queen voice.

I flashed my badge and he flashed a gold tooth smile that had me a little uneasy. He flipped a magical switched and allowed the drawbridge to give us safe passage to the magnificent castles.

"I think he likey," I said as we drove pass.

"You're just so fucking irresistible Logan," another one of Webb's pearls had been unleashed upon my weakened psyche, "Jesus Christ get over yourself, not everybody wants you."

"I didn't say…"

"You didn't have to. Guys like you, oh forget it…"

At the end of the block we drove around a cul-de-sac and arrived at One Blair-Way. Her tone disguised a deep seeded outrage. *Another woman scorned; another man ultimately at fault.* This time the bulls-eye was squarely across my forehead. *Sorry Tamara, sorry you got involved with a married man. It's entirely all my fault and I take full blame, never mind the happiness we brought to each other's life. Forget about the good times and focus solely on the bad. I'm your justification for all your failed relationships, past, present and future. I am solely responsible for the unhappiness that weighs your heart down like a lead balloon. I've brought nothing but misery. So why do you get so nostalgic for my pathetic, selfish, unfulfilling company? Why do you always look for me to save you?* I stretched my legs out; vacated the truck and made my way over to Detective Santiago.

"Fuck."

"Yeah J.T., I know; caught me on a bad day?"

I coughed into my hand and followed him inside as he led me around two towering redwood doors. I could never hope to afford this type of luxury on six times my salary; it almost made you wish something mischievous had happened to the previous owners. A Baby Grand with untouched pearly whites sat beneath an opulent crystal chandelier and granite countertops with graphite specks twinkled as though they were stars blazing thru a dark Brazilian sky. Jealousy couldn't begin to capture the essences of my disdain. After tonight this house will be a sunken treasure ship stripped barren of its riches. No matter how regal, an empty house is just an antiseptic shell. The foul odor of death permeated every room in the house; penetrated your soul and tore at your humanity. My stomach churned and bones ached as I fought back the realization of the stark brutality yet discovered. A hand carved staircase with elegant railings made of ash and cork guided us to the basement. The mind can only endure so much before it sinks deeper into the quagmire of delusion and emptiness. *Am I on the verge? Could I find my way back?* His first tangible message to the outside world had been written on the wall in blood. And its meaning was as convoluted as the murders themselves.

YOU WILL FIND GOD HAS FORSAKEN YOU YOUR SOUL IMPRIOSONED BY RELIGIOUS ZEALOTS YOUR MIND YOUR BODY NOT YOUR OWN ONLY I CAN RELASE YOU SET YOU FREE!

Connie had been slain and posed in an apparent mockery of Christ upon the cross and now this.

"Does it mean anything to you Logan?" Officer Eddie Kedison stood on the second floor balcony; his voice suddenly lost in a wave of panic, we turned in unison and bounded up the staircase.

They were all trained professionals hardened by child rapists, suicides and decomposing bodies. They stood around the kitchen and resembled children holding their noses. It was a failed attempt to squash the foul smell of rotted meat and rising tension. A young male officer meant to turn on the light above the stainless steel sink and granite countertop, but in his hubris flicked the wrong switch. I yelled in vain but the sound of my voice trailed off as the garbage disposal sparked to life. It barfed out a montage of marbled bone, bloody meat, intestines, fingers, toes, matted hair and a gush of indescribable goo. The walls and ceiling were painted with thick human sludge that rained down upon us. The vomiting ensued, set off by the young officer, but by no means contained to just him.

"Ladies and gentlemen meet Mr. Ryan Beliford! And please tread carefully so as not to contaminate the evidence!" I barked out orders as the heave fest persisted.

"How do you know its Ryan?" Tamara quizzed as she stood by my side.

"I just do," I turned, her forehead was tagged by a piece of raw flesh; she looked understandably queasy, "You feel like you need to…"

"No. No Logan I'm good."

TODD ANDREW DAVIS
EYE OF THE GATE KEEPER
CHAPTER XXI

Exiting Connie's end of town; I soon had the same eerie sixth sense. *How could they have found Ryno so fast?* This couldn't be; I figured it would have taken the authorities' days. *Someone must have alerted them, tipped them off. It could have been the 911 calls or perhaps one of the bevy of bitches accumulated on his cell. I should've kept the phone instead of annihilating it.* I sat outside the all too familiar cul-de-sac an engraved lacquer plaque that read One Blair-Way.

The bony white maggot manned his glass sandbox and stunk of petulance and cheap cologne. He had draped himself in an olive colored silk costume and on his face sat a hideous black wisp of a mustache trained obediently to stay in place. The man's entire persona paid homage to dear departed gay actors of the silver screen. He thought himself of regal importance but was nothing more than a carnival clown caught in the wrong decade. *What could he have told the pigs?' Could this tinker bell be my downfall? Even if they confiscated the surveillance video and I couldn't be identified; the car would stand out.* My anger rose. *This wasn't my fault. For what purpose did he choose this location? He wanted to up the ante and intimidate the wealthy by making them shake and shiver. He needed me, not everything was instinctual and some things could get problematic very quickly if not attended to in the proper fashion.* The gate keeper flicked the lever with his dainty white gloved hand and allowed the pigs to enter. They promptly joined the festivities at the top of the hill.

My complete transformation mainly occurred during the killing stage and on previous occasions I'd only been granted the privileges of voyeurism. However, lately I had been more of an active participant and it constituted a new found era of trustworthiness. With this new accountability critical attention had to be paid to the minutest of details. This was my first real challenge. Even if the cops hadn't retrieved the tape from Winston Howard V, how the fuck was I going to gain possession of it now? It would seem protocol would dictate that it was a lost cause. The Chevelle would have to go, I could leave it in the ghetto and it would be dismantled by day's end. I had intended to wait outside the gate for my two little piglets, but before I knew it I was knocking on the booth. The cops were mere blocks away and within earshot of the screaming queen. I had to act soon. I decided.

"Hello friend," I said in a low seductive voice.

"I'm sorry do I know you?" The queer bit his bottom lip. I'm sure he thought it was probably from a chance encounter at a rest stop or bathroom stall.

"We've met before," I said but he still seemed puzzled. With all the commotion the cops had caused swarming around and my sudden reappearance, I could see the thoughts register in his mind. "Cha-ching," I extended my forefinger to my nose, "very impressive and you didn't even wet yourself."

"I didn't tell them any..."

"You didn't mention me because I so graciously slipped you a hundo? Perhaps you figured letting a killer in for such a nominal fee was a bargain? I'm sure deep down you detest this gated community. Your only hope of associating with these people was through servitude. I'm sure you have plenty of secrets with the lifestyle you chose and some you intend on taking to the grave." A wicked smile crossed my lips and he displayed a retched uneasiness. The booth window was partially open and he had made no attempt to close it.

"What do you want me to do?" pouted the winged ferry.

"Let me in," I snarled.

"I… I… I didn't…" he visibly trembled in his snake skins.

I turned the knob, found the guard's door unlocked and in one motion put all my weight against it forcing it open. The edge of the door caught him above his Jew nose, blood began to flow and the hysterical little ninny flew into a wild frenzy.

"Open it," he urged me through blood and pain as he frantically pointed to a wood stained cabinet, "It's what you want."

His outlook on life grew brighter as he realized he'd sparked my interest. My eyes never wavered from his while I grasped the brass handle. A distinctive clicking noise originated from within the bowls of the cabinet and a black VCR stared back like an unopened Christmas present.

"I lied to them. I told the officers the tapes for the cameras were in a different location and that I would personally hand deliver it to them."

"You did this all for me?" I saw the youthful exuberance return through his bloody flesh and I put an end to it before he could eagerly spell out his deception, "Saving me is the furthest thing from your little fag mind. I'm not going out on a limb by saying that I'm not the only man who you've allowed inside. You had a dilemma. I'm sure some incriminating homosexual shit has been going on for months inside the confines of your little glory hole. I bet you seduced your fair share of these snotty rich punks. A little alcohol to entice a teenage boy's libido and you were off and flying down the Hershey highway. I bet that's closer to the truth huh? You probably had them suck you off on bended knee as you raised the gate to let their parents in. You tried to save your own ass out of shame. See, you're not that typical fagot that's tolerated by a portion of mainstream society; you're the deviant fuck that good Christians fear will turn their children into sexual hedonist. Yes it's true you're not at fault for making them queer; you just satisfied their kinky curiosities."

I slashed his aorta and the plexiglass was awash in reddish brown syrup. His hands in prayer begged me to spare his life. *Who's this atheist fooling?* No worry, he'd bleed out soon. I gazed off into the distance as a whimsical mixture of blue and red lights danced with the morning glory. The overcast shadows brought by the clouds had dissipated; the sun would soon cleanse our daily sins and we would be born anew. My hands trembled as I pressed the ejector button on the VCR; the motor strained then seized. The anticipation had been excruciating, the door opened an out popped a video tape. *Holy fuck!* I wiped my fingerprints off the VCR button and door knob with my shirt sleeve. I paused to soak in the glorious mess that had once been the attendant; it was a cow led to the slaughterhouse. His neck was bent at such a crude angle that his body physically formed a question mark. His horn rimmed glasses lay in a pool of shit and his olive colored outfit turned dark maroon. I backed away from the growing pool of blood. His left arm had been pinned underneath his body and appeared as though it had been ripped off and tossed away. His face was twisted into a frozen mask of horror and his green eyes had turned murky, opaque, and dead. *It happened so quickly how could there have been so much carnage?* I expected him to die in the fetal position clutching his jugular; instead the animal channel couldn't have done this scene justice. I had to look away. I didn't envy the people who had to work this insidious crime. I was wrong, so very wrong. For a few seconds I glanced at the aftermath and was nauseated. I thought I'd welcome this, but now I realized why I had been speared. I can think of myself as a demon or a monster, but I would never fully understand what I had become.

"Human emotions will weaken you," said the voice inside as I stepped into the crisp morning air. I was trying to make the best out of this shared soul; I need not think too much. I had to maintain my composure; after all I had come so far. Let him kill, let him fast and I will keep us from the hangman's noose. I should have been thrilled; my salvation lay in my hands. Instead, I stepped back into the booth and tried to recall a time before he entered my life. There had to have been a pivotal moment when I conjured up this demon to do my bidding. The second I arrived in Illinois I had this inkling this had once been home for me. *Had I ever been in control? Why can't I remember anything before the teenage whore, the headless bitch and her little sister?*

A myriad of pig-men in Crown Vic's, Suburban's and other unidentifiable vehicles began the long descent down the twisting hill. I had been in the booth for over a half hour, but it had seemed like minutes. The crap colored pig mobile was situated in the middle of a conga line. The sun grasped the early morning hours by the throat and choked out the last remnants of darkness. I used the guard's pickle green vest to clean the carnage off the window, pressed the lever, engaged the gears and watched as the mechanical arm rose. I allowed the invited guests and the Serve and Protect community of Blair-Way to pass by while obscuring my face from scrutiny. They sunk their heads and a defeated expression was etched across their once jubilant faces. Most hadn't noticed me or my wicked smile. Some glanced over, some acknowledge my presence, but the beat went on with every passing vehicle. Even our hero was too preoccupied. *How could they not realize the killer they sought was in their midst? I guess not even the craziest of psychopaths would dare enter the enemy's camp and intermingle the way I have. Is that what I am? Do I really believe that I am a psychotic killer on the rampage? No. Not me.*

I ran a finger across my weary temple; I was so much more than your run-of-the-mill killer. I would rain blood down upon these pathetic souls. Even in their disgust they would worship me as the last trail blazer who cast a shadow over their perpetual hope and everlasting moral righteousness. I scoffed at their ineptitude. *Christ this was becoming too easy.* A euphoric high is described as an 'exaggerated feeling of well-being or elation' and it exemplified my mood precisely. I had the distinct advantage of living in a civil society. Those who were blessed with good looks, athletic ability, fame, fortune or a working knowledge of the human mind have the unique capacity to elevate their status in life. Ants are ants because it is God's will to make them so. Evolution may alter the food chain but every one of us is a meal not yet devoured. Death is a wondrous thing and the architects of death should be highly commended. It is a celebration and the makers of death are arbitrarily chosen to uphold the natural order of things. I walked over to my car, turned the ignition switch, engaged the clutch and shifted into first.

TODD ANDREW DAVIS
BY DAWNS EARLY LIGHT
CHAPTER XXII

Sweat dripped from my forehead and my temper at its peak made worse by the choking and stagnate air.

"We have no other choice than to take another approach," echoed Detective J.T. Santiago.

He had his own theories on how we should proceed. "Detective Santiago," I motion for him to take center stage.

"Thank you Detective Crenshaw."

I was tired, short of breath and glad to be out of the spotlight. *He wanted it, he's got it. Fuck them all! Ignorant mother fuckers! Two faced cocksuckers! I can play their game; smile as I slip the knife into their backs. I heard the rumors; saw the contemptuous looks on their faces. You think you can do better? Have at it dirty ass kissing wetback, this ain't the Barrio.* The murders had my juices flowing, but the media and public's constant yammering soured my devotion. I'd sought out the limelight and got it tenfold. I received death threats on a daily bases and the FBI went from threatening to take over command to insisting on protecting my well being and yet here I stood next to a man I fucking loathed. I had my arm around his shoulder and a look of confidence beamed across my lying face. I hated being phony; I hated being one of them. This

BY DAWNS EARLY LIGHT

day was inevitable. The pompous bunch of ingrates known affectionately as my taskforce had lost sight of the goal.

They read the newspaper clippings and panicked, watched the nightly news and soiled themselves; they listened to neighbors and friends that the world was coming to an end. We had turned on each other and now they would cut the head off their leader. That was exactly what the killer wanted. I was the albatross weighing down the righteous and everyone else was blameless and untouched by the wickedness. Divided we fall and the body count will rise. *Have fun at the top; bean-eater.*

"Furthermore," stated Santiago, "I believe there are two killers who are joined at the hip. Perhaps a Professor and student whose relationship evolved into this sick collaboration. This duo obviously is extremely sophisticated and skilled in the art of deception, just like any good magician who's honed his craft. They wanted us to concentrate on the heinousness of the crimes. This teams' relationship is one of uncle- nephew, father-son, brothers, cousins, friends, roommates, lovers. These two share a unique bond that makes them inseparable. They're trying to unnerve us, break us and make us quit. We cannot allow this to happen." He was more politician than cop. He paused to sip water from a white Styrofoam cup, "My theory revolves around two men, mentor and protégé; one a stone could diabolical killer the other a meticulous and calculated submissive who keeps them safe."

Why reinvent the wheel. I had conjured up a thick Mexican accent and barely listened to Santiago's dissertation.

"So why should we reinvent the wheel when we already have a sound blueprint brought about by good solid detective work! These individuals are criminals; highly educated perhaps, but eventually a mistake will occur and their collective minds will fracture." Santiago cleared his throat, "I can't emphasize this enough rely on your instincts and training. There is an outside agency leering over our shoulders. These are our people, our communities. It's unacceptable to me that unseasoned officer's and first responders are mucking around in the evidence and trampling the crime scene. We need to focus, not only on the brutality of the crime, but the particulars of the data. We will uncover their methods and the killers will be revealed. They're draped in human flesh, blood and bone just like everyone in this room... with the exception of Logan of course," laughter erupted from the officers gathered. "Now is not the time to cower but respect the oath, the badge and catch these madmen!"

Santiago was a hypocritical asshole. He'd sent Darlene and the kids to her mother's in Kansas. He was as shallow as the deep end of the kiddy pool and had been handpicked by our fearless leader Captain Oliver 'Ollie' Hill; mainly to babysit me I suppose. He wanted his moment in the sun and in a nutshell the plan was to divide the task force. My team would concentrate on sisters Jessica, Jennifer and Laura's dead boyfriend Allen and Santiago's team would concentrate on Connie, Ryan and the Jane Doe hooker found in the motel fire.

"Back to the drawing board people; forget what you think you know. I want two separate profiles. I want the thread that links these cases together. Logan and I will have control over all of the boxed evidence, crime scenes photo's and reports."

He wanted to prove he was right and wanted me to struggle like an untrained monkey. *Well game on Chico.*

"I know everyone will do whatever it takes to close this case. Ends justify the means and how you accomplish those means are of no consequence to me."

I knew he thought I was a miserable dumb redneck cracker who had his chance and screwed the pooch. *Drinking again Logan? Fucking someone instrumental to the case? Yeah you racist prick; I'm your worst nightmare, a brown skin who's showing your dumb lily white ass how to do his job. Bet you thought you'd never see the day.*

"Detective Logan and I will be extremely receptive to any ideas you have to offer," said Santiago. "Pound the pavement, go door to door, video surveillance, security guards, vagrants, streetwalkers, juveniles; anyone could be a potential witness or a suspect. I want as many interviews at day's end as you can handle. It's all fundamental police work, what we were trained to do. Flood the streets; show up in force. They will try to operate perfectly, they will fail and we won't. Let's take back our neighborhoods ladies and gentlemen, street by street!" With that, Santiago walked among the task force's rousing applause and standing ovation. It was a beautiful speech and not being one for the rah-rah motivational bullshit theater, I'd never felt so inspired in all my life.

I guess my mind had drifted back to this morning's speech as sort of a protection mechanism against my fear of claustrophobia. I stood over the bludgeoned body of the gatekeeper. Technically it fell under Santiago's jurisdiction and I would be stepping on his toes, but there were a few unanswered questions that I needed answered. His approximate time of death was during or shortly after we departed the Ryan Belafiore crime scene. *Was it possible that while Ryan's remains were being scrapped off the ceiling, Winston Howard V was dismembered? Could this killer be so brazen that he'd opened the gate for us on our way out? That's preposterous!* I felt a sense of unease as I stared at Winston's battered head; it was a grapefruit that had been stuffed with spaghetti and meat sauce then violently splattered. His eyes two jumbo sized olives plucked from his skull, and placed inside a cabinet drawer. *Forgotten souvenirs?* If Winston had taken the time to fill out his organ donor card then it would have been a colossal waste of time. He was already small in stature but now he could easily fit inside an airplane carry-on bag. Bits and pieces of black and silver plastic were embedded in his flesh; the autopsy would confirm it was a Panasonic VCR. There wasn't a distinctive pattern to the blood splatter that hinted at a point of attack and the shoebox interior was plastered with reddish-brown goo. We dressed head to toe in white Hazmat suits complete with full-face respirators to keep from contaminating the crime scene and ourselves. A marbled mound of splintered bone and partially eaten intestines were stacked in a pile underneath the console, parts of him were either missing or beaten beyond recognition. Winston was a blood born biohazard and his lime green sports coat with matching fedora were some of the few things used to identify the poor slob. We hoped for traces of saliva or vomit in the partially devoured carcass and yet not a finger or shoe print found in or outside this isometric cube that could be attributed to our killer. I felt the onset of a panic attack coming.

The diminutive quarters won out, I felt claustrophobic and the protective clothing combined with the respirator made me lightheaded. A sausage grinder could not have tenderized Winston any more efficiently. It was nonsensical to not attribute this hellacious scene to an overactive imagination conjured up by a provocative special effects tech. The movie tech however would have been laughed out of the business for going ridiculously too far in his portrayal of death. Winston's right hand and arm were flattened to the point where they could have squeezed underneath the door. His head was void of ears and teeth; his eyes and lips were purple in color. The broken tile that lay beneath him had buckled due to the force of the blows to his body. Only nubs remained on his left hand and I pictured his fingers being bitten off one by one. I rotated my torso and hips to view the slaughter rather than walk through the slippery sticky muck. I'd been the third person allowed inside and was given explicit instructions to keep my feet within the path of my predecessors. It was a daunting task to say the least. It was hard to keep my feet from sliding out from beneath me. Unfortunately my size thirteen shoes were too large for the hazmat suit and I had to remove them and could feel the warm slick blood through the suit's thin membrane and it squished between my toes. *How much time did the killer afford himself in this booth? Was he aware that he was surrounded by cops or was he in such a rage that he blocked everything out? How could he of gone undetected? Had he followed us... or me?* He tried to prove he was invincible and that he held all the cards in the palm of his hands. *Was he a cop?* It seemed more plausible with each passing day. Winston was a shot across the bow to all those who waded too far from shore. A killer shark lurked and feasted on anything with a pulse. There's neither rhyme nor reason just insanity. No motive or single profile that fit. He was simply death incarnate. *How do you stop such a thing?*

The cold muzzle of a double barreled shotgun was pressed firmly against my abdomen and shook the last remnants of REM sleep from my weary head. The Winchester 12 gauge made it hard for oxygen to infiltrate my lungs. I wanted to snatch it from him and bash him to death with it. Most of all, I wanted to know who he was and what he wanted from me. He exuded calmness an aura of confidence as though it wasn't the first time he had stood toe to toe with the Devil. I'd been caught off guard; sleep deprived my body had simply shutdown.

"Do you know who you're fucking with?" I blurted out.

His eyes were hidden by the brim of an old Stetson cowboy hat and his body cloaked in the darkness. I sat up on the edge of the bed and planted my feet firmly on the cool surface of the ceramic tile. I started to stand and made my second mistake. The butt of the riffle slammed into my left temple and I thought I heard something break. The room pitched left then right and I slipped into a dark oblivion. *Was I being tortured for all my sins? Would my Savior still come to rescue me? I aimed to be legendary.*

Was I being dragged back from whence I came? My Maker would never allow this. My God... My eyelids were heavy and I focused on a single light above the stove. My muscles had tightened up; every movement stretched them like a rubber band. The acid in my stomach burned as hot as an open flame. I prayed for a chance to strike, that's all I needed and I would teach this ingrate what true suffering was about. *I'll skin this one and stuff his rotted flesh down his throat. There won't be a drop of blood found in his corpse.* The pleasantry of my thoughts gave me great solace in a time of ambiguity. *So make me suffer; bring on all the sadistic torture you can fathom. They'll pale in comparison for what's in store for you.*

"Liam," he spoke as he moved closer.

His hand tilted my head to the side so I could take a sip of tap water from a cup. I gulped down nearly all of it and immediately was alerted to an unfamiliar aftertaste not native to Chicagoans. The water had been tainted. *That's how he kept his advantage over me.* I closed my eyes and listened as he moved about the room. The name Liam rang as hollow as church bells cascading down from a wooden steeple. His voice droned on until I faded back into another time, another world. I was led down hells corridor by a beast nearly eight feet tall. His back was covered in a sweaty mass of coarse black wiry hair and I could detect brown skin underneath his mane. A bevy of scars marked his face, a pungent odor wafted from the unwashed brute and his massive limbs dangled pass his knees. His neck sloped due to the weight of his oversized head; however his beastly appearance betrayed his intellect and gracefulness. Most of his identifiable human-characteristics had eroded over the centuries but some mannerisms still held slight traits. A human pyramid was embedded in the walls above the staircase we descended. Flesh faced and white boned gargoyles barked as we passed; jealous of all those who wore human skin. I couldn't allow my chains to drag me down and knew my freedom lay in his grotesque and

179

disfigured hands. I kept up with his pace, eager for the privilege of meeting my creator.

I wanted the opportunity to prove my worthiness and unwavering loyalty. I was devoted to him, shed my morality and cast away the confines of societal bounds. I did it all in the quest for his acceptance and now I would kneel before him in his exalted honor. *Who was this beast of burden; this soulless creature who held my chains? Had he once been an obedient soldier: was this his reward?'* My mind was fraught with emotions that needed to be vanquished. I was naked, sweat boiled on my skin and my nose gushed a thick vile sludge that threatened to choke me, but my resolve remained steadfast. I was not just a seeker or a Devil worshiping novitiate whose punk music and simulated anarchy had been a youthful phase. I wasn't an obnoxious piece of shit spawned from a lack of parental control, henchman or lost soul out for vindication. Nor was I a martyr for those lip pierced, tongue impaled, nose ring, head-banging degenerates who couldn't get laid. I was a God who walked among all of earth's subhumans. By no means was I his equal and I shall be humble in his presence. I did not suffer from a lack of absent minded obedience. Quite the reverse, I appreciated the fact that I was chosen; through the grace of him go I. Hellfire's toxic inferno blended white, ginger and scarlet flames into a human-like apparition. My lungs were excruciatingly inflamed by the intense heat.

"Liam," it called to me.

My system had been shocked back into its mortal state and I lay before the Stetson wearing parasite. He was nothing more than a petty insult thrown in my direction. I seethed with hatred and vowed to dispose of him in time. My mouth was cotton dry; but I learned my lesson drinking from a poison chalice. My body convulsed as my lungs tried to assimilate to the rush of free flowing oxygen.

"This is the story of your re-birth; a night that changed all of us forever," my captor talked about a point in time that held no relevance. "Our parents were sadists and prayed on the innocents of the neighborhood children. Their lust for blood and young flesh were a ghastly demonstration of how the Devil can corrupt one's mind. Nothing good ever spawned from their covenant. They were destined for each other, a bond unbroken in life as well as death. We had no chance at the moment of conception and we three were forever doomed; abortion would have been a more acceptable fate. The stink of death fills our lungs; the blood of human suffering stains our souls. We were bred to be killers, born to dine on flesh."

He lit up a cigar and surveyed the apartment. The smoke blurred his identity as it floated pass his face. He tilted another refreshing glass in my direction; I wanted to resist, but I found myself reluctantly drinking the bittersweet elixir. It was a different concoction that nonetheless temporarily quenched my thirst.

"Our parents' violence radically grew over the decades," he continued with his story, satisfied with his act of kindness. "One fateful day, dad beat a young girl so bad her screams were heard a mile away. The guest bed was turned into a torture rack. You can't even begin to appreciate the amount of pain a child can endure until you see it firsthand. A childhood friend was so terribly abused that she became a virtual empty shell and with their sense of gratification gone, they took turns suffocating her. The rumors abound and our parents had no other remedy but to turn their insanity inward. They were partners in debauchery and we were the targets of their rage. One day it all ended and you took the full blame. We share a unique bond as blood and being triplets makes it so much more special. Liam, I'm your brother Lucas. I took sole custody of your daughter and she's safe and living with me in Charlotte, North Carolina. I will take you to her after we've finished The Plan."

The Plan, stick to The Plan; it was a faded echo that ricocheted throughout my brain ever since I had come back to Ravenswood. *Had he been there from the beginning? Was his the voice that burned inside my subconscious? No. He was no warrior; he hadn't stood before the Devil and offered up sacrifices. Yet, he knew of The Plan.* His care of my child was inconsequential and it changed nothing of course, I was still goanna kill him. I wondered if he could sense that fact. I had endured humiliation at his hand and he would atone for his blasphemes ways. I wasn't bound by human compassion and would not feel the loss or guilt for slaughtering this lamb. My brother would simply be a source of nutrition.

Just because I was laden in flesh it didn't mean I wouldn't cannibalize the entire human race. He would die on the cross as a tribute to his fallen Messiah.

"You've been institutionalized for the past twenty plus years Liam. A lie stole your freedom and turned you into a fiend. After you were committed they tested experimental drugs on you and destroyed your memory. While you valiantly pleaded your innocence the testimony of one person sealed your fate. He turned his back on us and condemned you, a fifteen year old boy left alone to cope with the brutal slaying of our parents. The little town of Ravenswood had been tarnished forever. They shipped you to Waco, Texas hoping the legend would eventually die along with you. You survived and became a master manipulator. The drugs worked, they'd cast out the demons and made you whole again, but just beneath the surface a killer lurked and waited. That's all I knew, that's all they ever reminded me about. You've heard those voices in your head ever since I could remember. The drugs kept them at bay and by the time of your twenty-fifth birthday you had partial access to the mental facility. You worked as a dishwasher and custodian; a reliable little robot. You survived for years without incident that was until the Lolita Nicole had been admitted; otherwise you might have made it as the Cedar Homes poster boy. The black nympho bitch was suicidal and you homicidal; it wasn't a very good combination. When they learned you got an underage girl pregnant your privileges were revoked and the administrators looked for a more suitable place to dump you off." He rested the long barrel of the Winchester on his shoulder, "Nine months later your daughter was born and I was contacted. Nicole had her baby taken away and sunk into a deep depression. She severed a cord from a television set and hung herself in her room. Gossip, rumors they all centered on you, perhaps you had a hand in her suicide. Once again you were a pariah, an outcast, but this time in a world of the mentally insane."

We sat across from each other as the morning sun lit the smallish interior of the motel room. He got up and walked across the room; his left hand pushed the blinds aside and he peered out the window. "You have a great view Liam, " he said as he stared across the alley at the back of Ledgers Hardware Store's brick wall. He fished out a small metallic flask from inside his breast pocket. "Like I stated, there had always been rumors that you killed her but there was never any substantial evidence. They forced you back into solitude and in that time spent isolated, your thoughts churned inside your troubled mind with no release. If you weren't mad before... I always believed in your innocence, not just about Nichole but mom and dad as well. I never stopped hunting for the truth."

His jaw line was an entanglement of old scars, masculine and square in nature. By contrast, his body was rather pudgy and unformed. Narcissism got the best of me and I hadn't been able to see a clear image of myself for quite some time now. I gathered the monster inside of me had permanently distorted my image and I could only view myself through a narrow prism. I knew my head sprouted long curly brown locks and that I looked youthful for my age. I thought I was unique in the world but standing in front of me in his low brim Stetson was evidence of my genealogy. Time had faded my memory of almost every aspect of my former self. I grew to accept that fact until my brother mysteriously materialized out of whole cloth and I could not afford to feel any human emotion, brother or not.

"Why are you here?" I heard myself ask.

He walked back over to the bed sat on the edge and said, "I am here simply to put things back on track."

"And what exactly does that entail?"

He placed his right thumb and index finger to his head and simultaneously in an opposite circular motion, massaged his eyelids, "Brother if you would just indulge me a little longer, I was attempting to shed light on your new found transformation and why after so long you came back home."

Home, I had felt it the moment I crossed into Illinois. I'd been drawn here and I needed to know why. The more the fog dissipated from my head the more I wanted to learn about myself. The festering beast inside had been subdued for now.

"Decades later I learned the truth behind your incarceration. You suffered the consequences of a wretched lie. Mom and dad beat you unmercifully that night and you bled out of every orifice. They raped you, tortured you and you would never be the same. Maybe you wanted them dead so badly you believed that you had slaughtered them. The brotherly bond that night was broken forever. Born triplets our third sibling committed the most egregious of all sins. He allowed his own flesh and blood to suffer for a crime he perpetrated. Logan's a cop, a big fish in a small pond and it just became infested with sharks. He's been living the good life Liam, a life of admiration and respect. That's why I came up with The Plan; simply put make him suffer for all his deceit. You've crippled this town, shut down their ability to function as a normal society. It's good versus evil; Kane and Abel. Expose him for the coward he is. You languished in purgatory while he turned his back on the both of us. Nobody in his world has even heard the slightest whisper of our existence. I stood by you, watched as they polluted your system with mind altering medications and listened as they condemned you of parricide. Their judgment of you was unjust, factitious, a creation and by happenstance, I arrived at the truth. I confronted Logan and his insipid denial was more than I could stomach. He lived while you suffered and now it's our time to flourish and right the wrong. You lost your child, your friends, your family and your soul. You paid for his sins with flesh and freedom and were shunned by all who gazed upon you. Logan needs to experience grief and humiliation. Nail him to the cross, inflict unspeakable misery on him, bleed him dry and make him suffer beyond eternity. Reign down upon him for his mortal sins, devour him and send him screaming into the depths of damnation!"

TODD ANDREW DAVIS
A SIMPLE MAN
CHAPTER XXIV

Winston's body lay in the basement at the police station morgue. We reconstructed the crime scene; minus the gate and fancy cobblestone drive. The guard's station, Winston's death chamber, was nothing but a glorified phone booth. The floors, ceiling and walls were plastered with two layers of six inch poly. A sophisticated decontamination unit (DECON) had been constructed, equipped with double entry and exit flaps and a shower to boot. Once again I had to don the hazmat suit and a (PAPR) Powered Air Purifying Respirator. I'd been instructed to remove all clothing, toss suit into the decontamination area upon exit, leave the respirator on and proceed through the maze then shower and dress. It was a lot to commit to memory. The booth was a spaceship in an ocean of poly and I a monkey in a spacesuit sadly adjusting to my new environment. As I moon walked toward Doc Henagar, several CSI's came into view. Every square inch of flesh, every drip drop of fluid from Winston was scrutinized. I continued my approach; in laymen's terms their sophisticated instruments appeared to be rubber spatulas and squeegees. The whole event would have been hysterical if not for the seriousness of the circumstances. What was left of Winston lay in pieces on the examining table. Lab Techs performed an artful microscopic reconstruction; the little wizards determined which mound of Humpty Dumpty's goop went where. His clothing tattered and stained was inspected just as painstakingly as his remains.

"Searching for a pimple on Big Foot's ass, I see," my voice was muffled and echoed back in a hollow imitation but

Doc managed to parse the verbiage with little effort.

"Logan," Henagar's lethargic voice was mirrored by his body language, "we'll get the Nobel Prize if we can isolate anything foreign and determine its origin." In a complete display of utter hopelessness he raised a glass vial, "His alligator loafers helped us identify his feet. Head to toe this man's body was beaten worse than a piñata."

"Keep me informed if you find anything Doc."

"Ollie told me Detective Santiago was in charge of this part of the investigation?"

"He is; I just need the basics," I turned to leave. "Oh and Doc, let's just keep this between you and me, okay."

I stuck to protocol as I emerged nude from inside the containment. The sanitary sandpaper towels were less than desirable. I was irritated with the lack of ability to ease the woes of my fellow colleagues and made it my burden, my mission to close this case. Today I saw firsthand how much the murders had affected the team. I had surfaced from Mars where time was irrelevant and I was just an obstacle inside DECON. I knew I was a self centered, self absorbed stinking bastard with delusional psychosis and hypersensitive paranoia; a self diagnoses of course. I was also armed and extremely dangerous.

Santiago's speech annoyed me because it forced me to question my own tactics. I could feel the pores on my skin open as I escaped the confines of the Hazmat suit. I signed out of containment using the safety data sheet and promptly jumped into my civvies. I made a beeline for the service elevator at the end of the basement. As I walked I realized that for nearly two months my mind had been consumed with death. A black cloud of perpetual doom hung over my head like an anvil. On the rare occasion I was home, I found little relief. I was emotionally detached to Kathy's mood swings and Lizzy's struggle for independence. It was next to impossible to get a sympathetic ear that is except for Laura. Sweet little Laura was different from anyone I'd ever known, but the longer the relationship went on the more trouble she would be; another fly in the ointment. *God how could I knowingly do the absolute wrong mother fucking thing and still march full steam ahead?* I rubbed my head with my hands as I pressed the freight elevator to the third floor. The industrial steel coffin sparked to life and a brownish glow materialized as the cockroach coach opened its doors. I felt as if I was sinking in quicksand. I reverted back to my happy place, being drunk as a skunk and that made me grin. I had never officially quit the booze; I just morphed into the status of a social drinker. Getting hammered takes on a different connotation when you're partying with fellow codependents. Out of the blue, I had a change of heart and hit the button for the garage level. I didn't want a showdown with superiors, Santiago or a run in with underlings for that matter. I needed a drink.

I was duly aware that I was racing down the street in an unmarked all for the sweet nectar of bourbon; I might have a slight problem. The bar was a mirage in my mind and with every turn I saw it just beyond my reach. It started snowing again and the wheels felt as if I were driving on air. I spotted a coyote from the corner of my eye and hit the brakes. The car fishtailed before I regained control and stopped in the middle of the road. The vehicle behind me slammed on his brakes, I waved him pass and pulled over to the shoulder while my eyes never left the coyote. I exited the squad and the animal slowly turned and walked away. I pulled my hoodie over my ears and followed; I was fascinated with the animal. He sensed my presence and his walk turned into a slow gate. *This is crazy Logan.* I vaulted the guardrail, snow and ice filled my shoes but didn't deter my resolve. He stopped at the edge of the tree line as if he expected me to turn back; the woods were his. I had been inexplicitly drawn to this magnificent creature, even though the snow grew deeper my bravery remained unwavering. I lost sight of him shortly after I had entered his domain, however fresh paw prints kept me on his trail. I was freezing and not suitably dressed for a winter hike in unfamiliar woods. I realized the foolishness of my ways about a mile in. *A coyote Logan, what the fuck were you thinking?* The paw prints had morphed into something altogether different; *I'd better cool it on the doctor prescribed meds. Was this another one of my crazy ass hallucinations?* I found myself on the east side of the lake and inside the land of my nightmares, lucid and wide awake.

The outline of the weathered barn was in sight and I shivered something awful. *I should turn around and head back roadside.* Instead, I trekked through virgin snow and closed the distance to the barn. My thinly lined hooded fleece coat, dress pants and shoes were utterly useless in the freezing wind and snow. My hands throbbed with pain and my toes were numb. *Whatever it was I was trying to prove to myself, I'd better do it quick.* I decided to forgo the barn and headed straight for the little rundown cabin.

It was as if every amazing detail in my nightmare had been reconstructed and laid out before me. It occurred to me that I had been here as a boy. It just seemed so foreign; a memory of my childhood that was best forgotten. I reached for the knob of the front door and had another vision. I saw myself as a child peering out the window. *Something real took place inside these four walls; another demon that needed to be dispelled.* I forced my way inside. Spider webs were strewn from every conceivable square inch of the interior and I was in desperate need of a bayonet. In the corner was an antique rocking chair that was missing several spindles and a pair of weathered men's army boots dangled off the bare fireplace mantel. I made my way over to a rotted out drawer where the wood panels had been partially eaten by rats. I rummaged through the rodent feces and wet black mold until my frozen fingertips seized its treasure. I returned to the fireplace and struck a couple of damp matches until the second to last sparked to life. The musky firewood in the hearth lit, I retrieved the drawer and tossed it into the budding fire. I knew things about this place, but it was like a classic song and I couldn't remember all the lyrics. I towed the rocker in front of the fireplace. I reluctantly removed my shoes and socks knowing that this simple act left me vulnerable, but my body thanked me almost immediately. The fire nurtured my soul. The wood burned white hot and the moldy smell began to evaporate. My mind was flooded with rabid thoughts of yesteryear. I was ten years old, alone frightened and hiding. *What was it that terrified me?*

"L-o-o-g-a-a-n," the decrepit voice crackled.

It was a distinctively male voice spoken with a rancid tongue. I poked my head up from below the windowsill and saw the oaks sway gently in the evening breeze. I was haunted by something unseen and sought the shelter of the dank cabin; Custer's last stand I suppose. It was a flawed idea from the get go. When I was a child I had been so scared and perhaps too young to remember the horror that stalked me now. I knew the menace would skin me alive and heard him as he circled the cabin with bow whip in hand. He wanted me to think about my punishment well before the sting from the strap tore flesh. My father had been an evil man with an innate depravity that surpassed the wickedness of the men of his time. I forced the sleep from my eyes; it was dark. In most instances my dreams faded quickly with every waking moment. It was unclear if it had been a memory or a nightmare; *leave it buried Logan whichever it was leave it be*. The coyote had drawn me here, my memories and my nightmares were haunted with ghost that need not be disturbed. I made my pilgrimage out of the woods and back roadside. It had snowed heavily throughout the night and finding my way out had been a bit of luck and my success had brought a sense of adulation. My thought's returned to a more simple and tangible goal; the Mud River Lounge.

TODD ANDREW DAVIS
DEATH HAS STRANGE BEDFELLOWS
CHAPTER XXV

I detested taking instructions from a neophyte or appeasing his feeble waste of an existence, but brotherly love had its upsides as well. I'd been infuriated by the way this sniffling twit had barged into my lair and got the drop on me. It was only when my ire subsided that I varied from my typical behavior and granted him permission to live. I'm in control and not the reverse. Now that I had a stranglehold on what was happening to me, I'd gather the strength, overcome my misfortune and set forth a new course. Blood will rain down upon all my adversaries, but for now my mission was as clear as crystal ice; The Plan. Logan, brother of Satan shall crumble, suffer, wither and die. I wanted him to stare into my eyes as every incision of my blade ripped away his meaty tissue. I had been imprisoned due to his ineptness and my life a casualty of falsehoods. I'd been summoned to exact revenge and had been knocked off course by my appetite for destruction. My hunger had single handedly blinded me. I'd been too eager to please, too afraid of retribution and hadn't realized that I possessed the power all along. Logan had been exposed and I would unleash the beast to deal with him. I wondered if my brother Lucas could read my thoughts; the beast would have him too. Once it was done I could be my old self again and assume my place in the world. I have only one master and could not be tricked into thinking differently. My quest had been revealed and everything else irrelevant. I shall not enter

Satan's kingdom until my time has come to pass. His hand guided the knife, pulverized bone and muscle alike. I begged him to be more than a bystander and I became more than a willing participant. I would never reconcile with God and never be his puppet. I knew my place was not at the foot of God and my honor lay in the fiery pit of hell. I have no regrets, I'll do what must be done and set things right. I'll devour Logan like a rat caught in a serpent's grasp and his flesh will be flayed from bone. I will bask in the glory of Armageddon and a new day of reckoning will come.

The sequence of events that had led me down this sanctimonious path can only be characterized as manifest destiny. I was overwhelmed with anticipation; being polluted by another's madness tends to weaken one's spirit. Now as the dominoes fell, I would reap the bounty. The stage was only big enough for one. I knew of course neither Lucas nor Logan would be able to appreciate the essence of the gift bequeathed. They would piss upon the very notion, but in the darkness there was power, fear and genius. I was the chosen one and I alone understood the magnitude of this illustrious honor. All who interfered must suffer and all who doubted were blasphemers. Christ perished for the sins of men and Satan ruled over them because it was ordained. Humans were never to be looked upon as their contemporaries; they were flawed, weak, sniveling little creatures. They obeyed commands and did not give them. They worship sundials, statues, bibles with passages spewed from fork tongued prophets. They sought out images of the Lord and Savior plastered across highway overpasses or in a bag of stale chips. Their inspiration was drawn from scripture and stood as a declaration to their ignorance. They were weak emotional peasants with minds full of mush. They were goats mired in their own dung and they desperately searched for a shepherd to guide them.

Faith allowed their souls to remain untethered. I will rule this land; convert millions to his cause and a legion of souls will fill his coffers. I walked among their ranks as the immortal prophet. A doomed species weakened by social conduct and religion. I will cultivate their minds with a greater knowledge and a new belief system and shall show them the ways of my God. I will be obedient and remain focused on The Plan.

The daylight hours flickered away and the temperature dipped below the freezing mark. Boredom crept in and it tried to divert me from my goal. I had been waiting for him to emerge from the bowels of the thirteenth precinct for nearly three and a half hours. My windows had iced and kept me concealed from the occasional passerby. I placed my left hand on the driver side window, made a circular motion and created a small portal to the outside world. It was the only indulgence I allowed myself. The cold was unbearable at first, but my body soon adapted to the conditions. I watched the little people as they came and went throughout the night; only a few women sparked my interest. I did not act upon my instinctual desires and expose myself to capture, perhaps my survival instincts had kicked in. Potential victims moved ever so close to my web without any concern for the spider that lurked within. My target emerged from the underground garage and the static in my head cleared. The car started on the first turn of the key, the hemi growled and the chase was afoot. We sped down unplowed ice covered roadways in an apparent suicide pack. I let off the accelerator as my car threatened to slide off the road for the second time. It was an easy task to keep track of his Crown Vic as traffic was sparse. There was a real possibility that I would break my neck before I had the opportunity to snap his. I stayed calm and focused; after all he was my main objective. For a split second he disappeared when a gust of swirling snow temporally blinded me.

Logan had stomped on the brakes and I almost plowed right into the cruiser; my life spared by my quick reactions. *Did he know he was being tailed?* I backed up and maneuvered my vehicle around his; the headlights disguised me. He stuck his hand out the window and waved me pass. I gripped the pearl handled knife. I crept slowly alongside my dear sibling and as I passed I wanted to feel his bloody heart pulsate in my hands. His window was open and his eyes studied a field off in the distance. I kept driving and checked my rearview periodically. The passenger side door flung open and my brother trekked off into the snowy night. His eyes were transfixed on something beyond my sight. I came across an old body shop; the sign above displayed a picture of a red tow truck and read, **'Dillon's Premier Auto body Specialist, we fix domestics and imports.'** I made a U-turn in his snow covered driveway, turned the lights off and spotted Logan's car within minutes. I looked through the windshield and made certain it was empty then parked up the street and entered into the crippling night air.

I walked back and cautiously approached the cruiser. The moon was frozen in the winter sky and a stiff breeze effortlessly pushed the tree tops back and forth as though it were slicing into a baby's tender skin. I searched the grounds and found his sunken footprints in the fresh winter powder. I kept my laced steel toed boots within his footprints and began my trek down the embankment and across the field. I scanned the horizon but could see neither hide nor hair of him. *Why had he stopped here and run off into the woods? No matter, I would spill his blood and make his body impossible to find. Out here there would be no one to hear him yell.* It was the first time that I could remember feeling an unexplainable sense of unease; something wasn't copasetic, I couldn't move, it was as though I were frozen in a game of Simon Says. My skin became colder, my heart tightened and goose pimples rose as sweat dripped from my brow. I was sick to my stomach and dry heaved. I muffled the coughing with my hands and stood at the precipice of the woods with a child's anxiety clutching at my soul. I experienced pure terror. This feeling rotted the roots of my being and rose from the pit of my stomach. My throat was raw and my vision blurred. I fought back the fear on weakened knees and thrust deeper into Mother Nature's womb. It was desperation if not foolishness to continue on in my pathetic state. I'd handed him the advantage and gave him the license to do with me whatever he wanted. For the first time my apprehension rendered me powerless. I was a lion among lambs, a God among men; I have been all these things yet I quivered like a child afraid of the boogie man beneath his bed. *Where was the moon?* I tilted my head skyward. A fever struck me and my body was racked with pain. *Had I crossed onto holy ground? Was this his God imposing his will?* He'd need a hell of a lot more to break my spirit. The wind whispered in my ears, but my focus remained resolute. I was on a sacred mission, one of vengeance and purity. I'd been shunned, banished from heaven and had been subjected to the similar fate as my condemned brethren. I will soar above the heavens as a phoenix reborn of ash and fire. I'll cut away angels wings; nothing shall keep me from the annihilation of God's precious species.

A barn rose from the depths of the frozen earth and I had the sensation of familiarity. I stared in awe like a child. My eyes shifted to a diminutive cabin that summoned me forth. Something unseen made my feet feel as if they were cemented in blocks and did not grant me permission to move. My world slid off its axis as vertigo spun me round and round.

I was entombed in snow; my jacket's inner lining, pockets, sleeves were filled with frozen ice. My head pounded; I could not regain my bearings and felt as if I had been struck in the back of the head. My fingers and toes stung with the onset of frostbite. *How long I'd been out?* I gazed up toward the tree tops; I knew how fortunate I'd been to have awakened when I did. I dragged my frozen limbs back to the car where I caught sight of Logan; divine intervention I suppose. Whatever it was that he found so fascinating no longer drew his attention. I was sure he would have seen me through the trees and winter thinned brush. He appeared disoriented; we were both vulnerable and incapable of mounting or sustaining much of an attack. I waited in the dark until he reached his car and heard it fight to turnover; then boom to life. Hobbled, I hurried to my car in excruciating pain.

TODD ANDREW DAVIS
IN THE WAKE
CHAPTER XXVI

The buzz from television invaded my sleep; the test pattern appeared on screen as the station signaled their programming had gone off the air. The forgettable show that caused my premature slumber had ended hours ago. I reached for the remote and inadvertently knocked a glass off the nightstand. I tried valiantly to catch it in midair, but my reactions were too lethargic to save it. A deep sigh escaped my lungs. Ever since Allen's murder I hadn't been quite myself and moped around the apartment in bunny slippers. I worked at the college library and had missed the last two days. I thought about my classes the past few semesters and how I'd basically phoned it in. I was surprised I did so well on my finals last week. I'd gone back to school after initially planning to take a year off and travel. After I graduated high school I needed a break. I wanted to discover the world and needed time to find myself. I found myself alright; almost two years removed from graduation, I was broke and unemployed in Ravenswood, Illinois.

I had made a deal with mom. I'd go to college and in return she and dad would pay for my housing. Ever since then I've had a loaded gun pointed at my head; I'd rather her pull the trigger than crawl back to Nevada. To get reacclimated into the wondrous world of academia, I scored a job as an Assistant Librarian at Ravenswood College.

I figured it would motivate me to take classes; it wasn't a well thought out process. The money and hours were shitty and the boredom was beyond belief.

Somehow, I eventually managed to matriculate into the college atmosphere and that's how I met Allen. I'd been thinking of him a lot lately. I never properly mourned him; I guess I'd been too ashamed. I took up a torrid affair with a married cop and if that weren't bad enough, every time I thought of Allen he morphed into Logan. What a bitch I am. The perplexing thing was that I'm not entirely sure I loved him. Now that he was gone, I missed him more in death. I was too young to have death in my life, I hadn't even started living yet and I guess that was what had made his murder so enraging. He had only begun to live as well. I hadn't told my parents about him and now I just couldn't. They'd hijack the first plane to Illinois and kidnap me for sure. My dad and mom were both avid news buffs, so it was hard to comprehend why they hadn't heard about the killings, but I was thankful.

I swung my legs off the bed and just milliseconds before my feet hit the floor; I thought about the broken glass. Tears streamed down my face and I felt a shard of glass rip deep into the sole of my right arch. The pain was agonizing; I hopped twice before I fell flat on my face. The blood flowed like a breached dam and the initial surge of pain forced me into the fetal position for nearly three minutes. I writhed in pain. I slithered on my belly to the washroom with only the backlight of the television to guide me. Every movement made the glass dig deeper into my flesh. *Giving birth couldn't be this fucking painful.* The tile floor was cold and unforgiving; I knew eventually I would have to convince myself to stand. I bypassed the wall light switch and made it to the commode. I used the vanity and the tub to hoist myself to my feet. I clicked on the florescent light; it wasn't bright enough to perform this critical procedure. I gently eased myself onto the foam covered toilet seat. A faint, but audible noise came from the kitchen. I held my balance like an uncoordinated ballerina on tip toes, raised my injured foot inches off the ground and listen intently. I'm fucked; I couldn't defend myself. I hopped over to the bathroom door, closed and locked it. I searched for tweezers to remove the glass from my foot. *Think Laura; last time you use them... eyebrows - shit plucking my eyebrows in the bedroom.* I hunted for a weapon in the cabinet under the sink. Rollers, curling iron, hairbrushes, combs, nail polish purple-lavender, green— machine and rock and roll red. I had a disposable package of razor blades, scissors and a box of half filled tampons that proclaimed; *'A Touch of Heaven in Every Stride.' If having a four inch finger jammed in your twat was a touch of heaven I'd rather bleed to death in hell.* I found a red and black screw driver my dad left that would make the most formidable weapon. I made my way back to the toilet with the scissors in one hand I situated my right foot on top my left thigh. I snatched a wad of toilet tissue from the roll then stretched out until my fingers met the faucet and dabbed the tissue under cold running water. Lightning shot up my spine as the steel blade grazed the embedded glass. I clenched my teeth and fought back the pain then listened intently for the intruder's next move. I grabbed a chocolate colored twelve ounce bottle of peroxide from atop the sink and poured a cap full directly into the wound. I took a second cap full and liberally doused the scissors. My toes grew numb and my hand shook. I dug my nails in first and the shard of glass made my finger tips bleed. Vomit surged then ebbed in my throat. I was burning up and all I could think of was infection and gangrene; *you can do this.* I thought I heard footsteps walk down the hallway outside the confines of the bathroom. Whoever it was would surely have spotted the light from beneath the door and then I'd be in a fight for survival. I grabbed the bottle of peroxide; I'd blind him with it then stab him with the screwdriver. I only had one chance. The intruder must have heard the loud clang as I dropped the scissors against the corner edge of the porcelain sink. I cut the lights. It seemed pointless to pray; so I waited with a bloody foot dripping, knuckles pale and eyes bulging. The silence was only broken by my erratic wheezing. I was ready for war, armed and dangerous.

No.... Shit, no. My fucking period came; maybe I'll die of internal bleeding. I should use it to my advantage and scream, *'I have a weapon and I'm on the rag!'* Ten minutes later, all was still quiet on the Midwestern front. My attention turned back to my injured foot and I dug out the shard of glass with the tip of the scissor's blade. I took my time cleaning the blood and fitting the wound with a bandage. My thoughts turned to work and all the sleep I'd wasted. I was too drowsy to care if I was going to be murdered. I hobbled into the kitchen; it was just the way I left it with a mile high pile of dishes that loomed in the foreground. I poured myself another smooth glass of raspberry lemonade then washed some of the dishes; towel dried and put them away. I paused at the closet. I felt silly, reached for the handle and flung the doors open. I clutched the neck of the vacuum and dragged it out. *Vacuum bags... I always forget to buy the bags.* I didn't want to wake anyone. However, the neighbors had awakened me once or twice to their sounds of passionate, okay hardcore fucking. I turned the light on in the bedroom, plugged in the vacuum and prayed I wouldn't have to deal with my landlord's bitching. I wanted to rest my weary head for just a moment and attended to the broken glass later. I fought that urged, picked up most of the glass with my bare hands and the rest I rushed my handheld vacuum over. It was 1:38 am when I pulled the covers tight. *What was it that had gone bump in the night? Ghost perhaps? Nice freak your ass out.* I checked to see if my alarm was set; it was of course. I didn't know if it was habitual or a ritual, but I checked every night before I settled in. I got only micro naps; resting my eyes and thinking rather than dreaming. In this state of consciousness everything was tremendously vivid.

Allen was fidgety and extremely angry with me; I recognized him by his body language. I shouldn't have jumped into bed with Logan; it tainted my perspective on things. Married men don't just leave their wives for a good fuck. It takes a little more than that; more than I was willing to offer. I wasn't looking for a commitment from Logan and I guess Allen's death made me want to feel alive. I wanted to connect with someone who could understand my feelings. I wanted warmth; I craved hardcore sex. I needed someone who could fuck the shit out of me and make me cum like the slut next door. Allen was a one trick pony when it came to intimacy. He'd been a missionary man and after the novelty of a new relationship waned; monotony set in from lack of spice. Allen was as bland as it gets. He'd been fastidiously anal about everything, self centered and incapable of pleasing anyone other than himself. Unfortunately, it was a tremendous waste of a nine inch penis.

Something wasn't right, I could sense it; there was someone else in the room. I knew it beyond a shadow of a doubt and swallowed my breath and listened. I could hear a shallow breath trying to synchronize with mine. He was in the far corner of the room or hidden under the bed. I had the advantage of being closest to the door and knew my apartment in the dark. *With my bandage foot could I out run him?* I had no other alternative. *Would anyone open their doors to the sound of blood curdling screams this late at night?* Somehow, I had to find my car keys, unchain the lock, click the deadbolt and... I heard a muffled cough escape his mouth and I was off and running. I leapt off the bed and my momentum hurled me sideways into the door frame. I jammed my left pinky toe; it felt broken but I didn't break my stride. I made it into the kitchen and in the pale light of the moon. I could vaguely make out the door chain as it hung dangling out of place. I decided to forgo the keys; I clutched the doorknob and opened the door. Goose bumps rose on my flesh as I heard him enter the kitchen. I ran south then east away from the parking lot, away from the other tenants who were oblivious to my plight and into the woods. There was a church or school on the other side if I remembered correctly. With every frozen footfall, I wished I'd grabbed my sneakers. All I had to do was reach down and pick them up off the floor, but fear compelled me not to waste a single second. I sported a long baby blue t-shirt and boy shorts; most nights it was either one or the other or nothing at all. I guess I should have been thankful for the little things.

The wind rudely whipped between my thighs, my skin burned and my feet were so cold I feared I lose them both. Nature had placed fallen tree branches, small rocks and frozen snow in my path to ridicule my predicament. I panicked and it cost me dearly. If I had shoes I could have run faster and further giving myself a fighting chance. I was lost out here in the woods; they were dense and completely unknown to me. Tears blurred my vision as I continued to painstakingly maneuver through the forest. Thorn bushes penetrated my exposed flesh. I ran until I was faced with a seven foot barrier and on the other side was the highway; I was sure of it. I had no reason to travel on the highway, but I recognized the oddly shaped designs that adorned the top of the sound barrier wall. The fence was high and I would have to make a running jump. I backed up five or six steps and felt my body bump squarely into his. Self-preservation demands you scream, scratch, kick and fight, but I was so cold; so tired. He had won and our little game of hide and seek was over. A hunter's knife hung low on his hip and the handle was encrusted with blood. It sent shivers skipping throughout my soul, but it was the way Logan stared at me that struck horror in my veins. His gaze was animalistic; a predator who had trapped its prey. This man who had meant safety had been the only person worthwhile in this miserable life. He brushed my face with his hand; then began to beat me unmercifully.

"You whore! You fucking whore," he shouted, "you're just like the rest of them!"

Electricity surged through my body and I heard a loud thump. My dream was so intense that beads of perspiration had formed on my skin. After I woke, memories of the dream quickly faded away. Lately, all my dreams had been intense or in some cases vulgar; nothing out of the ordinary I suppose. *But why did I have this sinking feeling of impending doom lurking around the corner?* Friends and coworkers tried to be considerate and delicate when they spoke of Allen and the television news made his death seem all too antiseptic and detached.

"My dad's a cop," the grocery store checkout girl said the other day, "and he was shocked; that redheaded boy was gutted like a deer. I heard him on his short-wave talking with his superior. His neck was at such a crooked angle and there had been so much blood that at first they thought it was an elaborate prank. The stuffing had gotten knocked out of that Howdy Doody lookalike." She gabbed like there was no tomorrow.

I wanted to grab her by her Mohawk and rip out her nose

ring, but instead of Allen I pictured a life sized rubber manikin lying in thick red cranberry syrup. I still had a difficult time of processing everything. I heard a second and then a third loud thump; it must have been the boiler kicking on. The doorbell rang like a banshee in the night. My heart began to pound as I lay uncertain of what to do. *Answer the door you dumb fuck!* I leapt out of bed and grabbed a white cloth robe; a gift from mom. I always thought she had gotten it from some swanky resort her and dad visited. The imagery and thought of how many other people had donned it, well it took several laundry cycles before I found it irresistibly comfy. The laceration on my foot still hurt and I wondered if it was worth it to get out of bed. I found one fuzzy pink slipper before I decided to kick it off and continue barefoot.

TODD ANDREW DAVIS
THE MUD RIVER LOUNGE
CHAPTER XXVII

The bar was a low key oasis off the beaten path. I took my gun in and left my badge in the glove compartment. Drinking was the last true bastion of freedom humanity had to offer and I was going to indulge. I moseyed up to the bar and rested my elbows on the brass railing that encompassed the whole shebang. Never fuck with a dog while he's eating or a man while he's drinking. I ordered a tall JD with a lime, minus the ice and straw; they just get in the way. That was one of my truisms as it were.

"Sade," I said, "leave the bottle. When I start flirting with you that's when it's time to take it away." Another truism.

She was an older lady with one of those great personalities; not particularly the kind of woman you wanted to wake-up to. All wounds tonight were goanna be self inflicted. I'd done a decent enough job of keeping my head above water, but tonight I needed to drink. The taste, the feeling; I craved it more than pussy. One time in this fine establishment I'd turned my back on a guy who snorted a line of coke right off the toilet seat; desperate times breed desperate measures I suppose. I would let him be. I didn't want to sully my reputation by whipping out my badge, ever since then I had taken to leaving it in the car. The good slow burn of alcohol and the anticipated euphoric state had lifted my spirits. My alcoholism wasn't a chronic dilemma but an occasional necessity. Drinking was a side effect of being a cop and not a career ender by any means. It just needed to be kept under wraps. With the media constantly breathing down our throats, hideouts like these served their purpose well. The air was thick with the condemnation of hearsay and fabrication. Articles were written in half-truths and the telecast beamed images of cops scurrying away from the camera's eye. They'd never let us forget how slow our progress was or allow us to escape the heat of the spotlight even for a moment. They tormented us and flashed their intellectual skills in Op-Eds. They would sell their mother's souls for a story and give up possession of their own. They're so called good intentions were always met with cynicism for those of us who played the game. *When you're a lone wolf eventually the pack will turn on you.* I hadn't completely isolated myself within the department, but I'd become increasingly antisocial. However, in my defense I didn't want my drinking to become water cooler gossip. I slow walked to the bathroom and after relieving myself, I returned to the table. I spotted a drop dead gorgeous brunette sitting next to two ugly mother fuckers. A pasty white piece of trash with half dollar sized craters on his shaved head and a chocolate skinned baboon in need of a fix. *Baboon baboonis babooni,* I chuckled to myself. I must be drunk. I finished off the last remnants of my drink; guzzled down two more healthy shots, found Sade, paid my tab and flashed the brown haired chick another look attached with a sinister smile. Our eyes met for a brief moment, expressionless she turned her attention back to the skinhead. The diseased whore wasn't worth my time anyhow.

Mother Nature's cold winters kiss shook the cobwebs from my head as I stepped outside. Normally I drove the SUV, but with the road conditions worsening I swapped the truck for the cruiser and let Kathy have the four wheeler. Funny, it had been truly the one tangible thought I had of her all night. A couple of good old boys were having an impromptu party around my Crown Vic and eyeballed me before they disappeared. They were curious and wanted to see the squad's owner and the company they'd been keeping. It was the perpetual sore thumb indeed. I flipped the ignition, eased out of the tavern and headed straight for Tella Hute. It was madness or at best intoxication that led me even further out of my way. I should have headed home, it was borderline ridiculous; just turn around. *You're drunk.* She'd smell the alcohol and turn you away in an instant, that's if she were even home. I had passed the magical point in time where I decreed it was pointless to turn back. My eyelids grew heavier as the roads were harder to navigate. I wanted to pull off to the side and sleep, but I kept driving until I saw the skyline of her complex. I was minutes from my destination and I feared that I had made a monumental mistake. I eased the car into a vacant spot, turned the ignition off and staggered in the falling snow. I was worse off than I imagined. My head throbbed and my stomach did Olympic style back flips. I knocked on her door; several minutes passed and I rang the bell. I rang it again and again like a madman embodying the spirit of Quasimodo. The starlit sky with her colorless full moon hovered high above me and was the last memory I had……..

The Mud River Lounge was a classless place in the middle of nowhere and a perfect hideaway from life's little irritations. His cruiser stood out like a redheaded stepchild. The conclusion I drew just from the exterior of the establishment intrigued me. *This ain't a typical cop hangout.* He must be chasing down a lead. I waited ten minutes before I entered; it reeked of beer, cologne and cheap women. The tavern was home to the sort of people who'd be none too happy to learn that my bro was a law man. I lowered my cap and surveyed the scenery. Out of my peripheral vision I caught my likeness sitting at the bar. His features differed from Lucas's; he was definitely more chiseled and his physique resembled mine. We were more of a carbon copy and that fact alone would definitely draw attention. Lucas had faded scars on his lower right jaw and a rather deep one that jetted from under his left eye to his cheekbone. Their eyes... our eyes were a bluish green and for a cop Logan wore his hair longer than most. Of course I didn't get close enough to see his eyes, but we were three of a kind with only subtle differences. I believed brother Lucas was bald under his Stetson, but I remained uncertain of my own facial features. My own image had always been distorted and I gave up believing that I resemble humanity long ago. I wasn't one of them anyway so why should I pretend to be part of their cabal. I was the jagged edge piece of the puzzle that didn't quite fit, but I could pass as one of them. Eventually I would have found myself on this path, although my methods were perhaps a little obscene. The decapitation and bloodlust had signified an undisciplined, uncouth approach that might become problematic in time.

I paid for my draft and avoided the bartenders gaze. I sat in a dimly lit section of the bar and kept the ball cap low just above my brow. I watched him; he had a bottle of Jack all to himself. My fingers wandered the inner lining of my coat pocket and struck gold. Lucas left me a powder formula of the drug he used to paralyze me. I had to figure out how I could slip A into B undetected. Three unclean individuals grabbed a spot in relative proximity; a skinny brown monkey, a white crack head and skanky dark-haired chick.

Within minutes of a loquacious discussion the dirt bags dealt heroin out in the open. The colored and whore seemed to be an item and the junkie was also masquerading as a dealer. I made my way over to their booth and took a seat. I reached underneath the table and placed my knife on the white boy's inner thigh. The tip nudged up against his prick or perhaps just a guesstimate of its proximity.

"I am goanna make this painful..." I lean into him and whispered in his ear.

"Listen asshole..." said the black skin, but white-trash motioned for him to close his wretched trap.

"What do you want Mister?" he asked nervously.

You would think I'd drawn blood the way his teeth clenched and his body squirmed. Their collective beady little eyes sensed danger. Blackie and the girl assumed I was packing heat and had stuck a gun into Skelators rib cage and he was petrified I'd cut off his manhood.

"You will be extremely old motherfuckers when your jail sentences are up," my voice trailed off. The girl wept as the colored tried to place an arm around her. I placed a plastic orange prescription bottle on the table, "Do this one thing for me and you'll see the sunrise from your own piss stained mattresses." Their feeble minds raced from the terror of being robbed, to a bust, to just plain confused.

"And if we don't?" asked tar baby.

"Aaron please," he paused as I dug the blade deeper into whitey's scrotum, "just do whatever the man asks." Spittle covered his dried cracked lips.

The way they interacted and the tenor of his voice as he spoke his name made me realize they were more than just mere acquaintances. The queers probably both did the girl as well as each other; needless to say, I didn't care. I devised a plan; my little cohorts would distract my brother and slip the powder into his drink.

"Go; the girl stays with me."

They were petrified, but were obedient little servants as was she. I moistened my forefinger, slid it under her jean skirt and past her thong underwear. As my finger penetrated her snatch, I advised her to dress more appropriately for the weather. Like a good little girl she made no effort to deny me the simple pleasure of masturbating her under the table. *And that's how one prolongs their life; others could take notes if so inclined.* She stared straight ahead unmoving, unemotional and a little wetter for the experience. My god, I envisioned her pink twat pounding away on my throbbing hard cock.

I grabbed her by the elbow and placed her hand inside my jeans. There was far displayed on her face like a lit Halloween jack-o-lantern. *If only I had time to fuck this one*. I needed to remain focused.

"You're good enough to eat," I proclaimed with a wink as I tasted my finger. I was a little rougher exiting than entering. The discomfort she felt took form in the way of tears and she quickly wiped them away with the back of her hand. She knew if I wanted her that she would have no alternative but to give herself to me fully. Minutes later, the boys returned to the table relived that their mission had been accomplished. I glanced toward Logan; he had just returned to his seat.

"Don't worry he had to take a leak," chimed pale skin, "Aaron never let him out of his sight and I slipped the shit in his bottle without being noticed."

"Dude quit saying my name," Tootsie roll interjected.

I watched Logan refill his glass twice and watched as knocked them back. It could be a ruse; they could have told him everything in the bathroom. Logan would have remarked, 'Act natural I am a cop, play along and I'll take care of this.' They could have devised a scheme to turn the tables; that is if they hadn't fried their trailer trash monkey brains in search of a new high. Closer to the truth, they were probably afraid I'd whip my dick out and fuck their little slut in front of them. I studied their dirty dumb fucking mugs and came to the conclusion that their brains had turned to pabulum long ago. The whore meant something to the two Neanderthals; possibly the only real thing they cared about beyond their addictions. So I did the honorable thing, kept my word, vacated the table and was on my way. I'd celebrate with young pussy after the mission was complete.

I waited across the road for another half hour until Logan walked through the doors of The Mud River. He made small talk with a couple of lowlife thugs who took residence on his cruiser. They were shooed away without incident and found another nest to squat. He slid behind the wheel, turned the key and threw the car in reverse. He eased out of the stall; flipped the shifter in gear and sped off. His driving was noticeably erratic as he bobbed and weaved down the roadway. I kept my distance, as if it mattered and filled my head with thoughts on how I was going to punish my brother. He had blatantly turned his back on me in a time of need. I should of lived my life in the sunlight and not been reduced to lurking among shadows. My memories were whitewashed and stolen from me; pumped full of drugs I wasn't capable of sustaining a lucid thought. I had no recollection of the exact events that shaped me today, although I was still hell bent on retribution. The institution that had so conveniently hid me away from society and extrapolated my soul will feel my wrath as well. I needed to be clear headed and focused; everything done to Logan would be by my hand. How I had ever been diverted from the mission was well beyond me. I drugged him so he'd be off his game, so I could exercise patience and cause his suffering to be etched in the nightmares of all who laid eyes upon him. A random thought of the forest and the cabin brought with it chills of the past. *Were the woods an inner-sanctum in which he felt protected? Why did it affect me so negatively?* I'd find the answers in time.

WELCOME TO TELLA HUTE *Population* **6,863** read the street sign. I wasn't going to let this providential opportunity slip through my hands again. Laura had less right to live than he did; this would be my finest piece of artwork yet. I'll be catapulted into mythology and neither man nor beast will unseat me. With his grace, Lucifer will smile upon my adoring face. My alliance with the God of the underworld will grant me treasures beyond all imagination.

I flicked on every switch I passed as I made my way to the front door. I held my robe tight. *I wish I knew where the belt was to this thing.* I pressed my weight against the door and peered through the peephole. I couldn't make out a thing. The glass on the other side was mucked up from the weather; I had noticed the dirty white film the other day and meant to clean it. I hated the way females were always portrayed as dizzy, dumb, sex craved, anorexic bitches in horror films. They always die just before or after the token black guy, so I amazed myself when I unhooked the chain, turned the deadbolt and stuck my head outside. As I opened the door, the weight on the opposite side threatened to topple me over. Once again, I astonished myself by not screaming at the top of my lungs. At my feet in the sparse glow of the moonlight lay Logan's limp body. Instinctively I reached for him, my first thought was that he had been shot and was dying and on hands and knees crawled his way to me. I smelled the alcohol and figured his wife had kicked him out. I dragged him across the threshold and like the cryptic lore told of the mythological vampire 'once you invite them in, you're screwed.' Even though he was unconscious I felt a little safer with him here. *Put him on the couch, on the couch.* I dragged his dead weight down the hallway and toward the bedroom. I undressed him and walked back into the living room. I quietly stepped to the front door, checked the dead bolt and lock, but both were secured. *Okay Laura, you're losing it.* I fished out a tin kettle; a gift I thieved from my parent's house. I suffered untold decades of physiological damage and they were lucky I hadn't snatched the Benz. *What was I gonna do with him? Was it a criminal offense to scan through a police officer's Blackberry? He hadn't responded, not even when I accidentally nailed his head on the nightstand; twice. Did he have alcohol poisoning? Should I call 911? Would he lose his job? He'd lose it. What would happen to me if he didn't wake up and died in my bed?*

I never really *looked at him; it had been dark when we made love.* I wanted to sneak a peek at his man junk. *Okay I am officially going to hell, although if the shoe were on the other foot I am sure he'd do more than look.* I intended to watch television, lay next to him in bed and monitor his breathing. I snatched up the TV remote and riffled through a half dozen infomercials, weather channel, news talk shows, romantic comedies, westerns and old black and white shit. I found another new 'Reality' show. *Gee, great!* I turned the set off, took another sip of hot ginseng tea and rested my head on his chest then worked my hand underneath his waistband. I was sleepier than I had thought, within minutes I was dreaming of far off exotic destinations. Allen was at times by my side, but as always kept morphing into Logan. It was infuriating, unless I studied photographs I couldn't picture his face; the camera never did do him justice. It was a guilt trip my mind played with me; he was nothing special I guess. So why did he haunt me? I needed to get far away from Ravenswood and for a second or two I mulled over the thought of going home to my parents. I had options, friends who had offered futons, spare rooms and I turned them all down in favor of being on my own. The truth was that I reveled in my independence. I squeezed Logan's balls and got a faint murmur; I'd force myself out of the humdrum existence one way or another, but he would be off limits romantically. I was understandably stressed out; even the occasional over the counter sleeping pill had little effect on me.

The last dream I remembered was the one where I was drowning or choking. I'd summoned up every ounce of strength to force myself to wake; I had this dreadful feeling. I assumed it was just part of the mourning process and that I needed to cope with the Allen's death. When my eyes opened I saw Logan staring back at me. He had maneuvered himself on top and forced his way inside. His right hand was clenched tightly over my mouth and he thrust his body with force. He spat in my face and his saliva mixed with my budding tears. I couldn't fathom why he was attacking me. He smacked me across the cheek and made me dizzy. He punched me hard in my rib cage and a tortured breath escaped my lungs from the recoil. He smelled vile; his nostrils flared back like a race horse coming down the final stretch. He had me pinned beneath him and fucked so hard he tore my labia. I tried to bite him, but he was able to fend me off. My body ached and I just wanted him to finish; not quite the fuck party I had in mind. His dirty brown curly locks dangled in my face. *His hair, what made me think this animal was Logan?* I wiggled my left arm free; I flailed wildly and struck Logan's lifeless body as hard as I could. He lay next to me, stone cold; he didn't move. A wild eyed imposter bore a demented expression of an inbred brutality; an innate ugliness that could never be corrected. This repulsive version of Logan shared none of the compassion of the man I knew. This Logan was a filthy creature enraged by his own meager existence. He had come to kill me; there was no mistaking the blood lust in his eyes. I prayed for God to intervene and I wanted the light to guide me to eternal peace.

The pain was excruciating and the weight of his body numbed my limbs. My prayers weren't being answered. The intense pressure caused my capillaries to burst. He placed his hand on my throat and threatened to suffocate me. He repositioned himself and forced my arms underneath me. My lungs begged for one last breath. I was dying and it hurt. No love ones whispered in my ears, Gabriel's trumpet didn't sound and angels weren't dispatched to sing and comfort me. I willed Logan to wake from his stupor. I struggled mightily and my backbone let out an audible crack that sent a white hot shockwave up and down my spinal column. The animal had no interest in easing my pain, but he feared that I might blackout. He wanted me to feel, he wanted me to see. I spit in his face, he licked it up and punched me again. He knocked the wind out of me and tore my nightgown open. I could hear a low vile laugh as he re-entered me and raped me unmercifully. He pulled out clumps of my hair by their bloody roots as his tongue sought mine through clench lips. He bit into my flesh and again my screams were muted by his thick hands. He snorted like a wild boar; his body burned so hot as if he was the Devil's son. This man could never have known the caring and the loving touch of another being; he's not human. I detested this disgusting beast; loathed the sight and smell of him. He toyed with his helpless victims. At any time he could have cut the strings and let me pass on, but it was all part of the game he played. I wished that I could be around when Logan annihilated this fuck. I wished I could see the day, but my fate had been sealed. His cruel eyes gazed at Logan and he flashed a hideous smile. He covered my mouth and stuck a finger up each nostril. I closed my eyes and gave up the fight. The willingness to submit angered him; I dared to sap the pleasure from him. His eyes reddened, his face contorted and he continued to beat me. I swallowed a bloody tooth. Blood and bile filled my mouth and I tried to choke myself on it, but he'd have none of it. My neck broke or fractured and it felt like as if an iron rod dipped in molten fire had been placed down my esophagus. *Why won't you just let go? Die already Laura, die.* I felt the crushing of my windpipe and started to convulse as my brain began to hemorrhage. The pounding in my scull sharply increased. There wasn't a molecule of oxygen allowed to slip into my dying lungs. I heard myself wheeze and I relaxed my limbs as the pain subsided little by little. There was an unrecognizable humming noise that echoed loudly throughout the room and then began to fade. I was scared, lost, afraid, relived, dea...

TODD ANDREW DAVIS
OPPORTUNITY KNOCKS
CHAPTER XXX

The voice had been clear and distinct; it didn't originate from inside my head, I don't think. *Why couldn't I tell the difference? What would happen if I disobeyed? What would happen if I listened?* A dilemma arose; I needed to vanquish him before he clouded my thoughts any further. The voice grew stronger and came from all around me. I felt his voice exploding through my speakers.

"Please I beg of you. Why now? How have I forsaken you?" My hands shook on the steering wheel.

A mind numbing white light flooded the interior of the car; I was completely impaired at forty miles an hour. The car pulled to the right as I pumped the brakes. My sight returned as my metal stead brushed against the guardrail. I had been on the verge of blacking out; my faculties slowly returned. *Who spoke to me?* They weren't my thoughts I was sure. I was befuddled. *Why had my mental process been so flagrantly disrupted? Was I running out of time? Was this another fly in the ointment or a cautionary tale of how delicate the balance between us was?* My brain felt as if it had short circuited, a migraine ensued and the nauseated feeling I experienced in the woods returned. *Was I rejecting this body? Did I need to seek out a new host?* The experience was exhausting and could've jeopardized everything I'd worked towards. I couldn't have this, whatever this was during a moment of battle. *Maybe my God was trying to contact me and encourage me on my quest?* So many voices, so many thoughts; it's no wonder I remained sane. I didn't pay much attention to the road and somehow made it unharmed to the apartment complex. I watched dare old brother stumble out of his car and stagger to Laura's door. He knocked; his body was hunched over and his legs were wobbly and when the door finally opened he collapsed.

Even in darkness she was a radiant vision; death wouldn't be so kind to her vanity. Two caged and lost souls; a deadweight affectionately known as my brother and the other a sinner. I found a spot in the parking lot and idled the car. The sky was backlit by a smattering of stars and the moon was a hammock strung across the stratosphere. This night was so quiet you could hear the angels sing; that heavenly harmony will turn to horrid shrieks soon enough. Their eyes will fill with sorrow and their wings will flutter madly as they fly away. *Tell your God I'm here! Tell him not to cower behind the clouds and face me! I shall spill blood this day and do unspeakable things. I shall not muzzle the screams of your children so that you may hear their cries. Face me, or are you frightened as well? I am the Devil's hand and I bring with me a message. You expelled an angel from your heavens with as much revulsion and contempt as he and his minions have for you.*

His inspiration was drawn directly from you. Your compassionless heart and wretched soul dispelled him from thought and condemned him to oblivion. I ask you, are your heavens now cleansed? Born Again or Saved, you still embrace sinners by the masses. Those who stand before you are made humble in your presence; for every two I send down, I'll be sure to send you one. He found me in my darkest hour and you shunned me; a decision you'll regret in this ongoing war. No matter how much we evolve, damnation is the final destination and is branded into the minds of the enlightened. Send back the child angel who watched me kill Ryan and I shall greedily bludgeon all in your likeness; let her witness what you are too terrified to see. I'll put on a good show for her; maybe even turn her into a woman before the night is done. It will be epic and from this day forth all who kill will measure their deeds by mine. I will never be replicated. I will receive nothing less than the admiration and worship from those of my kind. The fairy tale of Kane and Able will pale in comparison to the slaughter of Logan Crenshaw.

I openly defied God and it put me in the right frame of mind; he wasn't completely worthless. I had a purpose, to reign over the fallen, judge them accordingly and when necessary kill without prejudice and I excelled at it. I watched Laura drag Logan's lifeless body inside her apartment while her head whipped side to side scanning the parking lot. I made my way closer; the door was still slightly ajar. I was less than ten feet from her front door and could have charged in and killed them both in less than a hiccup. I hunched down below the hedges that grew along her neighbor's windowsill. I stopped and listened; one second, two seconds, nothing but the sweet sound of silence. I peered inside then entered and locked the door behind me. Once again, I took up residence inside the cramped hall closet. I heard the bitch toss and turn and an old fashion copper plated tea kettle whistle in the background. I waited until they were asleep in the bedroom before I made my move. *Was the sidewalk covered with snow or laden with salt? It was clear; I didn't track snow inside.* I didn't want to spook her or alert her to my presence; of course my trepidation could be easily remedied with the aid of a serrated blade across her larynx. It was humiliating being stuffed into this sardine box.

I preoccupied my thoughts with the savage imagery I would inflict upon her just to cope. I emerged a lion seeking the blood of Christians trapped inside the walls of the coliseum. I moved catlike down the hallway and stood at the edge of the doorway. I saw both of them lying in bed; Logan dead to the world and Laura's head rested serenely on his chest. A fire was stoked deep inside and burned hot embers of rage.

This was my night; this was my will. I slowly undressed and silently moved toward her. I was enthralled in virtual ecstasy and before she had even opened her eyes my cock was buried deep inside, hammering away. She had an expression of absolute bewilderment. I got her nice and wet before she realized I wasn't him. *How could my lover act this way?* She sobbed deeply and it heightened the sensation. Electricity surged throughout my body and was almost too much; under different circumstances she would have thoroughly enjoyed it as well. She thought I'd stopped after I came, but she was wrong. This was the final curtain call to the end of her short life. Curtsey sweetheart; take your encore and off the stage you go.

She struck Logan in the midsection and a moan escaped his lips. My fingers encircled her neck; she tried to fight me off, but it was useless. I stared deep into her baby blues and a tear escaped both our eyes.

"My face is the last face you'll ever see," I snarled.

The bitch spat in my face as a last ignorant attempt at defiance. I used my tongue to lap up the sweet nectar. I pinned down her arms and legs. I slapped her with an open hand and her head recoiled from the blow then landed a right fist across her nose. I clutched her throat with all the force I could generate from my hands as I sucked from her nude breast. She attempted to end our fun prematurely, by giving in to the dark embrace of death; I didn't allow it. I stared into her unblinking eyes with hatred and contempt before I allowed her to pass. Now that 'The Plan' had been set into motion, my attention turned toward my brother.

TODD ANDREW DAVIS
SHARDS OF GLASS
CHAPTER XXXI

"**F**uck! Fuck! Fuck me! Holy shit, holy fucking shit; this can't be happening." I ran down the hall buck naked and was able to get the toilet seat up before I vomited.

My eyes burned as my throat was inflamed by acid reflux. I was sweating profusely and dry heaving, slowly my death-grip loosened on the toilet. I made my way back to the bedroom on unsteady legs. The signs of traumatic stress were evident all across her nude body and her skin had turned a pale shade of whitish blue. Dried blood caked her nose and purple bruises encircled her throat; her trachea had been crushed. Streaks of thin red ruptured blood vessels clouded her eyes; she had been beaten severely. A pool of blood coagulated within her open mouth, her tongue resembled ground venison and my semen lay within her womb. My fingerprints were scattered all over her condo. I sat on the edge of the bed and stared at her. I couldn't remember the night, didn't even remember the sex. My hand brushed against the sole of her foot and the cold that emanated from her skin ricocheted throughout my body. My eyes walked up and down her naked flesh and I could clearly envision what had happened to her, but couldn't comprehend why. My phone rang; I didn't answer it right away. I was out of breath or had simply forgotten how to breathe. I struggled for oxygen; *inhale, now exhale slowly.* It was 5:00 am; I had wasted a good fifteen minutes feeling sorry for myself. I pulled on my boxers and found my sox entangled in a pink laced bra on the floor. I placed my hand over the palm print on her neck, a perfect match. *Wake-up,* I had work to do and plenty of it. I turned my back; it felt odd dressing in front of her. My mind played a cruel joke and breathed life back into her lifeless shell. My hands shook badly. *Shit, what have you done? Think or you're a dead man. The only life here that can be saved is yours.* My phone rang for a third time I think and I answered it without checking the caller id.

"Where are you?" the female voice sounded oddly familiar but I didn't know who it was.

"Kathy?" I guessed.

"Are you okay?" she asked.

"I told you never to call me on this phone!" I promptly hung up. Time was of the essence. *Think, think.* I went into the bathroom; the smell of my own unflushed vomit almost made my stomach convulse again. I flicked the lever, opened the medicine cabinet and searched for a razor. I checked the drawer and the cabinet under the sink, nodda. I pulled back the shower curtain, strawberry shaving cream and a men's razor sat on the edge of the tub. I snatched the razor, cream, filled a glass on the counter with water and returned to the room. I pulled my shirt off and positioned Laura in the center of the queen sized bed. I shaved her pubic hair, then her arms and legs. I voyaged back into the bathroom a third time and netted a maroon washcloth and fingernail clippers. I held her left hand and clipped the nails short. When I was satisfied with my work, I decided to clip her toe nails as well and that's when I spotted the dry blood on the sole of her foot. I studied the wound; I surmised that it was a rough cut made by glass.

Her deadweight gave me the chills, but I had no other alternative and wiped her down one more time.

Once again my cell sparked to life. "Hello," my voice was even toned.

"Logan, its Tamara can you pick me up?"

"Give me a half hour," I said before hanging up.

I scooped Laura up in my arms and headed straight for the bathtub; my eyes intentionally averted hers' as I carried her. I went back into the bedroom and gather up the bed sheets and pillow cases. I remade the bed with fresh sheets and a comforter from her linen closet. I neatly folded the soiled bedding and set it aside. I ejected the cartridge from the razor and tossed it on top of the pile then placed the razor and cream in the sink. The mirror reflected the worst portrait I could ever recall seeing. I placed a white towel over the sink, found a fresh cartridge for the razor and shaved my face. Murphy's Law dictated that I'd cut myself. I checked the medicine cabinet for a bandage and came up empty. The panic crept into the tiniest crevices of my mind. It almost convinced me to give up and turn myself in, but I regained my composure. *Just finish; return later and cleanup.* She stared up at me with glazed puppy dog eyes and I had to shut the bath curtain.

"I'm so sorry Laura..." I whispered.

Get a grip Logan; you've seen dozens of dead bodies; especially on this case. She is no different. A trickle of blood ran down my face and I doused my head and face with tap water. I used a man's spray on deodorant; presumably Allen's; rummaged through her closet and found one of his white collar shirts. I cleaned the drying blood from my neck with a cotton swab, pulled on my pants, tied my shoes, buttoned my shirt and grabbed her keys from the hook in the family room. I found a unisex hoodie hanging in the hallway closet and snatched my keys and jacket. I retrieved the blanket, bed sheets, deodorant, razor, razorblades, and washcloth along with the towel from the sink. I found a black garbage bag stowed under her kitchen sink and tossed everything into it. I entered into the morning light around a quarter past 6:00 am and locked the door behind me.

TODD ANDREW DAVIS
OPEN EYES
CHAPTER XXXII

I was ill and dizzy; my hands shook as I fought the urge to pass out. I was out of breath but couldn't stop pacing. I was infuriated, tired and even dismayed. My sole purpose, my only goal had once again been thwarted; that was until this tiny miracle appeared. I raised my binoculars to witness an unbelievable turn of events. I was in utter disbelief as I watched from my bird's eye view. My brother the saint was behaving like a sinner and then I understood the pure genius of The Plan. All the while I had been making a spectacle of myself and pitying my ineptitude. The thorn bush blooms another blood red rose. *We were truly three of a kind.* I'd had my chance to do away with Logan; her suffering had eased the hatred that burned within me. This was all part of a more diabolical scheme and his life was spared for now. His face displayed sheer panic as he ran naked down the hall and disappeared for several minutes. He sat on the foot of the bed, fought back his emotions and examined the thing that had once been his lover. *His phone, he didn't dial; incoming call.* He talked for a few seconds then promptly hung up. His face was flustered and filled with anger. He wore a path from her bedroom to her bathroom. *Upset stomach brother?* I watch as he redressed than undressed and stripped her down. *Necrophilia?* My curiosity was aroused and I laughed as he shaved her. *She's a tad hairy I do agree. I'm betting right about now that pussy is a little ripe too.* He shaved her legs as well as under her arms then got up again and left the room only to return moments later. Now her hands and feet drew his interest; he clipped her nails. He was trying to make sure nothing could connect him to the whore. Another incoming call and his movements were more frantic. He feared a cuticle, a pubic hair or a microscopic particle of his own DNA would be all that was needed to spell his doom. If at that moment I had called the cops, he would have been signed, sealed and delivered.

He carried her body from one room to the next. This was anything but official police protocol; this was a man who knew he was capable of murder. I listened for an ambulance and cop cars, but the wind was the only howl I heard. He fished out a dress shirt from Laura's closet; changed sheets and blankets and packaged the soiled. I made my way down the icy incline and caught sight of him tossing the incriminating evidence into his car. I crisscrossed the lot to my vehicle. This time as I trailed him I was a little more careful. After seventeen minutes we ended up at the female pig's digs. I could have plowed into the back of them without raising as much as an eyebrow by the way they were interacting with each other; she was probably giving him a hand job. I followed the pair all the way across town and back to the Thirteenth Precinct.

I waited a half hour then drove off and indulged in the simple pleasure of filling the tank. On my way back to my car I passed fresh meat; she was alone. *Waiting for a bus and all dressed up to go downtown?* I made a U-turn and drove ten feet pass the bus stop. I sat down next to her and politely asked her for a light. Before she could open her mouth to respond, I had already split her nose. She instinctively clutched her purse; her eyes knowingly feared the worst. She tried to fire up the old vocal cords, but I terminated her cry with an equally hard karate chop to the throat. My knife pressed lovingly against her cheekbone and stifled any other notion that popped into her pretty little head. I muscled her into the car and checked the rearview mirror; I couldn't wait to unwrap her like a Christmas present. Upon glancing in the mirror, I saw a tall thin young man with a cell phone camera recording the whole ordeal. White smoke billowed from my tires as if the Sistine Chapel had selected a new Pontiff. I shifted the gear into reverse and headed directly at him; he realized what I was doing and panicked. Three blocks from the Thirteenth Precinct he turned and headed toward the alley. His lanky physique and awkward running style reminded me of an injured giraffe on the discovery channel. I flipped the car into drive, pressed the pedal to the floor and shot down the alley. I was on him like a hawk and made no attempt to swerve or intimidate him. He didn't cartwheel out of the way or slam into the windshield, but was simply devoured by 3,700 lbs of metal and chrome. I checked the side mirror; Daddy long legs had been true to form and tried to crawl to safety. The girl was barely conscious; her head was slumped against the glove box. Neither the passenger door or window could be opened from her side; she would have to risk escaping via the driver side door. I took the keys from the ignition and kneeled next to Daddy long legs; my hand pushed down on his back and forced him to lie flat on the concrete.

"Where is it?" I clutched a handful of his hair.

He tried to conjure up the strength to answer through the pain of a fractured jaw and broken bones. The left side of his body had the imprint of the Chevelle's tire and his left eye hung from its orbital socket. I snapped the optic nerve, plucked it free and made him watch as I popped it in my mouth and chewed.

"Your phone where is it?"

Terrified he flexed his fingers on his left hand and that's when I saw it. The cell had imbedded in his flesh; phone and man had become one. His head had been partially cratered and his spine bore proof that his only movements would be involuntary from this day forth. I contemplated finishing the job, but my ire for his little stunt angered me and I let him lie in his own fluids. It was almost the humane thing to do; don't put the poor bastard out of his misery, leave him to doctors and scientists. He was no danger to me; his thoughts couldn't fill a petri dish. I got back in the car and the chick stared at me with tear filled eyes.

"You're not just gonna leave him there?"

I stared at him from my side mirror; his pathetic one eyed twitched in the late morning sunlight. Naturally I didn't want her to think I wasn't sympathetic to the poor man's condition. I reversed the car and split his head with the full force of a sledge hammer hitting a watermelon. Her face turned pale as she witnessed his execution through the tilted looking glass of the rearview.

TODD ANDREW DAVIS
SELF-PRESERVATION
CHAPTER XXXIII

A multitude of scenarios flashed through my head on the nearly twenty minute drive; none where I lived happily ever after. I knew deep down that I didn't kill Laura, I couldn't kill her. I realized whatever story I gave to the police, to Tamara, I would never satisfactorily vindicate myself. I was the villain they all sought and Laura's brutal death would end the moratorium on Illinois' death penalty. I know it sounds archaic, but she was a troubled girl heading down a troubled path. There was nothing good left of Laura's life to save while I could still salvage my own; better a guilty conscious than a death sentence cocktail. I had less than a twenty-four hour window in which to work and paranoia kept my senses sharp. The average slime ball gets caught when they trip up on their alibis and whereabouts. I've always wondered if I could furnish specific dates, times, places, people, faces, dogs barking, kids playing, conversations or phone calls if the tables had been reversed. I fished my cell phone from my pocket and dialed home.

"Hello," Kathy's voice sounded sad and dejected; I thought she'd had a miscarriage.

"Kathy; honey what's wrong?" my voice was laced with anxiety.

"Nothing I'm watching Oprah," she sighed.

I wanted to stop the car, turn around and strangle the bitch! "Baby you called me earlier and....."

"I know; I talked to Tamara, she said you were with her working on the case and you crashed on the sofa."

Fuck now I needed and alibi for my alibi. Tamara was a manipulative little cunt who would do just about anything short of a colonoscopy to get the truth out of me.

"Sorry about earlier, I was interrogating a suspect. The session got kinda heated. I didn't mean to take it out on you," I was less than five minutes from Tamara's and my mind was working overtime. "Sweetheart I just called to apologize. I have to go, I'll call you later, love you."

Think Logan, what the hell happened? Could I have been drugged? Had someone else been in the apartment? It was more plausible than the idea that I might have snapped, killed her and woke with no recollection of having done so. The thought of blacking out frustrated me more than Laura's decomposing corpse. The fog in my head began to lift as I pulled into Tamara's driveway. At this point the truth was more damning than any lie and until I knew for certain what happened I was better off burying everything.

"Hey Lo," a bundled up Eskimo opened the passenger side door and jumped in.

"Tam."

"Logan the full report says they found sperm and blood inside Connie, also blood droplets on the bathroom sink countertop and a sufficient amount in the elbow of the pipe underneath the vanity."

"It's Ryan's," I said bluntly, "the killer staged it," I was stunned with my own outburst but quickly followed up, "He's not all of a sudden gonna be careless. This guy is a pro in the same way were professionals. He just wanted us to take the bait, distract us for a while. He's planning something even more spectacular;" *like implicating the lead Detective.*

"Are you telling me he's so fucking clever and we're all a bunch of goddamn lab monkeys Logan?"

"So far; it's nothing personal. He's amused by the thought of our collective heads spinning like tops. Even though we can't see it yet, there's a purpose to his madness. He takes pride in his work. And if we salivate over every false lead and pursue utter nonsensical rubbish were doomed."

"Nonsensical rubbish, do you hear yourself Logan? We may just posses enough exculpatory evidence to bury him and you just dismiss it?"

"Exculpatory is a term used for exoneration…"

"Whatever Logan, you know what the fuck I mean!" Her face grew flustered as she leaned back in the seat. "What's with the cruiser?"

"I wanted to bring shivery back and ended up with a car that conked out on me."

"I didn't realize chivalry was dead," she smirked. "So you left Kathy with Mr. Reliable huh?"

The way she pronounced dead unnerved me, "She had a prenatal check-up this afternoon and I…"

"And you should be there for her Logan. If you want I'll drop you off at the house," Tamara placed her hand on my arm, "What time is her appointment?"

"I'll have to call her and get the time, but when we get back to the station I'll get a loaner from Joe, being stranded with you all night wouldn't be much fun."

"You could have called; I would've come to your rescue. Where'd you breakdown anyway?"

"Not too far from The Mud River Lounge. Ever heard of it?"

"Logan."

"What now?"

"You're not drinking again?"

"What are you my fucking shrink? Do I have to remind you that I am your goddamn superior! Shit Tamara, just because we were once lovers that doesn't give you the right to invade my life! I said the fucking car broke down! You just naturally assumed I threw away five years of sobriety just like that!"

"You're right. I'm sorry; I just care so much about you Logan. I didn't mean anything, honestly. It's just Kathy was worried….. "

"I don't need you making up shit to her either. You didn't do me any favors; you've turned the simple truth into a lie.

Imagine if I had told Kathy the truth; that I slept roadside in the cruiser and not on your couch," I was fuming. "By the way if you think that little doozy ain't gonna fuck me your fooling yourself; for god's sake Tam you might as well have told her we were screwing."

"I wasn't thinking. I didn't know."

"And you don't need to know."

We drove to the station in a silent nirvana, *perfect*. I started to smile and could do absolutely nothing about it. I wasn't being pragmatic. I understood how mixed up and unethical everything appeared. I had an affair with a girl who was tightly interwoven with my investigation. I was a married cop cheating on his pregnant wife with the aforementioned girl who coincidentally turned up dead. My career wouldn't survive the tabloids and my marriage wouldn't survive the truth. I would be linked to Allen's murder, labeled a jealous boyfriend and connected to all the unsolved killings in an attempt to quell the public's fears. It would be a carnival of madness and I would be their main attraction. Proving my innocence was nothing compared to covering up my involvement in Laura's death. *What if I wasn't so innocent?* Maybe I snapped. Maybe I was so incensed by Santiago's takeover of the investigation that I did something unspeakable. *What if I was the madman I was tracking all along?* I'm no killer, but how could I expose the truth? My behavior was a serious contradiction to the actions of an innocent man. *How could I convince anyone else if I had doubts myself?* The pounding in my head registered ten on the rector scale and my feelings for Laura had been superseded by sheer panic, or perhaps the preservation of my own life; call it what you will. My moral blunders although few were unforgivable. In most aspects I was a decent and honorable man; we're all sinners in the eyes of the Lord. I openly acknowledged my faults and my shortcomings. I was put to the ultimate test of my character and failed miserably; save your sorry soul Logan. *You've created a black hole that systematically sucked in everyone from your life. The lamb or the lion, it was my choice. Who did I want to be?*

Tamara stared out the vehicle lost somewhere in the horizon. She was special to me, but she didn't need to get involved any more than she already was. The killer could have targeted me from the very start of the investigation? I left an opening when I got stoned out of my head and was incapable of defending myself. Instead of taking my life, he planned on taking everything from it. He wanted to play a new game; he watched me fuck Laura and by killing her, he sealed my fate. I was boxed in and he was out there awaiting my next move. From now on I had to be cognizant of my every movement. *Maybe I can lure him in and escape unscathed?* I pulled into the Thirteen Precinct underground garage and before I set the car in park Tamara had bolted. I walked over to the service area; behind the cage was Joey Perilya, Head Mechanic; a hairy son-of-a-gun with an acute sweat gland disorder. He wore a wife beater T' with checker-board suspenders and stunk of cigarettes and coffee. Joe was grumpy, old and litigious.

"Can I help you Mr. Logan?"

"I need to swap out the cruiser; she broke down last night."

"What's wrong with her?" he stared at the navy blue Crown Vic in disbelief then skeptically eyeballed me and let out a deep groan.

"I'm not a mechanic Joe."

"How did she sound?" he gave me a no shit kind of smirk, "Did you have problems getting her to turn over?"

He had an intimidating way about him that made you feel two inches high and if you were uncomfortable with his inquiries he prodded even harder. Joe would have made a great prosecutor.

"Um, it stalled and wouldn't start back up; probably the cold weather," I tossed the keys on the counter. "Joe I don't have time for idle chit chat. I've got a hectic schedule today; just give me another vehicle and we'll work it out tomorrow?" He opened the door to the cage and headed for the cruiser. "Joe I have a prenatal appointment with Kathy and I....."

"How's she doing Mr. Logan?"

"She's doing fine, thanks and Abby?"

"Gabby," he corrected me, "Women are women, enough said right? I'll give her the once over tonight; take the blue one in the corner over there." His pudgy index finger pointed in the direction of an identical car.

"Joe my wife's going to go berserk with her hormones and all, she'll never believe I swapped out the old vehicle; she won't step foot in that one."

"What do you suggest I do paint it white?" he threw his hands up in exasperation.

"How about I take the brown one?"

"It's buried behind a sea of cars it will take me forever to get it out..."

"Thanks Joe, I'll be back around eleven," I turned my back to him and walked to the elevator. I could feel the weight of his stare.

I'd be back before lunch, grab the car, head over to Laura's and finish cleaning the apartment. I needed to buy cleaning supplies, bleach, gloves, mop; what else? Make a mental list; I can't afford to write anything down. Roses, I need to buy a dozen roses.

I sat behind my desk and eyed the clock; time stood still. *"Honey the library called and wanted to know why you weren't at work. Please call me back,"* I imagined Laura's mother calling and not being able to reach her, or perhaps her friends had stopped by to hang out. Could one of them have their own set of keys? *"Laura; Katie and Susan said they'd stopped by and rang the doorbell several times with no answer. Getting worried please call me when you get this okay; love you sweetheart."* My desk phone rang and I almost had a heart attack, "Detective Crenshaw, speaking."

Santiago's voice oozed through the telephone, "Logan; its J.T., I was disappointed you didn't return to the meeting. Listen I am not trying to step on any toes here…"

"I'm just a little under the weather," I abruptly interrupted him, "and with Kathy; I thought I'd be better off at home. No hard feelings."

"Of course not, sorry for the misunderstanding, give Kathy…."

I hung up the phone before he finished and spent the rest of the morning making myself visible. I went everywhere from the mail room to the examiner's office and even joked with dispatch. I went through the open case files and thumbed through Victims 1 & 2 Jessica and Jenifer Foster killed outside the Double Door Bar nearly a month and half ago, I had vowed to catch their killer, but I was still nowhere near closing the case. Then there was a possible Victim #3, the Jane Doe found in a raging fire inside the Paradise Motel. Victim # 4 Laura's boyfriend Allen Gross murdered outside Marcel's Coffee Shoppe, his death had brought her into my life and I regretted that I failed to resist the temptation. Victim #5 Sixth Grade Teacher Connie Jefferson of Glenmore Heights; hers was the only crime scene linked by DNA to our first possible lead, Ryan Beliford. Unless he stuffed himself into a garbage disposal and committed the most absurd act of suicide, Mr. Beliford was ruled out as the killer and checked off as Victim #6. And the body of Victim #7 Security Guard Winston Howard V outside Beliford's crime scene in King's Crossing. Wrong place, wrong time for Winston; what was left of him couldn't be viewed on a full stomach. I sat down at my desk half exhausted and eyed the large glass window of the Captain's office. I couldn't hear what they were saying, but Santiago was inside and they appeared to be in the middle of a heated argument. Ollie jabbed his finger into Santiago's chest and used it as if he had just emphasized a point. I knocked on Ollie's door.

"Come in," his Midwestern voice was raspy from years of smoking.

"Everything all right Cap?" I stood behind the half opened door.

"Yes of course, Mr. Santiago was just leaving."

Santiago was clearly surprised by Ollie's dismissal and wanted to respond but was dissuaded by the intensity of

Ollie's glare. He gathered up his field report, averted my eyes and coldly brushed by me as he left the Caption's office.

"Okay, what the fuck was that all about?" I asked.

"Nothing, just rack it up to Professional Disagreement," he leaned back in his high back leather chair.

His office walls were covered with pictures of himself and many of the department's brass; my eyes focused on the one we had taken in Key Largo nearly a year ago. We stood on the pier in front of a pulley that held our 9 foot, thousand pound swordfish between us; in the background was Ollie's boat aptly named *'Last Chance.'* And there it was, providence smacking me in the face. Tell him and forget about how crazy your story sounds; figure that out later, just say something, anything. It might well have been my last chance, but I let the moment pass.

"I'm going to take her out again this summer," Ollie noticed the direction of my gaze, "You're always welcome to come with me."

"Thanks but I don't think Kathy would be too happy if I took off for a week."

"You know if there was anything you wanted to talk about... Kathy, kids; anything. You can always come talk to me."

"What the fuck, you Dr. Phil now?" I smirked. "Are you charging me for a session Ollie?"

"Despite what you might have seen, if this is about Santiago my decision was in no way a reflection on your performance. It's just that we need to take additional steps to solve this crime."

"I agree. We need a fresh approach," I hadn't taken a step inside his office and he was blabbering like one of Saddam's henchmen. *Could you at least wait until I got settled before the torture begins?* "We need to be less radical and more analytical and I have heard just how anal Santiago is." *He spent a great deal of time with his head burrowed deep inside your rectum.* "I know you're under a lot of stress with the Feds breathing down your neck demanding to take over. Don't worry Ollie, we'll be able to function well together. We'll catch this guy and make you the hero." *The higher-ups will throw you a Mardi Gras style parade.* "Santiago's got a decent head on his shoulders; he'll flourish in his new role and you heard that straight from the horse's mouth. No hard feelings?" Ouch, I extended my hand and wanted to commit Harakiri, "We have twice as many squad cars in the garage as we do on the streets; I believe we need a show of force."

"Truth be told I don't care if we catch the bastard or not," he said; therein lies Ollie's infinite wisdom, "I just hope to scare him out of our jurisdiction."

The fat man was unequivocally the biggest media whore known to mankind. Ollie was my friend and one of the Mayor's top designated butt kissing brown nose flunkies. He pretended it hadn't gotten under his ever widening anatomy, except I knew this glory hound needed the Thirteenth to catch the bastard. Maybe he could mind fuck the rest of them, but I knew better. He chuckled and I smiled and we both stood wearing metaphorical hip waders in the middle of Shit Creek. I artfully disengaged myself from his presence by using the old 'short on time' routine. I needed an excuse to get-away, to get back to Laura's apartment and finish cleaning; time was of the essence. Back in my office an idea popped in my head and I dialed the home phone; it rang half a dozen times.

"Hello," she somberly answered.

"Hey sweetheart," I responded.

"Oh, hey hon."

"I want to take you to lunch at the Thai Palace in New Haven," I didn't let her lack of enthusiasm damper my demeanor.

"Today? Jesus Logan you honestly couldn't have picked a worse day if you tried. Mom is on her way over and Lizzy's sick; I'm picking her up from school. Plus, I've got the worse migraine ever," her voice showed concern. "What's the occasion? I've been bugging you for months to go there."

"Think about it; I'll call you back," I was almost ready to confess. *Wholly shit my life hung in the balance and I had to rely on my loved ones to keep me from the noose.* It was a snag in the plan I hadn't anticipated and my attitude quickly dimmed. I hung up the phone and dialed my mother-in-law.

"Hello?"

"Hello mom," I cradled the receiver to my mouth, "I need to talk to you about Kathy."

"Is there something wrong dear?"

"It's just that I was hoping we could get away today. She

deserves it mom… with the case and the baby, things have been a little rocky lately," I should have known better and chose my words more artfully when speaking to my nosey bitch of a mother-in-law.

"Rocky? She never mentioned you were having marital trouble? Do you want me to talk with her dear?"

No I don't you old crow, but you'll stick your filthy beak in as always, "No mom, Kathy would kill me if she knew I had said anything. I just need a favor?"

"Anything Logan I'm always here for you two."

"Lizzy's sick and I need you to babysit so I can take her out for lunch."

"Wouldn't dinner be more romantic?"

"Work won't permit me," I rubbed my temple. *Listen you old battle axe, I have to run clear across town to tidy up a murder scene, if I waited until dinner I'd be served my next meal in a ten by ten cell.*

"Could you call her? Tell her to be at the Thai restaurant by 1:00 that would be terrific. Love you mom."

"Of course honey. I'm thinking……"

"Gotta go ma," I promptly hung up; all this deceit was working up quite the appetite.

I checked my watch; *first* stop at *Laura's apartment and cleanup, then drive across town and meet Kathy for lunch.* I entered the locker room, unlocked the standard issued dull blue locker and retrieved a long sleeve popsicle green polo shirt and sand brown khakis that hung inside. I undressed, placed my clothes along with Allen's white shirt inside then took my shampoo, conditioner, soap and towel with me to the shower. As I lathered up it dawned on me that the items from Laura's condo were nestled in the trunk of the navy blue Vic: blankets, sheets, pillow cases, washcloth with her pubic hair, nail clippings and my blood on a razor blade. Haste makes waste. If Laura's bedding and DNA were discovered, I'd have to resurrect Johnny Cochran to save my lily white ass. The shower gently massaged my aching body. I'm a good cop; why can't I end this nightmare? I can't even find the words to explain my way out of this hellhole. I was sinking in quicksand the moment I stepped inside Laura's condo. I acted on my desire and ignored every basic procedure known to law enforcement. It was reckless, unethical and unimaginable for any officer to take center stage in a crime investigation. I was a married man with a child and one in the oven; it was the mistake of a lifetime and I had done it twice. There was no time to grieve for Laura or myself. What's done is done and I had to wiggle off the proverbial hook. *And how pray tell was I to accomplish such an impossible feat?* I was supposed to be the beloved detective, the man appointed to rescue the city from the grips of a psycho killer. Instead, I was a mere mortal who'd rolled the dice against the Devil one too many times and came up snake eyes. Once public confidence and respect was lost, the press would turn on me like a bunch of hyenas. Buffoonery was a dangerous thing and my career rested on a volcano of lies and a growing pile of smoldering failures. However, I had a different scenario for this never ending nightmare. I quickly succumbed to the realization that my team was overmatched by the whims of a psychotic killer.

My rational for leading this case and my ability to remain objective had been scarred; nothing in this investigation made sense to me. The killer possessed a unique ability to kill at will, remain shrouded in mystery and strike in what I believed an uncontrollable burst of rage. His body pumped full of endorphins, adrenaline, hate, steroids, drugs were fused together like a hydrogen bomb. Anything, possibly a memory that could no longer be repressed could trigger the killer and ignite a deluge of destruction. Finding the source of his hatred could extinguish the flame. Unfortunately I couldn't rule myself out and that was first and foremost job one; self-preservation at all cost. *Maybe the killer within me lay dormant for decades? The level of violence committed against my fellow man could not have been waiting to erupt without any signs of past madness.* Most of my childhood memories were long dead and buried; it always felt odd that I couldn't remember. When engaged in conversations of my youth, I'd joke with others using the standard banter of childhood anxiety and teenage jocularity. The absences of authenticity hadn't spawned any undue concern until now. Ever since I had set foot on Chancellor's Manor, memories had been flooding back. I didn't know why or what had unearthed them. I ignored most of my bazaar proclivities believing that every man had his devious impulses from time to time. The pure insanity of the crimes alone was enough to rule me out. If I had blacked out how could I have been so shrewd and meticulous? Even if I suffered from dementia or schizophrenia Kathy, my coworkers, the staff physiologist; somebody would have recognized the signs long ago. I knew it was insanity to risk going back to Laura's apartment. I had a queasiness in my stomach telling me I hadn't done enough; a little birdie whispered in my ear and told me to move the body off the premises. *Had my brain deliberately masked my culpability to murder concealing the truth from a fractured and delusional mind?*'

The shower had a medicinal effect; I was replenished and felt a little like my old self again. I emerged with a new and stronger vigor. I was determined not to allow Laura's murder to stain my reputation. The long and the short of it was that I had lived an imperfect yet decent life, or at least the one committed to memory had been. I had a beautiful wife, gorgeous daughter and my namesake on the way. I wanted this life, guilty or innocent it wouldn't keep me from my family. If I was broken I could heal myself; hell, I made it this long. I took the elevator down to the garage floor. Joe had the tan colored Vic washed, cleaned and keys in the ignition.

"Joe, I left some personal effects in the other car," I waved him over, "Any chance I can get them now?"

"You're referring to the bag and the blankets?" he asked.

I could double back; kill Joe in a random act of ....

"I placed them in lock-up, don't worry I took inventory of everything myself. It's all there. I figured you and the Misses probably kept them for the occasional picnic or beach rondevu."

Why was I having such difficulties and yet some of the dumbest criminals that were known to man got away with murder? *Yeah Joe I need the blanket, as well as the sheets, the bloody washcloth, razor, pubic hair, and my signed confession.* His sarcastic tone told me everything-he was on to me; he knew I had committed adultery and it disgusted him. *Oh yeah Joe, by the way don't fuck up the new crime scene you've just created. Make sure you get those big sweaty paws all over everything. You dumb lummox.* I would name him my coconspirator if I were ever taken into custody; we'd frog walk together down the cold hallways of the state penitentiary. I briefly thanked him as he retrieved the damning evidence and haphazardly tossed our lives into the trunk. I started up the car then sped off.

I stopped in two different towns and two different convenient stores; bought several gallons of bleach, a foot of rope, duct tape, an exacto-knife, scissors, latex gloves and a dozen roses. I placed the items in the trunk next to the black trash bag full of the contents of Laura's apartment. I then stopped at a department store and purchased a gym bag, leather gloves, a white nightgown with a detachable red bow and a pair of bunny slippers. I felt like OJ fleeing Brentwood California after a double homicide. I arrived in Tella Hute eighteen minutes later. I placed my booty into the bag, pulled the unisex hoody low and made sure the roses would be seen by prodding eyes. I counted one hundred and twenty three steps from my car to Laura's front doorstep. I hesitated and then exhaled as my fingers searched for her keys buried in my front pocket. I turned the key and stepped back into the realm of my nightmare.

A bittersweet funk permeated throughout the condo. I found a scented aerosol spray and votive candles. Nothing says I love you quite like the aroma of white orchid candles. Everything seemed copacetic. The windows had fogged and made me feel as if I had been entombed; however it gave me the liberty to move back and forth without being detected. I proceeded through the house and treated it like a crime scene. Even though I knew it was a futile task to erase all my fingerprints it was gloves on from here on. I had been here before legitimately on police business, so my main concern was the bedroom. Television remote, unwashed glasses, bathroom doorknob, toilet seat, sink basin, headboard, thermostat, medicine cabinet, garbage container, shampoo and conditioner, anything that stood out. I began wiping the handle of the razor when I heard a faint knock at the front door; the doorbell rang. I stood paralyzed in a perverted game of hide and go seek. After a minute, whoever it was gave up. *Did some meddlesome neighbor see me enter her apartment? A friend, family member or maybe it was the Property Manager checking on complaints of the foul stench?*

I doused the sink in bleach and generously poured it down the drain. I did the same with the kitchen sink and the toilet. I had something completely different in mind for Laura and the tub. I filled it with water and emptied a bottle of bleach into the fifty gallon tub. The thought of moving her and dumping her body on the Southside or far Western Suburbs resurfaced. I grabbed my coat form the couch and headed outside. I briskly walked to the car and popped the trunk, it was immaculate. The spare tire was covered by carpet and the tire iron and kit were neatly tucked inside the black netting that adorned the side wall. There was a litter of blue windshield wiper fluid and a funnel on the opposite side of the trunk. I removed the funnel and headed back inside. A couple of people walked the parking lot, but they were more preoccupied with the cold than my presence. I lowered my head and re-entered the condo. I threw my jacket onto the sofa, walked the narrow hall to the bathroom then pulled the shower curtain along the rod to expose Laura's submerged body. I undressed down to my underwear; slid my right hand under her buttocks and lifted her upward. Her slippery torso flopped toward me and her head clunked against the edge of the prefab tub. I felt somewhat unnerved as I watched her head slip under, her hair fanned out across the surface of the murky bleached water then wrapped around her face as her head sank. I uncapped another bottle; her feet and legs dangled over the side and I did my best impression of her gynecologist. I separated her vaginal lips, inserted the funnel and purified her internal cavity. My eyes stung from the vapors rising off the liquid chemical as it threatened to overflow and my back strained as my grip tightened around her hips; my thumb accidently slid across her anus. I hoped the unorthodox method would be better than Spermicide. When I was finished I was disgusted to find that I had a budding erection; I shook my head in utter amazement. *Maybe I didn't know myself; maybe I was capable of the unthinkable.* I scrubbed her feet, ankles, legs, thighs, vagina, stomach, breast, bruised neck and face. I flipped her over and repeated the process. I emptied the tub, cleansed the shower, dried her body off and carried her to the bed. I dressed her in the white negligee minus the detachable bow then cut semi-equal lengths of rope and bound her hands and feet to the post. Lastly, my hands diligently cut away her eyelids with the exacto knife. I snagged an empty bag she had from the outlet mall and gathered the bottles of bleach, knife and packaging for the rope. I gave the place a quick once over, stuffed the contents into the gym bag, slipped on my jacket and headed out to the car with plenty of time to spare to meet my wife.

TODD ANDREW DAVIS
DAZED AND THE CONFUSED
CHAPTER XXXIV

I made my way onto 290 and headed for the city. I could tell it sparked her interest; did she really think that I would let her go? Our drive took us pass a viaduct where a state trooper was busy rousting a couple of vato's chilling by their low riders. Damn bangers were everywhere.

"If you give me any trouble, refuse an order and you will be begging me to kill you," I said as I made a right onto Independence; half a block later I cruised down the street and got service with an attitude.

"You look like a cop," stated a fifteen year old Mex wearing a wife beater, blue bandana and a tattoo of an English Bulldog on his right bicep. He leaned his nappy afro head through the passenger window. "Who's the chic, she look scared homey?"

I unzipped her jacket and unbuttoned her blouse; she was shaking. I grabbed the boy by the wrist startling him. He obviously thought he was going to feel the cold sting of steel handcuffs on his wrist; instead I forced his hand beneath her bra.

"I need six and if you serve me quick, I'll let you get your fingers wet as well," I grinned. He pedaled his banana seat six speed as fast as he could with his growing hard-on then jumped the curb and disappeared behind a church. "Don't get any ideas. Take a good gander at the scenery; there ain't no good Samaritans out here. I hate these wetbacks as much as you hate me. These cockroaches would pull a train on you so fast you'd have blood in your stool for months and no self respecting white boy will want you after they're done. A little hand to hand combat and it's over and done; unless of course you wanna watch me end the punks life? No problemo senorita."

She shook her head no.

"Clean yourself up," I gave her a napkin.

Three minutes later he returned. I leaned across her lap and propped the door open so he could slide into the back seat. "Go around the corner," he instructed, "turn right, then right again at the alley." His eyes were constantly on the lookout for Narcs. "Here dude. Its brown shit primo yo; uncut. That's some wicked virgin shit unlike this puta," his pupils were the size of needle heads. "Can I fucker?" he asked as he slipped me six baggies of smack.

"How'd you like me to ask that question of your old lady?" I replied. He was too horny to want any confrontation. "She'll use her hand that's it." I handed him four fives and four tens, "Get in the back."

She was in her early to mid-twenties, nice figure despite the winter clothes. The cold made her complexion change noticeably into a red faced cherub. She reluctantly made her way into the back seat and into the lion's den.

"Sweet her shit don't stink neither," he was so busy pulling at her breast and forcing her jeans low that he didn't even count the money. He was enchanted lost in cholo heaven;

all he needed was a cerveza and a poncho. If his boys saw him give me the shit before he got the money, his classic whites would be dangling from a telephone wire by their shoestrings. Even in the jungle there were rules; I guess Caucasian snatch will do that to a brown skin. "Man my cock is hard like Rocky dude. I just want to go a few rounds; I got raincoats."

"She's my wife; don't ask me again."

"Sorry bro," he bit his lip; after a handful of moans and grunts we were square. He handed me two baggies on the house. "Bring her around again sometime. Ask for Spider I'll hook you up," he wiped the sweat from his brow and disappeared into the gleaming sun.

"See darling the rules are simple, adhere to them and you prolong your life."

She curled up into the fetal position and whimpered. I could have demanded that she sit up next to me in the front seat, but one white face in this neck of town was dangerous enough. The patty wagons and vice squad combed through the grease pit like the wetbacks combed through their oiled saturated hair. I circled around the block, made it to the on-ramp and headed back to the police station. By 10:35 am we arrived in front of the Thirteenth and by 11:00 am we were once again on the move. I got lucky; the clever bastard had changed cars. He pulled out in a brown Vic; if it hadn't been for his impatience and squealing tires I would have been none the wiser. In all honesty I wasn't convinced it was him I was following until he made his first stop. This time he only took the side streets and at our final stop my curiosity got the best of me. I parked at the far end of the lot and after a stern warning I walked the girl around the rear of the car and stuffed her in the trunk.

I made my way to the store's entrance; it was mildly populated. A greeter with Down syndrome asked me if I were in need of a cart.

"Why the fuck not," I said cheerfully.

He rolled one in my general direction and I headed towards the pharmacy where I picked up a bag of fifteen orange caped syringes and a bag of twenty-four count cotton balls. I snatched up a bottle of generic alcohol then made my way over to the kitchen isle and lifted two spoons from a box-set of stainless steel silverware. I strolled down the food isle, placed a six pack of spring water in the cart and headed to the checkout. I spotted Logan shortly after. He nervously searched for a line shorter than the one he was in. He looked right at me, stared at the eight items or less sign and shook his head. His cart had bleach, duct tape, rope and a host of other packaged goods that I couldn't make out. I saw Corky roaming around the store, got his attention and asked him to get me duct tape; it would have been quicker if I had done it myself. Finally my slow motion hero returned with three different colors for me to choose from. I patted him on the head and still checked out before my dear old brother. I dumped my cargo into the trunk of my car and fetched my prize from the dingy damp interior of the steel casket.

"What's your name sweetheart?"

"Angie… Angela," her voice quivered.

"You're doing really well so far, keep up the good work."

My smile was absolutely no comfort to her. She diverted her eyes and it made me paranoid; I thought she might be up to something. *I'm taking those eyes; I'm taking everything that makes her, her.* I tailed Logan back to the condo. I parked on the south side of the hill outside Laura's building and stayed in the clearing behind her apartment. I took out a baggy, syringe, matches, water and a spoon and prepared Angela's lunch. She squirmed and mistakenly thought she'd have to watch me shoot up, but my treat would come much later.

"This will make everything easier. If you fight me you'll break the needle off inside," I grew impatient with her, Logan and the whole wait and see game.

I stuck Angie back inside the trunk and waltzed over to my perch that gave me a view of Laura's bedroom window. The interior windows were obscured by condensation and I walked down the hill to peer inside; my vision slightly hindered from the film that carpeted the glass. My brother was quite the busy bee. *He'd make a good housewife.* He frantically wiped away evidence of his prior existence in Laura's home from everything and anything. I could barely make out the tiny orange flame from a candle he had lit. I moved away from the window and walked around the condo. The parking lot was void of prying eyes so I pressed my ear against Laura's front door and listened. I could hear the water as it splashed around the tub; my smile widened as I pushed the doorbell. There was a faint echo and I could picture the poor bastard shitting his pants. It was a childish gamble, but I sincerely doubted he'd open the front door. Everything confirmed my suspicion of my brother; the dumb motherfucker was convinced he had murdered Laura. The cover up only showed his morality was as skewed as the killer he sought and after a few moments of silence I heard him return to his chores. I leisurely strolled around the building and heard the front door open. I pressed up fully against the brick wall; my hand gripped the pearl handled knife.

DAZED AND THE CONFUSED

"Over here brother, over here," I whispered into the wind.

He walked the lot to his vehicle and I feared I had made a grave miscalculation. He's going to drive away and I didn't have time to get to my car. I was about to bolt into the woods when the trunk of the cruiser popped up; he wasn't finished after all. He dug around the trunk and held what looked like a funnel in his right hand. I snuck back to my post and waited. He undressed, left the bedroom for thirteen minutes then returned with Laura's nude body. He fidgeted around and I saw him actually dressing Laura through the clouded window; now I understood. He wasn't certain that he killed her after all; what was important was to make it look identical to Connie's murder. *Bravo brother well played.* During his encore performance he bound her hands and feet to the bedpost. I watched him summon the nerve to cut off her eyelids; it was simply a masterful performance. As he dressed I fired up the beast and waited near the end of the school parking lot. It was after 12:30 pm; a few parked busses and a handful of students and teachers stood outside the school's exits cloaked in a nicotine induced haze. Students poured into the parking lot and left the premises for lunch; I relaxed, the Chevelle blended in with the other hotrods and beaters. Some of them looked through my windshield to see if they could recognize the man behind the wheel, but that's what tinted glass was for. Finally, Logan was off and on his way in the shit brown mobile.

The most intriguing stop of the day was a little Thai restaurant in New Haven; we waited ten minutes before entering. The restaurant was poorly lit and the ambiance a tad overdone. The waitresses were petite boat people and the cooks sprouted long wiry hair and yellow teeth. They cackled to one another in their native tongue. It's hard to believe this dog cooking, roach infested dung heap was patronized by so much white clientele. *Send these dirty little island rats back I say.*

"Jacoat, haat."

"Jacket and hat," I repeated to the little toothless immigrant in proper English and I wasn't about to relinquish either. "Fuck that," I said to my date as I found a corner booth to my liking.

My brother and a new lady friend were chatting away several tables down behind a knee wall that enclosed their section. The woman's face was heavier than what I would have guessed was my brother's taste. She still had a defined beauty, not cookie cutter but charmingly unique. Her reddish hair, not quiet shoulder length was as radiant as her complexion. She was a real woman not like the children I had been reduced to fucking. The way he caressed her arm was intimate but did not overstate his affection and it made me realize she was something special to him. This wasn't someone whose corpse he'd let rot like week old meat. She's wasn't a lover, sister, or a friend, she was much more than that.

After our Thai tea and curry roasted duck, I watched him excuse himself and leave her with his credit card. A kiss on the neck, a peck on the cheek and he was off. I initially wanted to scoop Angie out of the booth and onto her feet in hot pursuit, but when the check came I relaxed. His woman was in my sights and when she stood I almost yelled out she's pregnant. She was his wife, not a divorcée or a fling or a woman on the outs. She had his credit card and was someone more intimate rather than a mere exchange of body fluids. Fresh off a meal of exotic cuisine my appetite was quenched so I went head hunting. Angela had a few cc's left in her system and had been more of an annoyance than anything. I was happy; my brother's pregnant felines lead me straight to their homestead. Once again I played the dreadful waiting game, this time I made Angela give me a blow job for all my efforts. I didn't cum though; I was saving this hard on for prego. She said her goodbyes to an older lady, who proceeded to her car. She drove right fucking pass me while Angie was still slobbing my knob. If the old bag had just glanced in my direction she would of known something wasn't quite right. *Why was I parked here for starters?* I pulled Angie off my cock and slowly drove down the rocky path that led to the driveway. A decorative homemade sign was painted on their mailbox and was engraved, '***Logan and Kathy Crenshaw; Home Sweet Home.***'

TODD ANDREW DAVIS
THE GUILT OF INNOCENCE
CHAPTER XXXV

It had been nearly 36 unbearable hours before the first call came into the station concerning Laura; I had almost phoned in an anonymous call to get the ball rolling. A squad was sent to the condo and the preliminaries were coming across the wire. I went about my day unaffected until Tamara entered my office babbling hysterically.

"Logan! Logan!" she squawked out of breath, "Laura... Allen's Laura, she's dead."

She was my Laura too, until I murdered her. I had to watch my words carefully; how I responded mattered. I was a bit perplexed and it wasn't from the lying and deceptive practices in which I had to partake but the uninterrupted, undisturbed and all around good night's sleep I had. I had imagined the possibility of being haunted by two ghouls from beyond the earthly world but truthfully, all the craziness had effectively tired me the fuck-out. I felt at peace; that was until Tamara made her over dramatic entrance and then I was in a tailspin sliding down an icy double lane highway. I was not entirely positive what my reply had been to Tamara and I couldn't afford to have a flippant comment dangle out there.

We raced down Port Road with sirens bellowing. Tamara was driving and my eyes caught an unflattering profile.

THE GUILT OF INNOCENCE

The case had been arduous to say the least but the toll it took on Tamara had robbed her of some of her beauty. I was curiously enthusiastic about leading an investigation where at the crux I stood as suspect numero uno. I was nervous; I needed to know if I'd done enough to ensure no clues were left behind to incriminate me. Following standard modus operandi was one thing and it was quite another to whitewash a crime scene to protect yourself.

No matter how certain I was that I hadn't missed a thing, doubt ebbed at the edges of my mind. When you were you twenty-four seven anything out of place no matter how miniscule could interrupt your happy medium and the lies you told would unravel. *How do you imitate you?* We all have telling quirks or mannerisms that are unto ourselves. *How can I replicate myself beyond suspicion? 'Logan you're so quiet. Logan is everything okay? Logan, are you feeling sick? Logan you're not yourself today; do you want to talk?' 'Yes as a matter-of-fact I do. A couple of days ago I cheated on Kathy with this beautiful young thang; you know Laura whose boyfriend Allen was slain. Anyways, not only don't I remember banging the little trollop, but turns out I don't remember killing her either and for the past couple of days I've been playing cover-up.'*

"Logan, you okay?" Tamara's asked sincerely.

I busted out laughing; an outburst she obviously didn't expect, but after several moments of loud uncontrollable guffaws she loosened up and joined in. Moments later we arrived at the parking lot of Laura Jean Miles. The overcast clouds were dense slow moving marshmallows and the dashboard thermometer read a bone chilling three degrees. The wind chill was like needles on the exposed skin; hell bore icicles. I convinced myself that I would be fine once inside the warm confines of Laura's place. We were greeted by the customary tin badges outside the crime scene and it only prolonged my discomfort; it showed visibly. With all the murders on the docket it had become second habit for the herd of buffalo to gather and wait for the bull to take charge. The swirls of white steam from cups of coffee mingled with plumes of cigarette puffs and exhaled breath.

"The weather keeps the vultures to a minimum," said Officer Elliot Cordele. He referred to the small band of spectators that were cordoned off by police tape.

I barely acknowledge him as I stepped inside. *Okay; I felt okay.* This was my turf and I had home field advantage. Inside I was greeted by more detectives with fake smiles and handshakes. I pretended to take in the lay of the land not wanting to give the impression of being overly familiar with this place.

"The bedroom?" I extended my index finger toward the narrow hallway.

"Yes sir, it's straight ahead and then to your immediate right," replied an officer.

Webb hovered nearby and I acted causally as I stared at some of the photographs that hung on the wall. She was understandably a little aloof since our minor blowup we had a few days back, but her silence served me well. I'm sure the questions popped off in her brain like fireworks on the 4th.

"Chlorine, bleach, you smell it?" I asked Tamara.

"Yes."

I stated the obvious and in my humble estimation the voluntary insight left me with nothing gained or lost. I entered Laura's room; she lay on top of a neatly made bed adorned in a white negligee. *Fuck why did I make the bed?* They'd hunt around the apartment for the soiled linens or conclude that they had been taken; it was something that would ultimately tie the killer to the crime. Dumb, dumb, dumb. Through trial and error they'll figure out the bed was made after the murder. The blood soaked mattress and the blood pattern on the comforter weren't consistent. Two plainclothes excused themselves as I pulled on my latex gloves. They reminded me of Apollo Astronauts in preparation for the first Lunar landing; I'm not entirely sure why. As I moved closer the lump in my throat mutated into an almost unconscionable act and I fought with all my fiber to suppress the rising bile. Amazingly among the barrage of colorful bruises Laura remained beautiful almost angelic.

"What do think Logan?" Webb raised her nightgown. She gestured to the discoloration of Laura's exposed clitoris. "I think the sick fuck ejaculated inside her, panicked and bathed her in bleach. You can smell the stench coming from the bathroom. I don't understand, why he's now so concerned with covering up? The need for good housekeeping is puzzling don't you think?"

I studied her feet, ankles, thighs, vagina, midsection, breast, neck and face, before I offered my opinion, "Her entire body shows signs of discoloration. His message was one of purification, not self-preservation. It was a premeditated act not an afterthought. You're wrong, I don't think he had sex with her then in a panic tried to destroy evidence; our guy doesn't get unnerved or make mistakes. He dressed her up and posed her spread eagle.

He knew the distinctive odor of bleach would linger, if he'd fucked-up he would have dumped her somewhere; the woods behind her apartment would have been a good spot. This was Allen's girl and he was keenly aware of that." I placed a gloved right hand over the purple and yellow impressions on her neck. "This madman is sending us a message and letting us know he's watching. Her eyelids were painstakingly cut away and her hands and feet bound in the same way as Connie Jefferson's," I was oddly proud of myself.

"Maybe he has latent homosexual tendencies."

I shot her a look.

"What? You act as though your offended Logan."

"No I'm not. Go ahead, let's hear your rationale."

"Well, all the female victims have been spared the beatings their male counterparts suffered; except Jennifer who he decapitated. Allen, Ryan and the Gate Keeper suffered epic trauma. The killer was so enraged that he tried to obliterate them from existence. I think in some way it's perversely connected to his sexuality and the women were an attempt to steer us away from his intended target. I'll bet he was sexually abused by his father or uncle or someone he trusted and his docile mother didn't intercede out of fear or whatever, I'm just grasping at straws."

"No. No, go on," I prompted.

"What if we went straight to the media?" Used code words like repressed and latent homosexual tendencies; notch it up a bit and call him a faggot or queer. He's probably operating in the gay community and we should put them on the lookout as well."

"Have you lost your ever-loving mind? We're not living in the Middle Ages; we'd be adding fuel to the fire. Every man in that community would have a target on their back. It would be open season on them and anyone suspected of being homosexual; a literal bloodbath. Do you really want to demonize a community who's been persecuted as much as they have? You might as well throw a live grenade onto State Street during the Gay Pride Parade. You of all people should know better," I wasn't quite finished with my examination of Laura and as I looked at Tamara one thing became all too clear. "You've spoken to someone already?" I didn't give her the chance to respond, "You report to me! You don't fucking going off the reservation and spout your goddamn theories without checking with me! You're not a psychologist; you're pissing in the wind like the rest of us. Who the fuck did you speak to about this?"

"Logan, you haven't been focused lately and ….."

"Who!" I could hear the other officers rummaging around outside the bedroom. I passed Tamara and slammed the bedroom door shut; enraged I repeated the question through clenched teeth.

"Cap."

"You pulled rank; beautiful," I smiled in disgust, "you're the last motherfucker I'd suspect of mutiny. You want my job! Huh Tamara; cause you can have it!"

"Logan, I am sorry. The idea was shot down; you're right I should have come to you first."

"So I could have marched out in front of the firing squad with your repackaged idea?" I rubbed my chin with my bicep, "I hope Santiago wants you because you're off my team."

"Logan you can't be serious?" she protested. "All my leg work, all the man hours I've put in." Her voice trailed off.

"We were a mistake from the beginning," I didn't give a shit whether she thought I was referring to being part of the team or our relationship. It didn't matter either way.

She opened the door and silently slunk away with her tail between her legs. I was a little saddened, but more relieved. I knew her report would wind up on my desk first and I'd have the opportunity to alter it without repercussion.

I took out a scrapper and worked underneath Laura's toenails and fingernails then slipped the contents into a silicone pouch and slid it into my pant pocket. Her wrist and ankles were severely gashed from the restraints. I inspected her mouth and under her swollen tongue. A splintered bone that was as white as winter snow protruded from her neck. Only when I swept her hair back could the harshness of her injuries be appreciated. Blood pooled in her lower extremities with the majority settling in her lower back. I turned her on her left side. I could hear the liquid swish around inside and it reminded me vaguely of a washing machine on rinse cycle. I probed and foraged for alien hairs and tissue. I knew full well the naked eye was no match for inferred, but I owed it to myself to be as meticulous as possible. My stomach was nauseous. When I'd had all I could bear I ordered the body to be removed and the room processed. I was satisfied that my earlier attempt to cover up my tracks were complete. I peeled off the gloves, made my way pass the throne of officers and let the outside air wash over me. The sidewalk and adjacent parking lot were filled with news vans, satellite trucks, crowds of onlookers and a horde of cops. Maybe our fearless leader Ollie could give a press conference. 'The fagot is on the run; don't fear good people of Ravenswood we've got him by the balls.' I couldn't have a sympathetic thought for Tam, it was intolerable the shit she pulled. I breathed a sigh of relief as I pulled out of the parking lot and onto the main road. I hadn't wavered and I was confident that I didn't play an instrumental part in Laura's demise. The real killer was out there and I had to find him. I needed to retrace my steps and without Tamara up my ass I'd have a chance to investigate freely. I just hoped the trail hadn't grown cold.

Back at the station a detailed written report listed three bottles of generic bleach had been found underneath the kitchen cabinet. At this stage of the investigation they were presumed to be the same type that was used to flush the poor girl's insides clean. A notation at the bottom stated: curiously unlike the other murders the killer had wiped everything down. The toilet seat and lever, showerhead and faucet, door knobs, glasses in the sink, toothbrush, paste and tweezers, even the television remote. Another anomaly was the bedspread and sheets underneath Laura were relatively clean. So what happened to the soiled laundry? The lack of evidence suggested Laura may have had a relationship with the killer. She let him inside, made him green ginseng tea, watched TV, shared her toothbrush and took a shower or bath together. For some reason on the night of her murder her lover snapped and forced himself on her after or during their love making. What had gone wrong? No screams or shouts heard, no turned over nightstands that signaled a struggle only a broken glass found in the trash.

An elderly lady described someone who had entered Laura's apartment; a man carrying flowers, red she thought, but her cataracts had made her vision blurry. She said she was an insomniac and had been watching the Late Late Show and was too tired to care about someone's gentleman caller. She was confused and redacted her prior statement. 'I think I saw him about one-thirty in the morning, but the more I think about it, well it could have been around twelve in the afternoon that day,' she was just unsure; age had robbed her of more than her vision. A little Hispanic girl across the way remembered hearing her dog bark late that same night. She had hushed Dixie, the three year-old Pekingese and returned to the land of make believe. Both parents gave the impression they dabbled in cannabis as well as other illegal substance s and were of no use to the investigation. There was a suspicious indentation next to the hedges outside Laura's door. I could have told them it was a knee print from where I collapsed that night, but I didn't feel much like aiding to the investigation. Some witness told stories of a Crown Vic, but when pressed admitted they'd seen an abundance of them in recent days due to the new police initiative

'Take Back the Streets Program.' The program had stirred up more shit than anything. There were several unfounded accusations of officials making Ravenswood a police state. 'We're living under a military style lockdown,' a quote that was attributed to one of the Mayors republican rivals. Fresh prints were found in the snow behind the building. The perpetrator had walked the premises to and fro via the same impressions. As he retraced his steps the toecap had obliterated the heel and instep of the shoe prints, but molds of the impressions were taken nonetheless.

Bread crumbs puzzled the CSI's until they calculated several different species of animal prints were collected inside the molds. When they started analyzing the crumbs, I smiled to myself and realized my secret was safe. They were turning over so many stones that they created a mess.

They marched around like crossed eyed zombies having a miserable time deciphering all the excess bullshit; being overworked and underpaid made the lab fertile grounds for mistakes. They'd forgo the benign and concentrate on the sensational. Watch the left hand wave the wand as the right deceived you; he had them and I had them right where we wanted.

I returned to my office emotionally and physically drained. I needed to capitalize on the chaotic mess that had erupted. Too much medaling would be perceived as suspicious behavior, however leaving things to fate wasn't settling my nerves. I faced a precarious dilemma; how to throw the game without drawing attention? Getting Tamara reassigned was an ingenious first step, but I needed more of a diversion, a scapegoat. I had to be careful not to over think or over react; I'm the last person anyone would suspect. *If I had to eliminate the little girl with the dog and kill the old lady with the bad eyesight could I? Was I capable of murdering both of them in cold blood? I would do whatever was necessary to protect myself. Should I conduct interviews with both or was it better to hang back in the weeds? Logan you need to get a grip. Think.* I dialed Kathy's cell, several seconds later she picked up.

"Hey babe, thank you again for lunch the other day."

"Kathy, listen. There's been another murder. I think it would be best if you took Lizzy and stayed with your mother......"

"For how long?" she screamed, "A week or a month?

When will you catch him Logan? Why are you doing this to me now?"

I wanted to yell at her. *'You're in danger; the woman I was cheating with is dead and I might have killed her. I might be the deranged animal, if I was it would only be a matter of time before I kill you too.'* Deep down I didn't believe I could ever harm my wife and daughter.

"I'm worried about you; it's just not safe."

"We've talked about this Logan. We both agreed that uprooting Lizzy wasn't the best decision and with the baby coming she already feels neglected. She loves school, her friends; she's safe and I limit the places I go. I'm always with Terri, Naomi and mom comes over twice a week, so I appreciate your concern, but honey there's nothing to worry about." Kathy was exhausted and refused the idea of compromise, "Will you be home late again tonight?"

All couples have that innate ability to be loving and caring as they twist the knife in deeper. On the night of Laura's death I hadn't come home at all. Covering up the affair with Tamara was beginning to fester and when discovered would eventually become a full blown war. I knew then and sensed it in her voice now.

"No sweetheart I plan on being home at a reasonable hour. I have a lot of work, but I'll do my best to keep it from being too late." *Besides I needed to keep up the appearance of a loving and kind family man. You probably want me and Lizz out of the house so you can bring your Jezebel home. You just want to get rid of me, was that it? It would be Sodom and Gomorrah.* Sometimes I wondered whether a certain priest had clued her in, "I have to get back to work. I'll see you tonight."

"Love you."

"Love you too."   There was one more thing that I had to take care of. It was already mid-afternoon and it was time to make amends.

TODD ANDREW DAVIS
THE CONSUMPSTION OF ANGELA
CHAPTER XXXVI

I patted the steering wheel, dropped my hand down to the gear shift knob, threw the car in reverse and headed for the Royal East Hotel. This was a good day and it deserved commemoration. I was elated as we raced back to my little bungalow. The traffic wasn't too intense and we were making excellent time. I stopped at a liquor store; got a double barrel of JD, a pack of cigs and some cheese doodles. I had visions of Logan's lovely wife and my cock was ready to split the bitch. This mission was based on how much pain I could extract; how much sorrow and despair I could inflict. Even though the course I followed occasionally deviated, The Plan was more suitable to someone of my stature. I helped the bitch out of the car then towards the elevator and up to the seventh floor of my piece-of-shit hotel room. It was a definite upgrade to the transient paradise where I had previously stayed. The cops did their customary raids on the hookers, pimps and junkies who called the Royal East home. I shoved the whore onto the bed and gave her another taste of the heroine until she was flying high like a space cadet. I locked up, went into the bathroom, tied myself off and altered my state of being. I stripped down, jumped into bed and slammed that pussy hard enough to crack her pelvis. She didn't scream or cum, but I got off on the tears that streaked down her face. She was hot and moist with every thrust. I dismounted, bound her hands and feet with duct tape and sealed her mouth shut.

I held her foot and with knife in hand I devoured the first of her toes then drank the sweet nectar from the open wound. I placed the remaining two toes in an ice bucket and dangled the third from my mouth like a cigar. I bandaged her up; the fright in her eyes was a clarion call of fear. The night had just begun and her blood just started to flow. It was all so intoxicating; the heroine, the whisky, the VIP invitation into my brother's world. I made an incision into the sciatic artery and her veins gushed forth a Texas oil strike. The bed was flooded with blood, my cock at attention; I pulled her body closer and fucked her in the ass. She was a treat for the ages, her body nicer than I had envisioned; I was thankful that I took the time to indulge. My mouth fished for a finger and when I snagged one she let out a muffled yelp. I bit down hard and violently thrashed my head side to side. I could feel her finger dislocate in the grip of my jaw. I pounded her ass harder as I tore my prize free; warm sticky blood coated my face. I pulled out, flipped her on her back and tore her left nipple completely off; mother's milk. I wanted more; I wanted to taste her insides but most of all I wasn't ready to cum, not yet. It would have spoiled the sensation and I wanted to feel her body writhe with pain and pleasure. I leaned back and admired my work then punched her in the face as hard as I could. I wondered at what point she had finally come to the realization that there was no hope left for her. Maybe it was when I first cracked her one at the bus stop that she sensed it wasn't going to be her day. This gift would be her finest moment in her short life and I acknowledged that, even if the concept of sacrifice had escaped her. She had made the tedious formality of spying on my brother more gratifying. It had been so long since I fed that you would have thunk I was on a diet. I emptied my whisky bottle on her stomach and lapped up every drop, every hemoglobin and every morsel until I was full.

She was done; her life withered away as her last breath escaped her lips. I finished cutting the rest of her fingers and toes and placed them in the tiny compartment in the hotel freezer. I felt an overwhelming sense of déjà vu. I paused and tried desperately to hang on to the feeling, but the sensation passed as quickly as it came. I carried her body to the tub and I continued dismembering her in sections. I decided to take her with me until I found a suitable dump site. It took a few hours to properly package Angela. I removed the sheets, flipped the mattress and did some general tidying up. The blankets were okay to place on the bed but the bed sheets were beyond ruined; I would have to grab another set from the maid's push cart. Angela parts were stowed away neatly in the inner compartment of my duffle bag. I went to the bathroom, washed then slung the duffle over my shoulder with her body dangling low at my side. I casually walked to the service elevator and pressed the button for the lobby. The maids were of Hispanic ancestry and nodded politely in my direction. They acted coy and uninterested in drawing attention to themselves; maybe they knew what I was. Irregardless, trouble sought is trouble found. One little tight ass rode down three flights with me avoiding eye contact and conversation, maybe she thought I was with INS. Lucas had his annoying tendencies; he thought he had kept me on a relatively short leash and with a few exceptions I had adhered to The Plan. In the end I was a hunter; I had to kill, I had to feed and I hated being banished to the darkness or feeling like a neutered cat. "Anonymity," Lucas said, "that's what will keep you free. Your problem is that you're too reactionary." He didn't want me to take too many chances or kill without thinking. "Adhere to The Plan." He was right not to offend me so I played his game; I was a lion with natural born instincts that could never be tamed.

TODD ANDREW DAVIS
PREACHER BOY
CHAPTER XXXVII

True Wiseman seek-out others in a time of disheartenment. I didn't know why but I couldn't shake the feeling Father Daugherty had the answers to what was happening in Ravenswood.

"You know Logan there isn't a man that walks the earth that I fear, but whatever's taken to slaughtering people like cattle has shaken me to my foundation," said Father Daugherty, "The number of parishioners that show up every Sunday has been dwindling and the panic that fills them is unsettling… I don't know how to console them anymore. My words are no match for the blood that has been spilled in our streets. I want to help you Logan but I am afraid what I have to tell you would do more harm than good."

"Tim I'm out of options. If there is anything you can do to shed any light I would greatly appreciate it. I know lately things between us have been pretty shitty, but we've been friends forever and legally were still brothers. I apologize for my behavior the last time around; my actions were repulsive and I hate the thought of losing your friendship." I slowly exhaled, "Tim, I know somehow what happened at Chancellor's Manor years ago has something to do with the killer stalking Ravenswood today. You know something, I saw it in your eyes; I need to understand what's happening to me."

We walked alongside the dimly lit street lamps on One Downy Street three blocks away from St. Joseph. It seemed that every dog in neighborhood barked at us from atop front porches and behind mesh gates. The sun had set long ago and the cold kiss of winter was glued to our backsides.

"Logan, the evening you asked me to go with you to the Mansion struck me like an anvil," Timmy's face was solemn, "I saw the sincerity in your eyes, I didn't refuse you out of sheer fright or reluctance to help. I was stupefied."

"Padre you're not making sense."

"Let me finish."

"Sorry."

"I was in disbelief. The Mansion had once been your family home," Timmy placed his hand on my shoulder, "Logan I truly apologize. I had hoped you had been able to vanquish all those horrors from your childhood, but I never forgot."

"I have brothers?" I asked, but knew it as fact.

"Liam and Lucas; you were one of triplets," he said in quiet disbelief.

The gears clicked in my head and it all began to make sense. The ghost of the little girl I'd seen in the mansion was a child my parents had kidnapped; she had escaped a particularly torturous session before begin dragged back to their room. I was about ten and I knew whatever had happened it was better her than me. The bald man who had got the drop on me in the basement of the mansion was Tobias; a hideous demon who was also my father. Everything I saw in that house happened during different points of my life. Sara, the ghost that attacked me in the woods, bore the image of a girl my dad had stashed in his torture chamber. I was thirteen when my father wanted to make me a man; I refused to fuck her and he beat me unmercifully then showed me how it was done. There were probably dozens of bodies scatter underneath the grounds of my birthplace. I remembered that my mother's mind had been just as twisted. She fully participated and even added to his depravity. My brothers and I were bait used to lure innocent children from the sanctuary of their yards and into the darkness of their graves. Of all the dead Sara had haunted my dreams the most. She wasn't just another guinea pig, but one of my father's prized possessions. A beautiful girl who wasn't a day over fifteen; she had lasted longer than most of them. I was in the cabin in the woods playing army when she had bolted from the main house. She'd assumed she had stumbled upon a safe harbor far away from the horrors of the mansion. I can still see the doorknob violently turning as she rushed in; her legs gave way and she crumbled to the floor. I leaned against the door and pushed it closed. Her plaid skirt had been torn and streaks of blood and excrement ran down the inner portion of her white thighs. Her face was swollen, her eyes lost and when she saw me her heart sank. I knew the immorality that had been bestowed upon my brothers and what they must have done to her. She was petrified of me, but I convinced her of my heart's innocence.

Lucas burst into the cabin before I could ferry her to safety. He was enraged and his eyes burned wildly, "Dad in here!

Dad!" he screamed and moments later both my parents

stepped through the doorway.

My dad wrenched Sara's shaking body from my arms and pulled her out by her hair. Her wrists bore deep grooves of handcuffs and that day was the beginning of the end for her. I sat up on the floor and tightly held a piece of Sara's torn blouse; Lucas smiled wickedly then kicked me in the right temple. My mother comforted me by spitting in my face and stared at me with utter contempt. I raised my head; Liam had his trousers down and squatted over my face, "You're lucky faggot I wasted all my shit on her."

The door slammed; I lay on the floor with my eyes closed and head spinning. I realized I wasn't alone; my father belt in hand kicked and punched me, "You motherfucker! You Goddamn motherfucker! I give you everything! And you're nothing! A fucking coward! The weak link. I would have killed you long ago if it weren't for that cunt mother of yours!" His breathing was extremely erratic, "Test me again boy and you'll see how far my charity goes." He punched me repeatedly in the throat.

I don't know how long the beating lasted; I just remember spending the next couple of days balled up on the cabin floor. I knew it was pointless; the cabin in the woods was just another extension of my parent's playhouse. *Why I tried to help her was beyond me.* 'Sara Jane Carter,' her name smoldered within me. The name on the gravestone; the ghost I had followed into the woods. The old graveyard predated the Civil War and made the house and property a landmark safe from demolition. What people hadn't realized was that most of the occupants were from the twentieth century and it had provided my dad with easy access to a dump site. His victims were buried in that graveyard sometimes two or three in a single plot. Nobody would ever be suspicious of a man tending to his own land while preserving the history of this great nation. Their sexual perversity was the tip of the iceberg and inflicting as much pain as humanly possible was what really got them off. They'd use pliers to snap fingers and toes; my mom would sit on a child's chest while my dad pulled teeth or plucked eyes from sockets. They would castrate young boys and rape little girls. They had special rooms for different activities and encouraged our participation. It was where I differed from my brothers, anything I did was forced; I didn't have the backbone or the stomach. Liam was all too eager to please them and took pride in luring innocence's into the jaws of madness. I hated him as much as I did Lucas. I remember my dad building a special torture rack. He bound feet and hands with chains and used a hand crank to stretch limbs beyond the brink. Just for Sara's punishment, he retrofitted his torture rack with a motor; 'That's what you get for running away.' A horrible mad man who had antiseptically devised a plan to maximize the amount of pain he could inflict on a human being with no more emotion than filling out a crossword puzzle. She'd been stripped nude, laid spread eagle with her feet strapped and he fucked the virginity out of her. You would rather be sold into slavery than be on the wrong side of my father's hatred. He once exclaimed that they were better fucks during torture than before or after. Her suffering went on for endless hours which turned into unending days.

"Please stop, please make him stop!" I covered my head with a pillow in an effort to block out the sound of her pain. In the end I did help her; I released her. I snuck in her room one night with a screwdriver and wrench in hand. Her face was purple and her neck battered and bruised. I shifted my eyes back up to hers and tried with all my might to break the chains; my hands bled from the effort. After several failed attempts, I did my best to console her. There was nothing left to do so I went back to my room and returned with the pillow I used to block out her cries. She looked at me and at first was terrified.

"You'll be safe now, he won't hurt you anymore. I promise," I placed the pillow gently over her head and with the full weight of my body held it in place.

Not long after Sara's failed escape my mother started to have panic attacks and feared our family secret would be exposed. My dad agreed to no more outsiders and that's when their insanity turned on us. Most of my childhood I had wished my parents dead and one day poof, everyone disappeared and I was alone. When they were gone so was the boy that once bore their name; I was free, free to become anyone I wanted. Tim didn't speak another word until we made it back to the church. He knew I'd been locked in an eternal battle with my emotions. He put his hand on my shoulder as he walked by my side. Our goodbyes weren't deeply heartwarming or memorable. I got in my car and drove aimlessly into the night. I had locked it all in a vault and left it to rot. It was just a matter of time; I was a ticking bomb. I was born with the DNA blueprint of a killer; it was who I was and my life's blood was forever tainted by insanity. *What was it that triggered my madness? Had it been the wink of an eye Jessica gave me at the bar? Did she remind me of all those fair haired girls my dad brought home? Did she remind me of Sara? Laura, sweet, sweet Laura is that why I killed you too? Had Allen been a casualty of my affections for her?*

I needed to determine a new timeline; one that involved me. I had to revisit each murder, each crime scene. It made perfect sense internally, I was subconsciously protecting myself. *What have I done?* Would I really collect the evidence to seal my fate? I didn't need a high powered attorney who could plea bargain it down to insanity. I wanted it, needed it over. Even Kathy didn't know the real me, just the made up mumbo jumbo parts I let her see. I invented this new Logan and my surname Crenshaw was Tim's mother's maiden name. His father had nothing to do with the wayward kid from across the tracks; however his mother had enough influence on her own to legally adopt me. There were always rumors and questions: 'How did my parents die? How screwed up were their sons? It was charred embers from another lifetime and from the ashes I was reborn, but to be born I first had to die. And I was more than willing; I saw a multitude of psychiatrist, physiotherapists, hypnotherapist, child advocates, counselors, doctors and was probed and prodded as if I were a captive of an alien abduction. I survived it all and had lived a good life; my brothers on the other hand bore the fruit of a rotted tree. Liam tried to cut the craziness from his veins, but in the end he became one of them. I had forged my life from the fires of hell and was left with no blood ties to the earthbound world. Lucas and Liam were dead to me, the deep wounds healed over even the atrocities of my childhood kept secrets which rivaled Nazi death camps. Tim was the only one who knew the truth outside the family and no one ever told a soul. We had kept our parents' secret even in death; like good sons, sons of the damned.

Where were my brothers now? I knew Liam was a lifer in a mental institution in Texas and there was talk of Lucas raising Liam's fucked up child in Virginia or South Carolina last I heard. I was truly blessed to have Tim and his mother enter my life at that crucial time. I was homeschooled, until the twelfth grade and finished my senior year in a new school where I met Kathy, stole Kathy from Tim, married her and moved away from Ravenswood.

I'd gone to the police academy and was a well respected, tough no nonsense cop in New Rachel. I had carefully sculpted the perfect family and erased the memory of my former self. Nobody knew my identity when I returned home almost two decades later; not even me. Once again a psychotic killer had the body count rising in Ravenswood and this time I realized it might be me. I was just like my old man after all and now the words of a friend, holy man, my only true brother, may have unlocked the vault to a murderous past. The walls around my psyche had crumbled and unknown to the both of us was whether the old me was back in Ravenswood or something much worse had been let out.

TODD ANDREW DAVIS
THE PRODICAL SON
CHAPTER XXXVII

I was jazzed after the slice and dice I preformed on my Angie; out of sight and out of mind, however I still had plenty of work to do. I walked into Pedro's a Mexican restaurant; the establishment had its customary wetback employee's to give it that special authenticity that gringos alone couldn't pull off. Carlos, the beady eyed bastard chef was banging Rachel, the blue eyed waitress bimbo. I wasn't about to stick my dick were that cockroach had been so the job was purely professional. I hunted Rachel with Angie's sweet smell on my clothing. She was a decoy, a clay pigeon and her only purpose was to keep the pigs fat and fed as the final stages of The Plan emerged. I preferred to do my own scouting, but Lucas told me she was an easy mark and if he was wrong it didn't matter I was prepared to hack my way out of trouble. She was pleasant to look at and her fluent Spanish enabled her to communicate with the help and patrons. She was defiantly my type, young, blonde and her legs went on forever. I was so tempted that I might actually fuck this one despite the health risk. Rachel and Carlos lived together in a little bungalow across town, she got off around eleven and he stayed to mop up after hours. I'd have nearly two hours to kill before her little brown boy came home. The drive took twenty-five minutes and the neighborhood had me locking my doors. I could hear and feel a boom box's thumping base emanating from one of the haciendas. A couple of Mexicono's were scattered throughout their lawns, driveways and porches and made the ability to isolate myself a logistical nightmare. There was no place to take shelter or alley to hide so I followed her up to her doorstep.

"Rachel?" I said.

She turned; her arms were full of packages of food she'd pilfered from the restaurant, "I'm sorry, do I know…."

She had inserted the key into the lock and when I punched her throat she staggered backward and we were inside her house. I juggled her food for a second as she released her bags and fell to the floor. Tears filled her eyes and she screamed. I kicked the door shut and in the darkness, I beat the living tar out of her. I dragged her limp body to the bedroom bound, gagged and blindfolded her naked body before she came to.

"Carlo's says you like it rough," I shook her head. "What not talking to me? That's okay, you will."

I flipped her on her side and fucked her chocolate cherry until it bled, didn't take long. I inserted my knife deep into her shoulder blade and the blood squirted everywhere. I punched her hard in the back of her head just to settle her down. I rolled her over and gave her a nice permanent four inch scar on her right cheekbone. She thrashed around as I bit the tip of her tongue. I removed the bandana from her head. Stark panic and tears flooded her eyes. I jerked off on her face then hit her so hard I knocked her out. I retrieved a white negligee and my exacto knife from my car. I dressed her, strapped her down and posed her like Connie. Then I cut away the thin skin on her eyelids. When I finished I checked her vitals, did some minor house cleaning and disappeared into the night. *I knew I'd fuck her;* I laughed and left her alive just as instructed. Now it was time to refocus. Again the moon was my companion. The Plan was mandated, ordained by the Devil and I could feel the electricity coursing within. This would be unlike all the others; it was the beginning of the end. I left my car at the top of the hill and walked the rest of the way. Lucas had spelled out everything in great detail. He told me that Satan had spoken to him directly and devised The Plan. I was at his command; the perfect executioner to see the deed done. A good and loyal soldier must obey without question and kill with purpose. A good solider rises steadily in the ranks and reaps in the spoils. Lucas preached to me that I couldn't allow myself to be distracted; I must learn my place. He was always persistent and cautioned me to focus; be mindful of the details. I was dumbfounded. *Why did Satan choose a court jester like Lucas? I should have his ear. I am a true warrior. Dear brother you're treading on thin ice.* At this stage this was what I wanted; what we all wanted. *Am I a fool? Was I just a pawn?* I had to keep my wits.

I strolled down the dirt path, my palms slick with anticipation. My focus was solely on Logan's suffering; that was more like it. My brother would endure the pain of shared misery and bear the scars just long enough to know he was responsible. I was a wild animal that had been set free to do what I do best. I walked to the front door and pressed the doorbell. Ding dong, I heard her scurrying around and a minute later the door slowly opened. Her expression was priceless; *if only I had a camera.*

TODD ANDREW DAVIS
LIVING IN A BOX
CHAPTER XXXVIII

"So what is he teaching us? To love one another, family, community, we are not alone in this journey called life. Experience it, breathe it in and accept life's trials and tribulations for what they are. Some wallow in self-pity, and are mired in depression and who see burden instead of fulfillment. Christ taught us through his deeds as well as his words. No man is greater than any other; from the peasant to the powerful, your station in life has no bearing in God's Kingdom. We're all sinners and we're all blessed for having such an understanding Lord and Savior. I realize how difficult recent times have been and as I look around I see my flock has waned." Father Daugherty banged his hand on the pulpit, "The economy has affected us all. The blood of our neighbors has been spilled, but we know life is not about earthly possessions, fast cars, big homes and huge 401ks. Because if that's what motivates you, sustains you, gives you the reason to live, then you haven't learnt the lessons Jesus taught. We search for answers, but the wickedness brought into God's House was delivered by us! We've created the things we detest. Cries in the night go unanswered because they are not cries of our children or our love ones; somebody will console them. Someone with more time, more patience, more love to give than I. We're reaping what we sow: the abused children, the teenage runaway who becomes the pregnant teenage prostitute, the outcast little boy who becomes a murderer. You think God brought the Devil to our shores? No! We created him by turning our backs to the words his son has preached? We're a society of addicts; whether its cable tv, prescription medication or the gazillion other comforts we mightily cling to. If only we held as tight to our children or to the bible these horrid killings could have been prevented. All of us our culpable, our blame is evenly shared." He stared at a few of the faces that seemed to pious, "Oh so you think you're not the sinner and your neighbor is? That it's okay to pass the blame after all, I donated to the victims of Katrina or Haiti so I'm absolved. The sickness grows in all of us and flourishes in those forgotten. They're the ones who desperately need to hear God's voice. If you allow evil to fester it will, if you leave evil unchecked then a wide birth of destruction will lie in its wake. It feeds off our weakness, our benevolence, our ignorance. Evil in its purist form is an equal match for good. It can extinguish God's flame and turn our hearts black as coal. Fear evil; beware of its daily temptations. Evil is powerful and its greatest advantage is complacency." He sighed deeply. "These four walls, built of wood, glass, brick and sweat are just a blanket for us to hide. Stay under the covers long enough and evil will go away. Hear no, see no, speak no, if only it were that simple. If we do not listen to the cries in the night or look into the eyes of a desperate soul or speak of the injustice we see then evil will visit all of us in forms you can't even imagine. Your beautiful child grown and behind bars, your adulteress spouse, your money grubbing family, lying lawyers, crooked cops, judges and politicians are products of a failing society. This is a test, one we're miserably failing. Heed my words, the Devil will not lie down, he will not rest, he will not stop until each and every one of us has denounced our faith. He is unrelenting, unrepentant and in certain sectors of society," he leaned over the pulpit, "some which are represented here today in this very congregation, he has won over to his side.

The writing is on the wall, but we're too illiterate to read it. I have given you the words; preach them, teach them, believe in them and our treasures in heaven will be preserved or let him in and let him win. Let the darkness fill your souls like an eclipse, let the hunger of knowledge be the steel against the hell in which your survival will depend. His army grows, his conviction strengthens and his boldness is no longer tempered. We sit in the path of his destruction and the total annihilation in which he seeks." He held his hands out, "God bless my children, all my children, rich, poor, Caucasian, African American, Native American, Hispanic, Asian, Pacific Islander," he paused, "Did I leave anyone out?" Brief laughter erupted from a congregation that sat enthralled and had the devil driven from their souls. "I can't underline strong enough the seriousness of our plight," Father Daugherty tapped his finger on the bible, "and even if I were standing at the pulpit with my voice raspy and only one soul out of an evaporating sea remained I would not stop. My words mimic his and his word I shall continue to speak. In the face of evil I will not falter, I will not sway; I am a pillar, a white column holding this House of God up for all to see. I am a beacon of light that guides God's humble servants to his doorstep. I am his voice, inspirational, motivational and I am his personification. His spirit bleeds into me and nourishes my soul so that I can teach you his wisdom. I inhale his breath as my tongue speaks his word. My body houses his spirit and his hand guides pen to paper to create my sermons. I am him, he is me."

I waited thirty-five minutes after his arousing sermon. His parishioners were from all walks of life; a cornucopia of souls who listened with bated breath. As they filed out of the church they stared at me incredulously; *judge not less thee be judged.* I must have been a mess; Laura's murder had my brain on in maximum overdrive. Admittedly it was a rush at first; the thrill of the crime was part of the allure I guess. What bigger thrill ride is there than murder? It's an intolerable crime in which the final outcome may result in death of the perpetrator. *Would a true gambler place a wager on his life?* Murder was a high stakes game of Russian roulette. Your physical being was at stake along with your reputation and livelihood. If I escaped prosecution, the stigma attached to my good name would outweigh any exoneration.

"Logan," Tim extended his hand and sat down. I scooted over; his body abused the pew as it absorbed his weight. He sank down next to me more tired and drained than I was.

"I would have given you a standing ovation if I weren't so exhausted."

"I thought you were an atheist Logan?"

"Shhh, he might hear you," I pointed heavenward.

"That's the point now isn't it? I need all the help I can get," Timmy smiled and every time it made its scheduled appearance it rang hollow, an imitation, a forgery, a bad one at that..

"You're decent enough salesmen, but you're not going to be able to convert this old roadster, I have too many miles."

"Lately you haven't been able to get enough of this place. I was hoping I was rubbing off."

"I have a high tolerance for pain," I observed his demeanor and listened intently to the slightest inflection in his voice. He knew I hadn't come back just to throw barbs at each other, "I have a confession to make. Ummm, how do I go about this?"

"We can move to one of the confessionals if that would make you more comfortable?"

"It wouldn't, but thanks for the offer. I'm trying to sort out where I should begin. I'm not seeking absolution Tim," I knew he was disappointed. "How about we go to your office and polish off that shitty brandy you have stowed away?"

"That shitty brandy has guided me through plenty of shitty times."

We left the hard wooden torture racks and walked to the back of the church. The wind had been taken out of his sails and his step wasn't as lively as I'd been accustomed to. He fished his pocket for a key, unlocked his office and plumped down in his leather recliner.

"It was a donation," he mused as he rubbed the chair's arms, "and a damn comfortable one indeed. So Logan, what's troubling you this time?"

"I was about to ask you the same thing," his phony baloney grin returned. "When we talked earlier…"

"Yesterday? The day before last? Last week? Specify Logan."

Tension bubbled just below the surface. He was on defense, yet I hadn't called a play. There was no fake attempt at an apology and the brandy didn't make its customary appearance, just the two of us sizing each other up. It was a shame cause right now I could have used a stiff drink.

"You were extremely helpful the last time we spoke," I changed my approach; the fucking snake knew more about my life than I did. "My memories of events are much more lucid now. I just had a couple of things I needed to put to rest." The desk drawer opened and he placed two shot glasses side by side. "Thank God," I said joyfully.

"I'm in the beginning stages of Parkinson's Disease," his hands were unsteady as he poured. He felt the burn of my stare. "My coordination eludes me at times, I'm just grateful my voice remains strong and I am blessed that I can still carry out my duties. Unfortunately, things have been getting progressively worse." His voice struck a somber tone, "I guess it's the price we pay for growing old."

"Older, we're not old yet. The graying temples are a distinguishing mark, not the onset of senility. Yes it's true we aren't kids anymore; children can be unwittingly deceitful, they don't know what it means to be honorable in the true sense of the word," I took a sip of the brandy. "I'll get straight to the point. You knew my parents..."

"Logan, enough already, you need to move on."

"Hear me out Tim," I put my hand up and he nodded his head reluctantly, "there are certain facts unique to this investigation. Two of the victims were posed and dressed in white negligees. I remember my dad....."

"And you're suggesting?" He relaxed, "Coincidences happen Logan, or has your father miraculously risen from the dead? It's ludicrous. Are you listening to yourself?"

"I think there is an overwhelming probability that someone who had experienced the horrors of that house has become a copycat to those crimes. What I am about to tell you never leaves this room; understood?" He nodded his head in agreement; my eyes searched his for understanding. "I woke up next to one of the victims. She had been strangled, windpipe crushed, and beaten to death. I'm a fuck I know; I had sex with this girl and for the life of me I can't remember what happened the night before. I have been twisted and jaded by this investigation; all the evidence points to me as the number one suspect. I'm sure locked away there were more memories festering, waiting their turn to drive me to the point of madness. There are only two other people besides me that knew the depths of my parent's insanity. The white clothing the victims wore is symbolic of purity, virginity and all of them were posed suggestively. The white clothing is a link, a message, sent from beyond the grave and not even the killer knows why he does what he does. I dressed Laura and copied the crime scene from another victim I may have been responsible for named Connie. But now I think I might not have invented a crime out of whole cloth, but it was something I learned."

"Logan, first and foremost you're no killer."

"I appreciate that Tim, honestly I do, but I fabricated a crime scene specifically Connie's. Why? I think subconsciously out of all the murders, it seemed right somehow."

"That's kind of a leap to say one death makes you responsible for all the others, it doesn't prove anything, nothing at all Logan."

"I am aware of that, but for whatever reason I have this gut feeling. I practically confessed a murder to you. I haven't been in the right frame of mind as of late, but I know that somehow that house has something to do with all of this. I can only base the evidence of this case in what I know is reality. Right now, I'm trying to track down Liam and find out his status and whereabouts. Lucas created an alternate identity for himself a long time ago and disappeared off the grid. If anyone found out who I was, what I was... because of how sensitive this is it can't go through the department."

"Logan, I'll help you where I can, of course, but my resources are limited."

"Am I being punished?" my voice was filled with uncertainty.

"For what Logan?"

"The shit I put Kathy through and my infidelity for starters."

"By whom are you being punished? You claim to be an atheist so God certainly isn't punishing you. Listen, only you can place this much sorrow in your own heart and only you can release it.

You need to reconcile with yourself. Speak with your brothers, except them into your life; you're not the only one lost. They also live with the scars of their childhood. They needed you then and I am willing to bet they still do."

"I need to speak with her."

"What? Who?" His brain finally registered, "No way Logan, that's fucking out of the question."

"She's the only one who can help me, please Tim I'm begging you."

"Mom is barely coherent, she mostly rambles; for God's sake she suffering from Alzheimer's."

"I went back to the house," I said; his eyes widened as if a breeze had passed through his soul and he became even more uncomfortable. "It's not my imagination running wild. That house is more than wood, brick and mortar; it embodies much more than that." I sat with elbows on knees and rubbed my eyebrows with my fingers, "What did you see when you went inside?"

"You know Logan you really haven't been to church this much in years," he chuckled disturbingly. "It's not what I saw it's what I felt. The sadness, the pain, the suffering, that house made me a man of God, not the betrayal that you and Kathy dealt me."

We sat silently across from each other, the church all but empty now. Incense filled the stagnant air, candles were lit to adorn the Alter of Christ and in his House we brought forth the demons that wished to vanquish him. Only in the House of the Lord did Father Tim feel safe and protected. This wasn't the bull-shitter, the prognosticator, the forever optimistic God fearing preacher I had known. This was a scared little boy of yesteryear, a boy of time past, time forgotten; this was my old friend.

"I had no way of communicating the unspeakable," he began to talk, "there are no words for such a haunting experience. Even when you told me the pains you suffered I couldn't express the evil that entered my soul. I felt a war inside me and an urge to deny all things created by God. With the simple turn of the wheel I could have been Satan's executioner; I was teetering in the wind. The mansion is a kind of purgatory, a weigh station for the soul and it forces you to choose sides. I learned that those with little faith were forever doomed. I observed a sequence of heinous crimes and my faith was tested well beyond its limits and was given a choice of which path to follow. I bounded the staircase to the second floor and watched two ghastly demons torture a little girl without remorse. I had been made to bear witness and petition for your parent's souls. I was their conduit, their jury and their judge before God. Only before I could enter judgment, I became the boy they sodomized and hung upside down from his penis. Mercifully your mother slit my throat; I remember it as if it were yesterday. A child skinned alive, a girl raped by your father; I wear the scars of the evil perpetrated against the young and innocent. The fate of their souls was placed in my hands."

I couldn't believe what I was hearing. I was confused, angered beyond belief and too afraid to interrupt. I feared Tim would change the subject or clam up; I sat silent, motionless.

"When I went to see you one summer's day, Lucas answered the door. He wore white tennis shorts and was barefoot and bare-chested. I thought nothing of it, it was smoldering outside," he paused to remember things in the correct sequence. "I asked if you were home. 'No!' Your brother always had a way with words. In the background I could see Liam's head tilted back and a tissue stuffed in his nostrils. I knew it was him right away, your hair was a lighter shade than your brothers from the sun drenched summers we spent bike riding. Your mother scolded Lucas. 'Don't just stand there like an idiot invite him in.' Looking back I should've left and gone home. Then I saw her," a glib frown emerged, "your mother had a beehive hairdo and her arm was around a beautiful girl with long strawberry blonde hair; I'll never forget her face. In hindsight I realize she had been a ploy and it worked. I was introduced to her, but her name escapes me. Your mother brought me fresh squeezed lemonade and implored me to wait five minutes for your return. Nearly fifteen passed and I was ushered into the back parlor; suddenly your father appeared in the passageway. He was shirtless as well; I remember his handlebar mustache, bald head and sweaty body. His words dripped from his lips, 'She's ready now.'" He fell silent for a moment. "I was escorted to another room and I saw a girl bound and tethered on top a massive marble table. I felt dizzy, the lemonade had been spiked. I wasn't me, I wasn't myself and before I knew it your mother slid my shorts past my hips. She manipulated my penis with her hand and she performed orally. The white dress the girl wore was torn off and I was forced to lie on top of her. 'Please just you,' she whispered in my ear as I penetrated her. 'Their monsters; a family of fucking monsters,' she cried. Your mother chanted, 'Fuck that bitch raw.' Your dad joined in, 'Fuck that virgin pussy! Fuck her good boy! Fuck her, fuck her, fuck her, fuck her!' they all chanted in unison. 'He came already,' proclaimed your mother, 'you owe me ten daddy. I told you they were both virgins.' Your dad grabbed me by the waist and hoisted me up in midair. The girl and I were taken upstairs and tossed inside the master bedroom. I got on my hands and knees and begged her for forgiveness; she lay on the bed nude and traumatized. I tried to make amends, but I failed to realize what she already knew. When your parents returned they took pleasure in repeatedly raping the both of us. I had never been so humiliated in my life. They attacked us like wild animals, snorting and growling and throughout the horrible ordeal she held my hand and stared deep into my soul; 'it's okay.' She saw how petrified I was and tried to console me. I never intended to hurt her; my heart sank as I gripped her hand tight. Even that filthy pig Lucas did his worst; he pressed his naked body on top of mine. That was my memory of being thirteen and the day I became one of them; I never told anyone until now. Blood was on me, I grew cold inside; I had my own nightmares to contend with. I had nowhere to turn so I internalized the hatred with suicidal thoughts. I was a good Catholic, went to Mass and the whole nine, but I never confessed. It ate away at me and rotted my soul. I always figured it had been my fault; I violated her, regardless of my youth or level of intoxication. I should have refused."

He poured himself another shot, "I realize now if not for Liam intervening on my behalf, my wound up on the side of a milk carton. That incident, that moment in time kept me from ever achieving a relationship with Kathy, or any other woman. I had been so ashamed that any kind of physical intimacy was out of the question. I couldn't even find the words to tell you. That fateful afternoon, years later when we egged each other to go inside Chancellor's Manor it wasn't my bravado that was on full display. The summer of my sixteenth birthday my friends didn't have an inkling of who you were; by then you had been living with my family for nearly three years. I figured you of all people would balk at the notion of entering that house. I guess you had successfully washed away the past, so I didn't chicken out like the others. I thought the house was calling out to me, reclaiming me," he sighed. He arched his back, sat up straight and I could physically see Father Timothy return from the revulsion of the past before he spoke another word.

"My soul needed to be cleansed. Over the decades the creeps and ghouls that once inhabited that house had less and less to do with the Logan you've become. When I entered, I felt the dead cry out and heard the tacit words of the Devil. There is evil living and breathing in all of us and he offered me false compassion. I contemplated my life; I would of committed suicide if I could have summoned the courage. God didn't swoop in to save my soul; he was nowhere to be found. So why didn't I let the darkness eclipse my soul? It was his test. A test of my faith in God; the Devil only tempts the weak. God has faith in all of us. The sickness in your parents was an inherent evil; their souls were corrupted long before they took their first breath. God helped me excise those fucking demons and send them back into the blackness they crawled out of. I overcame my hedonistic temptations, overcame the urge that tugged at me night and day. God made me free; I had sinned and had been sinned upon. Jesus died for the absolution of all our sins; in God's infinite wisdom he knew the tribulations we would face. If we cannot see the light, it's because our backs were turned, our hearts guarded, our eyes closed; we need only to believe. Is that so much to ask for? The ability to experience true happiness as well as gut wrenching pain: living, breathing, seeing, touching, loving, dying there all such wondrous gifts given to us by a merciful God and yet we want more. We're forever in his debt, for God has chosen us, among all others."

"I didn't come here to be preached to," I started to get up.

"Logan, I began my transformation from boy to man when my heart found God. He absolved my sins and welcomed me into his flock. Now, I see evil on a daily bases; beaten and battered women and poor hapless children from all walks of life. I've seen destitute men incapable of finding their way out from under their burden. I've seen utter hopelessness and I've lived it. My job is to bring hope back into their lives; I am God's voice, his vessel and will never relinquish the fight. I feel God in these rafters above, shining through the panels of the stained glass, his gaze at the altar and his spirit moves me as I write my daily sermons. As strong as I feel the presents of the Lord in my church, I felt the darkness in that house. Satan dwells in that horrid place. It's a breeding ground, an abyss and my skin still crawls from the mere thought of it. I've prayed for you and continued to do so. I can see you're a good man and feel it in the depths of my soul. I've led the fight to tear down that unholy stain upon humanity and reduce it to a pile of rubble. But, that's another battle for another time; perhaps another man. However you cleansed the horror of your childhood, you're better off letting things be. I am and always will be your friend and brother Logan. If you seek answers that might aide you in your investigation, I am here for you."

"I can't turn back the clock and I can't shut down the memories; maybe I am beyond saving. Maybe I am tainted by the Devil's touch and the good in me died long ago. I don't have the same faith as you claim you have in me. I need to stop this killer, even if we're one and the same. And for reasons I quite don't understand myself, I need to see mom."

"I think she would actually enjoy seeing you again, but not regarding this matter. I wish you had stayed in touch with her, after all she is your mother too."

"I know, a badge makes you an officer of the law it doesn't turn assholes into saints; that you have to work out on your own."

Inside I was fuming that this pompous ass of a human kept the truth from me. It angered me beyond words that he had been a victim of my parent's debauchery and was just as willing to take it to the grave. His hand disappeared below his collar; he retrieved a gold chain and dangled a copper key. Father Tim removed the necklace and with one beefy hand motioned for me to follow. We took an elevator down two flights. I stayed close as we walked by torch light through an extravagant maze of tunnels. A set of lockers came into view and Tim held up the combination padlock to locker 442. He rotated the dial right, left, and then right again. The metallic lock dangled by one arm, he popped the door open and made the sign of the holy cross. He reached inside and pulled out a black steel case the size of a breadbox and handed it to me.

"Mom gave me this," he said almost too quietly to hear; "I've never opened it. She said it was yours and that one day you might want answers to your past. She can no longer provide the knowledge that you seek but, maybe what's inside here can shed some light on your past."

Part of me wanted to slug him. I'd been tormented, guilt ridden, lost. I had turned to him on several occasions and all along he held the trump card. I couldn't imagine the secrets that may be held within the contents of that box, but after reliving the past twenty-five years with a man who had withheld vital information, I wasn't about to open the box in his presence. I took the key and pocketed it and saw the disappointment in his eyes. The thing had become as precious as a newborn to him; I clutched the box to my chest and we returned topside.

.

"Logan, I meant what I said, you should see mother," he wrote down the name and address of her convalescent home. "I'm always here for you if you need me."

He was dying to know what lay inside; it was evident in his voice as well as his eyes. He had his chance and should have taken it long ago; I would have. "Okay Tim and thanks again," I tapped the box and its metallic heart echoed in response.

The salt trucks were fanning the major roads, whoever the genius was who had the idea to skimp on the salt and use sand on the side streets should have been tarred and feathered. I was angry, and mad at the world. What I truly wanted was the answers that the black box couldn't provide; they were locked away inside a diseased mind. I slowed and pulled over to the shoulder. My fingers tapped loudly on the box and I moved it from the passenger seat to my lap. The key felt as light as a feather and as slippery as an eel, I inserted it and turned the lock. The top angled back like a retro lunch pail and the inside was overstuffed with newspaper. I sifted through them thinking they were only used for packing, but I soon realize they were clippings and articles about me and my family. My original birth certificate and a letter were among several other official documents neatly tucked away. I turned the overhead dome light on and read details about my history.

Date July 1994

Dear Son:

Writing this letter pains me, it is not something I wished to do but as you can see I am a coward. This letter is to be read by you, upon my death. I have always thought of you as my biological child. The love Timothy has for you convinced me that you would be a welcomed addition to our family. I was so proud when you entered the police academy. You always went out of your way to help others. I use to joke; I had a son in the academy and one in the seminary, now just try and keep me out of heaven. You boys brought me the greatest gift a mother could ask for.

Over the years I watched as my boys grew into men and it warmed my heart at the thought of what great men you've both become. I did my very best to shield you from your past. No one outside the immediate family ever learned of the monstrosities you endured. There were unsubstantiated allegations; never convictions, just inquiries into the lives of your parents. I hope the contents contained within can not only help you with your past, but convince you of the kind and gentle soul you are. I hope I haven't caused you any undue pain for that was never my intention.

I love you with all my heart Logan.

Mom

I dug through English and European newspapers. The first one that caught my eye was Dutch; I opened the glove compartment and reached for my reading glasses. I inhaled, braced myself then began reading.

Belgique Chronicles (Belgium Chronicles)

3 December, 1953

Dumitru and Constantin Vasilescu two Romanian born citizens were questioned today concerning the disappearance of five year old Christen Bernhard Leitner and several other children who disappeared over the past several years. The couple operated a Brussels Orphanage for wayward children. "They were good people," one of the staff members commented yesterday morning. A source who wishes to remain anonymous reiterated, "There is a staff of twenty-three; anyone could have done this. It's prejudice to treat them like Gypsies, they came here to make a new life. They were inspirations and a testament of true love for all God's children, even the forgotten. Godspeed Constance and Dmitri, Godspeed. And this too shall pass." One boy, one poor soul's demise may have unearthed the real truth about the Vasilescu's. As of now they are awaiting extradition back to Romania. How did this tragedy happen in our backyard? Every child is a gift from the heavens. We are their protectors, each of them were our moral responsibility. We let down Christen, Melba, Crina, Haden, Claude, Susan, Andrea, Bella, Benjamin, and Camellia. Undoubtedly the mass grave discovered will continue to add to the list of missing children. The story will fade away overtime and everyone will return to their happy lives. However, tonight for our collective failures each and every one of us has blood on our hands. So when you fortunate tuck your little ones in tonight, say a prayer for the dead.

Konrad Mertens, Journalist:

Belgique Chronicles

România Times
16 March, 1963.

In God's House.

The founder of In God's House Dumitru Vasilescu and wife Constantin were under a three year investigation. The nearly one hundred strong congregation was fraught with rumors of incest, rape and polygamy, Young women told stories of the occult, Devil worshiping and animal sacrifices. Even human sacrifices were much ballyhooed. As in much of these abnormal society's adolescent boys are threats as the reach puberty. Vladimir Cerenkov, Lawyer for the Vasilescu's said, "There is no truth to the unsubstantiated balderdash that had been spat. They were never tried or convicted of a 1953 witch hunt that turned up several other prime suspects. In fact they were vindicated of any wrong doing and received an official apology from the Prime Minister himself. These ruthless allegations have haunted the Vasilescu's with absolutely no merit and now in their beloved Romania, they are being crucified all over again. These are good God fearing citizens. There is no cult, no wife swapping, incest, or any other ridiculous charge the government would have you believe. They want to live in peace and not be treated like mad gypsies who wish to corrupt all of us. I've been to their so called compound and there were no masked gunmen, just happiness and love."

Styiles Martian, Reporter:

Romania Times

LIVING IN A BOX

Ravenswood Beacon

August 4, 1988 The Socialites

So much has been made of the family on Bellport Drive. There are our lives, and then there are our 'real lives.' The ones we keep safely hidden from prying eyes and the narrow prism in which we all wish to be viewed. The Creeps of Ravenswood secrets were dark twisted nightmares that festered beneath the surface. The rumors of incestual deviance and their proclivity for young children has forever tarnished the reputation of Ravenswood's wealthiest class. These hidden truths came courtesy of stories across the Atlantic. Tales of the terror and blackened souls. Only their captives really knew the depths of degradation that brewed at the bottom of the family caldron. As a society we were blinded by the disguise they wore. Why did City Officials allow the community to become a breeding ground for child killers? Questions without answers, even the Mayor remains tight lipped three years later. Only the inhabits of Chancellor's Manor can tell the full story and they're nowhere to be found. What made a young son kill his parents in the middle of the night? And where was he being held? Why was there so much secrecy? Conspiracy theories abound and the sordid past remains buried in the tombs of the Chancellor. What other horrors dwell in the subconscious and warped psyche of their surviving heirs. Reported evidence destroyed that could have helped solve this mystery and others. Rumors that the family had donated a substantial amount of money to the development of Ravenswood during its infancy; perhaps that's why officials looked the other way. What lay within the walls of Chancellor's Manor? And where are the boys now? The house has been left abandoned, but is a part of a living trust and I am sure it will remain empty long after we've passed.

Armstrong Blackwell, Editor;

Ravenswood Beacon

I read so many articles that I was light headed. I opened my birth certificate: May 13, 1967 Good Samaritan Hospital, Chicago Illinois, Born 11:58 pm, five pounds six ounces, baby boy. Father Tobias Chancellor, Mother Abigail Constantin Chancellor. Lucas had been born fifteen minutes before me, and Liam at midnight. I leaned back into the leather bucket seats; Chancellor's Manor, their names had changed but the abuse had carried on. My parents were fucking parasites and they got exactly what they deserved. I came across another document that jumped out at me from Cedar Homes, Waco Texas. I skimmed through it, Liam Jarred Chancellor admitted September 1986. I didn't give a shit about his prognosis, his treatments; I wanted a phone number and address.

Something was off; I'd been so exhausted it hadn't even raised an eyebrow during our conversation. I staged Laura's crime scene and it was predicated on mimicking Connie's. The position of the body, the white negligee, Tim had witnessed the same thing. The girl inside my childhood home; the way her feet and hands were bound. According to Tim she wore a white dress. *What if that one symbolic gesture was formulated decades earlier in the psyche of the killer and manifested itself in Connie's murder?* I had been absent from the debauchery that took place the day Tim had described, but Lucas and Liam... and Tim were there. I knew that the girl had turned to maggot food long ago, but I was unaware of Lucas's whereabouts and unsure whether or not Liam was still institutionalized. That left me with Tim; an insane thought that couldn't be ruled out, after all Tim had been sexually abused by my family. *Logan would you listen to yourself; Tim was a priest for God's sake and your brother and friend.* We're all monsters; the difference is I know what I am. Maybe I had things backwards, it might be that our bloodline was defective and was something that I might have to remedy later. Other than exhausted, I wasn't sure how I felt after I'd left the church. The stars twinkled a little brighter, but did nothing to quell the uneasy feeling that I was getting closer to the truth. Tim's detailed recollection of the girl in white placed him squarely in my sights. The collar gave him the luxury of moving undetected and a priest had access into every corridor of society; people would have felt safe around a holy man. He was big enough, strong enough and crazy enough as I recalled, but his anger would be focused on me or my family and not toward society in general? There had to be a link between all the victims, perhaps the church was where he found them. The Connie Jefferson and Ryan Beliford murders didn't fit the Task Force profile of the killer; they were well beyond his circle and neither had lived in Ravenswood. Maybe they had relatives in the area? Church raffles or donations were also a couple of ways to attain personal information. They could have been volunteers, he could have been an altar boy or she attended Sunday classes. The more I mulled it around in my head the more sense it made. Had Tim informed me about his diagnosis in an attempt to gain my sympathy? If he figured his illness would convey weakness and frailty and keep him off the suspect list, he was wrong. I hadn't seen weakness in him during my previous visits. My head was spinning, I wanted to unwind and I wanted to get rid of this case all together. I stopped off at the liquor store grabbed a bottle of Pinot Noir and headed home.

"I'm Logan's brother Liam," I said. The resemblance must have been uncanny. Her jawbone quivered slightly and her emerald eyes were wide as saucers. I desperately wanted them for my collection.

"Come in," she said in stunned disbelief. "I'm sorry, Liam?"

I realized the bastard must have forgotten to tell her he had identical brothers; we had a lot of catching up to do. She escorted me to a plush tan suede couch. "Is there someplace I can put these?" I offered to remove my shoes.

"No, that's okay. I'm sorry I don't know where... Logan never discussed family; he told me he grew up in foster care until he was adopted. That's how I met him actually, through his adopted family."

"Well that's not entirely untrue," I lay back on the couch. The Plan as it were had deviated. The job would still get done of course, but I would add my own personal touches to it. I could see she was shaking like a crack baby left on a church stoop. "After our parents died, we were shipped off to an orphanage. Logan was just luckier to have a caring family take him in. Not too many were interested in a package deal; I guess he was the handsome one." My laugh felt too counterfeit; I'd have to work on that if I ever planned on interacting more.

She chuckled uncomfortably; her laugh was just as unpolished.

"Twins?" I asked.

"I beg your pardon?"

"You're obviously pregnant."

"Oh no, God no; we already have one child who is quite the handful, I couldn't even imagine...." She nervously fumbled with a button on her shirt, "I'm sorry, where are my manners? I'm Kathy by the way.

Would you like something to eat, or drink?"

"Maybe later," I smiled. I got the distinct impression she wished later would come sooner.

"Boy or girl?" my hand glided across her stomach and she tensed under my touch.

"Um, it's a boy; we have a little girl already," she regretted the words the instant they escaped.

"So where's hubby?" I sized up the place; the house wasn't that big; I'd find the little one easy enough.

"He's a cop," Kathy blurted out. "You know, he should be home shortly."

"I would love to get reacquainted with my brother," I controlled my smile this time, "he's six minutes older than

I am; unfortunately I haven't seen him since we were children."

"Amazing, I can't believe Logan never told me. Wow, I'm flustered can you tell? We really don't keep secrets from each other."

"Sorry to be the one to inform you, but were actually triplets," I clenched my fists, "I never had the opportunity to live the charmed life he did; have a beautiful wife and kids. I don't mind fucking whores. But it sure would be nice to have a family to come home to; a home cooked meal. Ain't it a pity that God has altered our plans?"

"You're not serious?" Kathy exclaimed then quickly followed. "Of course you're not, I apologize, but I think you should go now," her voice was a noticeable octave higher.

"Kathy, you knew the moment you let me in I was here to stay."

"Listen…"

"Lower your voice Katy-bear; you don't want to wake darling little

Lizzy, do you?" I enjoyed the fear produced by saying the child's name. The great white whale tried to rise and I pushed her back in her seat. She was about to scream, wanted desperately to warn her child. "Do you want to watch me gut her?" I pressed an index finger to her lips, "I can't imagine you want her to see the things I'm going to do to you, it would give the poor girl nightmares; let her sleep."

"I... I.... Why are you?"

"I have abandonment issues," I grabbed a healthy handful of her hair. She let out a whimper as we navigated the staircase. We reached the second floor and I politely asked, "Where's big brother's room?"

Her legs were spaghetti; I flung her over my shoulder and continued down the hallway. The glow of a nightlight shimmered from beneath a door we passed. *I'll see you soon sweetheart.* My cock was locked and loaded. I strapped Kathy down and she was ready for the taking. I stuffed a wad of cotton in her mouth and disappeared into Lizzy's room; Lucas had wanted her death to be as painless as possible. I watched her with her teddy bear wrapped in her tiny arms. A Norman Rockwell painting couldn't capture this angelic little angel. I stopped in the doorway. As I moved closer to her bed, a light shone through the window and I froze in mid-step. The far wall was brilliantly illuminated and sliced through me as it darted towards the north corner of her room then vanished into darkness. My breathing was heavy as the air replenished my lungs. I could hear Kathy struggle to free herself.

"Wake my child," I leaned close to her face. Her tiny eyes opened after I gently rocked her. It took a second for her to realize I wasn't daddy. I picked her up by her throat. "I have unfinished business with you. I'll see you in Hell!" I threw her prepubescent body against the wall as hard as I could. Her screams came to an abrupt halt and her little frame ricocheted off the dresser before coming to a rest at the foot of her bed. Her neck had snapped on first impact. She should be thankful, very thankful. The headlights of the car alerted me to the fact that I had limited time. I marched back into my lover's room; with knife in hand. I cut away the bitches clothes exposing her breasts then slid

I pressed down hard on her pregnant belly. "How does this feel bitch?"

"You're going to burn in fire and ashes; I can smell the sickness in you. Can you smell death?" her mouth sprayed blood with every syllable.

"You're nothing but blood, urine, and cum," I pulled out of her and ran the knife over her belly. "You're a diseased pig, all you wretched whores are the same! Let's see if this piglet resembles me, shall we?" I cut the boy from her belly and held it up by an underdeveloped foot. A mixture of blood and slime dripped onto her face. "Look what you made me do," I said, her breathing was fast and furious. I mounted again for one last ride. "What's his name?" I demanded, but there was no answer. I flung the fetus on the floor and rode her into the fiery pits of Hell. Playtime was over. I checked on the girl, she was as dead as a doornail and what was left of her mother passed ten minutes ago. I walked downstairs with junior's body flopping on each step while I dragged him at my side. I had an idea; it was a clever twist on an old move. I found a nice sized pot and filled it halfway with water.

"Hope you can swim." I tossed him in and turn the dial on the stove to simmer.

Headlights blazed the interior of the kitchen. A vehicle started up the driveway. I ducked behind the L-shaped counter top. In a vase was a dozen withering roses like the ones he had bought Laura; what a guy my brother. A white unopened envelope rested upright against its base. I heard the front door open as I unlatched the back door and stepped out into the pale moonlight.

TODD ANDREW DAVIS
THE FORSAKEN
CHAPTER XL

I quietly snuck into the house and paused with the bottle of Pinot Noir in hand. I stood still on the stairs; something wasn't right. The lights were on and it was silent, dead silent. I had a sick feeling in the pit of my stomach. I dropped the bottle and it bounced than broke as I ran up the staircase.

"Kathy! Kathy!" I yelled louder, "Kathy!" still nothing.

I stopped at Lizzy's room first and flicked on the light switch; her bed was empty. I ran the rest of the way to the master bedroom. My hand scrambled for the rocker switch and it took a second to transfer everything to my brain; I went numb. I froze in place, tears stung my eyes and my heart inflamed. I couldn't breathe, lost my balance and on hands and knees crawled to my wife's bedside. I pulled myself up by the comforter and an avalanche of blood rained down on my head. I tasted her bitter sweet blood and vomited. I willed myself to stand, my eyes tightly closed and fists clenched; I stood over her. *I failed to protect her; she needed me: they needed me.* I sobbed and every inch of my body ached. My eyes lingered on her body; she'd been butchered. Her face had been brutally beaten; her eyes were swollen and gave the appearance of being closed. Her nose was a gruesome mess; what her killer had left didn't resemble Kathy in the least. I could feel her spirit in the room. I climbed in bed next to her, held her tightly and drifted off to sleep.

"Daddy, throw me the ball," Jason pleaded.

"No throw it to me!" Lizzy screamed at the top of her lungs.

"Lizzy," Kathy fired back, "lower your voice."

"It's okay babe."

"You're always spoiling them Logan."

"I try my best to spoil you too," I joked, the expression on her face warned me away from getting to sarcastic. "Lizzy, listen to mom."

Kathy cracked a half smile and I knew I was on the way to a solid comeback. My hand was instinctively drawn to her stomach, my eyes opened. I could feel deep inside her open belly. I sat up, got out of the bed and made the slow march to Lizzy's room. The glow of the nightlight was visible from the doorway and I could make out her toes protruding from the foot of her bed. I scooped her up in my arms, her head bounced; her neck had less fortitude than a rubber band. I took her body to her mother and gently laid her down on the king sized bed then dialed Tamara. Her phone rang a half a dozen times.

"L...." she checked the caller ID to make sure, "Logan."

"They're dead," I heard myself say, "Kathy, Lizz..." My movements were lethargic, my eyes closed and I collapsed on the bed holding my two girls.

'It's okay daddy. Please don't be sad,' Lizzy voice echoed from beyond.

There were dozens of cops in my house. Tamara and another officer helped me undress down to my skivvies and packaged my soiled clothes into evidence bags. Someone had thrown a blanket over my shoulders as though it were Superman's cape. Tamara held my hand and questions were shot at me left and right, but I disregarded all of them. I could feel panic sweep through the air.

"Logan, there's something you need to know," Tamara knelt in front of me and kept her voice low. "Santiago's been asking a lot of questions about you. He had his suspicions; he thought for some reason you weren't following all the leads to their end. He's been trying to get Internal Affairs to open an investigation on you, but Ollie's been blocking him. He said Santiago was crazy and that you were the best cop on the force. Santiago believes you know more than you're letting on about the Laura Miles case. When you brought your cruiser back to the garage Joe had taken some objects from the trunk. Some of the items listed, the blanket and sheets seemed odd to him. There were stains on the blanket and it was sent out to the lab," she lowered her head and couldn't look me in the face, "A call came in from West Granada and Santiago and I took it. A waitress from Pedro's Restaurant was beaten severely. The description of her attacker matched those of our previous victims, only she survived. When I heard her description of the assailant it sounded like she was describing you; Santiago thought so as well. I'm afraid it looks bad Logan, with Laura and what happened here... Santiago personally went to Judge Carter to get a search warrant for your house and he's on his way over tonight."

"I swear to you Tamara I had nothing to do with Laura's

death and I would never harm my family," I said sternly and she nodded her head in compliance. She was conflicted, unsure whether to believe the story of a man she'd known for years; she walked away.

"Holly fucking shit! There's a fucking baby boiling on the stove," a disembodied voice shouted from the kitchen. "My God what the hell happened here?" His voice was ambient noise, nothing penetrated my soul. The familiar aroma of coffee and tobacco saturated my nostrils.

Tim held me as a mother would a child, but I was ridged and unyielding to his compassion, "Logan," he spoke in a heavy baritone, warm and inviting yet cold. The dialect was alien at first, I had forgotten how to communicate with the human race and I shook as the first syllable penetrated my armor. "I can't take away your pain and suffering or ease the loneliness or guilt that will threaten to consume you. Every life eventually comes to an end, we need to rejoice in the allotted time given to us and we need to understand the frailties of the human condition. I am your brother, your friend and your sorrow cuts me deeply as well."

He produced a metal flask from an interior coat pocket and offered me a sip. I cupped the brandy gently in my hands and took a healthy swig. The smooth burning sensation warmed my blood to near human status.

Before I could ask for another taste he kindheartedly returned the flask to my trembling hands. Tim stayed with me that night and shepherded the last officer out of my house. The morning light would bring with it a plethora of unanswerable questions an unavoidable speculation, but before I could express my intentions Tim was one step ahead of me.

"Let's go for a drive, get away from the house."

He helped me dress; I remained quasi mute as we descended the porch steps and into Tim's vintage brown Cady. I expected to find an 8 track buried inside the retro gold leather and wood paneling interior. I was disgusted and guilt ridden. I knew my recent conduct had brought the carnage to my front door and I felt dead inside. Tim rambled on about God and salvation without much pause; I was elsewhere and nothing mattered. In my mind I had severed the connections to a miserable life and faced with this monstrosity, I wanted my life to be over as well. I saw more than my fair share of death and it left behind a visceral rage and a lust for revenge. My sickening behavior had cost Laura her life and ultimately my family's lives as well as my own. I wasn't the madman lurking among the shadows, I knew it from the moment I saw them. I was capable of great evil, but I would never have harmed my family. We passed cars parked curbside waiting for their owners to spark them to life and I watched the branches of tall oak trees sway in the winter breeze. The night was a dull gray, void of all color. I saw the world through a different prism as the victim. *Now tell me your God exist; tell me how kind hearted and merciful your Lord and Savior is.* I peered up toward the black sky; was this God's master plan? My spirit lay dismantled among the wreckage that was my life. There was no comforting me, nothing could unburden my soul and it will remain forever black; pity and understanding were meaningless words. Humanity in its entirety disgusted me. My head throbbed, I was unbalanced and a sensation of motion sickness washed over me.

"We're almost there Logan; the end of the road," Tim spoke clear and concise, but seemed miles off in the ether. "The mixture is potent," a wicked laugh escaped him and warned of impending doom. "I can't believe you were so blind. I laid it all out in front of you and you simply ignored the signs."

A rainbow of colors spun in my head until it emptied down an unseen drain; only blackness was left and then I was unconscious. I awoke some time later unsure whether or not I had imagined the absurd conversation with Tim. My body was paralyzed and I lost the ability to speak.

"Did you know I was a cadet?" Tim said casually as if our repartee had never stopped. "It's true; after you and Kathy took off to New York I joined the academy. I dabbled in many different careers before I realized I was better served in the House of the Lord. It was a long arduous uphill battle for me Logan; the church was never a place of solace for me and my spirit had long ago been ravished by maggots and purged of its innocence and vitality."

Kill me! Kill me! I welcome death, I embrace it. Release me from this cruel joke, set me free! I no longer cared if Tim was a serial killer and whether he butchered my pregnant wife and murdered my daughter. I didn't care if he continued to inflict his madness on every living creature in Ravenswood. I just wanted this to be over; I wanted the undying grief to stop. The thoughts of vengeance and exacting pain and suffering on the monster that had stalked my nightmares evaporated with the loss of my family. Killing Tim meant nothing to me and I would do nothing to escape or thwart my impending demise. I had taken too many chances as a man and as a cop. At nearly forty-one my death seemed long overdue and without my family it was void of purpose. You reap what you sow and I was paying the sum total of all my sins.

"You'll never learn Logan," Tim reached for something in

the back seat and slapped my face to get my attention, "your brother Liam has been just as easy to manipulate." He placed a worn Stetson Cowboy hat on his head and checked the review to make sure it sat just right. "As dear old Fad'er Daughtery friend of da family, 'twas easy to get Liam released in ta my custody," he exclaimed in a faked Irish accent, "and as dear brother Lucas all I needed to do was point Liam in the right direction. It's funny, once I took him off his medication he was like a pit bull ready to kill any dog that came into the yard; I just needed to find the right dogs.

We drove slowly up the cobblestone driveway in front of Chancellor's Manor; Tim put the car in park and got out. "We're here," he produced a large ring key holder and unlocked the giant iron gate, "home sweet home; the place where it all began, the place that changed all our lives." We parked near the garage and he forced me across the lawn then shoved me through the front doors. The foyer was filled with buckets of nails and screws, hammers, band saws and a host of other construction material. "And let there be light," he flicked on the switch that lit up the grand chandelier. "I told you I tried for years to get this place torn down. City Hall called this place a landmark because it was centuries old and wanted to restore it to its full glory. Can you imagine that? I filed suit against every building permit, building code and land permit, but I was overruled by bureaucrats. Call it providence if you will, but one of my parishioners was a wealthy Texas oil man. I convinced him to buy the property and I agreed to be the community liaison and oversee the construction. They started work a month ago and have restored much of the building's foundation. Unfortunately, it's forced me to move my schedule up."

He led me through the hallway and into a great parlor

room. At the far wall was a giant stone fireplace that my father had imported from Avon, France brick by brick. The heads of two large lions sat on the mantel at each end of the 15 foot firebox and it had always intimidated me as a child.

"Liam showed me every nook and cranny, every secret passageway of this house," Tim said as he pushed me inside the mouth of the fireplace. "In about three weeks the contractors would have thoroughly gone through this house and found these hidden little gems." His fingers searched the ash covered brick and found a hidden lever that opened a fake wall. Inside an iron spiral staircase ran four stories from basement to attic. The moonlight illuminated most of the stairs above our heads and left the section beneath our feet in blackness. "After decades you came back to this house as Detective Logan Crenshaw and surprised your brother and me. His natural instinct was to kill you on first sight, but you were babbling incoherently about demons taking you to hell; killing you in that state would not have been satisfying. When you started asking me questions about Chancellor's Manor, I thought the fog of your memories of that night had cleared and you had figured it all out, but you're just as fucked up as he is. On a good day your brother has a few hours of lucid thought creeping into his diseased mind. You on the other hand suffer from a few hours of complete insanity. I begged him not to kill you, but he picked you up and headed down the stairs to your parent's torture chamber. It took three tranquilizers to knock him out and stop him before he had the chance to fillet you from head to toe."

Tim held out a lantern and shoved me up the staircase; it was déjà vu and I felt as if the stone skulls embedded in the walls would tear my flesh apart. My eyes were glazed and I focused on not letting my bowels evacuate. My ears popped, knees buckled and my body threatened to collapse like an accordion. *It will be over soon.* Tim's arm snaked around my waist and he practically carried me to my parents' bedroom and tossed me inside. Surprisingly, I remained standing until he hit me on the back of my head. I felt the cold sting of the handcuffs lock my wrists behind my back and he tossed me on the bed. The mummified cadavers of a man and woman rested side by side underneath the soft green cover sheets. Their skin was a thin leathery brown and dark shriveled lips revealed dull white teeth. The eyes were deformed like runny eggs having lost their shape. They bore no resemblance to the fiends I had once known, but I instantly recognized them just the same.

"You did some of your best work here Logan; I have to hand it to you. I discovered where the authorities had buried your parents and had your brother dig them up for me. I've dreamt of this moment for years and now we're all together as one happy family. Everything's coming full circle and I will have my retribution," his voice was euphoric. He sat down in a wicker captain's chair next to the bed. "My life's been a nightmare! You knew the sickness inside your family and never warned me and I became just another faceless victim sodomized by those freaks. Your silence destroyed my childhood and cost me my manhood and there's only one way to excise all those demons." He spun the large key ring around his finger, "After the incident I lived with my Aunt in Kansas. Nobody knew what was wrong with me. I was antisocial and a bit of a recluse; I kept the secret and never told a soul. My dad was so enraged by my drastic change in behavior that for a short time he disowned me. Mother sent me to a top child psychologist and even he couldn't unlock the truth. It was a mystery as to why a healthy thirteen year old boy had stopped communicating with the outside world. After several pointless sessions without progress

I was shipped back off to Wichita and lived on my Aunties farm the rest of the summer. But the sickness was still deep inside me. I used a farm hand's knife to carve the marks on my face and neck, a byproduct of self loathing. If the doctors couldn't help me I'd tear out the disease an inch of flesh at a time," He opened his shirt and revealed raised scarification in the shape of a cross just above his heart. "You know what an elastrator is? They used the device to castrate farm animals; it's a long rubber band that ties off the scrotum just above the testicles. Once it's tightened and left on for hours the scrotum dies and you cut off the testicles with very little blood or pain. Extreme I suppose; it ruined any chances that I could have a normal life with Kathy or any other woman, but it was the only way I could stop myself from becoming something like Liam...or you. After my fix, all my thoughts were internalized and I began the slow process of mentally and physically self healing. By September everyone thought I was back to my old self.

My hatred for you was buried deeper than even I was aware and our friendship resumed unfazed."

"You always thought you were a better man than me," I slurred my speech, "but you never had the balls."

"When your parents were brutally slain it only made things between us more complicated. I hated the fact that mother wanted to adopt you and my candor got me beaten and grounded for nearly three weeks. How dare I turn my back on my best friend? She believed that you had been a good influence on me and never speculated that your family had been the source of my change. What would make an educated well respected woman want to remain utterly clueless? You embody a sinful nature that infects everything you touch. I despise you, I cringe when I hear your name. All your boyhood memories may have faded, but tonight I'll make sure you pay for the suffering you and your family have burned into the souls of Ravenswood. I'm not a fool Logan and I am a patient man. You were always a selfish fuck, but I practically handed Kathy to you and you lived your life without remorse or regret. God led me to Liam's lost soul; 'Isaiah 40:29 He gives strength to the weary and increases the power of the weak.' The drugs given to him in the Waco asylum tainted his memory and I became his spiritual inspiration. The so called experimental treatments were barbaric and he slowly lost touch with all reality. I wrote letters to the board on his behalf and even took parishioners to protest the inhumane conditions of the facility. We almost succeeded in getting it shutdown, but with defeat comes determination and eventually I was able to get Liam and ten others released. He did not recognize me or that I was the young boy he helped sodomized; I was a forgotten child's toy. He was left with the mind of a dimwitted adolescent. I took him in and each day I decreased his dose of medication until he was convinced the Devil had taken control over his soul. I forged the heated metal, hammered it into shape, hardened and tempered the steel for I was the sword maker and Liam was the hand that would wield destruction. Unfortunately there were times when he escaped and when he returned confessed to the murders of Jessica and Jenny as well as others and for that I am truly sorry. The church and God's words were no match for the evil that lurks inside your brother. I was taken in by his hypnotic charm, but Liam could not serve two masters. He would no longer listen to me so I became your loving brother Lucas and in return I struck a better deal with him than God could ever give. He promised to make you suffer for your sins. Your hyper-libido provided the conduit that ultimately led to your demise. He killed Allen on his own free will, but as Lucas, I spoke the words to Liam which sent Laura to her death.

When you confessed to me that you thought you were the killer; God it took so much restraint not to burst into hysterical laughter. Her death still left an unsatisfied feeling in the pit of my stomach. I took pride in devising The Plan for Kathy, Lizzy and your unborn child. I would have extended your misery much longer, but regrettably your brother has become more difficult to control. And now we have just a little unfinished business to attend to and you will be reunited with Liam soon. I had toyed with the idea of having him visit the genuine Lucas and the rest of the family clan, but I was afraid it might be too confusing for him and I didn't know how he'd react if he learned the truth. After he's finished with you, I'll make sure there's enough pieces left of your body to implicate him in your killing. Liam will be confined forever inside the walls of a nut house and I the aggrieved preacher returned to God's."

"I'll kill you and drag you down to hell with me! You made yourself a pathetic unick. You ran from girls and into the arms of God to keep your hatred under control, but all that was a waste because you're worse than me and you're worse than Liam!" I surprised myself with the intensity of my outburst. His body recoiled, the preacher man flinched he was scared of me; I prayed I would have the strength to kill him.

"There is no difference between you and Liam; you were born that way," Tim grabbed me by the collar, "You've lied so much that you can't even tell what is real anymore."

"Fuck your sanctimonious bullshit; you're no more a man of the cloth than I am. You're Pinocchio dreaming of being a real boy only you never will be."

"And what about you?" Tim bent down and stared me

square in the face, "You're a killer and a pathological liar. Remember, you confessed to murder long before I became a preacher. Poor, poor Logan, the way mommy and daddy mistreated you; fucked the innocence out of you. No one could blame an abused teenage boy for killing his parents while they slept, but letting Liam take the blame was truly cold blooded. If you had only killed them before they got their hands on me things would have been so different for us today."

"You really don't expect me to believe that crock of shit," I chuckled, "Even as a teen I was no killer or rapist so save your lies for Liam's twisted mind." *I know me, I know who I am. It was just more mental abuse before the physical fireworks commenced.*

"Liam loved your parents; he vowed to do anything for them and he did. He was your mother's favorite. No Logan, you killed your parents and you blamed Liam. Even after the asylum corrupted him with the pills, shock therapy and medicated lobotomy he knew you were responsible. He would've been better off if you'd slit his throat as well."

"You're a sick and delusional fuck trying to screw with my head before you unleash your Frankenstein's monster on me; bravo Tim, well done. You know if you take these handcuffs off me I'd be happy to applaud. Face it Timmy, you should've been bunkmates with Liam in the loony bin, strapped down to your bed 24/7."

Tim went to the bedroom window as he heard the Chevelle's loud hemi roar up the driveway then watched Liam step out with a black bag in hand. "It's almost time," he checked the handcuffs and placed a damp cloth over my face.

"Logan wake-up. Are you just gonna to sleep the day away?" asked Kathy. She still made quite a scene in her red bikini; my wife was officially a MILF. White beaches, water 72 degrees and a small fire burning at my feet; who says you can't enjoy a family vacation in paradise. The kids dashed in and out the water, Jason desperately tried to impress his big sister and I was the luckiest man on earth. I just needed to unwind; I was run down and just so god-awful tired. I didn't want to miss out on the good time, but my body wouldn't allow me to participate. Out of the corner of my eye I saw a lanky black teenager make a beeline straight for my cabana.

"I have a package for you sir," said the kid.

I signed for it and left a small gratuity. The manila envelope was stuffed to capacity and the return address was marked Ravenswood Police Department. I shook off my wife's attempted to socialize, vacated the swanky lounge area and headed straight for our room in the resort. Fresh linens were on the bed, the double bay windows were wide open and the cream colored curtains fluttered in the breeze. I open the envelope and spilled the contents on the queen sized bed. There was a letter attached to a myriad of photographs. Ollie's childlike handwriting was scribbled across the top of the page:

LOGAN HE'S BACK.
I'M SORRY TO SPOIL YOUR VACATION AND I KNOW IT'S BEEN SEVERAL YEARS SINCE YOU LEFT THE FORCE, BUT IT'S THE SAME M.O. AS THE SUBURBAN SLASHER.

The pics were of numerous victims that ranged from old to young from black to white to all of the above. My eyes were glued to the most disturbing set of photo's I had ever seen. A photo of our bedroom where Kathy's face was bruised and her mouth agape lay in our blood soaked bed. A photo of Lizzy's room; her neck had been snapped and a bulging bone protruded through her skin. There was a picture of the kitchen where a boiled fetus with loose white skin hung from its tiny skeleton. The last photograph was of the resort; my body lay in a bathtub overflowing with red water. My head was tilted back, throat brutally hacked to ribbons and a knife had etched Liam's name across my forehead. I inched over to the tiny bathroom, took a deep breath and put my hand on the door; it slowly squeaked open. In an instant I opened my eyes and woke to a dingy low lit room that stunk of cheap Cuban cigars and cheaper cologne.

"Good you're up Logan, I thought I might have given you the wrong concoction," Tim rolled a cigar between his fingers. I laid on my right side, the left side of my head ached and I could feel the slow trickle of warm blood snake down the back of my neck. I tried freeing my hands to no avail, "You son-of-a-bitch. Why didn't you…"

"Why didn't I what Logan? Kill you?" asked Tim. "You haven't figured it out yet have you?"

"What, that you want to fuck me first? I always knew that was your style. You're nothing but a homo priest who can't get it up unless you're victims are strapped down; sorry to disappoint you Tim, but I'm no queer."

"Even when you're about die you're a real asshole aren't Logan?"

"I have nothing left to live for, you saw to that."

"I am the victim here! Don't you ever forget it!" Tim jumped on top of me and held the tip of the cigar close to my eye, "I was defiled in that madhouse that spawned you." He released his grip; agitated he began to pace.

"Kill me already damn you! You preach God's word, but you're nothing more than a blasphemous pig. Liam has to do your dirty work? What's wrong Tim lost your cojones and your pride?"

"Why make things so difficult Logan?" He snatched my ear like a Nun, "You'll die soon enough. I've waited an eternity for this day and I refuse to allow you to ruin it for me."

"My apologies Father didn't mean to damper your spirits."

"The Devil does exist and I'm not talking about Liam or the other scum in your family, I am living proof; I traded my eternal spirit for the chance at revenge. I bided my time and polluted the world with the word of God. There is no great redeemer, no rescuer and no prayer that can save your miserable life. You're as blind as those I preach too and I laugh at their ignorance. I am the almighty and on bent knee you shall beg for my forgiveness.

"You claim to be God, but you're afraid to kill me; you're a voyeur, a pariah and nothing Liam does will ever give you the revenge you seek. A true God isn't passive as the bible says: 'And when you hear the sound of marching in the tops of the balsam trees, then rouse yourself, for then the Lord has gone out before you to strike down the army of the Philistines.' Instead, you hide behind a man-child with a fractured brain. Do you think he's even capable of feeling one tenth of your hatred for me?"

"Deliver me, I pray, from the hand of my brother," Tim looked up to the heavens, "from the hand of Esau; for I fear him, that he will come and attack me and the mothers with the children." He stared at me, his face shone no emotion, "Bible lesson's over."

Three loud knocks silenced the banter. He taped my mouth shut and made his way over to the door. He adjusted the Stetson and with my Beretta in hand, unlocked the door then stepped sideways and ushered my brother into the room. Liam wore a familiar red cap and a black leather jacket. He had in his possession a large black duffel bag that he placed gently on the floor. He removed his jacket, shirt and jeans and unveiled a freakish physique. When he removed his cap, long curly locks of coffee bean colored hair dangled over his face and he swept it aside to keep it out of his eyes.

Tim turned on the light and walked back to me and the giant slowly followed. His movements were mechanical and his mussels taught. His eyes locked onto me and I knew it was over. Tim stood at the foot of the bed and watched as the monster's enormous hands clasp around my throat and lift me off the bed as if I were a child. Eyeball to eyeball his face was youthful, but had a searing hard edge to it. A six inch scar barely visible ran from his brow to his upper lip, a testament to my dead mother and her wire hanger beatings. His jaw was slightly off center and protruded out further than normal; his nose had been broken so many times that barely any cartilage remained. The blood had rushed from my head and I was in danger of passing out when he released his grip. I gasped for breath, my eyes watered and my lungs struggled to take in the stagnant air.

"Kneel before your master," Tim ordered. "Hallelujah your time has come."

"Once he's done with me, I hope he starts in on you," I murmured through the loose tape.

Tim was enraged and hit me with the butt of the gun. Unfortunately, I was still conscious and my head was throbbing. I watch Liam dig through the duffle bag; he walked back to the bed and covered the mattress with plastic wrap. He then retrieved a pair of needle nose pliers, a hammer and what looked like a bone saw, clamp, goggles, latex gloves, three jugs of a Lyme based chemical and a pearl handled knife. I watched mesmerized as he neatly organized all his tools; it was exactly the way my father had done. With my life in the balance, visions of childhood memories buried in a haze began to fully dissipate. I remembered Liam. I hadn't visited him in the Waco asylum; I shut his memory out with the rest of my past. I had once loved Liam more than any soul could love their sibling, but when we were kids I never tried to protect him or save him from the ruthlessness of our parents; I had failed him. I had tried to save the girl in the cabin, the girl whose face haunted me. Lucas shouted out our whereabouts. My parents knew only punishing me would do nothing so Liam bore the brunt of the beatings; he was tortured and violently raped throughout the night. His body bled from head to toe and his groin was soaked in urine. I bathed him with a dishrag, bandaged his wounds and helped him into bed. It was all clear now, before the sun rose the next day I had made my way down the hall to the master bedroom. I held the knife in my hand, crept to their bedside and plunged the blade deep into my father's chest then cut his jugular. He let out an audible moan and my mother screamed as I leapt across the bed, tackled her on the floor and tore her white nightgown open. I hesitated, her eyes desperately pleaded with me and I cut her throat then drove the knife into her heart again and again and again. I ran from the house and hid in the cabin in the woods for nearly two days. When I returned I found the driveway full of police cars and news vans. An officer had wrapped a blanket around Lucas's shoulders and knelt to console him. Liam, head down was led from the house in handcuffs and into the back of a squad car. I wore the blood stained clothes of that horrible night. I could have confessed and saved him, but in that moment I turned and sought the anonymity of the woods. I walked away from my past forever. I thought I was finally free, instead I'd imprisoned Liam. He became a vessel of pure evil. Liam's movements, gestures and the way he maliciously aligned his instruments of torture told me he had planned to exact a great deal of pain. All the innocent lives he had taken and the brutal way he did so was his way of showing me his tormented soul and the horrors he wanted to inflict upon me. I knew the pain would only grow in intensity and they would keep me alive as long as possible; it triggered the kind of fear I had growing up in a house of insanity. Death was no match for Tobias, my father; now inhabiting the body of Liam rose from the grave just as Jesus had done before him and I was all too familiar with his brand of justice.

"All this time apart and you have nothing to say to your brother," Tim laughed. "How does it feel to finally be reunited?"

"Looks like you sprang the wrong freak, that ain't my brother you crazy asshole!"

"Really," a dumbfounded expression crossed Tim's face, "if he's not your brother who is he?"

"I'd hate to spoil the ending for you Preacher." I watched as he tried to compose himself; he was visibly flustered.

Without warning Liam snatched the knife from the table, tossed me onto the bed and pinned me down. He ran the blade across my chest as he made his first incision. "I'm going to pull your organs out one at a time," Liam giggled as the knife continued its descent down my abdomen, "Just like you did mother." Spittle dripped from his lips and stung my eyes.

I stared into Logan's face and was startled by a cold breeze that raised the hairs on the back of my neck. A young girl stood watching me. It was the demon witch; my father's favorite pet who had witnessed the butchering of Ryan. Her skin was translucent, her eyes black as buttons. She was the sole reason both my parents were dead. I wanted to lure her close and destroy whatever was left of the apparition. I froze in place, Jenifer and Jessica stood near the window with hatred burning in their eyes. *It can't be; it isn't real.* The black beauty Connie seemed lost and worried as she called out for her son then disappeared into the wall. Allan and Ryan stood by the table and rifled through the knives, hooks and hacksaws; their hatred for me burned from beyond the grave. I heard fingernails scraping on the ceiling tile above me; part of it fell and revealed the charred face of the dead hooker. Even through her smoldering flesh, she was eager to take part in her share of retribution; eye for an eye. I fell backwards and placed my hand in something sticky and slimy; Daddy Long Legs inched his crushed body and flat head across the floor leaving behind a trail of blood and innards as my little treat Angela held his leash. "Go away!" I shouted, "Please, go away!" I shut my eyes, but it only forced me to listen more intently. I heard Logan's daughter Elizabeth weeping, his baby crying and his wife trying to console them both. I braved a look and saw Laura sitting on the bed next to Logan. She rose to her feet, her broken bones clicked and popped and she fell to her knees. She crawled to me and placed a bony hand on my thigh. Her veins emptied of blood, bulged from beneath her pale skin and I could see something moving underneath her flesh. She opened her mouth and vomited a horde of maggots on my feet and the bugs and beetles crawled up my legs; I recoiled in fear. She leaned her broken neck in close until she was face to face with mine. My eyes stung and I turned my head slightly from the stench of bleach on her breath. "Deceiver," Laura turned her head and pointed a finger at Lucas, "deceeeeeiver!"

"Snap out of it you big dumb retard!" Tim held the gun loosely in his hand and pointed it towards Liam.

He dug inside a small bag that lay in a chair next to the bathroom and pulled out a small bottle of clear liquid and a syringe. He had turned his back and within seconds Liam's hand was around his throat; the two struggled violently. Liam grabbed a five inch serrated edged hunting knife from his belt and drove it into Tim's shoulder.

"God damn you mother fucker!" Tim swung the butt of the Berretta, cracked Liam on the forehead and he fell to the floor. "Son of a bitch," his hand raised to the open gash and he bent over and screamed, "aaaaahhhhhhhhhh!"

I was still in a daze, but was able to swing my legs off the bed and onto the floor. I tried to take a step and fell to my knees.

"If you want something done right," Tim turned his rage back to me, clicked the safety off my gun and placed the barrel next to my head.

I closed my eyes, braced myself then heard the sharp pop of the gun fire and my face was sprayed with blood. Stunned, Tim reached up towards his head, his ear dangled limply; the cartilage destroyed.

"Put the gun down now!" Tamara and Santiago stood in the doorway; her gun was pointed directly at Tim's chest. "Next one goes straight through your heart."

From his knee Liam threw the hunting knife and split Santiago's chin; the tip of the blade pierced his temporal lobe. He raised his hands to his face by reflex, but was dead before he hit the floor. Tamara didn't have time to refocus her aim onto my brother as he slammed his full body weight into her and they crashed into the wall. Two more officers entered the room, the younger jumped on Liam to prevent him from pummeling Tamara to death and the older took a step towards me. Tim emerged from behind the entry door, coolly raised the gun to the officer's head and blew his brains out. He rushed into the hallway and I heard an exchange of gunfire. Liam got to his feet with the young officer on his back. He tossed him like a rag doll against the far wall and he crashed down on the table. My brother jumped on top of the cop's prone body, grabbed the hacksaw off the broken table and raked it across his face. He took the pearl handle hunting knife and a small hatchet and ran out of my parent's room. I ran to Tamara, she was unconscious, but I could see she was still breathing. I sat down facing away from her body, scooted myself next to her and fumbled around her waist band for a pair of keys to the handcuffs. After a couple of awkward and failed attempts, I was able to unlock them. I wondered if she thought I was trying to escape when I left the house. I had given her plenty of reasons not to trust me; in the end it didn't matter why she followed me I was just grateful she did. I picked up Tamara's Berretta and exited into the hallway; at the far end of the hall lay a cop flat on his back. I cautiously walked over to him; there was a hole in his lip and blood formed around his neck. I looked out the large bay window; below were the flashing lights of a dozen police cars and I saw several members of a fully geared SWAT Team enter Chancellor's Manor. The mansion was surrounded; there was no escape. I walked down to the far end of the hallway and spotted a trail of blood drops on the floor. I stopped at my father's library. The doorknob had a bloody palm print; I stepped back and kicked it open with my gun drawn. I found the latch behind the bookcase and it opened up to the hidden stairwell. I raced up the spiral stairs and on to the roof top. The cold night air helped clear my head. There was noise from the roadside that lay just a few hundred meters from the mansion and I heard the blades of a police helicopter chopping the air as it approached from the east. The roof was under construction and dozens of the dilapidated gables were in the midst of repair. Exposed wooden beams, piles of construction material and machinery cluttered the roof turning it into a maze. I had no plan, no idea where I was going, but I ran anyway. I stopped to catch my breath near a gigantic heating vent; a sign read 'Danger Unstable Beyond This Point.' I raised my arms just in time to block the metal pipe Tim had swung at my head. The gun flew from my hands and was lost in the night; he hit me hard in the liver and I fell to the ground.

"Always the hero, aren't you Logan?" Tim dropped the pipe and it clanked on the cement roof, "Only you were never a hero to me. You could have saved me, but you didn't."

"We were kids back then," I grunted through the pain, "I didn't tell anyone because I was ashamed."

"You saved yourself; you wanted me to suffer just like you had suffered. You were able to dispel your demons; I however, not so much. You had a good job, beautiful family and I took all that away from you."

"There's no way out," I sat up, "SWAT will be here anytime now. You'll never make it off the roof alive Tim; its over."

"Maybe," Tim pointed the gun at me, "maybe not, either way you'll never know."

Liam slammed into him; they fell with Tim landing on top. Liam's left hand gripped Tim's hand that held the gun and with his left Tim bashed in Liam's nose. Liam tried to block the punches as they rained down. He reached up, gripped Tim's dangling ear and tore it off his head. Tim's fingers pressed against the gaping hole and lost his balance; in an instant Liam was on top of him.

"I'm gonna send you and all your ghosts back to hell for good," Liam slashed Tim's face with the hunting knife and on the back swing cut his chest.

Tim raised his knees, got his heels on the madman's waist and kicked him off. Liam lunged forward, Tim fired the Berretta and Liam stumbled backward over a 4 foot knee high wall. Tim was a bloody mess, his looks whatever he had thought of them before were a horror show now. He staggered to his feet and peered over the wall. Liam had torn chunks of the rotted shingles away as he slid down the 90 degree angle of the gable roof. It was 30 feet long and tapered off into a flat low slope with a 15 foot skylight.

Liam lay on his stomach halfway down and breathing heavily.

"You don't remember me you stupid fuck," Tim touched his bloody face, "I'm not Lucas; I was your brother Logan's only friend… the one you raped. I just thought you should know before you die." He pulled the trigger but the chamber was empty. "Fuck me!"

I crashed into Tim and heard both his legs break as we flipped over the knee wall and tumbled down the gable roof. Our bodies knocked Liam from his perch and we slid onto the center of the large glass skylight.

The rusted pins that held the old frame in place popped, it dropped several inches and dozens of the glass panels shattered on the empty swimming pool, four stories below. We lay still; Liam on his back, Tim on his side and me on my stomach.

"Logan!" Tamara shouted from the ridge side of the roof,

"Hold on we're coming."

"Stay back!" I could hear the old aluminum frame bend under pressure, "The roof can't support any more weight."

It dropped again and the glass under us gave way. I reached out and caught my brother by the shirt collar and Tim by his hand. I lay flat with my legs wrapped around the grid beam, my face pressed hard into the cross beam and the two men dangled below. My arms were strained; the muscles near fail and my fingers felt the little pin pricks as blood rushed out of them. The beam 2 feet in front of my head began to bend and separate from the rest of the frame.

"What's it gonna be Logan?" Tim held onto my hand with a vice grip, "You can't save both of us." I knew he was right. "We can start over you and me," he spit the overflow blood out of his mouth; four blocks away he could see the 'Jesus Saves' neon red sign. "We can forgive your brother for his horrible trespasses if we stick together."

What would become of Liam if I saved him? He would be confined to the asylum the rest of his life, punished for his crimes, shot full of drugs and maybe given a well deserved lobotomy. If I saved Tim he would plead for the mercy of the court; a man of the cloth forced to play his part in a sadistic game devised by two psychotic brothers. Hell given our past, even I would set him free. And myself, my true identity was bound to come out and be front pages of every newspaper in the country. My career was over, my reputation in tatters and with my family gone my life was nothing. I grunted loudly and used all of my remaining strength to pull Liam up; his fingers anxiously reached out and took hold of the crossbar. He looked me in the eyes, not sure what to say he kept silent. I had walked out on him when we were kids and took away the parents he so desperately loved. I guess in some sort of a twisted brotherly love gesture, maybe this was my way of making amends. In the far corner of the rooftop Laura stood as though she were floating over the city. She was just as beautiful as I remembered; her skin creamy white, her eyes full of love and life she stretched out her arms signaling that everything was alright. She wasn't my angel anymore or Allen's but she was an angel and she was real. I saw her; we saw her, Liam and me. I gazed toward Tamara, her eyes filled with tears she mouthed the word no and turned her head away.

"No Logan!" Tim realized what I was thinking; he

panicked, his fingers dug into my flesh as he desperately tried to climb up my arm.

A loud groan came from aluminum frame and the skylight buckled once again, I unlocked my legs from the cross beam and Tim and I began our free fall. I closed my eyes and I was back on the beach of that beautiful island paradise. I sat in a lounge chair with a small fire near my feet. I watched fully content as Kathy, Lizzy and my son Jason played in the surf. Out of the corner of my eye, I saw a young black teenager make his way over to my cabana.

"Message for you sir," he said and smiled when I handed him the tip. "Thank you very much sir."

The envelope was stuffed with photographs and had Ollie's childlike scribble written all over it. I sat up, kicked off my sandals and wiggled my toes in the warm beach sand. I looked at my beautiful family and watched them play as though they hadn't a care in the world. I felt the weight of the envelope in my hand; fear or the feeling of being completely at peace kept me from opening it and I tossed it into the fire.

The End

www.ingramcontent.com/pod-product-compliance
Lightning Source LLC
Chambersburg PA
CBHW021444240626
47153CB00001B/294